NEEDLE I

"Whoever parked this car e
Graham heard the chief insp
on Russum's face, that came
fication was traced to a bogus Canadian alias, its stolen Mass
plates gave it away."

"We're just glad you found it," Russum said, pulling his
Geiger counter from the trunk of his car.

"Do you think there may be any radiation?"

"We'll see soon enough. No time like the present to find
out. How 'bout popping the trunk?"

The inspector watched as Russum moved a wand sniffer
device back and forth across the Taurus's trunk. He seemed to
dwell in the nooks and crannies, the places where the air remained stagnant, but turned up nothing. The Geiger counter
remained silent.

"What do you make of it, Mr. Russum?" the inspector
asked. Graham looked on quietly, but knew the answer in advance.

"In all probability, this automobile did not carry conventional nuclear materials or weapons."

"That's a relief," the inspector sighed, but then he noticed
Russum didn't share his feelings. "Conventional nuclear materials? Is there any other kind?"

"There is now."

Praise for the novels of Bill Buchanan

Berkley titles by Bill Buchanan

VIRUS
CLEARWATER
PURE FUSION

PURE FUSION

BILL BUCHANAN

BERKLEY BOOKS, NEW YORK

THE BERKLEY PUBLISHING GROUP
Published by the Penguin Group
Penguin Group (USA) Inc.
375 Hudson Street, New York, New York 10014, USA
Penguin Group (Canada), 10 Alcorn Avenue, Toronto, Ontario M4V 3B2, Canada
(a division of Pearson Penguin Canada Inc.)
Penguin Books Ltd., 80 Strand, London WC2R 0RL, England
Penguin Group Ireland, 25 St. Stephen's Green, Dublin 2, Ireland (a division of Penguin Books Ltd.)
Penguin Group (Australia), 250 Camberwell Road, Camberwell, Victoria 3124, Australia
(a division of Pearson Australia Group Pty. Ltd.)
Penguin Books India Pvt. Ltd., 11 Community Centre, Panchsheel Park, New Delhi—110 017, India
Penguin Group (NZ), Cnr. Airborne and Rosedale Roads, Albany, Auckland 1310, New Zealand
(a division of Pearson New Zealand Ltd.)
Penguin Books (South Africa) (Pty.) Ltd.,
24 Sturdee Avenue, Rosebank, Johannesburg 2196, South Africa

Penguin Books Ltd., Registered Offices: 80 Strand, London WC2R 0RL, England

PURE FUSION

A Berkley mass-market edition / published by arrangement with
the author

PRINTING HISTORY
Berkley mass-market edition / September 2004

Copyright © 2004 by Bill Buchanan.

For information, address: The Berkley Publishing Group,
a division of Penguin Group (USA) Inc.,
375 Hudson Street, New York, New York 10014.

ISBN: 0-425-19254-7

BERKLEY®
Berkley Books are published by The Berkley Publishing Group,
a division of Penguin Group (USA) Inc.,
375 Hudson Street, New York, New York 10014.
BERKLEY is a registered trademark belonging
to Penguin Group (USA) Inc.
The "B" design is a trademark belonging
to Penguin Group (USA) Inc.
PRINTED IN THE UNITED STATES OF AMERICA

10 9 8 7 6 5 4 3 2 1

*For all who protect us; those with an unshakable resolve
to make sure that nothing like September 11th
ever happens again.*

*Complacency: A feeling of satisfaction
with the way things are while oblivious to danger.*

In the early nineties, Sam Cohen, the inventor of
the neutron bomb, warned us about the dangers
of red mercury.

This book is based on one simple premise: He
could be right . . .

PART ONE

Out of Balance

Winter, 2010

CHAPTER ONE

Angel of Death
Friday, Feb. 5, 9:21 A.M.
Hama, Syria

For *Times* correspondent Wyley Ramsi, it all started in Hama. Once Syria's most scenic city, today the Orontes River meandered lifelessly through town under a dreary, overcast sky. As for its western bank—well, he'd been instructed to follow the west bank to the barricades. So far, except for dead fish and scavenging dogs, it'd been practically deserted. It was a cold, drizzly-gray winter morning, the kind where damp wind and rain leave you chilled to the bone. Exhausted and shivering, Ramsi wished he'd never left home.

Rumors on the road to Damascus were running rampant—chemical weapons, water poisoning, tribal genocide, drug-related mass murder—but at this early stage of his investigation, only one thing was certain: Something horrific had happened here three days ago, in the middle of the night, and Syrian President Bashar Assad had banned the press—until today.

Wyley drove the 120 miles from Damascus to Hama early Friday morning and even then, after talking with dozens of refugees along the way, he didn't know exactly what to expect. He knew it was bad, but no one really knew what had happened. He'd brought enough clothes, food, and water for a week—didn't want to risk contamination—a notepad, a laptop computer, three camera bags crammed with photographic equipment, a case of batteries, two tripods, a lead-lined bag filled with a hundred rolls of film, a parabolic dish, a portable satellite uplink, and a phone. His midsized car was packed full. Still, nothing could have prepared him for this day.

Being there, experiencing Hama firsthand, would change

Wyley forever, and yet, this was only the beginning.

Slowing to a stop alongside the river, he studied a hand-drawn road map sketched for him by a refugee. *This is about as close as I'll get,* he judged, squinting in the dim light. Dry contacts bothered him and he reached for eyedrops. Feeling his shirt pocket empty, Wyley sighed. *Figures.* He'd left them back home in his Beirut office. Blinking, he formed tears, then studied the street signs. Marked intersections were few and far between in this part of town.

He parked the rental car in a dank honeycomb of narrow alleyways, just short of the military barricades surrounding the old Barudi neighborhood. *One thing about deserted city streets,* Ramsi observed tiredly, *the dogs are quick to move in and take over.* Sliding his pistol into his trench coat pocket, he grabbed his 35mm camera bag off the front floorboard and started walking down the west bank.

Rounding the first bend, Ramsi stopped cold in his tracks. Squinting to focus, he took in the scene. It looked like an old black-and-white picture from the German concentration camps of World War II—bodies heaped on top of bodies, hundreds of them dumped willy-nilly along the west bank. He'd been told the Hama cleanup was complete, yet these corpses hadn't been taken out of the city. *Like father, like son,* he thought. *Assad wants me to see this; he wants the world to see.*

Instinctively, Ramsi mounted a wide-angle lens, moved closer to the riverbank, and framed the shot. Looking down-stream, dead fish and human bodies extended off frame, seemingly into infinity. He had to get close-ups; their faces, who were these people?

His pace quickened, his energy renewed. Moving nearer to this horrific scene, he swapped lenses on the fly, mounting his favorite face lens, the Nikor 50-135 zoom. His breathing was rapid now, when suddenly the wind took his breath away. A nauseating stench washed over him unlike anything he'd ever experienced—rotting fish and flesh.

And it only got worse.

The nearer he drew to the dead, the closer he looked, the more vividly real their deaths became. These people could have been Wyley's family, friends, or relatives. At second glance, these weren't like Nazi concentration camp deaths at all. Closer inspection revealed these people had been treated with dignity. There was no blood, very little anyway, and no look of death agony on their faces. Most looked asleep, a few expressions revealed shock. Women remained adorned with clothes and bits of jewelry, their faces covered in the Muslim fundamentalist tradition; men still had their gold teeth.

Unbelievably, Wyley heard a groan. One corpse near the surface of the heap shifted, raising an arm and opening its eyes. Wyley froze. It was a middle-aged man. Any reporter— or CIA field personnel—worth their salt would have seized the moment, but Wyley couldn't move.

Lying on his back, near the top of the pile, the heavy-boned, dark-haired Syrian began vomiting uncontrollably, gasping for air. Gazing in total disbelief, Wyley looked on, paralyzed, unable to muster the courage to climb the body heap and help a fellow human being in need.

The Syrian man turned his head, their eyes met, and for a few moments, time stood still. His gaze revealed a profound hopelessness. Wyley, feeling the man's death agony and over-whelmed by the situation, wept openly, tears streaming down his face in the mist.

Seconds later, the Syrian lost focus, gagged on his own vomit, suffocated, then quietly stilled.

Finally, Wyley could stand it no longer. Instinctively, he lifted his camera, knowing it would shield him. Focusing on the dead man's eyes, deliberately blurring the surrounding background, his heart stepped out of the picture and his hands took over. One shot, the motor drive sang, another, then another, bracketing each exposure without conscious thought. Running on photographer's automatic, in the distance, maybe a half mile downstream, Ramsi saw something moving through the eyepiece. It looked like black diesel smoke rising from twin exhaust stacks; might be a front loader working bodies, but through the mists, he couldn't be sure.

Struggling to hear the engine noise, Ramsi held his breath, his attention suddenly shifting toward the old neighborhood across the river road. The cold stillness was punctuated by the sound of wooden wheels creaking. The sound lasted ten seconds or so, then, except for the distant howling of dogs and wind racing down the alleyways, Hama fell silent once again.

As best he could judge, the sound came from an alley. He couldn't be sure which one.

Cautiously approaching one narrow street, a cold chill shot down his back. *The Syrian army*. Soldiers carried corpses, one after another, out of neighborhood apartment buildings, loaded them onto wooden pushcarts, then dumped them alongside the river. The Syrian army was in charge of the cleanup, clearing the dead from the west side; but from the looks of them, they were only boys, kids really; couldn't've been over sixteen. Kids or not, they were integral cogs in Assad's mechanized body-disposal apparatus.

But where's the regular army? And the officers?

Ramsi wanted to know exactly what happened in Hama, how it happened, and why. It had been twenty-eight years since Assad's father—often called "the Lion of Damascus"—first purged Hama of the Muslim Brotherhood, an underground coalition of guerrilla groups. Even today, no one knew how many fundamentalists his regime killed during the 1982 massacre, but Amnesty International estimated ten to twenty-five thousand civilians dead, thousands more homeless. To make sure the job was done right, Hafez Assad crushed the troublesome neighborhoods with bulldozers, plowed up their rubble, then flattened them like a parking lot.

Like his father, Bashar Assad didn't destroy one of his own major cities every day—murdering countless thousands of his own people was reserved for special occasions—and Wyley believed if this could happen in Hama, no one was safe anywhere in the Middle East, perhaps anywhere in the world.

Wyley metered off the building shadows and grimaced. There wasn't enough light for a good body-cart shot in the alley. He needed a faster lens and his big flash, so he set up as he approached the boy soldier clearing the block.

On seeing Ramsi, the boy put on his sternest, most commanding expression and raised his weapon. "Halt!"

Dropping his camera and big flash, Wyley raised both hands, palms open toward the soldier. The bulky camera assembly fell like a full gallon of milk swinging by a tether and knocked the wind out of him. Its long lens rotated downward, bouncing off his lower abdomen. Pressure from the neck strap caused his head to throb.

The young soldier approached cautiously, looking for bullets or grenades on Ramsi's bandoleer. Across his chest, outside his trench coat, Wyley's bandoleer was festooned with rolls of film, extra batteries, and magnetic disks.

Wyley watched the boy's face, all the while keeping a close eye on his gun barrel. Normally, he never stuck his neck out for anyone and wasn't about to get gunned down by some frightened, trigger-happy kid. Even in the dim light, he could see stubble on the boy's lip and chin. *This kid's barely shaving.*

The boy soldier pointed his rifle barrel toward the bandoleer. "Empty it."

Wyley did so, laying out a dozen film canisters on the street.

Immediately, the tension in the boy's face relaxed, and Ramsi felt the immediate crisis had passed. Behind the boy's thin facade of toughness, Ramsi sensed sadness and age beyond his years. His eyes conveyed anguish, having already witnessed more death than most would see in a hundred lifetimes.

"Papers," the boy demanded.

Wyley handed over his *New York Times* press pass stamped BEIRUT BUREAU CHIEF. Not surprisingly, there was no mention of the CIA or any affiliation with the United States government. The soldier nodded approval. "We have been instructed to assist you in every way possible, Mr. Ramsi."

Once the boy lowered his weapon, Wyley lifted his camera, relieving the pressure on his neck. "You could start by telling me what happened here."

"I don't know. I'm not sure anyone knows, not yet anyway. We were given orders to empty these apartment buildings and bury the dead in a long open trench outside the city."

Wyley shot the young man a skeptical glance.

"I'm sorry to startle you, Mr. Ramsi, but we can't be too careful. We aren't welcome here."

"I can imagine." Wyley nodded understanding. "Are you, or any of these soldiers, from Hama?"

"No."

"I'm sure that's no accident. How many died?"

"I don't know. Every hospital's overflowing; people're still dying and the doctors don't know why. It's like a black plague epidemic or some sort of killer stomach flu. Most of the injured feel sick and puke a lot."

Wyley agreed at first, then, remembering the Syrian, he shook his head from side to side. "No, that plague idea doesn't explain the dead fish along the river bank."

"You're right," the boy agreed. "Dogs died too, rats, mice. I dunno, hundreds, maybe thousands of 'em. We haven't begun hauling dead animals out of these buildings and I hope we get more help in here before we do." The boy went silent, trying to decide to what extent he should trust this reporter.

Wyley guessed the young man was overwhelmed, but at sixteen or so years of age, he didn't have the experience to recognize it. After all, as a sixteen-year-old male, you're practically immortal; you'll live forever and can handle any situation. Ramsi decided to pick the boy's brain. "What parts of the city were stricken?"

Suddenly, the boy's expression conveyed relief, as if the weight of the world had been lifted off his shoulders. "I'll show you." The boy laid out his city street map and pointed to their barricaded sector. Marked with blue highlighter, it stood out as a square about two thousand yards on a side, bordered by the river. "This area, here in the center, nearly everyone died. We called it the dead zone." The soldier swept out a circular region near the middle of the blue sector, about one thousand yards across. "Outside the dead zone to the barricade, some lived, some died, and some're still sick. It all stopped at the river. Doesn't make sense, does it?"

"No. No, it doesn't. We're missing something important somewhere. Did you check the water?"

"They checked it first thing. I'm told it's as good as it gets in this part of the city."

"How about poison gas? I heard talk of chemical weapons on the road to Damascus."

"The Syrian army had nothing to do with this." The boy spoke in a defensive tone. "They're already overextended, spread out across the Turkish border. I know; both my brothers are there."

"I wouldn't want to fight the Turks," Wyley said. "But what about the gas? Did you check anyway? Hama could've been attacked."

"A team came through earlier today and found no trace."

"What about radiation?"

"We were trained for that and checked it first thing. Background radiation levels were normal."

"If someone set off a nuke, we'd know it," Wyley concluded. "The fireball telegraphs it to satellites around the world. We've all seen the pictures. There'd be a blast, fireball, debris, and radioactive fallout everywhere. Is there anything else you've seen? Anything else you could add?"

"I talked to many of the survivors, Mr. Ramsi, and nobody knows anything."

"There's no devastation," Wyley observed. "No cratering, no evidence of any blast or fireball, no trace of radiation or poisonous gas, only the sick and dying."

The young soldier looked down for a few moments, then raised his head, never looking Wyley in the eyes. "Nobody saw anything, nobody heard anything, nobody's claiming responsibility, and nobody's talking. It's like the death angel passed over Hama and these people just died."

Wyley hurriedly jotted down what the boy had said, verbatim. It took a few minutes, but the boy was patient. Once he'd gotten it on paper, he read it back and the young soldier concluded, "That's the way I see it."

After a few moments' thought, Wyley said, "I need to see the mass grave before it's . . . closed."

Focusing only on the here and now, the boy seemed surprised by the idea. "You're thinking about where to go from here? What's next?"

Wyley nodded.

The boy grimaced as he spoke. "Pictures?"

"Yeah, pictures."

"You're probably safer if I go with you. You'll need directions anyway."

"Thanks, thanks a lot." Wyley smiled for the first time. Now his expression telegraphed relief. "I could really use your help. Do you have a car?"

"No, they dropped us off here for the day."

Ramsi studied the soldier's street map. "Mine's back here, just outside the barricades. You have any other suggestions?"

"If you're determined to understand what happened, visit the hospitals. They're jammed full with the sick, dead, and dying, but there doesn't seem to be much anyone can do that really helps."

"They've been working around the clock for three days now. Maybe the doctors have come up with something, maybe they've got some idea what's behind this."

This time, the soldier shot Ramsi a skeptical glance. "I doubt it. Hama hospitals are the place people go to die."

Dreamboat
Tuesday, Feb. 9, 4:38 A.M.
Ashburn, Virginia

"Daddy, Daddy!" Turning on the light, Dr. Graham Higgins's six-year-old daughter bolted into his bedroom with news that could not wait. "Somebody's at the door."

Startled out of a sound sleep, Graham covered his eyes with a pillow, struggling to make sense out of the energetic little whirlwind that just blew in. He'd been in bed only two hours when the storm hit. Downstairs, he heard the muted sound of the doorbell ringing.

"Who could it be at this time of night?" Graham's wife muttered. Regrettably, she hadn't escaped the disturbance either. Before Graham could speculate, the phone rang.

"When it rains, it pours," Graham said, picking up the portable. *Must be an emergency.*

"Hello . . . Hello . . . Is anybody there?" It was a man's voice, unfamiliar with a distinct Texas accent. The call was odd, because Dr. Higgins's residence was unlisted.

"Who is this?" Graham demanded, pulling on a robe to head downstairs.

"My name's Russum, Billy Ray Russum. I work for the government, Counterterrorist Center. I apologize for waking you, but my business is urgent. Could I speak with Dr. Graham Higgins?"

"Speaking, but I think you've got the wrong man. I'm a civilian now, a surgeon."

"You were in the Air Force, right . . . specialized in the medical effects of neutron radiation?"

Taken aback, Graham was quiet for a moment. The mention of neutron radiation stopped him in his tracks. For a moment, he forgot about the doorbell. Years ago, when he had been hungry for tuition and the United States military needed doctors, the Air Force had paid for his medical training in exchange for time in blue. He'd served his hitch then, but periodically it still haunted him. "That's true. I specialized in neutron radiation injuries."

"I understand you pioneered work with bone marrow transplants from mismatched donors. From what I read, your work's helped save thousands who were unable to find suitable donors."

"My transplant procedure was an extension of existing work, but tell me, please, what exactly do you want?"

"If you'll take a look out your bedroom window, sir, you'll see me. I'm across the road waving a cowboy hat. I need to speak with you in person because we can't discuss this matter over the phone. I don't mean to alarm you, but those Marines standing outside your door are pretty tough hombres. They're here to make sure nothing happens to you." Higgins parted the curtains and looked out the window.

"Marines? What's the Navy got to do with it?" From a distance, Russum's appearance reminded Graham of a Marine drill sergeant: a tall man in his late thirties, with massive forearms; his bald head and thick neck combined to form the silhouette of a fireplug.

"Everyone in Washington with a need to know is keenly interested in this one, I assure you."

"Oh, I see." A pause. "Am I being drafted? You know what I mean, roped back in again to active duty?"

"No, not exactly. Like I said, I need to talk to you in person."

"Well then, Mr. Russum, if I'm not being shanghaied, you'd better understand one thing. People's lives are depending on me tomorrow and I've gotta get some sleep. I'm scheduled in surgery all morning and—"

"If I could interrupt, Doctor. We've taken care of your hospital commitments, so don't worry about tomorrow's surgery."

"The hell you say! You had no right to interfere with my patients. What exactly do you mean taken care of my hospital commitments?"

"We had a talk with the chief of surgery and explained the situation. Like I said, we're here in the hopes that you'll help us. He'll cover for you tomorrow and you have his complete support if you come with us. You can call him anytime you like and check out our story, but I assure you we're in earnest. Now, we're freezing our butts off out here so can we come in?"

"No, not until you tell me one thing first. Are people's lives at stake here? Don't give me weasel-words—a straight yes or no will do."

Russum released a breathy sigh into his phone. "Yes."

"Very well then, pull out your ID for me. I'll meet you at the door." Graham hung up the phone and spoke to his wife and daughter. "You two may want to stay up here."

Puzzled, his wife asked, "Why? What'd they want?"

"Those men downstairs are from Washington. They want to see me immediately and they say it's important. I don't know what's going on yet, but my gut tells me the Navy's had a reactor accident, probably a big one. They're looking for someone who knows about radiation sickness."

"Not again. They're not pulling you back on active duty, are they?"

"After what happened last time, not without my kicking and screaming."

Hearing the tone in his voice, Graham's wife was not convinced. Approaching him, she got out of bed as he hurriedly threw on some clothes. "You're not going with them, are you?"

"No, I doubt it, but it's too soon to know for sure. It all depends on the situation. I mean, if our boys were hurt and they really needed me, I'd go. I'd have to; somebody's gotta do it."

Russum entered the house first, followed by Wyley Ramsi and three uniformed military officers—one admiral and two generals, all three from military intelligence. Wyley carried a briefcase filled with photos and his laptop computer. Graham led them into the kitchen, where the six men sat down around the table. Outside, eight armed Marines wearing night-vision goggles silently dispersed around the house. One minute they were in plain view under the front porch light, the next minute they'd simply disappeared.

Russum took off his hat and introduced Wyley Ramsi as a *Times* correspondent. He didn't mention the CIA. Ramsi bore the dark, distinguished features of an Arab from the Middle East. Thick black hair and mustache; dark brown, nearly black eyes; and massive bones formed his solid, five-foot nine-inch frame. Graham couldn't be as sure about Wyley's age, but ballparked him at thirty-five.

From almost any perspective, the conclave looked extraordinary. One sleepy-eyed, middle-aged doctor sitting at his kitchen table surrounded by this high-powered government entourage—three uniformed, silver-haired intelligence officers, a Middle Easterner, and one barrel-chested cowboy doing most of the talking. When Graham had gone to bed that night, he'd never have believed he'd be in his kitchen surrounded by military top brass at five o'clock in the morning. *Normally*, Graham mused to himself, *midnight meetings like this were reserved for American history books*.

Without wasting words, Russum summarized the background behind the ghastly situation in Syria. "Something's happened in Hama and we've got to know what. Assad's regime has been under siege for the past year. Once a week, the Muslim Brotherhood sets off a bomb outside some government office building or official's home, several of his officials were gunned down in broad daylight, even his secretary was abducted and tortured. Two weeks ago, assassins tossed several live hand grenades at President Assad inside the official visitors' palace at Damascus. He escaped unharmed, thanks to a bodyguard and his own quick thinking. One bodyguard was killed smothering a grenade while Assad kicked two others away."

Graham listened, but was neither moved nor impressed.

"So, what else is new in the Middle East? Assad's not popular—why should I care?"

Russum paused, thinking how he might best convey the essence of their concerns. "The rebels backed him into a corner, wedged him between a rock and a hard place. His troops were already overextended across the border and he couldn't redeploy them to put down this uprising without jeopardizing his Turkish front."

"And?" Graham's patience was short.

"We think he may have nuked his own people—wiped out the rebels' stronghold in Hama—to stay in power."

Graham's jaw went slack, his expression revealing disbelief.

"This type of revenge is not without precedence. His father and uncle did it before. In 1982, they claimed responsibility for killing thirty-eight thousand people in Hama for the same reason. They used their latest weapons back then, against their own citizens, to maintain control."

"No, no. That happened forty years after World War Two; it's too fantastic to believe." Graham considered Russum's story, then focused on one obvious conclusion he felt he should challenge directly. "You're telling me Syria's got nuclear weapons?"

"We're working on confirmation with the Russians, but our latest information out of Hama leads us to believe they do. That's where Wyley comes in. He was one of the first reporters on the scene after Assad lifted his ban on the press."

"And they used these weapons against their own population?"

"Yep. That's about the size of it. Wyley'll pick up the story from here."

Showing countless photos along the way, including a poster-sized enlargement of Hama's city map, Wyley summarized his observations. Folding the human aspects into the story as only an eyewitness could, his delivery was both passionate and heartfelt. Once he'd said what he needed to say, he told Graham what was on his mind. His plea, an emotional call for support, concluded with, "No one is safe anywhere. If this can happen in Hama, it can happen here."

Still, Graham was not convinced. "What's this got to do with me? Syria's halfway around the world. I don't like it, but if they want to blow themselves off the face of the earth, there's nothing I can do to stop them."

Graham heard Wyley say these people needed help, they were dying by the score. He was shocked at the images of human devastation, though the massacre seemed like a bad dream, something that happened in a history book a long time ago, someplace far away. Graham didn't know these people, didn't know their families, didn't understand their culture, values, or religion. Sure, it was a tragedy, every story that comes out of the Middle East is a tragedy, but he didn't feel any immediate threat to his family or the security of the United States.

Sensing the pulse of his one-man audience, Wyley recounted his interviews. "Speculation was rampant regarding what happened, and conflicting eyewitness reports were everywhere. One thing I learned is especially important because it clears up some of the inconsistencies. No one trusts the Syrian army, so what survivors told them and what they told me privately were two slightly different stories. Many survivors recount hearing something like an explosion or sonic boom, but we can't say with any certainty where it came from. Most said it came from the old Barudi district, a few survivors insisted it came from overhead, some couldn't say where it came from but they heard something, others considered it an act of God against the unbelievers. These people insist an explosion erupted from the enormous Barudi mosque, but left their holy structure untouched. I checked out the mosque firsthand and there's no crater, no shattered glass, no evidence of blast damage of any sort."

"Show me its location."

Wyley pointed to the center of the dead zone.

Graham looked puzzled. "And no lingering radiation?"

"No. Syrian soldiers were working without protection and they assured me radiation levels were normal."

In conclusion, Wyley recounted his hospital visits. Instantly, he sensed a shift in Graham's interest level. *No surprise*, he thought. *The man's a doctor.* "The hospitals are in utter chaos."

"I can imagine. How long since this happened?"

"One week ago today."

"Can I assume you brought medical information you'd like me to review?"

"That's right. I brought enlargements of some records and translated them for you. These people were the first to die." Wyley handed over a considerable stack of 8 × 10, glossy black-and-white photographs.

"You pretty much read my mind," Graham told him, scanning the records. "First off, I need to know the leading causes of death." Hurriedly, in handwriting only he could read, the doctor constructed a table on a separate piece of paper, then summarized his findings. "Respiratory failure, brain edema, and shock."

Everyone nodded agreement.

"Time till death?" Graham looked to Wyley.

"Some died immediately, others died one or two days later."

Next, Graham reviewed their symptoms and his expression turned grim. *Ataxia, a complete lack of muscular coordination, convulsions, tremors; lethargy; fever; anorexia, lack of appetite, dislike for food; respiratory distress; intermittent stupor; frequent and severe diarrhea, watery at first, turning bloody.*

"Show me what else you brought."

"I left Hama on day five, so in effect, that's when these records stop." Wyley handed over a massive folder containing far more records than the first batch. "These people died in two to five days."

Everyone waited quietly as Dr. Higgins absorbed the information he'd been presented. After jotting down notes for almost half an hour, he set his records aside and summarized his results. "I don't want to jump to conclusions here, gentlemen: however, this preliminary evidence is very nearly overwhelming. I'm afraid your concerns are justified. I wish they were not. It's radiation sickness all right, very large doses of whole-body radiation.

"Pathological changes in the gastrointestinal tract are undeniable. Malaise, depression, and fatigue often show themselves for no apparent reason. Some people seem to improve for a few days, their symptoms temporarily disappear—only to come back with a vengeance. Changes take place in their blood-forming tissues, their early symptoms recur, followed by delirium, coma, and death. White blood cell counts—the neutrophils—are dropping off the charts. These neutrophils are formed by bone marrow and resist bacterial infection. You've gotta have 'em. Believe me, this is no laughing matter.

"I recommend you keep an eye on the survivors for the next twelve weeks. Many will lose their hair, but when you see an increase in deaths from hemorrhage and infection, your case for radiation sickness will be indisputable. White blood cell counts showed an increase for the first couple of days, but have begun to drop; some're already below normal. Fact is, if it's radiation injury, white cell counts will be all over the map. During the seventh or eighth week, the white cell counts should stabilize and bottom out below normal. God willing, an upward trend will follow for some, but complete recovery will require several months, maybe longer."

The general from Air Force intelligence spoke for the first time. "Any idea regarding radiation doses, Doctor?" Technically, the unit used to measure radiation dosage on the body is called a REM, an acronym for Roentgen Equivalent in Man.

Graham nodded grimly. "For this second group, and it's only a knee-jerk, somewhere between one to five thousand rems. I say this because, on average, circulatory collapse followed exposure within two to five days. The first group probably received in excess of five thousand rems. Neither group had any hope of survival."

Graham hesitated for a moment, looking desperately for something positive he could say. "People who survive more than a week or two have good reason to feel more optimistic. Keep an eye on their lymphocytes and platelet counts. Plate count is our best method for determining radiation dosage in the sublethal range. Using platelet counts, we can estimate their chances for survival by gauging their level of exposure.

The neutrophil count parallels the white blood cell count so we can't use it as an index."

"What are platelets?" Wyley wanted to know.

"A constituent of blood which helps clotting. You're familiar with the appearance of hemorrhage and purpura in radiation injury?"

Wyley cringed. "I'll never forget it as long as I live."

"Without clotting, you have hemorrhage, often visible beneath the skin."

Graham mentally shifted gears, assembling their story, recounting his experience in the U.S. military, drawing his own conclusions. Some important information was missing from this picture. He couldn't put his finger on it exactly, but he was sure of it. Three years ago when the Air Force recalled him from civilian practice to active duty, he'd been intentionally kept in the dark and he wasn't going to stand for it again. If he'd learned only one thing from government service, it was that he had to think for himself. He looked Russum straight in the eyes and stated flatly, "I think you're holding something back from me. You know something you're not letting me in on."

Russum didn't deny it. "You know the drill, Doctor. We're telling you what you need to know." Like many men with honor, he was a terrible liar and knew it.

"You want me to believe a nuclear bomb went off in Syria and somehow we were too blind to detect it? Nothing showed up on satellite?"

"Nothing conclusive, nothing even suspect, really."

"And no lingering radiation, no blast, no burns."

"That's about the size of it."

Graham addressed the group. "I think we need to understand each other, gentlemen. I wasn't born yesterday and I won't be played for a fool, not this time around. If you know something you're not telling me, you'd better come clean. Don't expect to keep me in the dark and get any help from me. From what you've told me so far, this is a weapon unlike anything I ever heard of."

"Nuclear weapons are my specialty, Doctor," Russum acknowledged. "I know some of 'em better than my own family. I follow 'em around the globe and this one's outta my league, too. It's got me stymied." Russum looked across the table to Wyley and his three military colleagues. They communicated without speaking. Their expressions read, *Go ahead, tell him.* "Our biggest concern is that Assad and God only knows who else may have gotten their hands on a new kind of nuclear weapon—a pure-fusion neutron bomb."

"Yeah, right." Graham almost laughed out loud. "Pure fusion? Not likely, not in my lifetime."

"I'm not kidding, Doctor. What I'm about to tell you is my own opinion based on publicly available information dating back to the middle of the twentieth century. This is in no way, shape, or form our government's official position."

"I understand," Graham said, feeling he was about to hear the heart of the matter for the first time. "You're laying your cards on the table." Russum hesitated and Graham took notice. For the second time, Russum would neither confirm nor deny Graham's statement.

Once he'd collected his thoughts, Russum began. "Russia started work on a pure-fusion weapon in the early fifties. Theoretically, we know it's possible and they published hard data in the early sixties that made us think they had it. In 1952, a Russian named Artsimovich reported fusion was possible during the compression and implosion produced by a charge of conventional explosives. He completed a series of experiments where fusion was achieved without using the radioactive fission trigger. As follow-up to Artsimovich's work, sometime during 1961, Colonel Pavlov published an article in a Soviet military journal about their plans for a neutron bomb. According to Pavlov, their neutron weapon's lethal radiation effects would reach out five hundred yards without destroying property.

"It could have been a simulation or misinformation, we couldn't know for sure, but it led us to begin work on the neutron bomb ourselves. We took the easy way out, though—a fission-fusion device destined for use against the Russians if they invaded Europe."

"Cheap and dirty," Graham observed.

"Radioactive as all get-out," Russum affirmed. "You need to understand, though, the Russians were in a different position than us. They didn't want to contaminate Europe if war broke out because in a blitz, they needed land they could occupy immediately. My bottom line is this: They needed this pure-fusion weapon in Europe and we have a wealth of circumstantial evidence indicating they pulled it off without fission. They certainly understood the principles and their military would be well served by such a weapon. Short of analyzing one, Hama may be as close as we'll get.

"If they did develop pure-fusion devices, their low explosive power and near zero radioactivity make it likely they could've tested 'em without our knowing it. Our official position is that we don't know what the Russians have accomplished since 1963."

"That's hard to believe," Graham interrupted. "What happened in 'sixty-three?"

"The Atmospheric Test Ban Treaty."

"Yeah, I guess that makes sense. Testing moved underground."

Russum sensed he had Graham's attention and continued. "Do the Russians have the neutron bomb? Sure, why shouldn't they? Have they achieved pure fusion? They needed it in Europe so what's stopping 'em? Nothing, not a damn thing. They began working on it sixty years ago. Their pure-fusion program promised a clean, dreamboat version of the neutron bomb, and ten years later, they showed a full understanding of its principles. We know they got off to a splendid start, then their technical work dropped off our radar screens. They've even published military doctrine which uses 'em as tank killers. We're talking about small, clean, tactical neutron weapons here. For any field commander who likes nukes, this is as good as it gets."

"That's fine, just fine," Graham said sarcastically, disgusted by Russum's enthusiasm, "but we were talking about Syria."

"Since the Russian bear crawled back into its hole, their nuclear arsenal's been run like a leaky bucket. They keep up with most of 'em, but last I heard, they can't account for over one hundred warheads. That's not to say they don't have 'em, it's only to say they can't find 'em. More troubling than this is the underground pipeline. It's generally understood there's a black market pipeline set up for delivering these weapons to the Middle East."

"That's a confirmed fact and publicly available information," the Air Force general added.

"Makes me feel a whole lot better knowing it's public information," Graham snarled, fed up with the whole insane affair. After recovering his composure, he asked Russum for the truth. "You're really only guessing, right? You don't have one shred of physical evidence, do you?"

"We don't have anyone on the inside, if that's what you mean," Russum agreed. "We have solid circumstantial evidence regarding Russia's pure-fusion neutron bomb. The whole world knows they're missing over a hundred warheads, but no one outside Russia knows the types. We've seen evidence of the pipeline, but have no solid trail of money changing hands, not yet anyway."

"So what do you think really happened in Hama?"

"Retribution."

"Based on what you told me, I expect you're right." Graham was not satisfied and continued to press. "What are you really afraid of?"

Russum scanned the poker-faced expressions of his colleagues. "We aren't at liberty to say, not yet anyway."

"I see." Graham rubbed his chin knowingly, as if to say he'd been in this situation before.

"That's our story and we're stuck with it." Russum forced a smile. "We're pulling together a small, flexible team to sort through this situation in the Middle East. If Syria's stockpiling Russian warheads, in all probability, they're not alone. Iraq, Iran, Libya, and God knows who else may be involved. In our worst-case scenario, some government-backed terrorist outfit buys the manufacturing technology, reverse-engineers a pure-fusion device, copies it, and puts it into production. Pure fusion requires virtually no fissile material so mass production is possible, but not likely. It'd be darn near impossible to manufacture one of these babies without our knowing about it."

Russum paused, couching his words more carefully. "At least, we think it's unlikely for several technology-based reasons. Fact is, we're depending on technology barriers to protect us from this nightmare. We've never gotten our hands on a pure-fusion device to analyze so we must eliminate this production possibility up front. Looks like special forces will be involved, and chances are we'll be going places we're not invited. We need a medical officer, someone with your background, who'll keep us out of trouble. Will you help us?"

Graham answered without hesitation, sensing he had the upper hand this time around. "I've got to push back on you fellas and think about this. A surgeon can't just pull out on his patients and I've got my family to consider. Three years ago, I was corralled back into active duty and spent twelve months sitting on my thumbs, waiting for an accident that never happened, thank God."

Russum nodded understanding. "Live and learn. I remember when—"

"That was different," Wyley interrupted. "People are dying as we speak and we need your help getting to the bottom of this."

At first, Graham didn't reply, as if his silence would make the problem go away. A few moments later, he looked at Wyley and spoke as compassionately as their situation allowed. "If you believe what you told me, get your family out of Beirut and do it now, today."

Wyley looked back at Graham, Russum, and the senior officers sitting across the table. "They're already on the move, en route to the States, but it's slow going. There's a mass exodus from the area and the place is in gridlock. Flights out are booked solid and car traffic's ground to a halt, the roads are crowded with refugees on foot. They've got my satellite phone, though, and we're in touch. They're out of harm's way."

"That's what's important," Graham said, feeling relieved. While escorting the men to his front door, Graham offered them an olive branch he hoped he wouldn't live to regret. "If you find out anything earth-shattering about those missing warheads and you're willing to tell me about it, let me know. Otherwise, let's consider my government obligation paid in full."

"Very well, if you're sure that's the way you want it," Russum said somberly, shaking Graham's hand on his way out.

"That's the way I want it." As Graham opened the door, rays from the early morning sun broke above the horizon, their glare reflecting off his snow-covered lawn.

A few minutes later, after everyone was gone, Graham's wife appeared at the bottom of the stairs. "Well?"

"Well what?" Graham was tired and simply didn't get it.

"Well, what'd you tell them?"

"I told 'em I gave at the office."

CHAPTER TWO

HAARP
Tuesday, Feb. 9, 12:10 P.M.
Gakona, Alaska

Peering through the twilight, Air Force First Lieutenant Gary Ellie surveyed the government research facility's antenna farm from the backseat of the station's snowcat. Its headlights reflected off the snow, cutting through the dusky, dim light of Alaska's winter sun. Even inside the heated cabin, condensation from Gary's breathing continually fogged the windows. It was cold, a flesh-freezing twenty-eight degrees below zero; still, despite the miserable weather he'd been impressed with the station's technology and for good reason.

Gary Ellie was a tech-head, a computer specialist, and his new assignment to Gakona's ionospheric research facility promised an exciting world of possibilities he'd never dreamed possible. He felt like a kid in a techno-candy store and life was good. If he'd lived a hundred years earlier, he'd never have had the chance to do any of this neat stuff. Sure, the Alaskan winter was cold, long, and dark, but Gakona station offered the finest facility of its type in the world; its closest rival was its twin sister site located on Kwajalein, an American territory near the equator. He was in the middle of his orientation tour now—he'd been here only two days—and yet he felt impatient, like he couldn't absorb everything fast enough. He wanted to get wired into the program and contribute immediately.

There was so much to see, so much to learn, and many new people to meet. Judging from the folks he'd come to know already, he knew he'd be looking over the shoulders of the finest minds in the world. With the exception of Lieutenant Junior Grade Eion Macke—his tour guide and a Navy friend he'd made during his last assignment—Gary had the disconcerting feeling that everyone here was smarter than he was. In addition, they specialized in areas he knew very little about. In some workplaces, that combination would mean misery and isolation for any newcomer, but not here, not at Gakona station. So far, his brief experience had been exhilarating. People invited him in as they would a family member, freely offering him the benefits of their experience, asking him for computer advice, hoping his transition would be a pleasant and productive one. From what Gary understood, this supportive attitude reflected the philosophy of Gakona's top management and chief scientist, Andreas Pappasongas. He'd met the great man only briefly, but felt his inspirational influence at every turn. *What a magnificent vision these people have created!* Gary thought, gazing across the vast antenna farm.

Run jointly by the Air Force and Navy, the business end of Gakona consisted of five hundred antenna towers uniformly distributed in a grid pattern spread out over thirty-plus acres of snow-covered Alaskan terrain. Each antenna was a high-frequency crossed dipole, which meant two thin horizontal poles crossed at right angles near the top of each tower. Looking down from overhead, each pair of crossed poles formed the shape of a large plus sign. In addition, alongside each antenna tower stood its own individual transmitter cabinet, each identical in every respect. Even to the uninitiated, the order and symmetry provided by seemingly countless rows of transmitter towers were an impressive sight. Overall, the cookie-cutter repetition of many large, complex, yet identical elements conveyed a feeling of creation and wonder. More important than this, HAARP (pronounced "harp"—High-Frequency Active Auroral Research Program) provided the United States the largest ionospheric heater in the world, a state-of-the-art high-frequency radio transmitter facility that could radiate ten million watts of energy skyward. A seemingly large amount of energy in human terms, but insignificant compared to the energy occurring in nature.

Tapping his friend and snowcat driver Eion Macke on his shoulder, Gary yelled over the roaring engine noise. "Antennas seem to grow pretty well here."

A pleasant sense of déjà vu washed over Eion. He smiled, repeating verbatim the same lines he'd been given during his initial orientation tour this past summer. "Ya know, you're right about that. New ones're sprouting up all the time; we grow 'em here year-round."

"What's the secret?"

Hearing the question he'd been waiting for, Eion responded with the canned script lines he'd first heard seven months earlier. "It's the soil. You can't beat this Alaskan combination of frozen tundra and midnight sun."

"What sun?" Gary retorted, gazing across the dimly lit abyss. "I can tell already, I'm gonna miss the daylight." Although near noon, it was an overcast midwinter day and there was no perceptible sunshine at all.

"It's not bad on the inside," Eion said optimistically. "Besides, you'll be so busy you won't have time to think about it."

"Yeah, that's true enough."

"You know, you jumped outta the frying pan into the fire with this new job of yours. Schedule-wise, you're already weeks behind the learning curve, and with sea trials coming up, you've got to ramp up practically overnight."

"Another case of trial by fire," Gary said, chuckling. "Been there, done that, ole buddy. Setting schedule pressure aside, by my way of measuring it, this job's as good as they get. Great boss, good group of people, excellent upper management, and interesting work. I tell you what: I'm looking forward to this little adventure. Fact is, I can't wait to get started."

"Like I told you, I knew you'd like the work. As for me, I can't wait to get my feet wet. I've wanted to go to sea as long as I've been in the service, and so far in my naval career, I haven't even flown over water. Soon as you're onboard, I'm headed to the Channel."

Gary nodded understanding. "I expect the English Channel's going to look pretty good for a few weeks. How long you gonna be gone?"

"The test plan's got some slack built into it, but assuming an optimistic sunny-day scenario, the sea trial'll run eight to ten weeks. I'll get back in time for midnight baseball, though, no matter what happens."

"What are you talking about, midnight baseball?"

"You might not believe it, but by the end of May we'll start playing baseball games under the light of the midnight sun. From what I hear, it's really cool."

"That's going to take some getting used to, but it sounds like fun." Gary smiled from the backseat, then for the hundredth time, cleaned off the scratched, foggy plastic window. Beyond the edge of the antenna field, inside the facility fence, he saw the outline of a substantial building illuminated by outdoor parking lot lights. They'd come full circle around the station's perimeter and their return destination was in sight.

Eion parked the snowcat in an outdoor equipment garage attached to the diesel generator building. Once he killed the engine, they climbed out of the cat and entered the station's power plant. Gary felt a rush of warm air as they entered the building, followed by the stench of diesel fuel. His next impression—cookie-cutter symmetry—felt familiar. Everywhere he looked he saw identical power generators, laid out in an orderly step and repeat pattern. Final thing he noticed was the quiet. Not one diesel generator engine was running.

That's strange, Gary thought. "Why's everything shut down?"

"It's not complicated, really; we're off the air today."

"What do you mean? How does it work?"

"All power for the radio transmitters comes from here, thirty million watts' worth to be exact. Around ten million's converted to radio waves; the rest is dissipated as heat inside the transmitter cabinets you saw outside. Like everywhere else, housekeeping power for facility computers, lights, and heat comes from the power company grid, but power for the transmitters comes from here."

"Computers?" Gary grinned. "Where?"

"Computers? You've gotta be kidding. We've got computers running outta our ears back at the main building. We'll get to them after my fingers thaw out, but you can see 'em from here, if you'd like."

"Sounds good. I'd like to take a look and see what I'm getting into."

Eion led Gary to a workstation near the rear of the building. He logged on and in a matter of minutes brought up a network map of the Gakona local area computer network.

Gary knew this network management system software and went straight to work. In less than five minutes, his jaw fell slack. "I thought we'd seen it all back at the Clear Water comp center, but this place, the computing horsepower in this place blows us off the map. What about this network? What's all the computing power good for anyway?"

"Did you ever see the movie *Journey to the Center of the Earth*?"

"Yeah, years ago when I was a kid."

"Well, basically, HAARP lets you see underground without digging. I've seen it in action over the past several months, and believe me, it's a tremendously capable remote-sensing tool. HAARP generates ELF waves that can be used to communicate with submarines, measure ocean temperature and current, or create three-dimensional images of objects beneath the earth's surface. Technically, when HAARP's peering underground, it's called an earth-penetrating radar and our comp center houses the signal-processing power that makes it all possible." Eion stopped to organize his thoughts, but before he could continue, Gary jumped in.

"I still don't understand how all this works. Even at a high level, my puzzle's got some pieces missing. I mean, like what's ELF got to do with it? I thought HAARP transmitted high-frequency radio waves, not low."

"You don't have to know what goes on in your stomach to enjoy a sandwich, do you?"

"No, but I don't follow your point."

"Well, I've been learning this ionospheric physics stuff in small stages, one layer at a time. Believe me, it works and over time you'll understand it in ever-increasing detail. You'll know more about it than I do in a few weeks, but for now, let me tell you what I understand. I'm no expert at ionospheric physics or anything, but the good news is you don't have to be to figure out what's happening. To start, HAARP transmitters modulate currents in the ionosphere which in turn create very weak, coherent ELF waves. Super-sensitive radios detect this faint signal near the remote site then ship it back to us over satellite link. We separate the signal from the noise and assemble the underground pictures in our image-processing lab." Lifting his hand in a friendly gesture, Eion pointed to a group of icons blinking on-screen. "And that's where you come in."

"How do the pictures look? I'd like to see some."

"Easier done than said." Moving in front of the workstation, Eion pulled up a color picture showing a cross-sectional view of an underground mine shaft. "This was made this past century, back in the nineties."

Nodding, Gary studied the screen carefully. "It's difficult to interpret without explanation." At first glance, it looked like a yellow circle laid over a red background.

"It's the first underground image HAARP ever made. It's an underground mine shaft near Fairbanks, buried thirty meters beneath the surface. If you read the story behind this picture, I doubt you'd believe it. Turns out, the first time they tried to image beneath the surface, it worked. Almost unbelievable: astounded everyone involved. It was a fantastic success story and it worked great, first time out of the box."

"It doesn't look much like a mineshaft to me."

"That's because the picture's resolution is limited by the long signal wavelength. Long wavelengths are good for penetrating the earth and sea, but they limit the size of objects we can detect."

"I guess that makes sense. In effect, if you're going to detect something beneath the surface, it's gotta be big."

"That's right. Within the limits of its resolution, HAARP provides a journey beneath the surface of the earth without going there."

"Amazing."

"It's better than that, as you'll soon see." Without hesitation, Eion went to his home page, where he'd stored copies of new underground image files. After a double-click, he displayed a 3-D picture that reflected the latest state-of-the-art advances in graphics and signal-processing technology. Each intricately rendered cube looked like a textured, reasonably colored, three-dimensional cross section of the earth's crust. Satisfied with his selection, he raised an eyebrow and clicked the ROTATE tool on-screen. The earth's crust began slowly turning about its vertical axis. Next, he clicked a tool labeled TRANSPARENT LAYERS and typed *"90%."* Instantly, the cube appeared semitransparent except for its solid black inner core. With no training whatsoever, anyone could see the lake of black crude oil buried deep beneath the earth's surface.

"You're sure there's oil there, right?"

Nodding, Eion clicked an eyeball icon, making the image layer named OIL DERRICK visible. "That's a computer-generated oil derrick, but the actual rig sits right there, squarely over the crude. Other wells're scattered all across the surface, but not shown."

Gary Ellie gazed in wonder at first, then his expression turned enthusiastic. "This is awesome, absolutely awesome. If I hadn't seen it with my own eyes, I'd never have believed it."

Grapefruit
Wednesday, Feb. 10, 10:49 A.M.
Langley, Virginia

Graham felt out of place and somewhat disoriented inside the CIA headquarters building, but Wyley escorted him through security straight to Russum's office without giving him time to dwell on it.

During their hurried walk, Wyley brought him up to speed on the Counterterrorist Center. "In a nutshell," he explained, "the CTC is the hub where all our terrorist experts and information come together. It's a nerve center combining law enforcement, military special operations, and intelligence."

"All that sounds very interesting," Graham responded, "but what do these people really do?"

"Most are high-tech, white-collar spies," Wyley chuckled, still moving at a quick clip. "They listen in on terrorists' phone conversations and trace their finances."

"How?"

"Intelligence satellites, communication sniffers, computers—lots of computers—and field personnel like me."

"So you eavesdrop and follow their money trails?"

"Yeah, that's right. Plus, most important of all, we track their people networks."

Graham's expression conveyed disbelief.

Wyley smiled, pausing at the elevator. "The CTC's bursting at the seams these days. We've expanded up to the second floor."

"I'm guessing that means trouble." Graham sighed.

"That's right, terrorist training camps spring up faster than we can possibly follow, let alone shut down. Ten years ago, the CTC tracked the top thirty most dangerous groups; today, we cover over three hundred worldwide. Some have over two hundred members. You've obviously heard of bin Laden?"

The doctor nodded.

"You got it. He's been sick. Some news reports even claim he's dead." Entering the elevator, Wyley punched Russum's floor. "Hussein offered him asylum years ago but he refused it due to their philosophical differences. After bin Laden was reported ill, they worked through their disagreements and were inseparable until the Iraq War. Truth is, we believe bin Laden's replacement, a man named al-Mashhadi, is running the show these days, but the word on the street is that bin Laden never died. Anyway, Iraq keeps his myth and terrorist organizations alive because they have been useful."

"A lot of good the Iraq War did us."

Wyley forced his lips together in a grimace. "It did help for a while. Believe me, we're much better off than we would have been. Hussein had been sponsoring terrorism for years."

"Wonderful," Graham groused.

"Well, as you might imagine, bin Laden and al-Mashhadi are big here in spook town. They've got their own separate department inside CTC keeping track of them and their terrorists organization. I feel like I know these guys personally and think they'd be pleased with the notoriety."

"Sounds like big trouble to me."

"You have no idea," Wyley sighed. "In some respects, bin Laden's like Saddam Hussein and Ayatollah Khomeini combined, if you can imagine that. To make matters worse, his own people love him, like he's some kind of messiah or folk hero or something, but don't get me wrong: Iraq and al-Mashhadi bankroll and organize terror on a global scale using two organizations bin Laden set up. One's a financial network called the *Foundation for Islamic Salvation*, which runs money through companies in the United States, Europe, and the Middle East. This money web directly supports *al Qaeda*, their network of terrorists."

"You're talking about state-sponsored, organized terrorism on a global scale."

"That's a pretty fair one-line assessment. We monitor more Islamic small businesses and charities than you'd ever imagine, all loosely linked to bin Laden. Along with the Treasury Department, we keep an eye on his wire transfers while the Foreign Assets Office works with other countries overseas to tighten the reins on his money laundering."

"This is some kind of major operation; I mean, it really involves a lot of people."

"And money," Wyley agreed. "The businesses, terrorists, and money all get intermixed, but once you separate them, you get a feel for how the man keeps his worldwide network going."

"Big Brother is watching," Graham observed, "but I'm glad he's there."

"We're more like a baby brother, really. We're not perfect, but our heart's in the right place," Wyley concluded, opening Russum's office door.

Almost immediately, Graham sensed tension in the CTC. The activity here gave the impression of importance, size, and substance. Something was happening here, something big. Corralled near the back of the room, Russum was talking to three senior officers; Graham thought the big Texan would look more at home on a horse. He looked like a fish out of water trapped in the confines of his pale-green government office, his bald head reflecting the overhead fluorescent lights like a mirror.

Russum broke off his conversation and acknowledged Graham immediately.

"I'm glad you could come," he said, shaking Graham's hand.

"You said it was important. If I remember your exact words, you said you'd learned something that would rattle my cage."

"The reason I needed to see you is serious as hell. Yesterday, the stakes shot through the roof."

"I got that feeling over the phone," Graham acknowledged.

"We learned more about those missing warheads from a highly placed source inside Russia's Weapons Intelligence Bureau. I spoke to him yesterday, face to face, and what I'm about to tell you must not leave this room. It's a political hot potato and it's too soon to predict the fallout. Anyway, he gave us information I felt would change your mind."

"I'm listening," Graham responded, obviously not convinced.

"The information's got three parts. The first's got to do with pure fusion—the Russians have it, they've had it since the early sixties."

"Like you suspected?" Graham looked for confirmation.

"Yep. Second, we showed the Russians everything Wyley brought back from Hama and they believe they know what happened, at least part of it."

"Okay, let me take it from here," Graham interrupted. "Pure fusion comes as no surprise and they've got over a hundred missing warheads—type unknown, until now."

"That's about the size of it. The Russians believe that son of a bitch Assad dropped one of their missing neutron bombs on Hama. Based on Wyley's information, they think it was one of their ten-ton pure-fusion devices, air-burst from its optimal kill altitude, lethal to a range of five hundred yards."

Graham looked puzzled. "Ten tons? That sounds kinda small. I thought you weapons guys talked about megaton explosions."

"Yeah, that's true, but the numbers are misleading when it comes to neutron bombs. Truth is, a ten-ton pure-fusion device releases about the same neutron radiation as a twenty-kiloton Nagasaki-size fission bomb, only its blast radius is much smaller. If you air-burst both weapons from optimal altitudes, the main difference between them is that the blast effects from a neutron bomb won't clobber the ground."

"But its neutron radiation will, right?"

Russum nodded.

"Sounds like less bang for more radiation."

"Yep, in the business, they're called enhanced radiation devices."

"But there's still an explosion, right?"

"Yeah, but like I said, in an airburst, the explosive blast effects won't destroy buildings on the ground, at least that's the theory."

"Exactly what Wyley saw in Hama."

"Yep, and no lingering radiation to boot," Russum added, unfolding Wyley's city map of Hama. "It's the Russian pure-fusion device all right, right down to the kill radius. Look at this ten-ton footprint. Dead zone averages two thousand yards across measuring from the river—a textbook case. I'm afraid it all holds together." There was no satisfaction in his voice, only sadness.

"Isn't technology wonderful?" Graham vented bitterly. "Okay, you figured out what happened, but Hama hasn't moved; it's still halfway around the world. So what's that got to do with me?"

"Well, for years we've been depending on technology barriers and the scarcity of plutonium to limit the spread of nuclear weapons. Fact is, we've been depending on this to cover our butts. Well, when red mercury came on the scene a few years back, our technology barriers crumbled and our luck ran out. We're exposed as hell."

Graham shot Russum a skeptical glance. "So red mercury was the straw that broke the camel's back. Must be mighty nasty stuff."

"Red mercury brought down the walls all right, threw the whole perverted mess outta balance. Let me give you the answer up front before talking 'bout the question. The bottom line is this. With red mercury, pure-fusion neutron bombs the size of grapefruit can be mass-produced, without plutonium, using off-the-shelf technology. You know—"

"God help us," Graham interrupted. He couldn't stop himself.

Russum paused then picked up where he'd left off. "You know about red mercury?"

"Thankfully, no."

"It's like this, Doctor. Conventional explosive triggers are the key to pure fusion and red mercury is key to the conventional explosion. Red mercury's a compound that's been exposed to massive amounts of radiation. When exploded, it creates phenomenal heat and pressure so intense it triggers pure fusion without plutonium."

Graham sat slack-jawed, hearing, but not fully comprehending.

Russum studied his expression and decided to spell it out at the risk of insulting his intelligence. "Heat and pressure from the exploding red mercury are sufficient to trigger a pure-fusion neutron bomb. Believe me, using red mercury, you can make these devices really small."

"How small again?"

"A softball-sized mini-nuke has a kill radius of five hundred yards. The Russians confirm this and now reluctantly admit twenty mini-nukes are missing."

Stunned and off balance, Graham felt the world as he knew

it shifting beneath his feet. He didn't know what to say, so he said nothing at all.

"If this doesn't sway you, nothing will."

"You're completely serious?" Graham prayed this was one of Russum's head tricks. He'd seen it before in isolated government circles—overstate the case for shock value, disorient the subject, and they'll become receptive, more accepting of a situation which might otherwise be considered nonsense.

"More serious about this than anything else in my life."

"I sure hope you're wrong." Graham sighed. "I gotta believe you're exaggerating this situation a bit."

"Damnit, Graham. I wish I was wrong too, but I'm not and wishing ain't gonna change it. I've seen pictures of 'em and I'm telling you these things can be smuggled into the States in a case of grapefruit. If we don't destroy 'em at the point of manufacture, there's not a damn thing we can do to stop 'em."

"Privately, Russia's admitted to producing stockpiles of red mercury and much of it's missing. If you've got a reactor, it's easy enough to make. They think some's legitimately lost, but most has been stolen and shipped throughout the Middle East. I said this before, but it's important. Before red mercury entered the picture, plutonium was needed to trigger fusion, but now all that's changed. I'm telling you red mercury means neutron bombs can be built the size of a grapefruit and they're lethal across several city blocks. In my book, we're talking about the ultimate terrorist weapon. Cheap, small, mass-produced mini-nukes. During Clinton's administration, U.N. weapons inspectors in Iraq found documents showing they'd purchased large quantities of red mercury. We were concerned then, and eventually fought the Iraq War hoping to put an end to this. We searched, but Hussein was smart. He cut a deal with Syria and moved everything across the border, knowing we wouldn't go there. Now, all these years later, Hussein is gone, but his malice lives on. That part of the world will never change, not in our lifetime; too much hate, too much pain, generations of death. Still, after this Hama incident, we're sincere. Bush was right. We've got to stop this at the source, before it crosses our borders."

"Who's on your hot suspect list?"

"Russia believes Iraq, Iran, and Syria have mini-nukes. At this juncture, I'd go with their judgment. How many they have, no one can say. We both expect they've reverse-engineered 'em by now and probably have them in full production."

For the first time, Graham spoke straight from his heart, his voice barely audible, but clear. "Jesus, dear God in heaven, don't let these monsters loose on our children."

Bull's-eye! Russum thought, following Graham's lead. "Our job is to locate their mini-nuke stockpiles and manufacturing facilities, then wipe them off the face of the earth. We're gonna start searching inside Syria and Iraq, and this time, we're not asking permission or broadcasting our intentions through the U.N. We're gonna do what we should 'a done years ago and rid the world of this scourge once and for all."

"This operation's already set up and approved?"

"It's being organized as we speak and my orders say exactly that. We've got approval from the top down and my only concern is that it may grow too big too fast. It could be a tragic mistake to put Syria or Iraq on alert too soon."

"After Hama, seems like they'd already be on alert. These people aren't like us, but they aren't stupid."

After pondering Graham's point, Russum asked, "So if you were Assad, what would you do after Hama?"

"Probably lay low and let the whole thing blow over."

Russum smiled. "Me too. I asked Wyley the same question and guess what, Sherlock? You hit the nail on the head your first try. These people aren't like us in some very important, fundamental ways and we can't change it. Wyley's an expert on the Middle East, he's lived there much of his adult life and understands these people. Know what he said?"

"No, but I wish you'd tell me. I don't understand how any Syrian alive could allow Assad to nuke his own people."

"Wyley said Assad would eventually take full credit for the massacre. His dad did it before and bragged about it in the process. In the Middle East, life is cheap, fear begets power, and power is everything. We can't make them value human life and they're not going to change because we want them to. In most respects, time simply stands still in the Middle East.

Sure, they've got high-tech gadgets and all, but the people haven't changed. Their thinking hasn't changed for a thousand years. They're not like us, and honestly, they scare the shit outta me. Best we can do is contain 'em, let 'em blow themselves to hell. They'd massacre their own kind if it'd keep 'em in power, and they'd wipe us off the face of the earth if they could."

"I'm not an expert on the Middle East," Graham said, "but I expect you're right. I mean, it sounds like something they'd do." The doctor committed Wyley's observations to memory because somehow he knew they'd be important. Moments later, he deliberately steered the conversation in the direction he wanted it to go. "You're not planning any sort of technology raid, are you? I mean, you're not bringing these things back to some U.S. weapons lab for mass production?"

"You're one suspicious fella." Russum smiled. "I guess if I were in your shoes, I'd ask the same question."

"Well, then?"

"No, there's no need for that. Our mission is one hundred percent seek and destroy. It'll be dangerous; special ops always are. Fact is it's getting more dangerous by the minute, but now that the red mercury cat's outta the bag, the Russians're being more candid about their weapons intelligence. They've offered technical support and committed to send us one of their mini-nukes."

"What about Israel?"

"We know they have 'em, but they're not our problem. They'll help us because it's in their best interest. In this case, it's obvious they want the same thing we do and this job's important. I have no idea how many lives may be at stake here, but any way you cut it, we're pitted against ruthless, government-sponsored terrorists with the ultimate weapon. It doesn't take much imagination to plant this thing on the steps of the Capitol and that puts it in your own backyard.

"Money's moving inside bin Laden's organization and we think something's coming down. We've traced four wire transfers over this past week, but at this juncture, that's all we know. After what's happened in Hama, we can't overlook anything."

Russum paused, then offered one final observation. "Like I said, I don't have much imagination, but you can't make this stuff up."

Graham looked up, staring Russum squarely in the eyes, a cold sweat beaded across his forehead.

His expression reminded Russum of a lost little boy, conveying a kaleidoscope of pain, sorrow, and loneliness all rolled into one glance. He could see Graham was scared, struggling to do the right thing, but he believed the doctor was destined to go with them. In his heart, Russum believed resistance was futile. Billy Ray Russum was a pretty good judge of character, and maybe in that respect, he knew Graham better than Graham knew himself. Instinctively, Russum shot him a reassuring glance, a kind of we're-in-this-thing-together look that let Graham know he wasn't alone, then he pressed for closure. "We really need you, Doc. You with us?"

Graham's spine stiffened as the feeling returned to his fingers. Nervously, he rubbed his hands together, every muscle tense, his head throbbing, his stomach knotted into an icy ball. He wasn't born yesterday; he knew better than this. It'd be dangerous, his future was uncertain; still, something inside him could not sit back and do nothing. He had to face it. Maybe it was the way he'd been raised, maybe it was the change that came with being a dad, or maybe it was his family; he didn't understand it. Maybe it was just who he was. "I'm in," he sighed. "Somebody's gotta do it."

CHAPTER THREE

Red Cross
Thursday, Feb. 11, 11:17 A.M.
Near the bank of the Shatt-al-Arab River
Basra, Iraq

Whop whop whop whop whop! The helo pilot was one of the best in the Iraqi army, but he flew like a wild man under fire, constantly checking his six. Strapped in tight, leaning hard to one side, he ham-fisted the stick and rotor collective with all the finesse of a butcher whacking out steaks with a cleaver. Looking out his bullet-riddled windshield, he spotted a large red cross painted on the hospital's helipad and cut a beeline to target. Jamming his feet against the rudder peddles, he stomped down hard, rotating his helicopter's tail through a full three-sixty, scanning the surrounding rooftops for snipers. Though already dropping like a rock, he steeply banked his aircraft, deliberately spiraling out of the sky at a near-suicidal rate. Fifty feet above the rooftop, he increased the main rotor's pitch, slowing their impact velocity at the last possible second. Downward force from the rotor backwash toppled every satellite dish on the roof, throwing them to the deck in disarray. Moments later, the helicopter slammed down hard against the concrete pad, but its oversized combat gear held fast.

Satisfied with the landing, the pilot surveyed his cockpit Plexiglas—no new bullet holes. They'd come down clean. He surmised this at a glance because every existing hole was patched with duct tape, highlighted with black marker. In theory, this type of unannounced, spontaneous flight should reduce their chances of taking sniper fire; still, with the leaks inside the Iraqi government, he never knew what to expect.

Low-level flying over Kurdish and Shiite rebel–infested areas of Iraq, especially along the Iranian border, was always a crap shoot. In an effort to improve their chances, their military chopper had been camouflaged, disguised to look like something it was not. Outside, except for two small clusters of gun barbettes bristling from its nose and tail, their aircraft appeared much like any other medevac helicopter. Inside, it was anything but.

Strapped down snugly near the rear of the bullet-proof cargo cabin, al-Mashhadi could feel the steady beat from the main rotor vibrating. Understandably, the big man was tense after the flight, but not overly so. After all, he knew the drill and today, so far, no one was shooting at him. As the prominent force inside the Iraqi cabinet and number one rebel target, helo-acrobatics came with the territory. The Iraqi minister of information had flown more low-level suicide finals than he liked to recall.

As the large, side-looking cargo door slammed open, six bodyguards armed with Skorpion machine pistols erupted from the dark cavern. Once the passageway between the chopper and rooftop doorway was secure, the menacing silhouette of al-Mashhadi's enormous hulk emerged from the black hole. Hunching forward, trying to clear the cargo doorway, he banged his massive head against the metal bulkhead with a dull thud. Undaunted, he moved down the steps to the helipad and stood upright.

By Iraqi standards, the man was a giant, a dark, shadowy figure who personified his motto—"Nobody hurts me unharmed." Towering above the others at six foot five, and shaped like the front end of a bus, al-Mashhadi knew he offered an easy target and wasted little time in direct sunlight.

As if on cue, once the big man cleared the rotor blades, the helo pilot lifted off and hovered overhead in one well-orchestrated, continuous cover motion, laying down a protective screen of rotor backwash, blowing smoke and sand. Less than thirty seconds later, the massive hulk had lumbered across the rooftop, entered the freight elevator, and disappeared into the darkness.

In the blink of an eye, the helo pilot increased his collective pitch, hurling his aircraft skyward. Slamming his stick forward, he punched the burners and disappeared in the distance.

Once inside the elevator, al-Mashhadi inserted his security key into the control panel, giving him an e-ticket ride to the otherwise inaccessible basement bunker. Less than two minutes later, al-Mashhadi and his band of thugs emerged to keep an unscheduled appointment.

Kajaz Hamandhani would never forget his first meeting with al-Mashhadi. The big man burst into his small office unannounced, surrounded by six heavily armed bodyguards. Once they'd judged the area secure, one bodyguard motioned that Kajaz should stand from behind his desk and move to one side. Looking down the wrong end of the gun, he did so without conscious thought.

The big man approached Kajaz, dwarfing him like Goliath towering over David. Stunned, the little man froze, unable to speak or move, his mind racing in a thousand directions. Finally, after what seemed like an eternity, Kajaz recognized al-Mashhadi's deeply wrinkled face from pictures he'd seen on TV. The man's skin was dark and weather-beaten from years in the sun, its texture coarse as old leather, his eyes dark, black as pitch.

Mustering his courage, Kajaz spoke to the massive form at the center of the storm, greeting him with the traditional Arabic salutation, *"Ahlan wa sahlan, ahlan wa sahlan"*—my house is your house.

Al-Mashhadi took Kajaz's seat without acknowledgment. Once the minister of information was comfortable, he surveyed the layout of the windowless office, looking through Kajaz as if he were invisible. The room was dim and cheerless, its bookcases lined with dank, smelly books about nuclear weapons, dating back to the dawn of the atomic age.

One book in particular caught al-Mashhadi's eye. Lifting the open book off Kajaz's desk, he studied its cover, *The Effects of Nuclear Weapons,* 1977. Behind his expressionless face, unseen by anyone, he smiled a thin, sinister smile. Below the book's title was a library stamp the man found ironic. It read simply,

Out of the corner of his eye, he noticed a plastic, circular slide rule kind of device, about five inches across, lying on the desk where the book had been. He picked it up, squinting to read the fine print around the outside border.

NUCLEAR BOMB EFFECTS COMPUTER

"What are you doing here, my friend?" al-Mashhadi asked, genuinely curious.

"Cleaning up Rashid's dust, checking his numbers." Rashid Al-Owhali was once one of Afghanistan's leading nuclear weapons experts.

The big man knew Rashid well; he'd helped bring him to Iraq and got him established as the head of its weapons development program. He probed further. "Why is this?"

"I don't trust anything he says without running through the numbers myself. So far, everything he's designed has been wildly optimistic with no margin for error. It's one thing to build a single prototype and make it work in the lab; it's quite another to manufacture them in volume with acceptable yields." Rashid was well known for stirring up a lot of technical dust, then leaving a trail of incomplete or marginal designs along the way.

"You learn quickly, my friend." Al-Mashhadi told Hamandhani to sit down and the two men continued talking. "Assad behaved stupidly. This situation in Hama has forced our hand, causing us to accelerate our deployment plans; we're pulling up the schedule effective immediately. We cannot risk discovery."

The Arab's expression showed some reluctance. "We're not ready."

"You must get these devices out of the country now. Timing is crucial."

"But it's the middle of the winter."

"The Halifax harbor never freezes. I have arranged a courier, a young machinist mate named Hakim Moussavi; his papers are ready, he'll be here within the hour, and he sails on the *Shell Udai* tomorrow."

"We weren't expecting this move until summer."

At this point, al-Mashhadi looked kindly at Kajaz. "You know, you are the image of your father. What a fine man he was, an honorable man. What a shame he's not with us today. *Ahlan wa sahlan.*"

Immediately, Kajaz understood he was being made an offer he could not refuse. As it happened, his father had been executed by an Iraqi firing squad during Hussein's rise to power. Back in the summer of 'seventy-nine, when Kajaz was a young boy, Hussein had considered his father a threat, tried him as a conspirator, then sentenced him to death by execution.

Kajaz considered his situation, then offered a carefully worded reply. "I will do as you request, but please understand, we have only six known-good devices and need half of them to prime the pump for our own engineering purposes. We must have them to stay on schedule and keep our manufacturing program moving forward."

Al-Mashhadi's expression turned to one of heartfelt concern for a friend. "Very well then, give Hakim every unit you can possibly spare. I pray you will be successful here, and soon."

Kajaz nodded, knowing his life depended on it.

Line in the Sand
Thursday, Feb. 11, 6:40 A.M.
Graham's house

"Eat your eggs before they get cold."

Sensing storm clouds gathering, Graham gazed down at his plate. From her tone, he knew his wife, Patty, was miffed, feeling put upon by his decision. "Guess I'm not as hungry as I thought."

"What about your patients?"

"They'll be in good hands and I'll talk to them all before I leave. Nobody's irreplaceable, but my job'll be here when I get back."

"Can you talk about it?—what you're doing, where you're going?"

"No, not really. I don't know many specifics about the mission, anyway. I'll probably get stuck on some ship somewhere, stranded out in the middle of the ocean. They told me about the problem to let me know what we're up against, but they're still working out the details. I won't learn much more until we're under way. From all accounts, it's a pretty hush-hush–type deployment and it's considered a black operation."

"That strikes me as suspicious. At least I need to know where you're going. What if one of the girls gets sick? How'll we stay in touch?"

"I asked about that, but turns out the answer's sorta complicated. Like you'd expect, we can write anytime but you can never plan on reaching me by phone. I'll have occasional access to a phone, but I'll never know when. Some days, I'll have e-mail, but I may have to go for an entire week without logging in. In most respects, I simply disappear."

"This sounds like cloak-and-dagger games on a shoestring budget. What's the problem with the phone? Why don't you just carry your cell phone with you?"

"They've got their reasons. My phone could be tracked like a beacon and give our position away. Besides, it doesn't work everywhere."

"Sure it does. You've called me from all over the world."

"I can't go into it, but believe me, if I could carry my phone, I would."

"This isn't another boondoggle, is it?" Patty's comments could bite when she wanted them to.

"I know it's hard on you after what happened last time, but I wish you wouldn't be so callous about the whole thing. I'm not even gone and I miss you and the girls already."

"But you said you wouldn't go."

"Yeah, but they learned more about the situation in the last couple of days. Things I couldn't ignore, not and live with myself anyway."

"What are you talking about? New information? What could be so important that it'd pull you away from your patients and family?"

"I can't talk about the specifics, you know that, but they've got a situation festering I couldn't turn my back on. Sometimes, at least since I've gotten older, I discover lines drawn in the sand that I never knew existed."

"I don't understand what you mean."

"I've discovered boundaries or limits inside me that must have been etched there when I was a kid. I don't know what else to call them, really. I mean, I never even knew some of 'em existed until they'd been crossed."

"You're talking in riddles."

After a few moments' thought, he tried again. "This situation violates something I feel very deeply about and it could threaten us all."

"It can't be that bad. Why don't you just ignore it?"

"Because if I do, people I care about are going to get killed. All night long I—"

"*Killed?*" Patty interrupted. "Who said anything about getting killed?"

"Well," Graham backpedaled, "in all fairness, I may have overstated my case a bit, but I slept on it all night long and that's how I feel. I wish I could ignore it, but it won't go away. We've got to contain this problem, make sure it doesn't spread or get any worse."

"It sounds dangerous. You're not on the front line, are you?"

Graham hesitated and his wife fired another round.

"Nobody's going to shoot at you, are they?"

"No, no, not likely, nothing like that. They don't shoot doctors. I operate from the rear as more of a consultant. Besides, they wouldn't trust me with a gun."

"Not if they know what's good for 'em." Patty smiled slightly. "What do you know about guns anyway?"

Graham shrugged, but didn't answer.

"So, is it some new disease?"

"Not exactly, but it's like a plague we've gotta isolate before it spreads."

"From what little you've said, it sounds like another American mission to save the world." Her voice rang cold, acerbic.

"No, nothing so grand as that. Maybe it's enough to say we're trying to make the world a safer, better place."

"Why you? Let someone else do it. Let someone else put their lives on hold for a change." Patty's eyes were cloudy now.

"I won't be gone long. Russum promised six to eight weeks tops. Once I get the new recruits onboard, I'm outta the program."

Patty released an exasperated sigh. "Graham, you're not in shape for this nonsense. I don't think you're up for it. You've never been the hero type. Other than walking to the car, you haven't done anything really physical since you got out of the service, and besides, you've got us to consider." She was scared, grasping for straws. It wasn't her words that hurt so much as the harshness in her voice.

"I have considered you; I always think of my family first. And the exercise'll be good for me—relieves stress."

Patty's mind was racing nonstop, running wide open with her ears disconnected. "Nothing anyone can do will make a difference. It never does."

Instead of keeping his head low and returning fire, Graham withdrew behind a wall of silence. After absorbing the pain and truth behind Patty's blow, he said what he wanted to believe. "I'm not blind to what you're saying and you may be right. God help us if you are."

Graham's words connected, shattering Patty's protective facade like a sledgehammer. He saw it in her expression and held her tightly in his arms. She lay her head on his shoulder, and for several minutes, their walls came down, their hearts touched, and emotionally they were one. Although trying to be brave, Graham felt her warm tears on his shoulder.

"I'm sorry," Graham murmured. "I don't mean to upset you. I know it's hard. I've been wrestling with this for days."

"I'm sorry, too," she said. "I know deep down you're trying to do the right thing, only it's tearing me apart. It's like you tell me sometimes: I'm feeling spread out all over the map. Worried, scared, angry, especially angry, only I'm not sure who to kick. I don't know, Graham, I'm having a lot of trouble accepting this. I trust you, I believe in you, but it's hard not knowing the whole story, not knowing how it's all gonna turn out."

"Tell me about it." Graham smiled. "I'm feeling like a scatter plot too, spread out all over. I only hope I'm doing the right thing. I pray we make a difference."

"From what you said, Graham, you'll make a difference. From what you told me, you've got to."

The Phone Call
Thursday, Feb. 11, 9:57 P.M.
In a studio apartment
New York City

"You're welcome to stay with us anytime," a soft voice said at the other end of the phone. "We'd love to have you and we're always here if you need us."

"I know, and I appreciate it very much, Dad. Maybe this summer, after Katie's out of kindergarten. I've been thinking it might be the best thing for Katie, and me too."

"Well, that sounds great to us, but it's your decision. Just understand that your mom and I would love to have you both back here with us whenever you're ready."

"I know, Dad, and I think you're right. It seems like I could have figured it out a long time ago though."

"No, don't think anything about that. Some lessons we have to learn for ourselves; sometimes we just have to learn the hard way. You know, I'm sorry the way your marriage turned out but it did give us Katie. I never liked the way he treated you, but Katie's wonderful."

"She is a little doll," Mary Marshall agreed quietly. "She fell asleep tonight on the couch when she was coloring."

"Please tell her we love her when she wakes up," Mary's father said quietly. "We miss you both and love you very much."

"I love you too," Mary said. "Good night."

Mary Marshall hung up her phone feeling a little homesick for her family, the New England seacoast, and the carefree life she used to know. Remembering their sunny days at the beach, she studied every feature of her tiny white-walled studio apartment by contrast. Like the beach, it was clean and bright, but that's where the comparison ended. Its walls were lined with Katie's most recent artwork, but the tiny space was hardly large enough for a single adult, let alone a mother and kindergarten-aged daughter. The apartment provided a small bathroom with kitchen and living area combined, but little else. Remarkably, she remembered, when she'd rented the place, the kitchen was considered a second room and now, only one year later, the tiny space was stacked nearly waist-high with boxes of colored construction paper, most of it adorned with Katie's priceless masterpieces.

Looking about the room, Mary took inventory of her belongings. Their family furniture consisted of a sleep sofa and chair, one child-sized coloring desk and rocker, plus a lamp.

As for the family treasures, Mary kept them squirreled away in those boxes.

CHAPTER FOUR

Voyage
Friday, Feb. 12, 9:23 A.M.
On the *Shell Udai*
Basra, Iraq

Hakim Moussavi had been raised and educated by the state, his parents having been killed in the Persian Gulf War. Fed a continuous diet of anti-American rhetoric, Saddam Hussein's picture adorned the walls of every school room he'd ever attended. Not surprisingly, he'd learned what he knew about the world jaundiced heavily by Hussein's perspective and bin Laden's terrorist training. At twenty-four years old, he'd been hand-chosen for this mission—ferrying three grapefruit-sized neutron bombs across the Atlantic—by al-Mashhadi because Hakim reminded the big man of a younger incarnation of himself. "Back off" was his credo and, like al-Mashhadi, nobody hurt him unharmed.

You couldn't tell his nationality by looking at him. *Another advantage,* al-Mashhadi had reasoned. If anything, Hakim looked European. Were it not for his dark hair, he could have passed as a Nordic member of Hitler's Aryan race—arrogant, with fair skin, square shoulders, perfect posture, and a look-down-my-nose-at-you attitude burning through his eyes. More important than this, he could be charming on demand and lied with all the passion of a polished politician. Speaking fluent English, sporting good looks and a quick, agile mind, he could easily pass for a rookie salesman or an American college student. On top of that, the young Iraqi agent possessed an extraordinary intuition for repairing mechanical things such as hydraulic pumps and engines, an invaluable talent for any machinist mate onboard the *Shell Udai.*

Al-Mashhadi's ship of choice for the voyage was no supertanker, but it was perfect for navigating the hazardous, often shallow waters of the Shatt-al-Arab River. Comparatively small as oil tankers go, capable of carrying 250,000 deadweight tons, the double-hulled vessel boasted state-of-the-art safety features, a shallow draft, plus every navigational aid available to the modern world. Navigation from Basra to the Persian Gulf was chancy, hazardous at best, treacherous at worst. In peacetime, with continual dredging, Iraq managed to keep its only waterway to the sea open, but just barely. Now fully loaded with heating fuel oil, the *Shell Udai* was sailing with what little tide there was, bound for Halifax.

On first inspection, there was very little telling about the contents of Hakim's duffle bags: clothes, shoes, papers, a few books, and food. Nothing surprising about that; still, the food, especially the cheese, looked good and, interestingly, there was too much of it for one person. In total, Hakim carried four Edam cheese balls onboard, each contained in a white, cube-shaped box, six inches on a side. Each box had been identically stamped in maroon ink with an official Wisconsin State University seal on one side and Bully, the school's bulldog mascot, strutting proudly across the top. Nutrition facts lined

another side of the box with instructions to refrigerate on arrival and store below 45°F. Inside each box, a red wax–covered
ball lay on a bed of green Easter-basket grass, and by all ap-
pearances, the Department of Food Science and Technology
had produced these babies, marking each with an individual
serial number. On the surface, the four balls were identical, except one had been recently cut, exposing its inviting contents
to anyone who cared to try it. On closer inspection, there was
something subtle, something different about this cheese ball
compared to the others. Though they looked identical in every
respect, their weights were different. This one weighed in at
five pounds, the others topped the scales at eight. Aside from
the weight, if American customs officials had inspected
Hakim's baggage, they might have found it curious that a
seagoing machinist mate would ship out from Basra for Halifax carrying four balls of American-made Edam cheese.

But this was Iraq.

Running Interference
Friday, Feb. 12, 6:25 A.M.
Irving mini-mart
Halifax, Nova Scotia

Kameel Belaidi paced nervously across the floor of his small
office, his eyes focused on an unexpected fax he held tightly
in his hand. Normally, Kameel knew, operations of this nature
required at least six months to set up inside al Qaeda. Under
no circumstances had he ever envisioned an operation of this
importance running on a short fuse in the dead of a Nova
Scotian winter. Like it or not, he had only a few days to run interference for a courier he hadn't anticipated until summer.
He'd worked through it a dozen times before, always planning
a summer tourist scenario when their chances for success
were greatest. Early June to mid-September brought tourists
and daily, regularly scheduled automobile ferries to Nova
Scotia. He'd practiced the primary route often enough, knew
every connection along the way, for all the good it'd do now,
in the middle of winter.

Kameel looked upward, earnestly seeking guidance from God. Then, in a fleeting moment of clarity, a vision of what he should do was revealed. Out of necessity, his revised plan would be simple, involving only as many people as absolutely necessary.

Kameel returned to his desk to study his map of Canada's Maritime Provinces. His primary route took the Marine Atlantic ferry from Yarmouth to Bar Harbor, Maine, but that was shut down for the winter, out of the picture now. His mouth twisted sideways, his gaze shifting northward to the Bay of Fundy. It wasn't his first choice, but the ferry from Digby to Saint John operated year-round. The three-hour boat trip could save hours, maybe days, of travel across snow-covered roads if bad weather set in.

Kameel looked up, letting out a sigh of relief. Perhaps this Digby ferry was a sign. From the manager's office behind his Irving mini-mart, he gazed tiredly through a frost-covered storm window overlooking the used car lot alongside his station. Radiant reddish pink sunlight flooded the sky, glistening off the snow-covered automobiles, saturating the new dawn with a rich, luminescent, almost indescribable color. *Praise be to God and blessings be upon Prophet Muhammad, his companions, and his kin.*

Inwardly, Kameel felt a sense of calm wash over him, for it was dawn, a time of prayer. As a Muslim, his life revolved around *Salat*—obligatory prayers—offered five times a day, every day of his life.

He pulled out his prayer cloth and bowed toward Mecca.

Once his mind was clear, he pulled out a map of the Atlantic Provinces and eastern Maine and began working through his revised plan.

Three nuclear devices, he thought. *Divide and conquer. The Marine Atlantic ferry runs from Digby to Saint John year-round. Perfect, praise be to God. Hakim'll carry two across the bay. I'll take my winter ski vacation, carry one across the border, and no one will be any the wiser.*

Belaidi knew America well enough to know it's a free country. Nothing could stop them. Unless they had a bad break, they'd be in and out of the country before anyone knew they were gone.

Gatekeeper
Friday, Feb. 12, 8:06 A.M.
Roaring River, Virginia

He wasn't the kind of man you'd normally consider inviting home for supper, but if your family were held hostage, you'd be delighted the United States Navy chose him to lead their rescue operation. On first impression, no matter what you might think about his appearance, language, morals, aggressive attitude, or swaggering bravado, you'd be glad he was on your side. If you weren't, he'd remind you *you should be*. The man was a warrior, he liked blowing things up, and this separated him from other men. Intimidating to behold, he looked like a bearded, long-haired, burly terrorist from hell with a big barrel chest and vise-grip handshake. Built like an offensive lineman, his massive forearms, broad shoulders, thick thighs and neck telegraphed a clear "don't tread on me" message to anyone within reach. Officially, John Perry "Buck" Harrison was the commanding officer of the Navy's Special Warfare Development Group (DEVGRU), an eighty-five-man organization devoted exclusively to covert counterterrorism. Unofficially, Commander Buck Harrison was the gatekeeper for black, special warfare, maritime operations. As a rule, anyone involved with clandestine counterterrorism had to interview the old man and meet with his approval.

Now thirty-nine, his men considered him a real Methuselah; still, they'd follow him wherever he wanted to go. They knew he was one of them. He'd risen from their enlisted ranks, understood their limitations, and breathed SEAL ops. More important than this, he didn't work under anyone's thumb, didn't jump when Washington said hop, and didn't accept DEVGRU missions that didn't match their specialty. He moved when he believed his men were ready, and to this extent, he remained forever an outsider. His men considered him a maverick and, in fact, so did his superiors.

Buck was an accomplished outdoorsman, a world-class

white-tail deer hunter, excellent marksman, parachutist, and swimmer. Extraordinarily sharp eyesight and ultrasensitive night vision gave him an edge over most riflemen and nearly any pilot. He would have made an excellent pilot too, had he put his mind to it, but he knew there weren't enough F-22 fighters to go around. *Too much time chained to a desk,* he'd reasoned about Air Force life, so he'd joined the SEALs and never looked back. Good with his men, well respected, he hated paperwork and the thought of being chained to a desk, even a Navy desk, continually tormented him. He was happiest in the field, defending those who could not protect themselves.

Buck had established modified appearance and foreign language standards for his organization to support their covert operations. *To take out a terrorist,* he'd reasoned, *you had to walk in their shoes;* so they did. Buck's entire organization looked, talked, and on occasion, trained like terrorists. Year-round, they maintained scraggly beards, long, oily hair, and during counterterrorism missions, some donned earrings. Further, after the turn of the century, DEVGRU operators required some fluency in a second, "acknowledged trouble spot" language. Though considered a band of competitive brothers, they looked like renegade bandits and were proud of it. As a result, Buck's organization was a continual source of embarrassment for the spit-and-polished top brass inside the Joint Special Operations Command (JSOC). In the final analysis, however, their unmilitary-like appearance, even their earrings, had been reluctantly accepted as a necessary evil of life in the twenty-first century.

Graham's stomach was tied up in knots. He'd been ordered to the newly revamped SEAL training base at Roaring River, Virginia, for an interview with Buck Harrison and had made the seemingly endless three-and-a-half-hour drive alone. He couldn't put his finger on it exactly, but couldn't escape the feeling he'd made a mistake. Driving the deserted backroads of Virginia in the middle of the night gives you time to reflect. Thinking back over his earliest experience with the military didn't help either. During Air Force ROTC, he'd always felt like a fish out of water, an outsider, never fitting in. On the one hand, the military had been good to him: he'd met some very fine people, both servicemen and civilians alike; they'd even sent him to medical school. On the other, he didn't understand what all the hazing, polished latrines, marching, physical training, and shaved heads were about. In retrospect, he could see some value, it did help young kids grow up, but on the whole he believed it did more harm than good. He vividly remembered dreading basic training and feeling glad when it was finally over. To this day, he was glad it was over, but couldn't help feeling he was back in it again.

It takes all kinds of people, Graham concluded. *I guess I'm just not the warrior type.*

Graham's heart sank as he approached the security gate guarding the entrance to the Roaring River military base. At nearly two in the morning, everything about the base looked bleak in the pitch black of night. From what Graham could see, Roaring River Naval Base consisted of two key attributes: a few lights that illuminated the small, one-man guard gate and a large chain-link fence that enclosed a whole lot of nothing. Graham parked his car outside the gate, got out, and approached the young military policeman. The place looked deserted as far as he could see.

"Not much traffic this time of night." Graham forced a tired smile.

"No, sir. Can I help you?"

"Dr. Graham Higgins to see Commander Buck Harrison."

The young man returned to his desk, checked his clipboard, then shook his head. "The CO's seen a good many new faces over the last couple of weeks, sir, but I'm afraid you're not on my list."

"That's just great," Graham mumbled, rubbing his forehead. He'd tried to anticipate every scenario, but the one situation he hadn't accounted for was being turned away at the gate. "Can't you call him? I'm supposed to meet him tomorrow morning, eight o'clock sharp."

The young enlisted man eyed the doctor warily, then grinned. "You don't know him very well, do you?"

.

Graham's innocent, blank expression conveyed everything the young man needed to know.

"I don't think that'd work, sir. Let me put it like this. I have a feeling he'd want me to exhaust all possible alternatives before calling him."

"I see."

"Could you show me your orders, sir? And I'll need some form of picture ID."

"I don't have any orders. I'm not in the military, I'm a doctor and outside consultant for the Navy's Special Warfare Group. Billy Russum told me to report here and said you'd find me someplace to sleep. All I know is we're supposed to set up a briefing and training program for some SEALs and Marines."

Scanning his entrance log, the security policeman's eyes lit up. "Well, sir, why didn't you say so before? Mr. Russum signed in earlier tonight, before I came on duty. He's staying in the BOQ with another civilian, a Mr. Wyley Ramsi. I'll give him a call."

After a short conversation, the policeman hung up. "You're all set, sir. Mr. Russum's got you a room next to his in the BOQ. Just follow the main drag about a half mile, around the bend beyond those trees. It's the only building on the right; you can't miss it."

With his head throbbing, Graham gazed beyond the gate across a featureless, infinite black abyss. He felt his heart racing in his chest, pounding in his ears. Instinctively, he checked his pulse. He had no idea what his blood pressure was, but knew it was shooting through the roof. He drew a deep breath, hoping to steel his nerve. *I know better than this,* he thought, staring into the darkness. He couldn't escape the feeling that he'd been here before and shouldn't come back.

"You okay, sir?" the guard asked.

Graham said nothing. He heard the young man talking, but didn't recognize the words as a question.

"Hello, Doctor, you in there?"

Graham triggered on the keyword *Doctor,* then responded, "Oh yeah, sorry. I was just thinking. This place brings back memories, not all of 'em good ones."

"That's okay, sir. You're not alone. A lotta guys feel pretty scared when they pass through these gates; it's like pregame jitters or stage fright or something. You'll feel better once you learn the ropes. Some SEAL recruits are so nervous they throw up right here before they go in, but don't tell 'em I said so. They'd skin me alive."

"Yeah." Graham smiled. "From what I hear, those guys even whip Marines."

"It's like another world in there, sir. You'll see things you'll never forget."

"I expect you're right," Graham sighed, "but I guess it's all necessary. It's a training base, right?"

"Training's a big part of it, sir."

"What else is going on here?"

"SEAL training, some amphibious assault. They keep most of their counterterrorist work under wraps."

"Pretty hush-hush, I suppose?"

The young man nodded, handed him a temporary pass for his car, then pointed to the gate. "Just follow this road, sir. You'll be fine. As far as I know, we haven't lost a consultant yet."

"Thanks, thanks a lot." He grinned. "Guess I'll have to trust you on this one."

"Good. It was a pleasure talking to you, sir."

"I enjoyed it too," Graham agreed, gazing out from the guard shack one final time. "Guess there's no turning back now."

The guard shot him a quick thumbs-up. "Go for it, Doc. You'll be fine."

Minutes later, Graham entered the Bachelor Officers Quarters, a musty-smelling, starkly furnished barracks. Sweating and sticky, he lay down on his dorm room bunk, eyes opened as wide as the steam heat in his tiny room. From all accounts, the BOQ furnace had only one setting—inferno. It was cold and damp outside, hot as a sauna in his room. When he could stand it no longer, he tried prying open the window, but it'd been painted shut. He saw scratch marks around the window frame and countless gouges across the sill, signs it'd been forced open before and often. Optimistic, he ran his small pocket knife around the window frame, and after several failed attempts, Graham's patience paid off. Wet, cool, moisture-saturated air rushed in.

Bone weary, he returned to his bunk. Above the hissing sound of the steam heat, Graham heard crickets singing inside the building. Though they might keep others awake, the melody was music to his ears, reminding him of his early childhood days in the country. Physically fatigued and mentally exhausted, he was lulled to sleep by their chirping in a matter of minutes. Graham slept better that night than he had for days, and it'd be the last good night's sleep he'd have for weeks.

Inside the base gym, across from the SEALs' indoor training pool, Commander Buck Harrison's temporary office reeked of chlorine.

Graham, Russum, and Wyley arrived early, hoping to see SEALs training, and they weren't disappointed. On their way to Buck's office, the trio passed a group of SEAL recruits in the pool, bobbing like corks. First thing Graham noticed was their wrists and ankles were bound. The instructor explained this was part of their survival training. They'd porpoise to the surface with their hands and ankles bound, grab a gulp of air, then sink slowly to the bottom of the pool until they needed to breathe again. There was no panic, no thrashing or gagging; they had the breathing cycle refined to an art and, remarkably, no one gave up.

Russum knew Buck, entered the CO's office first, and offered the introductions.

"Dr. Higgins, Mr. Ramsi, it's good to see you. Thanks for coming down. Personally, I'm damn glad you're here. Make yourselves at home, gentlemen, have a seat. Russum's told me a great deal about you both."

Graham shook the commander's large hand. Cold, calloused, and strong, it reminded him of a bear trap. Slightly stunned, he'd known Buck Harrison would look like a terrorist, but never imagined his own reaction. Graham stared at the dark, bearded, long-haired hulk of a man and didn't speak for a few moments. Something was wrong with this picture. Buck's voice and overall manner didn't fit his appearance. "I don't mean any offense, Commander, but if I were to meet you in a dark alley, I think I'd have a stroke."

Buck gave a laugh. "My mother doesn't like it either. She says I oughta shave, get a haircut and a real job."

After a brief getting-acquainted session, the four got down to business. Buck had read Russum's report in advance, so he was well equipped to absorb their detailed firsthand accounts of red mercury, neutron bombs, and Hama. The trio conveyed everything they'd learned through a series of pictures, medical records, and observations, and once their story'd been told, Buck barraged Russum with questions. "Where are these mini-nuke stockpiles anyway? Near some waterway? I gotta know if we're to take 'em out."

"Truth is, we don't know yet, not exactly. That's where your organization comes in. Syria and Iraq are our primary focus. Obviously, Syria's on the top of the list; Iraq's second because we know they bought large quantities of red mercury from Russia several years back. The first phase of our operation involves surveillance, some aboveboard, some clandestine. They're still working out the details back in Washington, but one aspect of the operation may involve inserting some of your people into both Syrian and Iraqi territory."

"What's the objective?"

"We've got to locate their stockpiles, weapons labs, and factories before we destroy them."

The CO's expression turned skeptical. "Oh yeah, that'll be easy."

"Ideally, we'd like to know how many of these mini-nukes exist before we destroy everything. We've got to know if we've got 'em all."

"You make this all sound like some kinda fuckin' accounting problem," Bucked vented. "Believe me, things aren't so neat and tidy with people shooting at you."

Russum fell silent. It hadn't taken long for their discussion to get up close and personal.

Once Graham noticed the muscles across Buck's temples relax, he broke the protracted silence. "We were sent to tell you what we know, ask for your support, and do what we could to help."

"Believe me, gentlemen, I don't shoot my messengers, but those smart-ass ticketpunchers back in Washington will get us all killed. How many times do we have to learn the same bloody lessons over and over again? My men operate in small teams with well-defined, limited objectives. We move in from the sea, take care of business, then return. That's it, end of story. We've trained for assaulting ships, aircraft, automobiles, trains, and shipyards, but we don't go anywhere to stay. Sounds like I'd better get my butt back there and kick some ass."

Russum chuckled. "Guess I'd have to agree with ya there. Everyone expected you'd wanna be involved with the planning from day one."

"The usual bullshit," Buck groused. "Mission planning cycle's already under way. I gotta play catch-up, then make some . . . corrections. Is Delta Force involved?" The CO was referring to the Army's special warfare unit.

Russum nodded. "Let me ask about that mini-nuke accounting problem. I need to understand where you're coming from."

"Sure. My thinking's pretty obvious, but I'll be more than happy to spell it out for you, gentlemen. As I see it, their small size is a show-stopper."

"It may be impossible to locate all their mini-nukes," Russum conceded, "but I think you'd agree we have to try."

"With devices that small, I wouldn't store 'em in one place. I'd disperse 'em around the country. If they were smart, they'd keep 'em moving around like a big shell game, or get 'em out of the country, or both."

"Yeah, I see what you mean," Russum said. "Frankly, I'm more optimistic about finding their weapons labs and factories. We've been monitoring Middle East hot spots for years and have a wealth of information about suspected weapons labs and production facilities. At this stage, we need to confirm our suspicions, then take 'em out."

"Why not have the Navy and Air Force take 'em all out? Why put my people at risk in the first place?"

"There're hundreds and hundreds of targets in Iraq alone. Thousands of targets across the whole of the Middle East. We've got to trim down the target list first, then take 'em out with a single decisive strike."

"They could tear down their factories, one machine at a time, and move 'em while we're futzing around trying to figure out what to do."

"Moving a production facility takes time, Commander, and currently that's exactly what our satellite surveillance folks are watching for around the clock. Still, I'm afraid you're probably right about their size. They're small and tough to detect. They don't contain radioactive plutonium like other nuclear weapons so they don't require the massive shielding."

"I'd say it a little different," Buck offered. "Unless these people are stupid, make a mistake, or we get lucky, we'll be damn fortunate to find any at all."

Reluctantly, the group acknowledged the commander's point.

"Don't get me wrong, gentlemen," the CO continued. "I don't mean to rain on your parade, but you gotta be realistic about this situation. Rest assured, though, once we pull together an ops plan that makes sense, DEVGRU is available on four-hour notice to deploy anywhere in the world."

"Most we can hope for," Russum concluded.

After a brief pause in the conversation, Graham asked, "What's next?"

"I'm really anxious to get started," Wyley added, shaking his head. "Hama caught us all by surprise, sent us scrambling, and I've got to believe we weren't alone. These people won't sit back and wait for us to come looking for them. They're terrorists. I mean it in the most despicable sense of the word. You've got to think of these people as government-sponsored terrorists. They'll strike without mercy, mark my words."

"Buck, I've got a sinking feeling Wyley's right," Russum admitted. "We're working against someone else's clock on this one."

Graham felt it important to speak. "I'm no expert on the

Middle East or anything, but it seems like Hama lit a fuse and we're already operating on borrowed time."

Buck thought a moment, then responded. "I've gotta assume you're right. Don't get me wrong, I don't wanna believe it, but we can't afford not to. Every minute counts. I'll fill you in on what you need to do."

A few minutes later, the three men nodded understanding.

"Glad to oblige," Russum closed, looking at Buck. "Is there anything else?"

"There's one other thing before I let you go." The burly CO looked across his desk and made eye contact with Graham. "I don't know if Russum mentioned this to you, Doctor, but I owe you one helluva lot."

"I'm afraid I don't understand, Commander." Graham was caught off guard.

"Ten years ago, my wife nearly died from leukemia. She needed a bone marrow transplant and had no prospects for a donor. Without your work, she would've died."

"I'm really happy to hear we could help her, Commander." Graham paused for a moment, then against his better judgment, decided to probe. "How's she doing now?"

Unknowingly, Buck telegraphed his loss through his eyes, but struggled to put a positive light on their situation. "We lost her, Doc, but you gave us six more good years together. Her doctors thought she'd outlive me, but no one planned on her getting throat cancer."

"Throat cancer," Graham whispered, visibly moved. "There's so precious little we can do that really helps. Was she a smoker?" He found it hard to articulate, but the situation with Buck's wife made the strangeness of this new world seem more familiar; somehow, the world felt a little smaller.

"She made some mistakes as a kid, smoked a few years as a teenager, but she quit long before we got married. Anyway, you gave us six good years together and I wanted you to know. Now, gentlemen," Buck addressed the group, intending to shift the subject back to business, "is there anything else?"

"I've got a favor I'd like to ask," Graham said, feeling a little embarrassed.

"Shoot."

"Could I get a tour?—and I'd like to meet your medical corpsmen."

"You want the fly-on-the-wall tour or ya wanna get your hands dirty?" Buck grinned like a Cheshire cat, as if he knew something Graham didn't know.

"I don't understand what you mean."

Russum piped in. "You said you'd like to learn to shoot, said your wife was on your case: well, this is your chance. The finest marksmen in the world get their training less than two miles from here; they shoot everything from pistols to flamethrowers."

"Really? I'd like the chance to try that."

"Good," Buck responded. "We've got some covert surveillance training going on that you don't wanna miss either. The VIPs love it. You fly little choppers no bigger than an eyeball."

"I'd like to try that too," Graham said, diving in with both feet.

"I expect they could be very useful," Wyley added.

"We'll set you up with an office this morning and you can get going. Once your briefing's on-line, we'll show you around, then take a few days to work you through some training."

"Thanks," Graham said. "I'd like that very much."

Wyley and Russum agreed.

"Excellent. What about swimming? No better training than you'll find here."

"I've been waiting for you to ask," Russum said. "We're not SEAL grade, but we've got our scuba licenses."

"Good. We'll show you around and you can sign up for what makes sense." Buck smiled beneath his heavy beard. "Welcome to the wonderful world of covert operations, gentlemen."

PART TWO

Our Own
Back Yard

CHAPTER FIVE

Working on the tunnel was like being buried alive.

From its inception, the construction project had been plagued by death. Leaks, cave-ins, electrical fires, and bad air had taken their toll on worker morale; still, following the Hama massacre, digging had been accelerated, their schedule pulled in three months. Equipment maintenance and safety had been sacrificed as a result, but then again, this was Iraq. Fear, bully-based management, and crash schedules were the norm.

Inside the access tunnel, al-Mashhadi was sweating like a pig. Deep underground, beneath the Shatt-al-Arab riverbed, the air felt oppressive, stale, and damp. More than this, with the overhead construction lights turned on, he could see the air he breathed. Almost unbelievably, it had a vile, gritty taste to it, like molded dust, leaving a nasty film on his teeth and tongue, coating his mouth with a sickening slime.

One hundred fifty feet beneath the river, the distinctive smell of mildew and urine reminded al-Mashhadi of an underground subway. At this stage of construction, access tunnel digging was nearly two-thirds complete and that was all that mattered to him. Two-thirds complete was enough. He needed it operational and he needed it now because the access tunnel included a spur that linked the basement of the Basra teaching hospital to his underground weapons manufacturing facility. In addition, once his manufacturing plant was fully operational, tunnel construction would provide a deceptive smoke-screen against prying satellite eyes. From the minister's point of view, the good news was that work on the main tunnel was only just beginning. Larger in diameter than the access tunnel, it'd take years to complete, and as far as he was concerned, the longer it took, the better.

Though work went on around the clock, progress on the access tunnel had been agonizingly slow, plagued by a relentless series of leaks and fissures in the overhead supporting wall. As long as the walls held fast and the seams remained dry, their gargantuan tunneling machine continued digging nonstop. Over and over again, however, it'd ground to a halt, the trouble directly related to the acidic polluted water of the Shatt-al-Arab River. Corrosive river water caused the tunnel's seals to disintegrate, resulting in a continuous series of moisture-related equipment failures. As with most computer-controlled machinery, their tunneling equipment was riddled with electronic sensors and computer electronics that didn't work well wet, if at all.

Nicknamed "the snake," were it laid out on the surface, the temperamental tunneling machine would look like an enormous, earth-eating worm with the head of a caterpillar. Made of three major assemblies, slightly larger in diameter than a two-lane highway, the caterpillar head consisted of a slowly rotating circular-disk–shaped bit, lined with hundreds of carbide-tipped blades that did the digging. Hydraulic rams inched the bit forward, guided by operators in the cylindrically shaped maneuvering room located immediately behind the head.

Every yard of dirt and rock digested—ground up and crushed—was transported down a fast-moving conveyor belt, expelled out its tail end, loaded onto narrow-gauge rail cars, then hauled away. At the entrance to the access tunnel, a continuous stream of dirt and crushed rock rolled out, while curved sections of steel-reinforced concrete wall were hauled in. Once inside the tunnel, the support wall was erected into position overhead, one piece at a time, using hydraulic arms located around the circumference of the snake's maneuvering room. After assembly, the curved wall sections formed a checkerboard pattern inside the pipelike tunnel structure.

Kajaz Hamandhani led al-Mashhadi and his bodyguards down the access tunnel without speaking. After only a few hundred feet, sunlight all but disappeared. Overhead construction lights were made dim by the dust, and noise from the tunneling machine pounded their ears until they began to ring. Aside from the smell and noise, the darkness struck al-Mashhadi as something difficult to overcome. Ahead, further down the tunnel, he saw lights from the maneuvering room and his pace quickened to an extent that his entourage had trouble keeping up.

Water dripped like rain from overhead seams, hitting the big man on his hardhat, soaking the shoulders of his robe.

Suddenly, the overhead lights flickered.

Al-Mashhadi glanced right, catching the eye of his bodyguards.

In the same breath, the digging machine stilled, then light collapsed into darkness.

Without warning, the big man's bodyguards shoved him hard, forward into the maneuvering room, behind a metal shroud, out of harm's way. He hit the steel deck with a thud, expecting a hail of bullets to erupt from the darkness.

Seconds later, emergency lights cut in, dimly illuminating the tunnel. Following a longer pause, a few handheld battery-powered flashlights came on, but aside from the sound of voices echoing down the tunnel, all was quiet. There was no gunfire.

With his white robe soiled, but otherwise unshaken, the big man raised his massive hulk, then directed his security forces into the darkest, most secretive man-made cavern of the tunnel. Once given the all clear, he continued his perilous journey past a series of heavily armored, vaultlike security doors, down the access tunnel's connecting spur, into his underground weapons manufacturing facility—codenamed the Pit.

Al-Mashhadi knew the Pit provided his key to power and, as a result, he rode shotgun over his pet project like a man obsessed. This was his baby, run his way, so either line up behind him or get out of his way. He'd masterminded the project, brought in the talent and equipment necessary to pull it off, selected its hospital-centric location, and organized the dig. The Pit would succeed—he'd see to that—and many had already died along the way to make it so.

Deep underground, al-Mashhadi listened intently to Kajaz summarizing construction progress on their neutron bomb

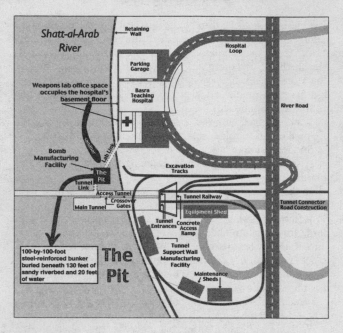

production facility. Surveying his Pit's construction up close and firsthand, the big man's head very nearly touched the ceiling. Its raised floors and dropped ceiling weren't yet completed, but what counted was that they had reliable, industrial-scale electrical power, fresh air, and, most important of all, it was dry.

Inside, overhead groundwater was used for heating and cooling the breathing air year-round. In addition, river water provided the plant an infinite heat sink, a cooling resource dearly needed for dissipating the enormous heat created by detonating pure-fusion pits, the seed devices that would trigger the neutron bomb's radiation burst.

"The last major hurdle is behind us," he heard Kajaz say. "Both the connecting tunnel and the computer network linking our lab with manufacturing are fully operational. Our weapons lab office space has been expanded to occupy the entire basement floor of the hospital and the connecting link tightly couples our development staff with manufacturing."

Al-Mashhadi crossed his arms impatiently, jutting out his chin in unconscious imitation of Mussolini, the Italian dictator during World War II. "Tell me about the heavy machinery. Where's the equipment?"

"Full rail access will be operational within one week," Kajaz explained. "Once the track spur is in place, we'll have the means to haul in the heavy, computer-controlled milling machinery necessary to fabricate the trigger." Kajaz was referring to the neutron bomb's innermost fusion trigger device, the peach pit–like central core of the bomb.

"One week." The big Iraqi rocked his head back and forth. "Why not today? Why not now?"

Kajaz went on to explain the plant rail and lifting crane requirements for moving heavy machinery into the Pit and eventually al-Mashhadi elected to back off.

Sensing al-Mashhadi's reluctant acceptance, Kajaz began rattling off a prioritized list of show-stopper problems, a list requiring immediate escalation. Manpower shortages topped his list, with equipment failures trailing a close second. The minister of information seethed at the seemingly endless list of problems, clenching his teeth so tightly the muscles on his face flinched.

"You tax my patience, Kajaz." Al-Mashhadi's eyes narrowed.

"We need laborers and we need them now. The snake is unreliable and manual labor is absolutely necessary to take up the slack."

"I don't want your problems, I want results."

There was a hiss in his voice, still Kajaz stood his ground.

"Deliver me five hundred Kurds and you'll get what you want. I promise you this on my father's grave."

Al-Mashhadi narrowed his eyes to a squint, considering this request. *The idea made sense to him—prison labor could provide their way out.* "Very well, then. You will have your rebels."

Rush Order
Monday, Feb. 15, 9:23 A.M.
FastTech Associates
Lexington, Massachusetts

Only fifty-five years old and bone weary, Ted Lewis felt beat up. He needed a way out of this rat race and couldn't imagine spending the rest of his life a slave to his job. For the senior production assistant at FastTech, it was a bitter cold, gray winter day, like every other winter day in Massachusetts. He'd arrived late to work after chipping ice off his front steps, clearing heavy, back-breaking slush from his driveway, then losing two more hours trapped in stalled traffic.

The only thing standing between Ted and his Florida retirement home was money. His kids were through college, his wife was willing, even anxious, and their move was years overdue. Ted was going to bust out of Massachusetts or die trying.

FastTech Associates, an electronics fabrication house off Route 128, specialized in rapid circuit board manufacture, assembly, and testing. Ted's desk was located on the factory floor, just beyond the noisy pneumatic printed circuit board assembly area.

His work area was surrounded by rows of flat-topped machines placing electronic parts on printed circuit boards. Beyond the component placement area, a solder machine finished the job of securing the tiny devices to the circuit boards.

Ted's shift supervisor intercepted him before he reached his desk. "We've got a hot one here, arrived in e-mail overnight. I already loaded it on your station. They want a dozen receiver, cable, and transmitter assemblies ready to go in three days."

"Three days?"

"We've done work for this backwoods New Hampshire outfit before, but never on such a short fuse. They're in a rush and they're willing to pay for it."

"O.T.?"

"Double time, plus they're willing to pay for pushing other jobs out of the queue."

"Sounds like they want it bad."

"Yeah, and I'll tell ya another thing, Ted. If we can pull this off, I expect you've spent your last winter with us here in Mass."

"Whatdaya mean?"

"If we can deliver, that retirement package we've been talking about's a done deal. We'll throw in five additional years of service to sweeten the pie, and you could be in Florida by April."

"Awesome." Ted smiled for the first time today, his mind running in a hundred directions. After a few moments of bliss, he grinned at his boss, recognizing they had to focus. "So talk to me. How's it look? Do we have everything we need in-house?"

"I went over the files this morning. We've got most of the parts in-house already. Pretty standard devices, all off-the-shelf. The cables use standard connectors, and the electronic description files they sent pass audit. All in all, we're in excellent shape. Both are laid out and ready for manufacture. There's two circuit boards required for each set, a small hand-held transmitter and a larger, odd-shaped receiver."

"Odd shaped?"

"See for yourself." Ted's supervisor pulled it up on-screen.

Ted grinned. "Looks like a donut with that circle cut outta the center."

"Yeah, it does. When I first saw it, I thought it might be something for Raytheon's missile division, but then again, they don't farm out their missile circuit boards to fast-turnaround houses like us."

"Whatdaya know about missiles?" Ted asked.

"When I worked there years ago, we made circuit boards that looked like that. It's shaped like a circular disk to fit inside the missile body, and that hole in the middle's for the warhead."

"That makes sense," Ted observed. "What is it anyway?"

"Just another black box, some kind of electrical subsystem, I suppose. There's no way to know what it's used for, but it's a battery-powered receiver, clock circuit, and programmable timer with some sort of control pulse distribution circuitry. Funny thing is all this stuff's available in commercial-grade parts from Radio Shack. The only difference is they've got a super-conservative mill-spec design here."

"Hmmmm." Ted studied the schematics on his large thirty-inch screen.

"They want it super-reliable," the supervisor continued. "Three nines availability over a huge temperature range. They want it to work 99.9 percent of the time under any conditions. In summary, it's a very simple, extraordinarily reliable circuit."

"Yep. I can see that," Ted agreed. "What's the plan?"

"Build 'em in two days, test 'em twenty-four hours in the heat tent, then ship 'em out overnight express mail. Can you do it?"

"Our biggest problem's behind us, right? We got the parts we need? Parts enough for three, maybe four dozen board sets? Working in a hurry like this, we're gonna build a lotta junk."

Ted's supervisor smiled. "We've got the parts covered. Junk's not the issue. We're expecting low yields, but we need at least twelve good transmitter-receiver pairs."

Ted ran through his checklist out loud. "We've got the artwork. They want surface-mount technology, components top and bottom. We can program our poke-and-place machines in half a day, starting immediately. Barring unforeseen disaster, we can do it with fifteen people rotating around the clock, three shifts, plus don't forget, we gotta have a minimum of four heat chambers without interruption."

"I've already cleared it with system test. Heat tents are no problem."

"That's it then, let's do it." Ted nodded. "I've gotta call my wife and get moving PDQ."

Smiling, Ted's supervisor handed him the phone.

Plates
Tuesday, Feb. 16, 2:08 A.M.
14 Phillips Circle
Andover, Massachusetts

One man, dressed in black, sat silently inside the drafty warmth of his rusting automobile, his gaze fixed on a large New England cape at the end of the lonely cul-de-sac. Seemingly at home with his situation, one glance in his trunk would have convinced any policeman this man was a well-equipped professional, completely comfortable with the idea of working alone. Checking the time on his dash clock, he knew the lights in the front den of the cape should go off any second now. Ten seconds later, the house went dark. The light timer in the Morrisons' home had been thrown off about four hours since the power failure from the last storm.

He drove down their freshly plowed drive and walked behind the garage to the rear of the house. For the sixth and final time this evening, he called the Morrisons using his cell phone. He could hear it ringing from outside their house, and after the fourth ring, their answering machine picked up. As usual, he left no message.

This would be easy; no stress, no strain. He knew the Morrisons had gone to Florida. The phone book hanging in a plastic bag on their mailbox post had telegraphed their winter hiatus to anyone interested enough to notice. He'd picked up their phone book several days back and had been casing their house ever since.

After cutting through the double-pane glass of the rear garage window, he unlocked it, lifted the sash, and simply climbed inside the garage carrying a small tool bag. Once inside, he turned on his infrared flashlight, invisible to the naked eye, and lowered his night-vision goggles.

Mr. Morrison's small Toyota was parked exactly where he'd left it last November. The intruder knew from his internet search homework that Art Morrison had retired from Hewlett Packard, a sales engineering manager with their Medical Products Division. Many engineers, he knew from past experience, were pretty particular about their cars. The intruder hoped Mr. Morrison was one of them.

The four-year-old Toyota sported Massachusetts license plates of the same age. Kneeling down on one knee, the intruder determined Mr. Morrison hated rust and one glance told him this job would be easier than he had any right to expect.

Mr. Morrison's front and rear license plates were attached using stainless steel bolts.

* * *

The Briefcase Bomb
Wednesday, Feb. 17, 2:50 P.M.
CTC headquarters
Langley, Virginia

Once Russian weapons experts arrived on American soil carrying their briefcase bomb, Los Alamos National Laboratory was asked to reverse-engineer it and publish their findings on an eyes-only government website. Working shoulder to shoulder with the Russians, CTC, FBI, and DoD weapons specialists had been operating around the clock for the past three days, dissecting the device, documenting everything they could evaluate without destroying the weapon.

Back at Langley, inside the secure walls of CTC headquarters, Graham, Wyley, and Buck looked over Russum's shoulder without comment, gazing at his large computer monitor. To their dismay, the big Texan meticulously examined every fragment of data on-screen with a fine-tooth comb, every studio-quality picture and X-ray he could bring up, first checking, then cross-checking the information from Los Alamos for consistency.

If Russum had had his way, he'd have been in Los Alamos working with the Russians, analyzing the device up close and firsthand. After all, this technology exchange had come about as a direct result of his efforts and the fact that the Russian government desperately needed money, lots of money. Aside from his professional interest in the device, he could have finagled a trip to Austin to see his parents, but in this day of instant information, remote access would have to do and, regrettably, it was good enough. Although initially intrigued by what he saw on-screen, Russum's mood quickly shifted to one of grave concern as he examined the images in ever increasing detail.

"The lab report's updated once an hour," Russum told the others, "so don't take it as gospel. It's only a draft, and that's why I gotta scrub it."

"Nevertheless," Graham added, "you need to give our boys credit."

"No doubt about it," the big Texan agreed. "They dissected this bomb faster than I ever thought possible and did an extraordinary job documenting it. In spite of everything, they got it all on-line in record time."

"You were right about one thing," Buck grunted. "That thing is small. You could hide it anywhere."

"Yep, but I'm afraid it goes downhill from here. Even though we've just begun looking at it, some alarming trends have already emerged."

"So spit it out, man. Whatdaya make of it?"

Russum sighed, chewing the stem of his empty pipe. "We think we're so damn smart. I tell you one thing, this technology is state-of-the-art. We couldn't do it any better if our lives depended on it. In some respects, this bomb's what I'd expected; from a distance, it looks like the pictures, but in other ways, humph . . . it wasn't what I expected at all. The physics behind the explosive may have been born in the early sixties, but this modular, integrated bomb assembly is bleeding-edge technology and damn scary. Its miniaturized detonator electronics are connectorized, computer-controlled, multifunction, and clearly capable of secure, remote activation. Any way you cut it, this spells big trouble."

After a few moments' silence, Graham asked the question everyone wanted to know, but was afraid to ask. "What's its estimated yield?"

"About ten tons of TNT."

"Compared to a megaton, that doesn't sound too bad." Always looking for a silver lining, Graham's tone expressed relief. "What does that mean in practical terms?"

"On a dry day, one of these babies would kill nearly everyone within a five-hundred-yard radius of the Capitol."

"Oh, I see." Graham looked down.

"What's humidity got to do with it?" Wyley wanted to know.

"Don't forget, it's a neutron bomb. Neutrons are absorbed by moisture in the air. Turns out, water makes an excellent shield from this kind of weapon."

"What about the fallout?"

"If this thing works as advertised, fallout's not a problem."

Wyley looked skeptical, so Russum continued.

"We won't really know its radiation footprint until we manufacture one and detonate it, but from all accounts in the Russian data, this baby's the real McCoy, first I've ever seen. Understand, though, if this had been one of our own mini-nukes, a fission-fusion device, winds would spread the radioactive fallout over Washington within hours."

Wyley nodded as if to say that's what he expected.

"All this theory is fine when your ass isn't hanging out," Buck groused in his deep gravelly voice, "but let's get down to brass tacks here. What do we have that'll detect this shit?"

Russum chewed on his empty pipe—his pacifier in good times and bad—then nodded. "That's a good question. No silver bullet, I'm afraid; nothing I'm aware of anyway. Aside from a metal detector or luggage X-ray machine, I don't think we've got anything that would sniff out these bombs. Originally, I had hoped a Geiger counter or dosimeter would be helpful, something to detect radioactivity, but hope's not a plan and the ionizing radiation around this device is so low they won't pick it up. The Russians claimed their pure-fusion device didn't use plutonium, and wouldn't you know it, this time it looks like they told the truth."

"Figures, don't it?" Buck grumbled. "How about moving 'em? How'll they get in the country?"

"If it were up to me, I'd drive. It'd be chancy flying one of these into the country, but our borders are wide open."

"So how the hell do you expect us to find them, much less count 'em?" Buck snarled, clearly understanding the position he and his troops were being asked to assume. "If you can't detect them as they pass under your nose, how the hell are we supposed to track 'em down when we don't even know where to look?"

"Yep," the Texan sighed. "Our problem just got a lot tougher."

The Promised Land
Wednesday, Feb. 17, 4:08 P.M.
Interstate 95 South
The Canadian–U.S. border into Maine

Hakim Moussavi lifted the hood of his Ford Taurus, filling the windshield washer with blue fluid. Once the job was done, he returned the gallon jug to his trunk, then he pressed on, shivering cold, but otherwise undaunted. He'd never seen snow before in his life, but he was a quick study and already knew he didn't like it. *How could anyone in their right minds live in such stark, cold conditions as these?* he wondered. The automatic temperature control inside his car was set to eighty degrees, but it felt much colder.

Hakim had been lucky so far. A winter storm was forming to his south, off the coast of Maine, but it looked as if he just might make it through before the brunt of the storm moved ashore. If you could believe the forecast, he had a six-hour window to drive the length of Maine before the weather closed in. Radio stations were few and far between in this part of Canada, but this close to the U.S. border, Maine stations bombarded the area with a nonstop countdown to the storm of the century. Judging from their constant talk about the weather, you'd think the world was about to stop cold, frozen dead in its tracks.

He couldn't be sure about Kameel's chances of getting through before the storm hit, but Hakim guessed he had at least a four-hour lead on him. It'd be close, but in the scheme of things, a one- or two-day delay in their plans was no cause for concern.

The sky was already an overcast solid gray, snow flurries were in the air, and a cold, howling wind was building. The once white snow piled alongside the interstate now looked dreary gray, brown, and dirty, beckoning another fresh clean coat. The road, plowed clear from a previous storm, lay open before him like a grave, silently awaiting another winter burial.

For people raised in the north country, accustomed to driving in the snow, Hakim's front-wheel-drive Taurus would have been adequate for these road conditions. But at twenty-four years old, Hakim had never seen snow before, let alone driven through a Nor'easter, a northeastern winter storm. Weather alone was enough to make him apprehensive, but as it turned out, the impending storm wasn't his biggest concern. He'd just passed the duty-free station, his last landmark before the U.S.-Canadian border.

Mentally, Hakim's mind was racing in a thousand directions. Nearing the border from the Canadian side, he recounted Kameel's guidance. "Once you pass the duty-free station," the older man had told him, "for practical purposes, you're at the border, so stay loose." Miles of beautiful countryside, uncluttered by exits, rest stops, and urban sprawl had been his only concern until now and, in retrospect, Hakim concluded Kameel had been right. He didn't want Hakim lulled into a false sense of security only to come unglued at the sudden sight of U.S. border guards.

Hakim cleaned his windshield with one prolonged spray of washer fluid as an antifreeze smell filled the passenger compartment. The fog that clouded his side windows had cleared now, his rear window defroster was working overtime, and he reasoned visibility into his car was such that it would not draw suspicion from the U.S. border guards. Remembering Kameel's advice, Hakim resolved to follow it to the letter. "Act pleasant and cooperative," he'd said. "When you're asked questions about weapons, you don't have any and you have nothing to declare."

It was ten minutes after four, almost dark, when Hakim saw the lights of the U.S. border crossing appear in the distance. On seeing them, he took a deep breath and tried to relax. He'd warmed up some, but his hands were still cold. The border checkpoints looked something like a series of interstate tollbooths, two lanes expanded into six, but only one was open and understandably so; he seemed to be the only traffic on the road with the exception of a few large trucks.

Hakim cleared his throat as bright lights from the open security checkpoint grew nearer. He could feel his heart racing, but did everything in his power to steady his nerves. America was a free country, Kameel Belaidi had told him. That was important because it meant he should expect to pass into the United States without suspicion, unless the border guards had been set on the alert. No doubt about it; it would be scary, alone in a foreign land; still, he had the paperwork to back up his story and chose to look on the bright side.

Best case, the storm might act as an incentive, Hakim thought optimistically. *The guards may even be helpful, actually anxious to get me home before the storm closes in. That's it*—he smiled, his confidence on the rise—*I'll ask for the benefit of their judgment; I'll engage them in my plight, throw my safety on the mercy of their counsel. Besides, cold weather should act in my favor because no one wants to search through a car in weather such as this.*

Hakim approached the brightly lit border gate and rolled to a stop as the ice, sand, and salt crunched beneath his tires. Looking out the driver's side, he saw a tall, frost-covered, glass-enclosed structure, but couldn't make out the men's faces inside. In a few seconds, one heavily clothed guard emerged from the booth with his face wrapped in a gray wool scarf. Before speaking to Hakim, the guard walked to the front of his car and cleaned off the snow from his Massachusetts license plate.

Spotlights flooded his plate with a bright flash, a snapshot was taken, and Hakim knew they were running a check on his plates.

After a few moments' delay, the silver-haired guard working inside the glass booth passed a clipboard and slip of paper outside to the younger man. Once the young guard had reviewed it, he approached the driver's side. Hakim lowered his window without prompting and greeted the young man with a warm smile.

"Hello, Officer."

"Could I see your license, please?"

Hakim had already removed his wallet, car registration, and insurance papers in expectation of this exchange. Pulling out his brand-new, but seemingly aged driver's license, he handed it over to the guard with a sympathetic smile. "I wouldn't want to change jobs with you today for anything in the world. You must be freezing."

"Tell me about it," the young man huffed. Every breath he exhaled into his scarf created a small cloud of fog in front of his face surrounding his cheeks. While the warm air was moist and kept his cheeks warm, it also condensed on his glasses, obscuring his vision. As a result, the young man was continually holding his breath, struggling to see, or cleaning his glasses.

After comparing the face in the car with the picture on the license, the guard cross-checked the driver's name and address with their records. *A match,* he thought. *So far, so good.* "Could you give me your name and home address?"

"Sure, it's Art, Art Morrison. Fourteen Phillips Circle, Andover, Massachusetts."

Exasperated with his glasses, the guard took them off and began to squint, studying what he could see inside Hakim's car. The backseat was empty except for a heavy coat and open cardboard box filled with snack food. In front, the guard noticed a small soft drink cooler and damp cloth lying on the console between the seats. "Is your travel business or pleasure?"

"Business," Hakim's grimaced convincingly. "I haven't had any fun since I started this trip."

"Where are you coming from?"

"Halifax. I've visited a hospital there. I'm with HP, Medical Products Division."

"I see." The guard squinted, making a note on his clipboard. "Are you carrying any weapons?"

Hakim shook his head. "No, don't own any."

"Do you have anything to declare?"

"Nothing. I'm carrying some exposed film from Halifax; that's it."

"Where're you headed?"

"Home, Officer, and I'm getting a little worried about it."

The guard nodded understanding. "You're about to run out of time."

"Yeah, I know. The radio's running nonstop about this storm. Do you have any suggestions?"

The guard thought about it for a second, then remembered something the driver said earlier. "I wouldn't want to be in your shoes, either. Are you dead set on making it home tonight?"

"I'd wanted to, but I'm not so sure now. I'm starting to backpedal a little bit."

"Good idea. Hold on just a minute." The young man disappeared into the guardhouse then returned. "You'll make it to Bangor all right, but I wouldn't push it any further; not tonight, not with this storm. The motels'll fill up early, and from what we hear, you'd better plan on staying a day or two, at least."

"Thanks, thanks very much," Hakim offered.

The young man nodded his head, smiling behind his scarf, feeling happy to have been of some help. After the barrier gate lifted, Hakim drove past the guard and officially entered U.S. territory.

Almost immediately, as soon as the border lights disappeared from his rearview mirror, the uncluttered layout of the land changed. Suddenly, a string of exits appeared, blanketing the terrain, illuminated by row after row of streetlights, congested strip malls, and storefronts. Hakim hadn't seen this many stores in all of Canada and the contrast was striking. From his vantage point on Interstate 95, one sign stood out above the others. As Kameel had promised, one sign towered high above them all.

He'd made it. He'd entered the promised land of Wal-Mart.

CHAPTER SIX

Whiteout
Wednesday, Feb. 17, 7:45 P.M.
St. John River Valley
New Brunswick, Canada

Checking his rearview mirror, Kameel Belaidi squinted from the glare, then looked away. That truck's high beams were blinding. All around him, snow was falling—the fine, powdery kind—at a modest clip, about an inch or so an hour, he guessed. Though driving conditions were acceptable, the winds were building and the Muslim sensed he was traveling on borrowed time.

In the dead of winter, a Canadian highway could be a cold, lonely place to die. Bin Laden's front man knew it well and took this winter storm warning seriously. His worst nightmare, like every driver's in this part of the country, was getting stranded at night, alone, in a Canadian blizzard, then running out of gas. He'd read about it happening so often this time of year, it was never far from his mind.

In Kameel's view, he was as prepared as he could be under the circumstances. Owning a chain of Irving mini-marts scattered across New Brunswick helped his feelings, but only slightly. He'd planned his route, running alongside the St. John River, such that he'd never be more than an hour's drive—in good weather—from any of them. In addition, he'd heavily loaded his four-wheel-drive SUV for a winter skiing vacation. Overhead, his rooftop ski rack was laden with a set of skis, poles, and snowshoes. Inside, he'd packed a wealth of warm winter clothes—boxes of them—so he wasn't about to freeze, no matter what.

In addition to outdoor winter gear, Kameel had something else going for him. Like many aircraft, his vehicle came equipped with two fuel tanks, a primary and backup auxiliary. Both had been topped off before he'd left Halifax so he was golden for gas. Unlike an aircraft, however, his SUV didn't carry any form of emergency locator beacon, so he'd brought along the next best thing. Looking down at the passenger seat, he saw them both blinking. His cell phone was plugged in, turned on, and roaming, and the handheld GPS receiver indicated sync lock, good signal strength, and his position within a few meters. He might be alone now, but help wasn't far away if he needed it.

When the storm hit, the ominous black night sky opened wide, laying down a dense blanket of snow.

Kameel topped a hill and saw it coming, an endless wall of snow moving toward him through the darkness like a great white wave. Unlike anything he'd ever experienced, a thunderstorm of snow—a literal downpour—blanketed the earth before his eyes, obliterating the road in seconds. Soon, drifts began accumulating as his windshield wipers worked nonstop, struggling to keep up. After a couple of miles' descent into the St. John River valley, unable to make out the road, Kameel found himself following vehicle tracks, mere ruts cut through the snow.

Sensing a bit of lateral slide, a slight fishtail to his right rear, Kameel engaged his four-wheel drive. Miles from the nearest small town, he forged ahead knowing full well he had no choice.

Suddenly, without warning, his SUV was buffeted violently as if shaken by the hand of God.

Instinctively, Kameel tensed behind the wheel, but kept moving.

Above the noise of his heater fan, he heard a violent, howling wind building in the distance, blustery at first, then getting louder. *Definitely getting louder,* he thought, roaring down the valley at hurricane speed.

Channeling the hundred-mile-an-hour winds like an enormous canal, the river valley served as a nozzle, focusing the brunt of the blizzard over the length of the highway. In a matter of a few seconds, the screaming winds were deafening, comparable to those of a hurricane, only this wind carried blowing snow.

There was no preparing for it, and when the winds hit, they hit suddenly.

The whiteout was instantaneous; he was totally blind.

In a span of seconds, Kameel's visibility collapsed to near zero. Minutes before, there'd been a plowed road stretching out before him. Moments ago, there'd been clear, textured ruts in the road. Now, only a featureless blanket of white remained. The road was completely buried, its ruts erased, snow whipping about and flying in every direction.

Kameel grimaced. *This is a bad one.* In the record books, the St. John Blizzard would come to be known as the storm of the century.

Low beams illuminated the blowing white mass—high beams made it worse—blinding him, reducing his visibility to less than five feet. He couldn't see the road or train tracks, couldn't see the ditch, and couldn't see the river. In the blink of an eye, he'd become totally disoriented.

Instinctively, his first reaction was to stop and stop quickly. *One thing about four-wheel drive,* Kameel lamented, *it'll go in the snow, but it won't stop any faster than a car.*

Attempting to pull off on the road's shoulder, Kameel slowed his SUV to a stop. Though buffeted about, whipped by the wind, he experienced reasonably even traction applying his brakes. *Good,* he concluded, believing he remained on the purple-rock asphalt.

He checked his compass, quickly recouping his bearings. Once oriented, he pinpointed his position using the GPS receiver, then plotted his position on a road map of the Atlantic provinces.

Without a moment's hesitation, he dialed the toll-free number for the Royal Canadian Mounted Police emergency rescue squad.

Busy.

He tried again.

Busy.

And again . . . and again.

More out of frustration than fear, he dialed the closest Irving mini-mart. Fortunately for Kameel, the station manager answered on the fourth ring. In a matter-of-fact voice, he relayed his situation, giving clear instructions to forward his exact location and cell phone number to the Royal Canadian Mounted Police. As he explained, there was no immediate danger, but it looked likely he'd be stranded for the duration of the blizzard. After giving his cell phone number to the manager, Kameel hung up, expecting the rescue squad would call him once his man had gotten through.

Next, as if running on autopilot, he called Hakim's cell phone to give him a heads-up regarding the storm delay. When it rang inside Hakim's Taurus, he answered immediately. Assuming the international call could be monitored, their conversation was purposefully generic, free of names, rendezvous location, and time. From the sound of it, Kameel could have been any vacationing motorist, temporarily stranded by the blizzard, calling a friend with news of late arrival and continued commitment to stay in touch. Anxious to keep his call short, Kameel tactfully brought their conversation to a close.

With his headlights on and motor running, Kameel gazed out the window, awestruck by the power of the storm. In the back of his mind, he considered calling his station manager to see if he'd gotten through, but elected to keep the line open until he'd heard from the rescue squad. After their initial contact, he imagined they'd call periodically to keep tabs on him; as he understood it, that's how they liked to operate in this type of situation.

Then, after a few minutes staring out the window, he detected a lull in the storm, a break in the hurricane-force wind. As suddenly as it started, the wind fell silent. It was the strangest feeling, an erie stillness like the calm before the storm, something like passing through the eye of a hurricane, but he knew it wouldn't last.

In an instant, his headlights revealed the wonder, the splendor of God's handiwork laid out before him. He saw snow drifting as he'd never seen it before, enormous drifts for such a young storm as this, torrents of snow blowing across the road in waves. Wave after relentless wave advanced across the open field before him; it just kept coming, then suddenly, the screaming wind returned.

A cold chill ran down his spine.

Then it occurred to him, like a snowy, blurry image suddenly crystallizing before his eyes: *He wasn't on the shoulder at all.* He was in the third lane, the slow-vehicle lane which allowed traffic to pass on the inside.

Without warning, two things happened in an instant.

First, an enormous, blinding wall of snow engulfed Kameel's SUV, racing up the highway at near hurricane speed, burying everything in its path.

Then, as this great snow wall raced up the hill, an eighteen-wheeler cleared the hilltop, heading straight for it.

Kameel's most significant revelation was disclosed to him in one final moment of clarity.

Trucks travel in this lane, he thought, but felt no panic.

It was an odd, almost surreal experience, much like he'd always imagined it would be, as if the doors to heaven were flung open.

Staring wide-eyed into his rearview mirror, Kameel became aware of a radiant light flooding his SUV. Frozen with disbelief, he heard something horrific, something deafeningly loud closing in behind him, but he couldn't be sure what.

Blinded by blowing snow and darkness, Kameel caught a fleeting glimpse of running lights as the jackknifed tractor-trailer skidded toward him. His heart stopped, now recognizing the sound—air brakes screaming their final, desperate, bloodcurdling cry before impact.

Suddenly, headlights appeared; they burned through first in the form of four white-hot suns. The truck's chrome steel bumper punched through next, followed by its checkerboard grill and PEI license plate.

Focusing only on the tag, Kameel's last conscious thoughts were of Prince Edward Island—emerald green grass, red soil, blue water, and heaven.

Inverted, a twisted mass of metal and shattered glass, the SUV plunged off the road into a ditch, buried beneath the eighteen-wheeler and an insulating mound of snow. Later that evening, one-hundred-mile-an-hour winds whipped surrounding snow into drifts ten feet high. Remarkably, there was no fire, as temperatures were cold enough to turn the tractor-trailer's leaking diesel fuel into a viscous gel.

The Calm Before the Storm
Thursday, Feb. 18, 9:35 A.M.
St. John River Valley
New Brunswick, Canada

Daylight revealed the full extent of the storm. Over three hundred cars and trucks were stranded that night in the St. John River valley, buried by gusting, violent winds and blowing snow. Best seen from the air, the string of snowbound vehicles snaking along the river road extended nearly ten miles.

With the high winds, snowplows were useless during the rescue. Front loaders had to come in and clear a path before rescue vehicles could enter the valley. Even then, some rescue vehicles were stranded overnight, literally frozen solid in the act of getting people to safety.

Thanks to local families and the selfless courage of rescuers who braved the fierce Canadian elements, not a single life was lost during the St. John Blizzard. Aside from two with serious injuries, all those stranded—hundreds of people—were led by rescuers into warm homes near the highway, a triumph of the human spirit, motivated by the worst of times.

As the truck driver would later explain, the whiteout happened so quickly he had no time to react. Admittedly, he was traveling too fast for the conditions—far too fast, investigators insisted—but he was also going downhill, negotiating a sharp turn alongside a bend in the river. What really mattered was his poor visibility; he couldn't see the vehicle until it was too late.

Instead of swerving, driving around the SUV to avoid collision, investigators concluded the driver panicked, locked his brakes, and placed his vehicle in a lateral, uncontrolled skid.

As the driver explained it, his steering simply stopped working. He turned his wheels right, then left, but his direction didn't change. Not surprisingly, the driver blamed the storm, claiming he lost control of his rig as a result of the whiteout, then jackknifed the trailer in the bend, crushing the SUV in its path.

Known to police and insurance companies alike for his long history of speeding tickets, by all accounts the trucker was a happily married family man who exercised good judgment in most areas of his life, except speed. Considering his record and the numerous driver rehab classes he'd attended, this good-looking young fellow was a big kid in a man's body, a wannabe race truck driver who'd not yet made it.

In the final analysis, investigators concluded he was simply driving too fast for the conditions, overdriving his headlights, not uncommon in this part of the country and often fatal.

But both men had been lucky. The truck driver's charmed life continued; he received only a single broken rib. Kameel Belaidi, on the other hand, didn't get off as easy. Although broken up pretty badly, what really mattered was that he had ducked in time to avoid decapitation.

Fortunately for Kameel, the Royal Canadian Mounted Police had his number and location. Their failure to contact him by phone quickly resulted in an escalation of his case. The Irving mini-mart manager insisted his boss was in earnest and urged them to take action immediately.

They arrived on the scene less than two hours later, as fast as humanly possible under the circumstances, then conducted their rescue and subsequent accident investigation with all the professionalism Canadians had come to expect from their police force—a national treasure by any standard. This was an extraordinary group of men and women who conducted themselves with great competence and demonstrated a high degree of professional curiosity. In fact, it was their thoroughness which would eventually put Kameel behind bars for the rest of his life.

Of particular interest to the Mounties was the contents of a white cardboard box. Curiously, though the box had been crushed by the impact, the cheese ball it contained remained intact—a perfect sphere showing only gashes through its red wax covering. Two things attracted the investigators' attention: It felt uncommonly hard—like a brick—and it was massive, weighing far too much to write off without further study.

Meanwhile, back at headquarters, the world suddenly seemed very small. As it turned out, Kameel Belaidi was more widely known than their infamous *race truck* driver. A quick database check revealed that their SUV casualty was of interest to law enforcement agencies inside both the United States and Canada. To the surprise of accident investigators and the rescue squad, their SUV victim was immediately red-flagged by the Canadian Mounties, FBI, and CTC.

Records described him as a Canadian businessman, Muslim fundamentalist, and suspected member of al Qaeda—bin Laden's terrorist organization—although no formal charges had been filed and nothing was yet proven. Another intriguing, though less threatening, aspect of Belaidi's business activities had been extensively documented, however.

Tax and financial records clearly established loose business relationships between the Irving mini-mart owner and several known members of bin Laden's financial network, the Foundation for Islamic Salvation; that much had been confirmed. As a result, in the minds of law enforcement officials, Kameel Belaidi was affiliated with trouble, if not an integral part of it. To the credit of Canada's finest, both rescue squad and accident investigators at the scene were notified of this development only minutes after the victim had been identified.

Putting two and two together, accident investigators placed the wax-coated metal sphere in an explosive transport container, then trucked it to the bomb squad's X-ray department for analysis.

Alarmed, X-ray didn't keep it long. They'd never seen anything like it. Within an hour, the device made its way to their weapons lab, where they determined it was, in all probability, an unarmed bomb of unknown type. Judging from its X-ray cross section, it may have been a miniature nuclear device, the deadliest component of an explosive package sometimes referred to as a briefcase bomb.

From that point forward, things happened very quickly. Everyone involved was amazed at the speed and escalation of the investigation. From the original pair of accident investigators, within four days the Belaidi case expanded to over one hundred fifty people in the Canadian provinces alone.

Less than one day after the device was brought into X-ray as suspicious, Canadians from the highest levels of government contacted both the FBI in Washington and Langley's CTC.

More remarkable than this, not one word about the briefcase bomb appeared in either the American or Canadian press.

Videoconference
Friday, Feb. 19, 11:30 A.M.
CTC

When a heads-up directive comes down from the president of the United States, people inside the government listen—especially when it's got their name on it. This particular directive read like an all points bulletin addressed to everybody who was anybody in U.S. counterterrorism: the heads of the CTC, CIA, FBI, the chairman of the Joint Chiefs of Staff, and the commander of the Joint Special Operations Command.

In plain English, it was a call to arms announcing a "must attend" videoconference with high-ranking law enforcement officials from Canada. There was no announced agenda, no attendance list on the Canadian side, no negotiation for a meeting time, just an emphatic directive to clear your calendar and call in—11:30 Friday morning. From the tone of the presidential edict, it was clear this was no drill.

From their videoconference room inside the CTC, Graham, Wyley, Buck, and Russum watched an array of TV screens, each divided into four window tiles showing a separate close-up of a single face, along with the person's name and position.

To Graham, it was the Canadian faces which were most telling. Looking drawn and fatigued, some had ashen complexions, others bore dark circles under their eyes. Many yawned as if they had missed their night's sleep, or just gotten up, but that didn't make sense. It was the middle of the day.

Aside from the close-ups—most looked like stodgy, white-haired bankers—one wide-angle shot showed ten somber Canadians sitting around a stately wooden table with a large red maple leaf carved in its center. Graham didn't recognize any of the faces except one, the prime minister sitting at the head of the table in front of the Canadian flag.

The prime minister started the meeting promptly at 11:30 by stating its purpose up front.

"Gentlemen, I will dispense with the introductions here for the sake of expediency. We can get to know each other later, once we put this threatening situation behind us. The information we need to relay is of a most urgent nature and to delay our communication any longer may border on the criminal. I need to make clear what we're here for, so please allow me to be blunt. We have reason to believe Muslim terrorists may have smuggled one or more small, cheese ball–sized nuclear bombs into your country across the Canadian border. I stress that these bombs may be nuclear, though admittedly, we're not sure yet and that's where your expertise comes in. The device we discovered is outside our experience. Frankly, we've never seen anything like it, although I've been told it resembles your old SADM device, only smaller. Now, please, hold your questions and let us tell you what we know."

A distinguished-looking, clean-cut gentleman—the youngest of those seated around the table—delivered the bad news, recounting the discovery of the bomb in Kameel Belaidi's SUV.

Labeled CHEESE-BALL BOMB, pictures of the gashed, red wax–covered device appeared on-screen. Coated in wax, and wrapped in an Ace bandage, the similarity between the Russian briefcase bomb and the Canadian device wasn't obvious at first. Yet, the sequence of images which followed quickly changed all that.

Within thirty seconds, an X-ray of the sphere, labeled EQUATORIAL VIEW, appeared on-screen. Before Graham had finished counting the modular connectors, the picture changed to a polar view of the device. A few moments later, Graham looked to Russum and mouthed the word *sixteen,* meaning a total of sixteen modular connectors were distributed across the surface of the device, exactly the same number as were found on the Russian explosive.

Russum, looking dismayed, acknowledged Graham's count.

Next, a series of dissection photographs were shown revealing a pile of red wax shavings, an Ace bandage, and finally, a close-up of the device itself. No doubt about it now, not in Graham's mind anyway.

Like a wife urging her husband to speak up, Graham nudged Russum in the ribs.

The Texan took a deep calming breath, then interrupted the videoconference call with the bad news.

"Excuse me, gentlemen. We can give you a positive I.D. on your bomb."

"And who are you, sir?" the speaker, Canada's chief lawman, wanted to know.

"My name's Russum, Billy Ray Russum. I'm a nuclear weapons expert with the CTC here in Langley, and I'm sorry to say, we know this device. We analyzed one for the first time earlier this week and we'd never seen one before, or anything like it for that matter. It's a Russian pure-fusion device; basically, it's a clean neutron bomb with a ten-ton yield. We think Assad detonated one of these over Hama earlier this month."

After the shock wore off, noise over the videoconference increased as everyone began talking at once. Once discussion of the Hama massacre quieted, Russum went on to explain pure fusion to the group; then he queried the Canadians. "Ours came armed, complete with detonator electronics, all packed in a briefcase. How 'bout yours?"

Canada's chief lawman referred the question to the senior accident investigator, who spoke next, delivering his firsthand account. Of those sitting around the Canadian maple leaf, Graham noticed the senior investigator bore the darkest circles. Fatigue shone through his eyes and heartfelt concern permeated his voice.

"We showed you everything relevant we recovered from the SUV. There were no detonator electronics and no briefcase, only a crushed white cardboard box containing the bomb. It's possible that there could be more debris buried beneath the accident scene, but we don't think it likely. We dug Belaidi and his bomb out from underneath a ten-foot snowdrift and a jackknifed tractor-trailer rig. The snow makes it impossible for us to know for sure, but we used metal detectors to comb the area and we think we have it pretty well covered. There is more to tell, however," the investigator explained in a strained voice.

"Beyond the bomb?" Graham whispered.

The speaker heard Graham's apprehensive tone and nodded his head. "It's got to do with why we believe these devices may have made their way to American soil." Once everyone understood where the Canadian investigator was going, his American audience sat absolutely quiet.

Another piece of evidence appeared on-screen, this one a picture of Belaidi's cell phone.

"Once we found the bomb, we did some follow-up work on Belaidi's cell phone calls. During this trip, he placed two calls to the same mobile phone and, unfortunately for all of us, this cell phone was on the move. We have no record of the conversation beyond its destination, time, and duration, but we classified both calls as alarming because the first call was taken inside Canada, the second in Maine. To be more specific, he made the first call at ten minutes till two, when this cell phone was located in New Brunswick, Canada, near Fredericton. Approximately six hours later, shortly before the accident, he called this same cell phone again, and this time, the call was taken in Bangor, Maine. Regrettably, recordings of the international call are not available. It was never recorded, so we have no voiceprints or additional information regarding the calls other than this one final point.

"We tried dialing the cell phone number to get a fix on that suspect's current location and got an answering machine. Apparently our suspect has turned off his cell phone because, according to telephone company records, the unit is no longer roaming and the voice mail account hasn't been checked for weeks.

"Anyway, as a result of these two calls, we believe one or more suspects working with Belaidi probably crossed the U.S. border into Maine sometime between 3:20 and 5:20 Wednesday afternoon. Considering the road conditions prevalent at the time and the distance between Fredericton and Bangor, we assumed they were traveling between twenty and forty-five miles an hour. In addition, we expect they kept on the major highways because they'd be plowed first and in the best shape.

"Both U.S. and Canadian customs officials have been working this case nonstop and we have records of every car and truck that crossed the border during this six-hour period on Wednesday. Further, like I said earlier, we have two other factors working for us that simplify our problem. First, there was a blizzard in the making so the traffic was less than average, and second, the Fredericton and Bangor calls give us a pretty good idea of our suspect's speed. Using this, we estimated the time our suspect vehicle most likely crossed the border and narrowed our focus to this two-hour interval. Though nearly three hundred trucks and cars crossed the border during this period, the task of checking these crossings is not insurmountable.

"With your cooperation, we're optimistic we'll find some inconsistency in their records. We have face and license plate photographs of everyone who crossed the border during this period, and we've already screened over two-thirds of them. In a nutshell, we eliminated almost all the Canadians from the list and narrowed it down to about one hundred fifty-five suspects, most of them American truck drivers and businessmen. We've prioritized the names and need your help checking out the rest of them. Of those remaining, only thirty-six percolated to the top as key suspects."

Without a moment's hesitation, the FBI director nodded to the directors of the CIA and CTC. They were in unanimous agreement. "We're on the case," he confirmed. "Just point us to your files and steer us to the right people; we'll take it from there."

CHAPTER SEVEN

Medusa
Monday, Feb. 22, 4:08 P.M.
Holiday Inn
Portsmouth, New Hampshire

The intriguing thing about the boxes from FastTech was their weight. They felt almost empty, as if they were filled with air, but Hakim knew each contained four sets of detonator electronics.

Hakim cleared the small writing desk of unnecessary clutter, then placed one of the boxes in front of him alongside his laptop computer. Earlier, Kameel had insisted bomb assembly was so simple a child could do it. Now, with him seemingly out of the picture, his words would be given the acid test, a form of trial by fire.

The first thing Hakim had to do was power up and test the electronics. Once he found a couple of good sets, he'd assemble two bombs by attaching separate detonator electronics to each one. There were several things he had to worry about along the way, but with a little luck, he'd find few surprises. Besides, if he got in a jam, he had FastTech's phone number plus access to their twenty-four-hour tech support hotline.

Carefully, with the patient, methodical conduct of someone twenty years his senior, Hakim opened one of the large
boxes from FastTech. In this respect, especially considering
his age, his slow, deliberate methods were extraordinary. Unlike many young people, this Iraqi terrorist was willing, even
anxious, to benefit from the relevant experience of others. If
he could learn what he needed to know the easy way, from
someone who'd done it before, he'd consistently go out of his
way to do so.

Remarkably, Hakim Moussavi defied the old adage "You
can't put an old head on young shoulders," and in this respect
alone, he was frightening, light-years ahead of his peers. Even
those who recognized his talent, those who knew the danger,
continually underestimated him because he never drew attention to himself. His overall manner, his innate ability to charm
and manipulate, was disarming. A bad seed born without con-
science, blessed with sound judgment and the immortality of
youth, Hakim Moussavi could charm his way into your life,
then gut you on the way out.

Inside the shipping carton, he found two half shells of
molded foam, each separated by an electrically conductive
pink plastic liner. Pulling up on the plastic, he removed the
top piece of foam. Examining it more closely, Hakim noticed
it looked like a cream-colored human brain. Although con-
forming to the square shape of the carton, it consisted of firm,
brainlike lobes and convolutions. After a few moments'
thought, he concluded the packing material had been sprayed
into the box as a thick liquid, then it had rapidly expanded,
surrounding the contents inside.

Ideal for mass production, Hakim thought. *Perfect for packing round bombs in square boxes.* He took several pictures of
the foam shell, planning to recommend it on his return.

Once he'd removed the top piece of molded foam, four
identical white boxes were revealed, each two inches deep by
ten inches square. Each box, labeled TRANSMITTER/RECEIVER
PAIR, held one set of detonator cables and electronics.

Without wasting any time, he removed one box from the
form-fitting foam. Scanning it for any information that might
be useful, Hakim saw only two serial numbers, and they were

short ones. Next he removed his pocket knife, slitting open one end of the box. Wedged inside, he saw a folded sheet of paper alongside a green circuit board assembly wrapped in pink bubble wrap. Carefully, he slit the center seam of the box, then laid it flat, exposing its contents.

To his credit, the first thing the young terrorist did was examine the paperwork. On top of the stack, he saw FastTech's Lifetime Warranty card. Smirking, he pressed on. Beneath the warranty, he found what he'd been looking for. It read simply, ASSEMBLY AND OPERATING INSTRUCTIONS, BATTERIES NOT INCLUDED. Further inspection revealed the box contained two items: something called a "frisbee" and the other a remote. The frisbee was a flat donut-shaped circuit board and cable assembly which required four D-cell batteries. The remote required a nine-volt battery and looked like the remote control for your garage door opener.

Next, he removed the donut-shaped motherboard from its pink bubble wrap. The frisbee was an interesting-looking contraption in that it had sixteen identical connectorized cables, each one foot in length, uniformly spaced and attached in a ring around the inside edge of the donut's hole. When Hakim lifted the donut-shaped disk from the bubble wrap, its dangling cables gave the appearance of jellyfish tentacles. In addition, Hakim noted four separate D-battery holders on the board, each positioned in a separate quadrant around the disk. Finally, he noticed a small keypad and display on the board as well as a plug-in connector for his laptop. Overall, functional but unremarkable. In truth, he'd been more impressed by the compact size and capability of his cellular phone.

After carefully laying out the motherboard's tentacles in a radial pattern, Hakim opened the remote control unit. Not only did it look like a garage door opener, it was one, inside and out, and a Stanley garage door opener at that. Nothing extraordinary here, and Hakim found comfort in this familiar handheld gadget. Stanley was a global company and well known in Iraq as the terrorist's weapon of choice for remotely detonating car bombs.

Hakim finished reading his instructions, front to back, to make sure he had all the tools, equipment, and supplies he'd need to assemble and test his two bombs. To his relief, Kameel had been correct in his assessment. It looked simple enough that a child could do it. Improving an already good situation, he found FastTech supplied a built-in test jig on each motherboard so, in effect, it could test itself. Once the board and cables were checked out, all Hakim had to do was attach it to an eight-pound cheese ball.

On paper, everything looked good, but you never knew until you went through it.

After returning with a bag full of batteries, Hakim installed them, then looped all sixteen cables back onto the board's test jig, a set of sixteen modular plug-in connectors, uniformly spaced around the outer edge of the motherboard. Once the cable ends were plugged in, Hakim attached his laptop, then powered everything on. In less than fifteen seconds, an ALL TESTS PASSED message flashed on the motherboard's small liquid-crystal display. From his laptop keyboard, Hakim clicked CAPTURE. Sixteen graphs showing sixteen separate pulses appeared on-screen. He selected COLLAPSE, then each graph shifted vertically, seemingly laying all sixteen pulses over each other.

Excellent. Hakim smiled. Sixteen precisely shaped detonation pulses, aligned to within a billionth of a second. They were perfect.

Satisfied, Hakim shifted his focus to the remote. He held it in his hand, aimed it at the frisbee, and pressed.

Nothing.

Pressed again.

Nothing.

Moving the remote next to the frisbee's eight-inch wire antenna, he pressed, this time squeezing really hard.

Nothing. Dead as a doornail.

Undaunted, he set his handheld remote on the desk, unfolded the instructions, and began to read. His revelation came quickly: BATTERIES NOT INCLUDED.

Come to think of it, Hakim thought as he shook his head, half smiling, *that remote did feel a little light.*

After testing a battery, he installed it in the remote and picked up where he had left off.

Pointing it at the frisbee, he pressed the remote.

CLOSE appeared on-screen.

He punched it again.

OPEN flashed on his laptop.

He checked its range from across the room, it worked; carried it down the hall, it worked; then finally, one floor down and outside from the Holiday Inn's snow-covered parking lot . . . it worked without a hitch. So long as the transmitter battery was fresh, range was not an issue.

Returning to his room, he programmed the timer, watched it count down, five, four, three, two, one, and suddenly, sixteen simultaneous pulses appeared on-screen. *God is great. Everything is as it should be.*

Not surprisingly, FastTech's operating instructions ended here. Regardless, Hakim was cautiously optimistic it couldn't be too tough.

Hakim removed one of the white Edam cheese boxes from his duffle bag and gingerly placed it on the desk. Opening the box, he lifted the red wax–covered ball off the Easter-basket grass and rested it on the rim of a drinking glass. After brushing all traces of plastic grass from the wax, Hakim opened his pocket knife and scored a circle around the sphere, like carving an equator around the globe. Deliberately cautious, Hakim kept his cut shallow. He could feel when he'd penetrated the wax, but, to his surprise, there was something beneath the protective coating and it wasn't metal. It felt like cloth, though he couldn't know for sure, not yet. Once the cut was complete, Hakim had hoped the two hemispheres would easily separate, cleanly lifting off the bomb; but to his disappointment, that was not to be. Without Kameel's help, Hakim was in unknown territory here, but he knew if he took it slow, he'd get through this wax removal without regret. *A child could do it.*

Once the equator was cut, he rotated the bomb and laid down a shallow, north-south score across the poles. Still, the parts didn't easily lift off or separate. Using his knife blade to start the process, Hakim began to peel back the wax like peeling the skin off an orange. What he discovered seemed reasonable once he exposed enough to understand what he was seeing. Beneath the wax, the bomb had been wrapped in a protective layer of Ace elastic bandage, the type used for wrapping sprained wrists or ankles. Once Hakim understood what he was up against, the wax came off quickly, in large torn sections. With most of the wax peeled away, he removed two metal clips securing the end of the bandage, then unwrapped it. At last, he saw the globelike, shiny metal sphere he'd been expecting. Distributed along lines of latitude and longitude, he counted sixteen plastic modular connectors.

Better check the fit, he thought, anxious to nail down this final assembly detail. Disconnecting the business end of a detonator cable, he aligned it with a connector mounted along the bomb's equator. The modular plug locked into place with a satisfying snap, then Hakim stood upright, examining his handiwork.

The first thing he noticed—sixteen detonation pulses, frozen in time, displayed on his laptop—caused his heart to stop, then panic! *The batteries are still installed!* The realization of what he'd done came crashing down around him and he snatched the detonator plug from its socket.

"Praise be to God," he whispered, visibly shaken.

Hakim knew he'd been lucky and wouldn't make that mistake again. He'd inadvertently armed the bomb without checking or setting the safety. The mini-nuke wouldn't have exploded with its full force from a single detonation pulse, but it most certainly would have killed him.

Facing this realization, Hakim felt as if he were about to explode. Instinctively, he picked up the ice bucket and took a walk to ease his tension. A short time later, he returned with a couple of cold American soft drinks. He liked the fizz. Once his nerves were back in check, he calmly thought through his situation, evaluating what he should do next. Minutes later, he picked up where he'd left off.

With the bomb sitting on the rim of a glass, Hakim attached the frisbee. Centering its hole over the top of the sphere, he carefully lowered it into position. Once stable, Hakim grabbed his tube of silicone and ran a ring about the seam with craftsmanlike precision. Within twenty-four hours, the silicone would set, anchoring the motherboard to the bomb. With the cables ends still connected to the frisbee, the assembly gave the impression of a small head wearing a hat of snakes.

From a distance, the assembly could easily have been taken for the shrunken head of Medusa.

Mismatch
Tuesday, Feb. 23, 10:12 A.M.
Russum's office
CTC

"More bad news," Russum stated flatly, then handed Graham a handful of pictures still warm off the color laser printer. "Take a look at these and sit tight. I need to round up Buck and Wyley."

Graham nodded and began studying the pictures as Russum hurried out of his office. The top page, marked SUSPECT'S VEHICLE, showed a late-model blue Ford Taurus, dirty and snowcovered, with Massachusetts license plates clearly bolted on its front bumper. The second was a poor-quality close-up of the driver's face taken with his side window lowered two-thirds of the way down. His nose and eyes were clear enough, but the driver's mouth was obscured through a foggy, frost-covered side window. As fate would have it, the closer to his mouth Graham tried to see, the foggier the window, the more obscure the image.

As Graham began examining the third page, Wyley rushed in, anxious to get up to speed. After a quick look over the first two pictures, Wyley joined Graham on page three.

The third picture revealed an enlarged, digitized full-page scanned image of the suspect's driver's license, filled with presumably relevant, but probably misleading information. Although the driver's picture was a blurred, washed-out face shot, you could better make out his mouth and chin.

Young, twenty-two to twenty-five years old, nice looking, clean shaven, probably just out of college, Graham thought. After a few moments, the doctor noticed Wyley looking away from the suspect's photo, seemingly ready to discuss it.

"What do you think?" Wyley asked.

"His name's listed as Art Morrison."

"I assume that's an alias."

"My wife would call this guy a hunk."

Wyley agreed, but wasn't smiling. "My wife and kids went to the Washington Zoo yesterday, and I'd be willing to bet you this: If we were to show her this picture, I expect she'd say that she saw him, or someone who looked a lot like him."

"I don't understand what you're getting at."

"Only this. Look at this guy's face. You can't figure out anything about him except his age. He doesn't have any distinguishing features that make him easy to identify. He could be an Italian, could be Greek, he could be Scottish for all I know; hell, who can say? He looks like a million other teenage heartthrobs. I'd describe him as a dark-haired, dark-eyed, good-looking young man. Like I said, you can't tell where the guy comes from just by looking at him and about a gazillion young men fit his description."

"I see what you mean." Graham studied the license, looking for some clue. Equally as important, the man's alleged name, address, and personal stats were spelled out in clear black print. Graham focused on his January 1985 date of birth first and whipped off a little mental arithmetic. "I'd buy this guy's advertised age. I'd peg him at twenty-five, but how about his eye color? They look almost black to me. What do you make of it?"

Wyley examined the man's eye color, height, and weight. "I can't know with any real degree of certainty, but brown is probably accurate. The suspect's eyes look almost black in the picture, but you have to take into account the light source and color printer. Most of the office printers around here are poorly maintained because it's cheaper to run those printer cartridges until they're completely empty. If you combine digital photography, tungsten lighting, and poorly maintained color printers, you sometimes see the colors shift slightly toward yellow or black. How about you? What do you think about his height and weight?"

"His height is listed as five foot ten, but judging from his low seat position in the Taurus, I'd say five ten is a stretch. I can't speak to his build or weight with much confidence working only from a face shot, but one hundred fifty pounds is a pretty reasonable weight for a medium-built twenty-five-year-old man maybe five feet eight or nine inches tall. Judging from what Massachusetts had to say, I don't think we should take any of this data at face value." Plastered like a watermark diagonally across the page in a large, light beige font, the Massachusetts director of Motor Vehicles had placed an official-looking state seal reading FORGERY — DO NOT REPRODUCE.

A fourth picture showed a detailed artist's rendition of the driver's face, in color, including official police estimates of the suspect's estimated height, build, and weight.

After studying the numbers, Wyley said, "Looks like the police agreed with your short call. They pegged him as a medium-built, five-foot-eight-inch male weighing one hundred forty-five pounds. From the account at the bottom of the page, this estimate and the picture were created with input from the customs officer on duty at the time."

"I'd take a firsthand account any day."

Next, they looked over a computer-enhanced rendition of the artist's drawings showing a set of face and full body shots. The pictures showed the suspect decked out with a beard, mustache, and longer hair. Also included were a series of pictures showing the clean-shaven man in a sweatshirt, blue jeans, and heavy jacket, and in a business suit as well. "They dressed him up like a Barbie doll," Graham observed, thumbing ahead to the next page.

That photo showed the cover of a road map labeled AT-LANTIC PROVINCES. At the bottom of the page were the words UNMARKED ROAD MAP RECOVERED FROM INSIDE BELAIDI'S SUV.

Before saying anything, Graham looked ahead to the final picture and, for a moment, he felt his heart stop. The page was titled simply. THE WASHINGTON CONNECTION.

"The Canadians raided his home and found these," Graham said, looking at Wyley.

This last picture showed a well-worn, marked-up city street map of Washington, D.C. At the bottom of the page were some handwritten notes plus a list of Washington, D.C.–oriented internet bookmarks. They would have been interpreted as the search results of a curious tourist had Kameel not been found with a neutron bomb in the back of his SUV.

About that time, Russum returned without Buck. Once he determined how far Graham and Wyley had gotten, he filled in the missing details. "We've narrowed the list down to six suspects, but our buddy Art here stands out head and shoulders above the rest."

Once he had the duo's attention, he continued.

"Art Morrison's story doesn't hold up. The guy's retired from HP; he and his wife go to Florida for the winter. An FBI agent interviewed one of his neighbors and immediately became suspicious. Come to find out, the lady was watching the Morrisons' house while they were away. At our request, Andover police checked out the house and discovered his tags missing. The real Art Morrison flew back yesterday and confirmed nothing else was taken."

After a short back and forth, Russum summarized the mood on Capitol Hill. "Both the president and Congress are taking this thing very seriously. They're talking about bringing in the military."

"Neutron bombs moving on Canadian soil with possible links to Washington. I guess I'd take it seriously too," Graham confirmed. "I can't believe it's really happening, playing out before our very eyes."

"Yeah, I've got a bad feeling about this one," Russum said in an uncharacteristically quiet voice. "Buck's been given orders to ship out in a week, once some political hurdles are cleared, and looks like we're going with him."

Under Siege
Wednesday, Feb. 24, 2:29 P.M.
Capitol Hill
Washington, D.C.

Something's gone wrong, Hakim Moussavi thought, gazing out the tour bus window. *Something's gone terribly wrong.*

Washington, D.C., looked like a city under siege. Between the White House and Capitol, Pennsylvania Avenue was lined with uniformed police and military personnel, deliberately visible for all to see. The image was one comparable to the late sixties, when National Guard troops were called in to protect Lyndon Johnson and Robert McNamara from the American people they'd sworn to serve.

Hakim's tour bus rolled to a stop near the northern white marble wing of the United States Capitol. After collecting his camera gear, he waited his turn, then stepped into the aisle and off the bus. Advertised as a Kodak moment, this stop offered a spectacular shot of the Capitol steps, but the terrorist in sheep's clothing sensed something was missing.

Lifting his camera, Hakim framed several quick shots. Through the lens, he repeatedly observed the same cold, lifeless pattern: a great deal of granite and marble, but almost no people, few civilians anyway. From the fenced-in White House grounds to the Capitol steps, what stood out in his mind was an inescapable sense of police state.

Beyond Pennsylvania Avenue, Hakim's impression was of the dead. To him, Washington felt like an enormous stonecold tomb, immortalizing the dead, death, and war. Seemingly everything he'd seen in Washington was named for the dead, nearly everything he'd read about was named for the dead, almost every building, monument, and memorial was named either for the dead or for some distant war from days gone by.

An exaggerated or distorted view?

Maybe.

Overstated?

Perhaps, but that was his impression nevertheless. Like it or not, Hakim thought of Washington as a mass grave.

Reminders of death and war were everywhere; you couldn't escape them if you tried. Even the park benches were dedicated to the dead and fallen. To Hakim, Washington seemed like a city more of the dead than of the living. Considering what he'd seen, it was understandable that people in a place such as this would foster death and war. Apparently, people living here worshiped these above all else.

Flatlander
Wednesday, Feb. 24, 7:26 P.M.
Holiday Inn, Georgetown
Washington, D.C.

Hakim surveyed the layout of his motel room. Three lamps, writing desk, phone, TV, several mirrors, two double beds, an ugly hotel-grade painting hanging by a picture window, clothes closet, shower, and toilet. At first glance, there was nothing extraordinary here, but first impressions are often intentionally deceiving.

Looking at the array of sockets behind the TV led him to the black coaxial TV cable. Following the cable to a splitter or Y-type connection, Hakim found one side ran to the TV, which was of no interest whatsoever. The other coax cable, however, ran to a modem-sized metal box with two green lights on the end and metal fins on the top. The green lights meant that the cable modem had connectivity back to a hub office, and through that office, Hakim expected high-speed, virtually instantaneous access to the internet. Cable modem internet access was the reason Hakim had chosen to stay at the Holiday Inn in Washington and he had every intention of taking full advantage of it.

Laying his briefcase on the bed, he opened it, removed his laptop, then set it on the writing desk in the corner, alongside the cable modem. As with all things internet, it never worked the first time, but after a few calls to the help desk, he was set, ready to run.

First thing he did was open Netscape. One click yielded an instantaneous web page, no waiting, no visible indication of download at all. He checked his e-mail, hoping to see some messages from Kameel. There were none; no new messages on the server.

Turning away from his laptop, he took one last pass through the pictures he'd taken on his bus tour of Washington. Lining Constitution Avenue from the Potomac to the Capitol he saw armed, uniformed troops patrolling the streets, as if they were purposefully placed there to thwart his mission. He couldn't know their total numbers, but estimated at least two soldiers per side street, maybe eight men per block. While their behavior wasn't bullyish, or immediately threatening, their presence alone was enough to make him think twice. Working in pairs, continually on the move, they sized up every civilian entering their territory as a possible target.

In addition to light weapons, he saw some carrying handheld cameras, working people on the street like the press works politicians. Gazing at a snapshot he'd taken of the Federal Reserve Building, he grimaced, knowing they'd gotten his picture at least once, possibly more. Toward the back outside edge of the frame, he circled the image of a soldier taking a picture of him. In a way, Hakim knew he was fortunate to capture the soldier in the act; it made his decision regarding what to do more straightforward. After looking over his pictures taken around the White House and Capitol steps, he concluded the troop density down Pennsylvania Avenue was much the same.

Since there was no mail, and since the president's cabinet was continually surrounded by uniformed military personnel, Hakim knew he had to communicate with al-Mashhadi. While he knew e-mail messages were continually monitored by the United States government, he also knew file transfers were not. As a result, communications between field agents such as Hakim—code-named Flatlander—and Baghdad were always encrypted and made indirect by way of a leased computer, a neutral proxy server accessible through the internet and located in Switzerland.

For Hakim and Baghdad to communicate securely, Hakim's laptop had to announce its presence to Baghdad's proxy computer then exchange its public, broadcast, and private encryption keys. Once the computers had finished chatting about security, each understood how to encode message and file information such that only they could read it. All Hakim cared about was that the broken key at the bottom of his browser transformed into a flashing, solid key, meaning his transmission was now secure. To crypto types in the business of secure communication, the method adopted by Baghdad was a slightly modified derivative of triple DES encryption. It had been changed in such a way that its crypto key was longer than that approved by the U.S. government. As a result, it would take National Security Agency computers longer to decrypt his files, if they chose to decrypt them at all, than he would be in the United States. As Flatlander saw it, by the time the NSA had decrypted his files, he'd be out of the country.

Hakim created a file, summarizing his situation, explaining the loss of Kameel and the military presence in Washington.

Once the message file was complete, Hakim triple-encrypted it then logged in to Baghdad's proxy server as Flatlander. Once logged in, he transferred the file to Baghdad's computer in Switzerland. After the file was in place, he modified his home page and uploaded it, adding a new pointer to his message file.

In Baghdad, computers immediately detected changes in Flatlander's home page; operators were notified, and they took action.

Rose in Bloom
Thursday, Feb. 25, 7:49 A.M.
The Pit

Overhead, a hoist gearbox ground to a halt, taking up the last bit of slack from the crane's lifting cable, stretching it ever so slightly under load, pulling its steel strands taut as piano wire. Down below on the railway flatcar, workers checked the cargo lifting harness one last time, then signaled the crane operator an all clear. Once again, the tension in the cable increased, gently lifting the last of the heavy milling machines up, then well clear of the flatcar. As the lifting crane's horizontal displacement motor slowly traversed the overhead I-beam, workers labored to position the heavy machine over the front ends of twin forklifts. Once the crane rolled to a stop, the operator loosened the brake grip slightly, slowly lowering the massive milling machine into position. Finally, once both forklift drivers were satisfied the load was evenly distributed, they signaled the crane operator and the lifting hook was released. Without discussion, both forklift operators climbed onto their vehicles and—one pushing, one pulling—they drove away into the darkness, down the connecting tunnel, toward the Pit.

Satisfied, Kajaz looked up at al-Mashhadi and said what he already knew. "That's the last of them."

Al-Mashhadi's eyes narrowed to black slits, communicating volumes without words.

Kajaz knew what he wanted to know and was quick with his answer. "Our operators are trained and our milling programs are complete. We'll be machining parts in less than twenty-four hours."

Al-Mashhadi gritted his teeth. "Like your father, you've been granted everything you requested and then some. Kurdish rebels have turned this situation around for you, so don't fail me now."

Out of the darkness, a technician approached al-Mashhadi and his horde of bodyguards. He spoke first with al-Mashhadi's head of security, who then escorted him to the big man's side. Clearly, he was apprehensive. "This message came from Flatlander, Excellency."

Al-Mashhadi read it quickly, then asked, "Where's your office?"

"Near the back entrance to the Pit, on the hospital side, room H-37."

"Our network's fully operational," Kajaz added, again knowing what the big man wanted before he asked. "You can signal Flatlander from there."

Al-Mashhadi looked to the technician for confirmation, as if doubting the word of his man in charge.

The technician nodded, adding, "That's right, Excellency. It's been operational now for weeks."

"Take me there at once."

The group piled into a small fleet of electric SUVs, then drove the short distance back to the Pit. Once inside the technician's office, al-Mashhadi looked over the man's shoulder, giving him directions along the way.

"Go to signals," he instructed.

The technician understood al-Mashhadi to mean log in to their remote web server and change directories to one named SIGNALS "Done," he replied.

"Look here." A large finger the size of an inch-diameter pipe pointed to a folder named ROSENBERG.

Inside he saw six files; five contained text, the other a picture.

"First, change the background on Flatlander's home page." The one-inch-thick finger poked at the image file named ROSES IN BLOOM. Once the roses were added to Flatlander's home page, the technician uploaded the change to their web server, then tested it. As expected, Flatlander's home page appeared with blossoming roses as its background.

Al-Mashhadi saw it, mumbled something inaudibly, then punched the log-in window again with his finger. "Show me all of 'em."

The technician double-clicked the text files and displayed them on-screen.

After a few moments' study, he pointed to the file named BLANK=_CHECK.TXT and instructed, "This one; send it."

A click, and it was gone.

Face Hit
Friday, Feb. 26, 9:32 A.M.
CTC

Graham, Wyley, and Russum stared in disbelief at a grainy color photograph, an enlargement of someone near the Capitol steps.

"He could be our man," Graham reluctantly agreed. "How'd they possibly find him?"

"We're in the business of finding faces, but the truth is we just got lucky."

"I just can't believe it." Graham felt stunned, almost dazed, as if his whole world were closing in around him.

"You gotta remember the CIA's in the business of identifying faces and they're really good at it." Russum was emphatic regarding this point. "Every day of the year, twenty-four hours a day, hundreds of CIA personnel watch news broadcasts from all around the world. It's almost unbelievable to me, too, but they sort through every broadcast, picking known faces out of the background. Most often, they find the faces we're looking for obscured by the background crowd in a news scene or newspaper photo."

"I don't get it." Graham looked puzzled.

"Generally, the people we're interested in don't draw attention to themselves. It'd be an exhausting, boring job to me—I hate bad TV—but these folks are really good. These same people have been looking for our terrorist around the clock since the FBI sent us his picture."

"Amazing."

"No, not really. Don't forget, this is hitting pretty close to home. Everybody's working flat-out, but remember, we don't have any confirmation that our terrorist even has a bomb." Russum was struggling to put a positive spin on a bad situation, but Wyley didn't buy it.

You've got to be kidding, Graham thought, but didn't say.

"The Japanese didn't confirm Pearl Harbor before they attacked, did they?" Wyley shook his head, clearly upset.

"So who took these pictures?" Graham asked in a long protracted sigh.

"These two were taken by a military photographer working the Capitol building, this other shot was taken by a military photographer working the National Mall."

"I can't imagine how anyone recognized him. I mean, he looks like another tourist to me, and besides that, he's grown a mustache."

"It's not a positive ID, but the FBI is looking into this lead. They're talking to the tour bus company now."

"What about all those other sightings?"

"The FBI's got their hands full all right. This guy's been seen all across the country: New York, Boston, Dallas, five places in California, and some small town in Georgia. Not too unusual, though, I'm told. The FBI's tracking down every lead, but these pictures have us mighty worried. What can we say? Our own photographers took these shots. They're not the best quality, but the resemblance to our terrorist is undeniable."

"It's a damn small world," Wyley observed bitterly. "My whole family's in Washington. Where the hell we gonna run now?"

"He might just pull it off," Graham acknowledged out loud for the first time.

"It's our job to make sure that he doesn't," Russum urged. "This little development's gonna delay our trip to Syria for a while and Buck's too. Hope you got refundable tickets."

"I did, but I still can't believe it. First, Hama, then that D.C. street map, now these pictures . . ." Graham sighed, feeling as if the wind had been knocked out of him. "That terrorist just might detonate this bloody thing in our own back-yard."

"So"—Russum looked Graham in the eye—"you got any more reservations about joining us?"

"No, not now, not anymore."

CHAPTER EIGHT

Blank Check
Friday, Feb. 26, 9:46 P.M.
Holiday Inn, Georgetown
Washington, D.C.

Beep . . . beep . . . beep . . . beep . . .

Hakim opened the door of his hotel room and found his laptop display flashing, going off like an alarm clock. One glance at the blinking mailbox icon told him something had changed since he'd left for breakfast.

Looking at the roses on his home page gave him a good idea of what to expect. His target had been changed, that much was clear, and for a moment he felt relief. More than this, Hakim knew roses in bloom could only mean one thing. If he couldn't shake up the president's cabinet, he'd rattle Wall Street by taking out the most powerful man in the world, Federal Reserve Chairman Jonathan Rosenberg, world-renowned czar of American economics and finance. Although a stranger to the United States, Hakim understood that when Jonathan Rosenberg spoke, rich and powerful people around the globe listened.

But he'd put an end to that.

Without further delay, he clicked GET MSG and opened his mail. *A blank check.* He smiled, knowing he'd been given free rein to use his own discretion, to do whatever it took. He could pick the time and place, then let the chips fall where they may. In this respect, it was a dream assignment, a death wish with no regard for expense or collateral damage.

Next, he opened his web navigator and looked inside his bookmark folder labeled THE FED. He had known before entering the United States that the Federal Reserve chairman was one of several possible secondary targets; however, he had a great deal of homework to do before the deed could be done.

His first task was to come to know his target, and in the case of the Federal Reserve Board chairman, the United States made it easy. The amount of relevant information on Rosenberg available at his fingertips was nearly overwhelming.

Since market analysts around the world needed to know and feel confident about the man at the helm of the Fed, the American government had adopted an open-door information policy about the chairman and his board of governors. You could get to know them through websites sponsored by Wall Street, national news, public TV, and government.

Straightaway, Hakim went to a government-sponsored website dedicated to the Fed and brought up a host of links, each pointing to biographies of the chairman and his board of governors.

Unbelievable, Hakim thought, dumbfounded at the extent to which this information was made available. Planning a murder in this country was quite literally becoming a point-and-click web-based operation. He almost laughed out loud and had trouble believing it could be this easy.

Next, he clicked the Rosenberg link and brought up his biography. Across the top of the page was a picture of his office, a stately banker's portrait of the man, and a lofty title which read: FEDERAL RESERVE BOARD: JONATHAN ROSENBERG, CHAIRMAN. This man had solid conservative written all over his government-sponsored persona.

With an ever increasing sense of confidence, Hakim was coming to believe he could change all that; he'd wipe that stodgy expression off the old man's face forever.

Below Rosenberg's picture was a host of files of different types: movies, audio clips, documents, and a photo library. Some were audio recordings of speeches; some were speech transcripts; others, hour-long biographies created by several learning and entertainment TV channels. For practical purposes, the list of professional information was endless, but admittedly, the limited personal information didn't reveal what the terrorist most needed to know—insight into the man's daily life, his habits and routine. He'd need time to acquire this information regarding his target's personal rut, but with al-Mashhadi's blank check, Hakim felt no pressing sense of urgency or need to rush, except . . . his stomach tensed into a tight knot.

Admittedly, something had gone wrong in D.C., though he wasn't sure what. He remembered a couple of nights ago when—almost by accident—he'd found his own picture and alias, Art Morrison, posted on the FBI's Most Wanted list. Hakim cringed, playing back the scene in his mind. According to FBI claims, their website was one of the most popular in the country. That single page alone took over ten thousand hits a day.

Wouldn't you just know it? Hakim thought, shaking his head.

He'd need to ditch his car, shift gears into his middle-aged alias, and stay out of sight for a while.

Still, this was America: land of opportunity and excess for anyone with money. He could rent a car for a couple of weeks or buy one with no money down, and no payment due until well after he left the country. Besides, money was no object; he could rent a limo. Too ostentatious? Maybe he'd take a cab.

Regardless, Hakim knew absorbing this internet information would take several days and he had every intention of enjoying it. Of all the stages necessary for murder, coming to know his prey was Hakim's personal favorite. In addition, neutron bombs gave him a degree of freedom he didn't enjoy with conventional explosives. As far as he knew, the bomb's five-hundred-yard kill radius didn't require pinpoint placement or precision anything for that matter; Rosenberg simply needed to be in the same neighborhood, so how tough could it be?

The terrorist wasn't as interested in Rosenberg's professional wherewithal as he was in his routine—his personal habits, family, women, and, most useful of all, his schedule. After a little more searching, the web-based answer to the chairman's schedule became crystal clear. Surprisingly,

Rosenberg's board meetings were scheduled and posted on-line for all the world to see. Even more remarkable to Hakim, they were organized months in advance and, to his delight, the next meeting took place not in Washington, but at the Federal Reserve Bank in New York. Unknown to Hakim, the meeting had been relocated to New York due to the Washington bomb scare. Hakim printed this page and considered it his personal invitation to join the board.

Without exception, Hakim found murder required resourcefulness, imagination, and location; location could make or break a murder and, so far, it looked like this one had New York Financial District written all over it. Hakim savored the thought, knowing his employers would be pleased.

In its planning stages, Hakim found murder exhilarating and, without fail, he found its execution a grind. Once visualized, walked through, rehearsed, and scheduled, the joy of the kill was gone. The murder itself became a chore, like reading a book when you know the ending. In a way, he believed a creative murder was in some ways comparable to a work of art— far more enjoyable when left to the imagination.

After a little more study, Hakim concluded Dr. Rosenberg was a man of numbers, a punctual creature of habit, and his scheduled routine would be his undoing. According to their agenda, he and his board of governors would be preparing their semiannual report to Congress. Following their meeting in New York, Rosenberg would testify before the Senate Banking Committee in Washington. As a result of these demands on him, he may well be preoccupied. Hakim could bushwhack him either during their meeting or in transit, whichever panned out. Detonation during the meeting would probably be easier, but he'd have to do a lot of homework up front to pull it off.

Next, he pulled up the internet photograph that seemed most revealing and studied it on-screen from the privacy of his motel room. Surrounded by his board of governors, Hakim noticed that Rosenberg sat at the head of a long, oval mahogany table. Though a small man, he seemed to tower above the others, like a child on a booster seat. After absorbing every relevant detail from the picture, Hakim grinned. *This'll put a chink in their armor.*

Over the next several days, Hakim continued studying the Fed chairman from a distance, examining his meeting schedule and workplaces using the internet. After the first full day's study, he circled Thursday, March eighteenth, on his calendar, his first and last meeting with the board of governors. The closer he looked into Manhattan's Financial District, the more apparent it became that there was a deliberate attempt to keep building-level satellite photos off the Web. It was like an information blackout; you could get close to the Financial District, you could see its streets, only not too close. He couldn't see its buildings and, like any good hunter, he'd need to scout out the territory for himself. An appointment with a real estate broker made sense; high-priced apartments and temporary office spaces were everywhere. No doubt about it, he'd need to take a trip.

Nineteen days, Hakim estimated. *It'll be tight, but that should do it. How tough can it be?*

In truth, he had no idea the enormous chasm he'd strike open with Rosenberg's death, nor the no-place-to-hide consequences which would inevitably haunt him the rest of his life.

Momentum
Wednesday, Mar. 3, 9:46 P.M.
Holiday Inn, Georgetown
Washington, D.C.

Five days later, Hakim couldn't sleep.

Following a trip to a large Georgetown bookstore, his head was spinning nonstop, like a top. His Rosenberg assignment was taking over completely, capturing his imagination, occupying his every thought. He'd wake up around three in the morning with the wheels in his head turning so fast that he couldn't rest. It was as if this Rosenberg chapter in his life needed to play out before he could relax again. He recognized he was becoming obsessed with Rosenberg's assassination, but it held such fantastic possibility. Without exaggeration, this hit would rock the financial foundation on which America stood.

He could visualize it now, the complete scenario unfolding before his eyes. This hit was possible. What's more, he believed he could do it; he was sure of it and his investigation only confirmed it.

He had eliminated Washington, D.C. as the hit location for several reasons. Working as a single, with troops on every block, tailing Rosenberg's limo without being detected was impossible. Aside from this observation, he'd learned a little about the man's route to and from work, and he could recognize Rosenberg's black limousine by its license plate and driver. But on the whole, the open expanses of Constitution Avenue, especially around the Federal Reserve Board building, remained buttoned up tight. By contrast, the cramped, narrow streets of New York City seemed wide open. Even the Federal Reserve Bank of New York remained accessible by street.

New York's Financial District security may be tight, but it's no police state, Hakim mused. *Besides, I'm not out to rob it.* As a Washington backup, Hakim knew he could always detonate one of his briefcase bombs somewhere. Be that as it may, it'd be riskier and wouldn't have nearly the impact as a direct strike against the heart of New York's Financial District, especially after 9/11.

Recalling the collapse of the World Trade Center buildings, he felt goose flesh crawling up his back. His achievement would dwarf all those who had come before him. In this, Hakim instinctively sensed he was plotting a new course through uncharted waters.

Quadruple the shock at one-quarter the risk, Hakim thought.

Normally, the Fed chairman and his board of governors met in Washington, but newspapers reported their next meeting had been moved to the Federal Reserve Bank of New York. In addition, it'd been rescheduled from Tuesday to Thursday because Rosenberg and his entourage would already be in New York City then to attend an international monetary conference. This was true as far as it went, but if the whole story were known, their meeting had been relocated behind the vaultlike walls of the New York Federal Reserve Bank for security reasons. More specifically, Hakim read that the board meeting had moved to the office of the New York Fed president. By this account, the move to the New York Fed was an admission of the Big Apple's dominant position as the nation's financial capital. As the *Washington Post* portrayed it, this board meeting was perceived by the New York Fed to be a matter of honor. The president of the New York Fed would offer his seat to the chairman of the Federal Reserve Board with all the dignity called for on such an occasion. The New York press would have a field day.

In his hotel room, Hakim had collected more maps and information about New York's Financial District than he'd ever imagined possible and it had been surprisingly easy. During his bookstore visit, Hakim played the role of a newcomer moving to Manhattan and found exactly what he was looking for. A Manhattan apartment sales guide, a New York traveler's picture book, Amtrak schedule, subway maps, and the internet all played a part in Hakim's planning. Looking back, the terrorist concluded that the money spent for Manhattan books and maps was the best investment he'd ever made. In a matter of a few days, he'd nailed down his apartment possibilities to three choices—one on John Street, another on Maiden Lane, and the ringer on Nassau. Liberty Tower stood out head and shoulders above the rest. He'd already contacted two real estate agents via e-mail and had standing appointments to see all three, but in the end, Hakim knew he'd occupy Liberty Tower . . . no matter what.

Adjacent to and towering thirty-four floors above the Federal Reserve Bank of New York, the Liberty Tower was perfect; it cost a fortune, but was ideal for the task at hand.

There was so much to plan, so much to do. At ten thousand dollars a month, he'd need a legitimate-looking business front, his new alias, and money, truckloads of money. He'd signal al-Mashhadi about that. Meanwhile, he'd change hotels and revert to his midfifties alias, Trevor Stevens.

Altering his appearance using a mirror and a pair of thinning shears, Hakim thinned the hair on the crown of his head to the point of balding. Next, he thinned out the thick hair across the top of his head, concentrating on what he could see near the front. Finally, he bushed his eyebrows slightly, then using a spray can of costume paint, lightened his remaining hair to near gray. In less than two hours, he'd aged easily thirty years.

Four days later, thanks to bin Laden's financial network, Hakim's music production front was established under the name of Trevor Stevens. As they arranged it, Stevens would be coming to New York to break into the music production business—a wealthy heir to a foreign fortune searching for new talent and hoping to open his own recording studio. In addition, both Stevens's New York and foreign bank accounts were in place.

The following morning, before dawn's first light, he'd left his car in Dulles's long-term parking, well away from the main terminal along the north service road. After some mental debate regarding his travel to Manhattan, he remembered his picture posted on the FBI's website. It wasn't a great picture, but it was a shock that he should be there at all, like watching TV and seeing himself on-screen. In light of this, he changed his mind at the last minute and took the conservative, low-profile approach. He decided to take a cab for the sixty-mile leg from Dulles to Baltimore-Washington International Airport; at BWI, he rented a car through Avis express showing only his Trevor Stevens license and credit card, then drove to Newark International Airport. There, he dropped off the car and took a cab for his final leg to the Millennium Hilton.

CHAPTER NINE

On the Air
Wednesday, Mar. 3, 3:40 P.M.
English Channel

Eion Macke stood inside the Combat Information Center of the USS *Yorktown*, an Arleigh Burke–class guided-missile destroyer modified to support geophysical surveying operations—

a new and still largely experimental type of military reconnaissance. Technically, this meant the ship's radio room had been upgraded with a seven-foot frame filled with brand-new ultrasensitive receivers designed to intercept radio frequencies between one and ten thousand hertz. Behind her, she towed a long cable array affectionately referred to as the squid. The squid consisted of eight long cables laced with magnetometers—ultrasensitive superconductor devices that measured magnetic fields.

Armed with an understanding of radio wave interaction with the earth, the *Yorktown*'s surveying team was considered a cutting-edge group of explorers who often peered into underground places no man had seen before. Privately, the United States government believed the team's success was paramount. For many big shots back in Washington, long-wavelength imaging was considered *the* linchpin surveillance technology for the beginning of the twenty-first century. To their credit, the heads of the CTC, CIA, and FBI had the foresight to believe it would eventually be an invaluable tool against state-sponsored terrorism.

Be that as it may, the surveying team's orders were phrased such that the heart of their mission remained obscure. On paper, the team's immediate task involved exploration of the subsurface geological structure of the earth beneath the English Channel. In truth, after stripping away the techno-speak, their sea trial was about imaging the EuroTunnel; the thirty-one-mile-long access and twin railway tunnels linking England to France.

During the next two months, this sea trial would have the *Yorktown* and three sister ships using long radio waves created over the equator and North Pole to image subterranean features such as tunnels, bunkers, and other areas of interest to U.S. national security. Beyond detecting these underground structures, military and national security leaders were always pushing for ever increasing detail. For better or worse, this next level of detail required identifying what was inside these underground structures, and sometimes, that became a problem.

At this point in the technology's development, the size of what could be identified underground was primarily determined by its depth and grounding. The deeper the object was buried, the larger it must be to be seen. In addition, an object touching the earth was easier to see than an insulated object. For example, a tank touching the earth through metal tracks was easier to discern than a truck resting on insulating tires because the well-grounded tank channeled current far better than the insulated truck. As a result, some metal hulks could be detected easier than others. Armed beforehand with maps of the tunnel and the Eurostar's train schedule, today Eion's team had hoped to image the tunnels and identify the well-grounded, half-mile-long trains as they passed beneath them.

Geophysical surveying using radio waves had been an established procedure in the oil and mining industry for years; however, civilian practices had been developed with the idea of locating areas of highly conductive material such as gold veins or other metal ore deposits. In addition, civilian surveying operations had been developed for use out in the open where anyone with eyes could see them. If an area was being surveyed, it was no secret, because technicians, trucks, computers, transmitters, and radio receivers were scattered about the surface of the area being imaged.

Understandably, the military brought a dimension of intrigue to the business of underground imaging because their surveying must often be accomplished in secret without alerting their quarry. In addition, the size and electrical nature of underground objects the military needs to image are very different from those of the civilian. Typically, the military looks for tunnels and bunkers—nonconductive voids and man-made structures—beneath the surface of the earth.

The mood in the Combat Information Center could best be described as one of restrained excitement. Gakona's chief scientist, Dr. Andreas Pappasongas, was on hand orchestrating the experiment, standing in the center of the activity inside the CIC.

"Here's the bottom charts you asked for, Doctor," Eion said. "They're a copy of the maps used when they constructed the tunnels."

"Thank you, son. That's excellent." Andreas had eyes that smiled with enthusiasm, and it was clear this experiment had his undivided attention. Dreams he had dreamed of his entire professional life were at long last coming true. After unrolling the chart on the table, he grinned and asked, "Are we there yet?"

"We're positioned here, about fifteen miles off the English coast, directly over the north-running tunnel." Eion pointed to the map. The three tunnels appeared as dotted lines running between Folkestone, England, and Calais, France.

"What's the depth of the channel here?"

"Sonar confirmed our bottom charts. The depth here runs around two hundred feet."

"How about the depth beneath the seabed?"

"We're directly over its deepest point, Dr. Pappasongas, like you requested. The north-running tunnel lies two hundred forty-six feet beneath the seabed."

"That's good. I expect we'll resolve tunnel details to within five percent of depth."

Eion thought Dr. Pappasongas's comment sounded important, but he didn't get it. "Could you run that by me one more time, Doctor?—in layman's terms. What exactly do you mean, five percent of depth?"

Andreas smiled at Eion, then sketched a picture of the tunnel buried beneath the seabed. Inside the tunnel, he drew two trains with different heights and lengths; one was a single, short flatcar marked five feet tall. The second was four cars long and taller, twelve and one-half feet top to bottom, to be exact. "What I mean is that the height of things we can detect beneath the surface varies with depth. If we look one hundred feet below the surface, we can see an object as short as five feet. At two hundred fifty feet deep, the train must be twelve and a half feet or taller for us to detect it."

"I see, so you're really talking about depth resolution."

"That's right. The deeper you go, the taller the object must be to see it. Five percent of depth is our rule of thumb today, but at the turn of the century, it was ten."

"What happened?"

"Happily for us, we had a breakthrough with our detection equipment. Superconductors radically improved our magnetometers and, for a while at least, we've got the lead. No one else can touch us. Still, even with improved detection, the deeper we look beneath the surface, the taller our subject must be to image it because the radio signal diminishes as it travels into the earth. Nothing's going to change the physics."

"I see." Eion paused for a moment. "What about length? How short a train could we detect?"

"Lateral size resolution depends mainly on the density of detectors at the surface. We're expecting to see sizes of a few meters with the squid. With the RPV, our lateral resolution should be about the same, maybe a little less." Dr. Pappasongas was referring to their remotely piloted vehicle, a model airplane which would fly over the EuroTunnel at low altitude and image it.

"I got it. Length is determined by the number of receivers and their spacing across the surface; height resolution runs about five percent of depth."

Andreas nodded. Eion's eyes revealed understanding, so the doctor continued. "What about our sister ships? Are they ready?"

"They're all on-line. Uplink is go. GPS—go. Receivers—go. We're ready."

"What about our seismic survey?" Andreas was asking the whereabouts of the ship they'd contracted from Petroleum Survey Services.

"PSS has one of their survey ships en route to us as we speak. They're coming in from the North Sea, so assuming everything goes as planned, they'll run their sweep over the tunnel tomorrow morning, weather permitting, and have the data to us by noon."

"What's the latest on the weather?"

"Still looks good, good for this time of year anyway."

"Excellent. PSS has been in the seismic data acquisition business for years. We can't get a better sanity check on our work than that outfit." Turning away from the charts toward a wall-mounted TV screen, Andreas spoke over satellite link to his lab director back at the HAARP site in Alaska. Judging from the background, and the fact that Eion's friend, Gary Ellie, was in the picture, they concluded the lab director was conferenced in from HAARP's computer center. "We're ready here. How about HAARP? Could you run down the situation at your end?"

HAARP operators and control room specialists knew the drill. "Power plant is on-line and prime power is go. All eighteen diesel generators are set to deliver full-rated power."

The voice over the conference call changed. "Transmitters are warm and stabilized, ready for air time."

"Every satellite data link is go. We're receiving your telemetry without error."

"Radio room is on-line; all channels have signal and frame."

"Comp center's on-line," Gary Ellie chimed in. "Recorders are running."

The lab director spoke last. "Ionospheric conditions are perfect. We've got the electron density overhead that we need to ensure a good run. Our signal propagation to the Channel should provide a splendid long-wave source."

"Excellent." Dr. Pappasongas then shifted his focus to their second HAARP facility located halfway around the world near the equator. "Gakona site is go. We're ready here. Could you run down your situation?"

There was a flurry of muffled discussion in the background. Although all the conversation wasn't audible, there was a distinct tone of optimism spilling over across the air waves. After a few moments, the director spoke for his team. "Kwajalein is on standby, awaiting your instructions, Doctor. Our HAARP site is ready, overhead airspace is clear, and ionospheric currents are the best we've experienced in days. Working in conjunction with Gakona, we can steer our beam over the Channel in a matter of seconds."

"Excellent. Does anyone know of any reason why we should not proceed?" Dr. Pappasongas looked at Eion.

He returned a thumbs-up. Over the TV monitor, Gary Ellie saw Eion's signal and returned a like sign.

After a long silence, the HAARP lab director from Alaska urged Andreas forward. "Gakona and Kwajalein sites are go. Conditions are perfect. Intent to transmit has been posted and overhead airspace is clear. We are go for max power, go for long-wave propagation."

"That's it then," Andreas said. "Everything is even better than we'd hoped, so I see no need to change our frequency plan. We'll image the tunnel using frequencies between one and one hundred Hertz. Bring both transmitter arrays from standby to full power."

Halfway around the world, inside the power buildings at Gakona and Kwajalein, the roar of the diesel generators shifted dramatically to a fully loaded rumble of heavy labor; yet outside to the naked eye, nothing changed at all.

"Yes! Yes!" Eion yelled. The vivid 3D image of the tunnel said it all. It looked so real you could almost feel the cold, steel-reinforced concrete walls against your skin.

"Marvelous." Andreas smiled quietly. "You can actually make out the seams and joints between the tunnel sections."

"Yeah, and their exterior almost looks wet."

For Dr. Pappasongas and his entire survey team, this was a sweet moment. Much like their first imaging experiment of the Fairbanks mine, this trial had rendered images with more textural detail than anyone had ever dreamed possible in their wildest imagination. Judging from the vivid clarity of the tunnel image appearing on-screen, they'd hit the first pitch of the game out of the park.

Still, this was only the first inning and, as everyone involved understood, the game wasn't over until it was over. They weren't home free, not yet anyway. They had two more tests to go before they'd be cut loose onshore.

After savoring the moment, Eion's thoughts turned to shore leave, foreign ports, luscious women, and sex. After all, this was the reason he'd joined the Navy.

Open House
Wednesday, Mar. 3, 12:46 P.M.
Nursery school classroom
28th floor of the Chase Manhattan Bank
New York City

Mary Marshall surveyed the long, blue, bustling classroom searching for one special face, her little girl. And there she was, at her small, child-sized table, sitting near a puffy white cloud painted on the far wall. Although surrounded by children in constant motion, Katie was sitting alone. With her fat red Crayola crayon in hand, she was concentrating hard, coloring, no doubt creating another masterpiece for her mother to admire.

As it happened, Katie loved to color and, more than that, Mary knew her daughter wanted her to love it too. As Mary approached, Katie looked up and beamed with delight. Impulsively, she jumped to her feet and bolted for her mother, hugging her tightly around her legs. Katie's love and enthusiasm filled Mary with a joy she had never known, and she kept these happiest of times gently tucked away in her heart. Katie's chipmunk cheeks, cheerful smile, and bright eyes kept Mary going and assured her that the birth of her little angel was no accident. This little one was her gift from God, and as far as she was concerned, they were inseparable, destined to be together. Mary prayed they would remain close, and couldn't imagine life without her.

Mary sat down on a tiny chair alongside her daughter, admiring Katie's wonderful artwork. After listening intently to her daughter's explanation of the big red kite, Mary explained that she'd loved coloring when she was a little girl too, and she'd had a big kite with a long tail, just like that one.

For a moment, Mary's thoughts turned back to a simpler time when she and her father flew kites on the beach at Plum Island. She remembered the smell of the ocean, running across the sand, the cool wind in her hair, and looking for seashells, but above all else, she could still hear her father's laughter as if it were yesterday.

Mary knew now that she'd been lucky growing up. Their family had been a happy one; they never had a lot of money, but she and her two brothers had everything they needed. They'd enjoyed all the love, support, and admiration anyone could want. No matter what she did, she found comfort knowing her mom and dad were always in her corner, rooting for her. Somehow, in her heart she knew they'd forever be her biggest fans. She remembered feeling discontent as a child, always wanting to grow up too fast and have her own place, but in retrospect, life there had been really wonderful. No bills, no worries, not a care in the world. Her mom had been there for her whenever she'd needed help, but more times than not, her dad was working. Now, through the eyes of a young adult, she fully understood her dad worked two jobs not because he loved it or wanted to, but to make it possible for her mom to be there for them.

Those were happy days too, and sometimes she wished she could turn back time, take Katie back there, and give her the sense of well-being that she'd experienced growing up near the saltwater marshes of New England's seacoast.

Thinking back on those wonderful days, Mary smiled. Most of all, she missed the laughter of her family, their teasing and good-natured humor, and couldn't help but feel that Katie would be better off closer to her grandparents and uncles. Mary loved walking the New England coastline, looking under every rock, and believed that Katie would love it too.

Looking down on Katie's soft brown hair, Mary recalled glimpses of her own days in kindergarten. Mainly, she remembered the wonderful storybooks—*Make Way for Ducklings, Blueberries for Sal, Stone Soup,* and a story about a little steam shovel who dug himself into a hole he couldn't get out of. *Life's like that sometimes,* she mused.

And then she remembered her drawing.

Her mother had saved her valuable artwork, boxes of it, and now Mary found herself following her mother's ways. Back home in their tiny studio apartment, Mary had box after box filled to overflowing with Katie's precious pictures.

But then again, I have no choice, do I? Mary thought fondly. *Katie loves to color, just loves it.*

Ballistic
Wednesday, Mar. 3, 9:45 P.M.
CTC

"What do you make of it, gentlemen?" Buck asked the trio huddled around the conference table in Russum's office.

"I don't like the looks of it, not at all. We've got big trouble staring us in the face and don't know what the hell to do about it. For now, I say we put Syria on the back burner and focus here at home."

"I agree," Wyley confirmed. "I'm afraid we're already running too far behind to catch up."

"Hold everything," Buck pushed back. "It can't be that bad. You're talking like the glass is half empty. At least we know money's moving inside bin Laden's network. That narrows the search one helluva lot; sure as hell beats running blind."

"And we're not alone here," Russum added, struggling to put an optimistic spin on the situation. "The Treasury Department, CTC, FBI, and military intelligence have people swarming all over this case. With the possibility of terrorists using nuclear weapons on American soil, no one's taking any chances."

A long pause followed as the four men reviewed the Treasury Department report for the fourth or fifth time. No matter how they read it, one fact was undeniable—large amounts of money were being transferred inside bin Laden's global terrorist organization and, historically, that meant trouble.

Finally, Buck looked across the table at Graham. "You've been mighty quiet over there, Doc."

Graham shrugged.

"Whatya thinkin'?"

Graham stared down at the table, hesitant about speaking at all. He felt a kaleidoscope of emotions, and had trouble sorting them all out. Increasingly, he felt a dominant sense of foreboding, an irrepressible fear and dread. He wasn't overwhelmed by it, but it was inescapable.

"Go ahead, Doc. Spit it out," Buck urged in a deliberately light tone. "We're all adults here."

After a long silence, Graham spoke in a whisper.

"Something's coming down here in our own back yard, I can feel it. It's like watching a fuse burn with your hands tied."

"Yep, we're all running on the same wavelength," Russum agreed, urging his team forward. "We gotta find that damn thing and snuff it out."

Broad Beam
Thursday, Mar. 4, 9:30 A.M.
English Channel

The seas over the English Channel were rough, but within operating limits of the *Black Gold*, a wedge-shaped seismic survey ship under contract to the U.S. Navy, operated by

Petroleum Survey Services. Broadest across her beam, her maximum width—half her length—spanned her stern, giving the *Black Gold* her distinctive delta shape. Her revolutionary hull represented the culmination of three decades of offshore survey ship design and was the latest delta-class vessel to emerge from PSS's newbuild program.

Inside her fog-bound bridge, the captain stood peering at an array of radar and TV screens. Forward, his radar revealed clear sailing with the *Yorktown* and her three sister ships positioned well out of the way, three miles to port. Aft, one large TV screen showed a GPS-based, computer-generated bird's-eye view of their towed sensors—a large acoustic array consisting of thirty-two uniformly distributed, mile-long streamer cables, and eight air gun clusters spread out like a blanket in a wide, rectangular pattern. From the air, the *Black Gold* looked as if she were towing water skiers; much like the large power boats at Cyprus Gardens.

All in all, towing the long planar array of cables through the current of the English Channel was a deceptively complicated, three-dimensional type of operation to coordinate because both the ship and the towed array had helmsmen. One group steered the ship along the surface, countering the crosscurrent using a set of thrusters beneath the ship's stern and bow, another group steered the towed array from side to side, another controlled its horizontal fanout, while a fourth group served as the array planesmen, diving the array like a submarine, maintaining its depth above the sea bottom.

Quietly orchestrating it all, the *Black Gold*'s captain looked on, but offered little guidance. In a sense, he'd completed one of the most important aspects of his job months ago, long before they'd arrived at the Channel. Through years of continuous classroom and on-the-job training, he'd seen to it that his crew were masters of their technology, not its victims. As a result, this morning's fog-bound, crosscurrent survey of the EuroTunnel was comparable to a walk in the park, simply another day at the office for the captain and crew of the *Black Gold*.

PSS operated a fleet of wedge-shaped, mine sweeper–like vessels outfitted for conducting 3D marine seismic surveys. Its fleet of delta-class vessels and its high-capacity seismic equipment gave PSS the ability to image subterranean features five miles or more beneath the seabed faster than anyone else in the industry. Remarkably quiet, this revolutionary delta class of ship was developed by PSS specifically for towing these large acoustic arrays and had become the de facto standard for seismic acquisition.

"Air guns are ready to blow, Captain, configured as a single source. All sixty-four are synchronized to within one millisecond."

"Very well. Are the streamers ready?"

"Hydrophone array is running at depth and true. GPS links are go, all receive channels are ready."

"Very well." The captain lifted his handset and spoke to the sonar room. "Pipe your signal over the intercom."

"Sonar, aye."

Looking across the bridge at his air gun operator, the captain ordered, "Set your source interval to five seconds and commence your sweep."

"Aye, aye, Captain." Sitting behind his computer console, the technician selected all sixty-four air guns with a sweep of the cursor, entered five seconds as their interpulse period, then clicked APPLY ALL. Five seconds later, an explosion erupted over the intercom.

BOOM!!!

Suddenly, computer screens all over the ship came alive with echoes flooding in from thousands of underwater microphones, then, almost as quickly, the array technician's monitor flashed CALIBRATION COMPLETE.

Five seconds later, BOOM!

In the blink of an eye, a series of 3D images appeared, revealing a quarter-mile-long section of the EuroTunnel.

BOOM!

Additional details were added to the tunnel images, one row at a time, from top to bottom.

BOOM!

With each subsequent blast of the air guns, ever increasing detail was overlaid on top of the images. In less than two minutes' time, the three-dimensional tunnel images looked so real they appeared to jump off the screen.

"How's it look?" the captain asked the head of his seismic team.

Their senior scientist gazed at the increasingly sharp images with delight. "The Navy's gonna love it."

"Good." Next, the captain punched the sonar room's line and lifted his handset. "Sonar, what do you hear?"

"There's a train coming, but it's out of our imaging range. Judging from its direction, I'd wager it's the 9:15 express bound for France."

"Good. Very good."

Without wasting motion, the captain rang the radio room. "Patch this video through to the *Yorktown*. They'll want to see this in real time."

Theoretical Limits
Thursday, Mar. 4, 9:33 A.M.
English Channel

Three miles away, inside the *Yorktown*'s CIC, Dr. Andreas Pappasongas, Lt. Eion Macke, and a host of survey team members gazed at their video monitors awestruck by the remarkable, lifelike clarity of the tunnel images.

"Are you thinking what I'm thinking?" Andreas asked Eion.

"An A-B comparison?"

"That's right."

"Let's relay this through to the comp center and bring Gary Ellie on line."

"My thinking exactly." Dr. Pappasongas lifted his handset and spoke to the radio room. Moments later, a continuous stream of digitized video data flooded skyward through a series of military relay satellites, halfway around the world, then downlinked to the HAARP comp center.

Almost as quickly, Gary Ellie's face appeared on the videoconference screen inside the *Yorktown*'s CIC. The first thing Eion noticed was that he looked tired; dark circles surrounded his eyes. Back in Alaska, it was roughly half past midnight, early Thursday morning, and at first glance, the long hours required to ramp up on this project combined with continuous twenty-four-hour duty were taking a toll on his friend. After commiserating a couple of moments, Eion explained their situation and Gary Ellie engaged. Once he'd finished a can of Jolt, he was ready for another round.

First thing he did was set up all his video connections so that the data flooding in from the *Black Gold* appeared on-screen. This data was considered their reference, and against this data, he would compare the *Yorktown*'s latest channel survey completed only a few hours earlier. In effect, both the *Black Gold*'s acoustic data and the *Yorktown*'s radio data had been converted to a series of three-dimensional spacial maps, comparable to a CAT scan. Acoustic and electromagnetic data sampled different properties of the subterranean landscape: acoustic echoes measured the earth's density; electromagnetic signal returns measured its electrical conductivity. Collectively, both types of information combined to provide a more complete picture than either taken separately.

On-screen, Gary Ellie saw the *Black Gold*'s 3D image of the EuroTunnel. On casual inspection, it appeared to be three pipes running parallel to each other, buried beneath the seabed. In a separate window, Gary Ellie swept out a short section of the tunnel with his cursor, then clicked, decomposing it into thousands of thin, ringlike slices, or cross sections. Conceptually, all he was doing with his A-B comparison was laying one tunnel map over the other, putting them both on a light table, aligning them, then looking for differences. In reality, once the composite 3D images were properly scaled and aligned, the computer compared the tunnel slices created by the *Yorktown* against the reference created by the *Black Gold*.

Once the *Yorktown*'s tunnel map lined up with the *Black Gold*'s, Gary Ellie ran a few spot checks to make sure the maps were aligned both north-to-south and east-to-west. Near the northernmost end of the maps, he clicked two cross sections—one from the *Yorktown*, the other from the *Black*

Gold—then compared the GPS coordinates of both. Their co-ordinates weren't identical, but they were within acceptable tolerances. One quarter mile south, he repeated the process, with near identical results. Satisfied, he kicked off the computer's automated slice-by-slice comparison program without prompting.

For the first few seconds, the progress bar raced across the screen showing the program slicing through their data like a hot knife through butter, then suddenly, the situation changed. Only moments after it began running, after comparing about two hundred feet of tunnel, an error window popped up out of nowhere and a flood of discrepancies began scrolling down the screen—thousands of errors in a matter of seconds.

Back on the *Yorktown*, Dr. Pappasongas looked concerned, but not overly so. He knew the physics behind the problem and understood its fundamental principles. They were on solid ground with this comparison, and if there was any problem it must be either a bug in the program or the tunnel's physical situation had changed. After a few moments' thought, he spoke to Eion.

"Apparently Gary Ellie's computer doesn't like our data." Forever the optimist, he forced a smile. "Any thoughts or recommendations?"

"I'm afraid it's going to take some time to sort it out, Doctor." Gary Ellie agreed with Eion's assessment over video link. "Either there's a problem with the software or something's changed inside the tunnel."

"A programming problem could take days to scope out." Gary Ellie sighed tiredly.

"Let's compare two red-tagged cross sections on-screen," Andreas suggested. "My gut tells me this must be something obvious. Our images looked too good to be this far off and our manual comparison with the tunnel construction maps was right on the money."

Gary Ellie and Eion nodded their heads in agreement, wanting to believe him.

Back in Alaska, Gary Ellie went to work with his mouse. The *Yorktown*'s tunnel cross section appeared on-screen first.

To everyone's eye, it looked perfect: three distinct, steel-reinforced concrete rings buried beneath the seabed. Next, he displayed the *Black Gold*'s tunnel slice. Differences between the two images were highlighted in red and all eyes focused on the single ring containing the bright red core.

After a few moments' reflection, the twinkle returned to the great man's eyes. "It's a train." As quickly as Andreas said these words, the pieces fell into place for his team.

"Yes, that's it, the EuroStar, that's the clincher!" Eion could see the problem clearly now and looked to his buddy.

Gary Ellie flashed an exhausted smile, then the rest of the story almost danced off the screen. The *Black Gold*'s data was being collected in real time, much like taking a motion picture of the tunnel. Consequently, when the EuroStar roared beneath the *Black Gold,* its data reflected the train as long as it remained in their acoustic field of view; the *Yorktown*'s did not. Gary Ellie breathed a sigh of relief praying, *Dear God, please don't let it be the programming.*

Unaware of what the others were thinking, Andreas calmly checked his watch and smiled. "Let's give it a minute or so."

Anxious, both Eion and Gary Ellie found themselves holding their breath for what seemed like an eternity.

Twenty-eight seconds later, the half-mile-long train had passed outside their imaging field of view and the bright red center disappeared. In its place, transparent fill revealed an empty tunnel and near perfect data match.

"Thank God it's not the software," Gary Ellie whispered over the videoconference line. All he wanted was some sleep.

The twinkle in Dr. Pappasongas's eyes spoke volumes about their success. After years of work and waiting, his dreams were unfolding before his very eyes. Only one test to go before wrapping up their EuroTunnel experiment. Washington would be pleased.

As Eion saw it, these results were fantastic. His bottom line—fourteen days to women and counting.

CHAPTER TEN

"Fifty-Five Liberty Street." Trevor Stevens smiled, reading the tall white building's address out loud. "This must be the place."

His real estate agent agreed. "Based on what you've told me, I think you'll find it's what you've been looking for. I can't wait to see your reaction."

"I hope you're right. So far, everything you've shown me has been . . . less than ideal." Craning his neck skyward, Hakim struggled to see the top of the structure. "It's taller and older looking than I expected. What style building is this anyway?" In truth, Hakim knew far more about the property than the real estate agent did.

"Its exterior is scheduled for a face-lift over the summer, Mr. Stevens. They rework it every twenty years, so don't let it deceive you. It was built in 1909, but inside it's immaculate. The Liberty Tower is a Gothic-style apartment building and its exterior is, or will be, white terra-cotta. It's one of the classics, if not the classic in the district. At thirty-two stories, I think you'll agree we saved the best till last."

The middle-aged Trevor Stevens entered the ground floor of the Liberty Tower apartment building behind his agent. The agent spoke with the building doorman, then they stepped into the elevator.

The elevator stopped at the twenty-eighth floor. Following a short walk down the hall, the agent opened the door to what Hakim already knew to be his new apartment. He feigned curiosity as the agent began his pitch. "As I mentioned earlier, this is considered a four-room apartment: 2 bedrooms, a living room, and a kitchen."

Hakim looked the agent in the eye as if to say, *And the price?*

"Ten thousand a month, twelve-month minimum commitment."

Hakim's expression revealed nothing as he walked to the window. One glance out the window told him everything he needed to know. He struggled to maintain his poker face. From here, he would watch Maiden Lane, and Nassau, William, and Liberty Streets, the four access roads surrounding the Federal Reserve Bank of New York.

And from here, he would detonate the bomb.

The Federal Reserve Bank was next door and he had an unobstructed bird's-eye view of Nassau and Liberty Streets. This apartment was better than he had a right to hope for. Looking out its large double window, Hakim slowly revealed his enthusiasm for the place a little bit at a time. "Tell me what I'm seeing here. I need to know the lay of the land and I'd like a little orientation tour. What's that short, squatty building next door? It looks like an armed fortress or prison with those iron bars. It's so out of place surrounded by these skyscrapers."

"That's the bank for banks, the Federal Reserve Bank of New York. Some people like the design, though honestly, I'm not sure why. Its massive stonework, those iron bars, and that turret make it look like a prison to me too, but at least the bars only cover the lower windows. That big building there to the right's the Chase Manhattan Bank, and that one there's the Marine Midland Bank."

"I think its the view and location you pay for here."

The realtor agreed. "The New York Stock Exchange and Wall Street are just down the street."

This is perfect, Hakim thought. Leaving the window, he walked into the bathroom and turned on the shower. "This doesn't look good."

"What do you mean?" the agent wanted to know, entering the bathroom to take a look.

"The water pressure's low, barely a trickle."

The agent smiled a reassuring sort of smile. "Not to worry, Mr. Stevens. The water tank's above us. They were doing

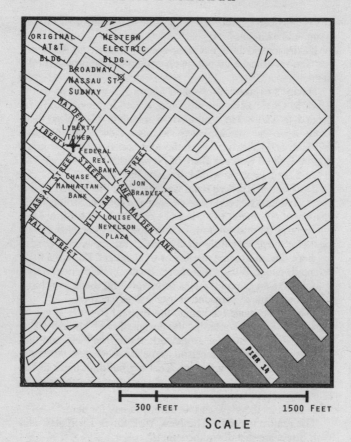

some renovation here in the last couple of weeks and must have left the water off. The switch to the apartment's booster pump is in the kitchen. Stay here and I'll take care of it."

In a moment, water gushed from the shower head with all the force anyone could ever want. And the drain kept up with the shower.

"That's great. This should do nicely. I think my apartment-hunting days are over." Hakim pondered his approach for a moment, then decided to offer his agent a carrot. "Now, if you can get me through the contract and in here without any surprises, I'd like to take a look at that commercial property we talked about."

"When would you like to move in?"

"Monday, the fifteenth."

The agent pulled a PalmPilot out of his pocket, displayed a March calendar, and counted days. "We could get you in here sooner if you'd like."

Hakim thought about the offer for a moment. "How much sooner?"

"The eleventh, that's on a Thursday, day after tomorrow."

That would buy me a little margin in case something goes wrong with the paperwork, Hakim reasoned. Smiling at the agent, he replied, "Excellent. Thursday would be perfect. That gives me the weekend to unpack."

Dreams Do Come True
Monday, Mar. 15, 1:55 P.M.
English Channel

Inside the CIC, Eion and Dr. Pappasongas studied one TV monitor in particular. Back at the HAARP site in Alaska, Gary Ellie watched the same thing. On-screen, they saw a jerky, bird's-eye view of the *Yorktown* transmitted from the nose camera of their RPV. In one respect, their RPV was like a miniature remote-controlled version of the Navy's P-3 aircraft. Its most telling characteristic was its tail boom, and, like the P-3, the RPV carried a cylindrical magnetic-anomaly detector sticking out its tail.

"It's a little like watching yourself on TV," the doctor mused.

"But I can't see my face," Eion quipped.

"And it's such a pretty face," Gary Ellie chimed in over videoconference. He'd caught up on some rest over the past several days and felt almost human again.

"I'm not going there," Eion responded, "but some things go without saying."

Eion shifted his focus to a separate screen and watched the

model airplane's cockpit instrumentation for a moment. It didn't change very fast, so he didn't dwell there long. Although computer generated, it looked remarkably real and reminded him of a flight simulator game he'd played as a kid. From the looks of it, the RPV was approaching the EuroTunnel from the north at an altitude of about two hundred feet.

In front of him sat the RPV's pilot and this guy was a trip to watch. His eyes never stopped moving, never focused in one place more than a few seconds. It was as if he were programmed to scan the horizon, check his overhead, read each instrument, then repeat the process. No doubt about it, this fella flew his model with all the care and attention he'd give a real airplane. He struck Eion as a little dramatic, but in a way, he was glad to have someone flying their RPV who took it seriously.

Across a row of four adjacent flat screens, Eion saw a panoramic, but piecemeal, view from the lightweight cameras mounted inside the RPV's cockpit. It wasn't like being there, but it was close, with each camera looking in a fixed direction, either right, forward, left, or overhead. Funny thing, though; really wasn't much to see—blue water all around, blue sky overhead.

As the RPV approached the EuroTunnel's GPS coordinates, the pilot signaled Andreas, then, following weeks of rehearsal, things happened very quickly.

In a matter of seconds, the Kwajalein and Gakona HAARP sites came to full power and, working together, they steered their long-wavelength signals over the Channel.

Inside the CIC, computer screens came alive with data, window after window filling with numbers and gauges showing signals from HAARP were arriving on station and in good health.

As the RPV flew over the tunnel, a picture began forming on the most prominent, centrally located monitor in the CIC. Compared to the tunnel images created by the squid and the *Black Gold,* the picture looked anemic . . . and it wasn't getting better.

Now there's a giant step backwards, Eion thought, but didn't say. He made eye contact with Gary Ellie and noticed he looked somewhat deflated, like his bubble had burst. All their testing, all their job-related cartwheels, all their personal sacrifices led them to this point, and for what?

What mattered most in the whole scheme of things was this test. In a sense, the RPV was their covert operations flagship, the vehicle they would need for most secret military surveys. All their eggs weren't in this basket, but most were.

Sensing their disappointment, Dr. Pappasongas asked, "Where's the beef?"

Both Eion and Gary Ellie shrugged their shoulders, but neither understood or broke a smile.

"It's a joke, fellas. You know the old Wendy's commercial?—the one with the little old lady?"

"Oh, yeah." Eion looked at Gary Ellie and flashed an expression signaling, *Don't say it.* Trouble was, Gary Ellie and Eion hadn't been born when the commercial came out; they'd never seen it, but they didn't want to make their hero feel old. "I musta been distracted, I guess, with the test and all. Seems like the picture's kinda fuzzy, or out of focus. What do you think happened?"

"You shouldn't expect our first flyby to gen up an image in any way, shape, or form as sharp as the squids. It looks blurred because it lacks information."

"What do you mean?"

"They're two things going on here. First, the synthetic aperture function hasn't been enabled yet, so our image isn't a refined accumulation of many snapshots, it's only a sequence of many individual shots viewed in rapid succession. Second, once the synthetic aperture processing is enabled, the image still won't be as sharp as the squids."

"Is that because of the smaller antenna? fewer receivers?"

"That's part of the story, but more fundamentally than that, there's a physics problem with our flyby; we can only measure magnetic fields from the air."

"I thought we always measured magnetic and electric fields."

"That's true with the squid, but from the air, we can't measure electric fields because our receiver's not grounded to the earth to complete the circuit."

"Yeah, that makes sense. So what do we lose without electric field data?"

"As you'd expect, we lose the ability to see some things beneath the surface. We can still resolve good conductors, but voids are tough."

"So we can see the train, but not the tunnel?"

"Well, not exactly. We'll see the train, no problem, but we'll also detect the steel rebar inside the concrete walls of the tunnel. I expect it'll look something like a wire frame. On the downside, we'll have a tough time detecting tunnels with dirt walls because they're more of an insulator."

"I see now. It seems to me, any tunnel or bunker worth hiding is going to have steel rebar in its walls."

"For the most part, I think you're right, and once we work out the bugs, we'll be able to detect them. You'll see, Eion. Don't lose heart."

"Didn't the North Koreans build a big dirt tunnel a long time ago?" Gary Ellie asked.

"That's true, the North Koreans built a tunnel under the DMZ back in the eighties, and I'm not so sure we could have detected it if it were left empty and deserted."

"I wouldn't think an empty deserted tunnel's much of a threat to anyone."

Andreas agreed. "Eventually, they filled it with trucks and tanks, so we could have detected their mischief before they were through. Come to think of it, I don't know how they dug that tunnel, but if they used any heavy equipment underground, we could have caught them in the act."

The Dark Side
Monday, Mar. 15, 11:11 A.M.
Liberty Tower

After returning to his apartment from the discount camera shop, Hakim opened a box containing his new Bogen tripod head and pulled out the instructions. They appeared straightforward. The pan-tilt head came with its handles dismantled; he need only screw them into place, then mount the head on the tripod's centerpost.

Once assembled, he removed the cork-covered camera mounting plate and bolted it to a bracket attached to his telescopic rifle scope. Next, after adjusting the tripod's legs to near full extension, he slipped the plate back into place and attempted to focus on the Fed's employee entrance on Maiden Lane.

Not good. From his perch on the twenty-eighth floor, his view of the employee entrance was blocked by the fourteen stories of the bank building itself. Well, this didn't come as a complete surprise. He'd been afraid of that.

Then he tried to focus in on the guards standing watch outside the garage of the Federal Reserve Bank.

Spoiled again. Their post was a few yards from the intersection of Maiden Lane and William Street, on the blind or shadow side of the building from Hakim's perspective. This wasn't going well, it wasn't going well at all.

After a little more study, Hakim began to loosen up. There were some useful patterns emerging below in the shadows. First thing he noticed—Maiden Lane was lined with trucks waiting admission to the Fed's loading gate. An armored truck was waiting outside the bank's steel garage door and a line of delivery trucks had formed behind it. Hakim could see the fronts of the delivery trucks waiting to enter, and as they moved forward one truck-length at a time, he could often read their license plates. He'd need to move in closer and check out this loading routine for himself. He had a hunch, but needed to stake out the garage entrance to check it out.

For the moment, what really mattered was that he couldn't see what he needed to see from his perch high atop the Liberty Tower. *A perfect place for detonation,* Hakim thought, *less than ideal for observation. You win some and lose some. This operation would have gone much smoother working as a twosome; I could really use Kameel's help about now.*

On the plus side, Hakim could see the public entrance on Liberty Street, where people toured the gold vaults inside the Federal Reserve. In addition, traffic flowed toward him down Maiden Lane and Liberty Street. That was a good thing, too, because it gave him an advanced warning of incoming traffic, and perhaps that's what he needed most.

There were also two restaurants opposite the bank's far diagonal corner on Maiden Lane and William Street, a McDon-

ald's and Jon Bradley's. They'd be open early if he needed to
stake out the corner.

Hakim taped his map of lower Manhattan to his apartment
window and studied it carefully, contrasting what he could see
from his apartment window against the layout shown on the
map. Within minutes, he noticed a second, potentially useful
characteristic about the Jon Bradley's location. It was situated
across the street from the Louise Nevelson Plaza, an open
space with a sculpture and a few trees, almost completely hidden on the far side of the bank.

That's perfect, Hakim thought. *I have some alternatives
and they could be useful.*

Once he'd seen enough, Hakim shifted roles from scout to
New York photographer. Reaching into his bag, he removed a
small, handheld digital camera and began taking a series of
pictures through the window of his corner apartment. His first
snapshot was the rooftop of the New York Federal Reserve
Bank. For his second subject, he chose the Chase Manhattan
Bank building located just across the street. Not surprisingly,
the tall structure wouldn't begin to fit in a single frame
through his 50mm lens.

Long-Term Parking
Tuesday, Mar. 16, 7:55 A.M.
Dulles International Airport

Hakim's Ford Taurus was cordoned off like a crime scene;
yellow and black tape surrounded it, setting its space apart
from all the other long-term parking spots at Dulles International Airport. Before Russum and his team arrived, the
bomb squad had been called in, combed through the vehicle,
and found it clean. The only obvious thing of interest—
a nearly empty gallon jug of blue windshield washer
antifreeze—stood immediately to the driver's right, on the
passenger-side floorboard. Although the glove compartment,
storage console, and trunk were empty, a quick inspection
revealed that its interior, hood, and door remained a gold
mine for prints.

"Whoever parked this car expected it'd be found eventually," Graham heard the chief inspector tell Russum. From the look on Russum's face, that came as no surprise. "The car's identification was traced to a bogus Canadian alias, its stolen Mass plates gave it away."

"We're just glad you found it," Russum said, pulling his Geiger counter from the trunk of his car.

"Do you think there may be any radiation?"

"We'll see soon enough. No time like the present to find out. How 'bout popping the trunk?"

The inspector watched as Russum moved a wand sniffer device back and forth across the interior of the Taurus's trunk. Clearly, the Texan had done this before. He seemed to dwell in the nooks and crannies, the places where the air remained stagnant, but turned up nothing. The Geiger counter remained quiet.

Next, Russum sniffed out the backseat and floorboard.

Nothing. The big man looked grim. "Humph."

Finally, he swept his sniffer beneath the hood, all four wheel wells, and two passes beneath the car.

Nothing. He'd suspected a gray result, but had to check out the vehicle anyway.

"What do you make of it, Mr. Russum?" the inspector asked. Graham looked on quietly, but knew the answer in advance.

"In all probability, this automobile did not carry conventional nuclear materials or weapons."

"That's a relief," the inspector said with a sigh, but then he noticed Russum didn't share his feelings. "Conventional nuclear materials? Is there any other kind?"

"There is now." This time, Russum sighed.

The inspector was stunned. After a few moments, he regained his equilibrium and pressed on. "What are you saying, Mr. Russum? In plain English."

"I'm saying we could still have a problem, a big one, and my Geiger counter won't detect it. I can't go into the details, but suffice it to say that we're looking for a bomb between the size of a grapefruit and a bowling ball. Do you have any other leads we could follow up on?"

"FBI agents are already swarming all over Dulles, speaking to every bus and taxi driver they can find, searching garage entry logs, videotapes of parking areas, you name it. They'll find out when the suspect entered the lot and, with a little luck, we'll get you a video shot of your terrorist. It's only a matter of time."

"Good, we sure as hell could use a little luck at this juncture. God knows we need it."

Behemoth
Tuesday, Mar. 16, 1:43 P.M.
English Channel

"From the looks of it, the RPV's making a pretty good showing of itself," Eion said. All three tunnels were shown as cylindrical wire frames on screen.

Every so often, Gary Ellie would click a button labeled RENDER, and the wire meshes would be filled with solid concrete-gray color and lit from a single source. Unfortunately, the computer-generated result looked like a computer-generated result, too perfect to be true, and overall it lacked the textural detail of the squid's imagery. Despite the results, the tunnels were easily recognizable and everyone could see the trains as they roared beneath them. "All in all, not a bad day's work for a toy plane," the computer master mused.

Andreas agreed, but remained focused on a long, large, stationary object apparently buried beneath one of the tunnels. "This behemoth intrigues me. From the looks of it, it's as wide as the tunnel. Why didn't we notice this before?"

"The tunnels were our target, so we ignored the data from beneath them," Eion spoke first. "I considered it clutter."

"I masked the background clutter from beneath the tunnel," Gary Ellie added, wondering if he'd done the right thing. "Our imaging software runs faster with less data per frame so I ignored it. Don't get me wrong; we recorded the raw data and all—we still have it—only I excluded it from our picture processing. We spent all our time looking at the tunnels, so it never occurred to me that I should process data we weren't scrutinizing."

"I see," Andreas acknowledged. "That makes a lot of

sense. Could you bring up this same section of tunnel from the squid's database and process the signal to a depth of four hundred feet? I'd like to double-check and see if this behemoth shows up on the squid's imagery."

"Sure thing, Doctor. But like I said, it'll take a while to develop an image that deep."

"I understand," Andreas said, then he spoke to Eion. "Could you do a little homework for me? I can't imagine what this thing could possibly be. It doesn't make any sense, but if the squid reveals the same carcass, we've got a little mystery on our hands. Could you talk to the EuroTunnel port authority and find out if they have any idea about this? Give them our location, whatever they need, but see if we can get to the bottom of this. There must be an explanation, but at this moment, I can't imagine what it could be."

CHAPTER ELEVEN

Hopes and Dreams
Tuesday, Mar. 16, 8:06 A.M.
Jon Bradley's Restaurant

"Whaddaya want?" snapped the young, hollow-eyed waitress in a put-up-or-shut-up tone.

"I'm new here," Hakim explained softly. "I've only just moved into the—"

"Yeah, so what's it to me?"

"I only meant—"

"Listen, I got no time to talk. There's fifteen tables in this place filled with hungry people and it won't be pretty if I keep 'em waiting. You want somethin' or what?"

"I just moved here from the Upper East Side and—"

"Yeah, so? I'm from Newark. Where you come from don't mean nothin' to me. Look, you gonna order or not?"

Hakim looked across the room at the pancakes and sausage resting in front of one of the bank's security guards. The man's ample American girth left the impression he ate here often. "I'll have what that gentleman's having over there." The gray-haired terrorist cut his eyes across the room, signaling the waitress without pointing.

"That's what put this place on the map, mister, that's the gold brick special; regulars eat it all the time."

"It must be good."

"Yeah, I suppose." The waitress rolled her eyes as if to say, *What planet did you come from?*

In an odd, self-satisfied way, Hakim revelled in the wretched rudeness of the waitress. He'd always found killing easier if he knew, and didn't care for, his victims. *I'm leaving the world a better place than I found it,* Hakim reasoned. *Like cleaning rats from the sewer.*

What Hakim failed to account for was that often, his victims had good reason for their behavior. This waitress, in particular, was exhausted and her feet ached from holding down two full-time jobs. She'd been on her feet nonstop for sixteen hours a day, six days a week, since she'd dropped out of high school nearly two and a half years ago. She reasoned that an honest, hard day's work was better than spending high-profit nights on her back, but what did she have to show for it?

Blisters and bills.

She should have never quit school. She knew that now, and as for the guys, none of 'em were worth it. Still, though she'd made some bad calls along the way, she'd accepted responsibility for her decisions and kept her pilot light burning. Above all else, she had her hopes and dreams.

One day, she'd go back to school. One day, and it would be soon, she'd wipe the dust of this crummy place off her feet and never look back. One day, she'd have a better life and there was nothing anyone could do to hold her back.

With her parents dead, her first husband long gone, and her two-year-old toddler in day care, she struggled just to make ends meet in her crummy Newark apartment. She'd seen pets—dogs and cats—who lived better than she did, and it looked as if her knight in shining armor would never find her, at least not in that armpit of an apartment where she lived. Hakim had no way to know this, but he had four times more living space in his Liberty Tower apartment than she'd ever experienced her entire life.

Still, when this young lady felt rested, she had integrity, strength of character, and the wherewithal to recognize that life was good, but it wasn't fair. On top of that, she had the resolve to one day escape this hellhole existence. One day soon her ship would come in, and when it did, she'd sail away.

But right now, in this time and this place, she was a waitress and her feet were killing her.

A few minutes later, she returned with Hakim's breakfast order. As she approached his table carrying a large shoulder tray, he noticed she walked with a limp, clearly favoring her right foot. Hakim pretended not to notice and continued looking out the window. His booth was on the ground floor, next to Maiden Lane, strategically situated where he had a clear view of both the bank garage entrance and the Louise Nevelson Plaza.

The smell of pancakes and sausage brought a smile to his face, and, seeing this, the waitress seemed genuinely pleased. "Do ya want anything else, sir?"

"This looks and smells delicious." Hakim smiled.

"I'm glad," the waitress said, implicitly apologizing for her initial rudeness. "Ya want somethin' to drink? Milk or coffee?"

"Orange juice would be nice."

"You got it. I'll be right back."

"And there's one other thing."

"Yes?" The waitress looked at Hakim, offering him a tired smile. "What'll it be?" This time around, the young lady took time to listen.

"Like I tried to tell you earlier, I'm new here and I was wondering if you could tell me the name of that little park across the street?"

"Sure, but I'd hardly call it a real park. That's the Louise

Nevelson Plaza. It contains one of her sculptures; think it's called *Shadows and Flags*. It's pretty neat if you haven't had a chance to see it."

"I've got a little time this morning. Maybe I'll do exactly that."

Moments later, the waitress returned with his juice and Hakim continued his study of the routine unfolding outside the bank garage doors. Today, like yesterday, a line of delivery trucks had formed down Maiden Lane, each waiting its turn to enter the fortress.

By 8:15, the line extended nearly two-thirds a city block, and then Hakim saw what he'd hoped he would see. The bank's queue rules operated with exceptions—most queues do—and now Hakim saw firsthand the black limo violation he'd hoped for. By Hakim's way of thinking, he considered this an almost humorous comment on American society. Without fail, when a senior bank executive approached in a black limo, they moved immediately to the front of the queue, the steel garage gates clanked open, and the vehicle disappeared behind the walls of the great fortress.

Between 8:15 and 8:40 that Tuesday morning, three limos entered the bank's garage.

The next day the same three limos entered the bank's garage during that twenty-five-minute period. Hakim recorded their license plates on a napkin, then committed them to memory so he'd be ready for tomorrow's main event.

Suicide
Tuesday, Mar. 16, 2:58 P.M.
English Channel

"No doubt about it, Doctor, the squid's imagery tells the same story, only with more detail."

"I expected as much." About that time, Andreas saw Eion entering the CIC, pocketing his Motorola satellite phone. Judging from his expression, he had something to say that wouldn't wait.

Holding up both hands, he announced, "Tunnel machine suicide."

Gary Ellie didn't have a clue where Eion was coming from, but Andreas was intrigued. "I expect your story will be a good one."

"Honest, Doc, you can't make this stuff up. Turns out, we're over the exact spot where the British and French first met when they dug the tunnel years ago. Believe it or not, that giant metal monster down there is a tunnel-boring machine. When the British and French boring machines met, they came together headfirst, and one of them had to die."

Both Andreas and Gary Ellie narrowed their eyes. Something was missing here. "Why?" they asked simultaneously.

"They couldn't go straight, they couldn't back up, and, as the story goes, the British behemoth was in a bad way, on its last leg. Following some political back-and-forth, the British machine drew the short straw and committed mechanical suicide, turning its nose down and burrowing itself even deeper underground below the tunnel."

"It just turned down and died." Gary Ellie grinned at first, then his expression turned serious. "I don't know. Now that I think about it, it sounds kinda harsh to me. After all, the thing was probably teaming with people—it carried them this far, didn't it?—dug its own grave, and was abandoned, left to die."

"That's right, cold as it may sound. It buried itself, but the bottom line was business; it was cheaper to leave it underground than to salvage it."

"Business," Gary Ellie scoffed. As a techno-zealot, he had enormous passion for technical elegance, and comparable loathing for profiteers. "It figures. Businessmen are like women. You can't live with 'em, you can't sustain life without 'em."

Eion felt strongly about this point and took exception. "Women have nothing to do with it. Work gets money, money gets women, and women . . . women make life worth the work."

Both young men looked to Andreas, anxious for approval, but the wise man simply shrugged and wouldn't bite.

"Whaddaya say, Doc?" Eion pressed, knowing him to be a happily married man with a large family.

"I have nothing to say."

The Commute
Wednesday, Mar. 17, 9:04 A.M.
Approaching the Broadway/Nassau Street subway station
Three blocks from the Chase Manhattan Bank

Good days for Mary Marshall and her daughter Katie were characterized by simple kindness and, so far this morning, their day had gotten off to an excellent start. Occasionally, on their best days, the Marshalls would board the New York subway and someone would offer them a seat. Today had been just such a day and their seat had been all the more welcome because, this morning, Katie was so sleepy she could hardly keep her eyes open.

Some days, Katie would color during their noisy subway ride, but today she slept in her mother's lap. It seemed Katie could sleep anywhere, and Mary often wished she could do that.

Mary watched the familiar subway stops pass by one by one, checking her watch repeatedly. Today, there had been no train delays and Mary believed she'd make it to work on time.

"Katie, wake up, honey. It's time to get off."

Her little one didn't respond at first, then released a tired sigh.

"Wake up, baby. You're a big girl now. Mommy can't carry you like she used to."

Katie's eyes opened slowly, reluctantly at first, but once they registered the image of her mother, a wide grin emerged. She stretched, hugged her mother, and began to stir as the train brakes screeched to a stop. Straightaway, the pair exited the subway at the Broadway/Nassau Street station and headed for the stairway leading to the surface.

Day after day, there was something magic about the light at the end of that stairway. Mary and Katie relished the sunshine and, this morning, the bright light at the end of the tunnel told them both that theirs would be a beautiful spring walk to the Chase Manhattan building.

* * *

"Yep, I hear you. Sounds like it could provide us with some helpful information. We'll download the video from your website and take a look-see. Thanks again." Russum nodded and hung up the phone. Without a moment's hesitation, he paged his team. In less than five minutes, Graham, Wyley, and Buck had taken their seats around his conference table.

"They found this video showing the Taurus being parked at Dulles."

On-screen, Russum played an mpeg video clip showing a gray-haired driver pulling into his long-term parking space. After a few more frames, the driver put on a winter hat, got out of the car, removed his luggage, and closed the trunk. After double-checking all the doors and backseat, he walked away. The only clue to trouble, and this was a stretch, was the fact that he double-checked everything: the doors, the trunk, the backseat, and, finally, the lights. Still, that double-check-it-all behavior was not that unusual if the driver was a better-be-safe-than-sorry type, traveling alone. Most people arriving at an airport early circled their car before heading for the terminal.

But the trouble with the on-screen mpeg image was size—it was too small, not even as large as a two-by-three Post-it Note. Wyley took control of Russum's mouse, attempting to zoom in on the driver's face, but to no avail. Once the bit map was enlarged, the blocky, tile-like nature of the picture began to dominate and it simply looked worse.

Wyley squinted in frustration. His contacts were killing him. Still, try as he might, the harder he looked, the less he could make out and the more irritated his eyes became. Finally, when he couldn't stand it any longer, he reached into his pocket and pulled out his rewetting drops.

Instantly, his eyes felt better, but the driver's face on the screen still looked like a blocky, digitized satellite image. He could verify the man's hair color was lighter than he'd expected, but that was about it.

After a few more minutes of wrestling with the zoom controls, Wyley vented his frustration. "This is about as productive as getting water from a rock."

"It's not going to happen quickly," Buck said, grinning. "So what else ya got?"

"A couple of cab drivers think they saw this man. We showed them our other pictures and one of 'em thinks they could be the same person. 'Something about that man's eyes,' the driver told the inspector. 'They were too young, too clear, for an old man and they were scary, like Rasputin's.'"

"Rasputin always made my skin crawl." Graham sighed. "Anything else? Where'd he go?"

"One driver carried him from Dulles to the Baltimore-Washington International Airport."

"Yeah, and?"

"The driver showed us his log; it checked out and his supervisor confirmed his story. Dulles to BWI's not an unheard-of taxi ride, but it's their policy to radio in and get backup coverage for Dulles while they're away. The supervisor's dispatch log showed this driver carried a fare to BWI approximately forty-five minutes after the Taurus was dropped off in long-term parking."

"It all holds together," Graham agreed. "What happened at BWI?"

"Our terrorist dropped off our radar screen, and so far, the FBI's drawn a blank. We got nothin' more outta BWI. Coulda headed any direction from there and his trail's grown cold."

"That's it? We've just lost him?"

"That's all related to this Dulles lead. The FBI's following up reported sightings all over the country, but this Dulles-BWI hit's on top of the list."

"What do you propose we do next?" Wyley asked.

"Stay the course. Focus on this domestic terrorist threat until we flush him out, then pick up where we left off with our flight to Hama. In a sense, it's just as well we're stuck stateside anyway because there's been some diplomatic snags with our trip. I don't have much expertise in foreign affairs, but I know a Syrian stall tactic when I see one. What the Syrian ambassador told me was that Assad's regime had some serious security concerns for our safety. They wanna give Graham and the rest of his illustrious medical entourage their red carpet treatment, but want to make sure the carpet's not stained with our blood."

"Good idea." Wyley nodded.

"On that much, I agree. They'd planned on welcoming us all as goodwill ambassadors, but because of this Hama instability, they want to postpone our arrival until they get these security concerns, uh, 'nailed down' was how he put it. I got the impression their security concerns had names."

"The way I read it," Wyley expanded, "is that Assad wants to eliminate these people before we're welcome in Syria."

Russum agreed.

"So where's the Syrian stall in this picture?" Graham wanted to know.

"The Syrian ambassador's story keeps changing. I told you only their latest pitch because it's my own personal favorite." Billy Ray grinned at first, then noticed Buck wasn't smiling at all.

"And what do I tell my men?" Buck vented. "Hell, I'm not even sure what we're up against here, so how the hell do we train? This whole operation's sounding less and less like a SEAL operation to me. You know what I'm saying; where's the water?"

"You're right," Billy Ray conceded. "We don't know what to train for. Still, I insist when the time comes, we'll know, and you'll be given time, whatever it takes, to prepare. If you don't buy in, they don't go in."

"Good." Buck was satisfied and gave a laugh. "Anyway, it's been one helluva ride so far."

"We can't seem to break clear of the States." Graham grinned. "Trapped like rats, bogged down in the Washington mire."

Pigeons
Thursday, Mar. 18, 7:50 A.M.
Jon Bradley's Restaurant

Thursday came and Hakim was there.

By now, he felt like a regular entering Jon Bradley's. He

didn't know any of the guards by name, but after three days, he knew their faces well enough to nod politely, say good morning, and comment on their breakfast choices. Looking across the restaurant, he caught the waitress's eye and mouthed the words *gold brick*. She smiled, held up five fingers, then directed him toward his favorite booth by the window.

It's a good life, Hakim thought to himself, feeling a little down at the knowledge that this was coming to an end. This would be the last time he'd enjoy "the Fed's favorite breakfast." If all went as expected, he'd change the complexion of this restaurant within a few hours. In a way, Hakim felt the excitement of the kill mixed with a nagging sense of loss he could not shake.

Suddenly, he recognized the Fed chairman's limo and license plate in the distance. At 8:00 A.M. sharp, well ahead of the others, the garage doors clanked open and license plate GOV 829 rolled into the bank.

Characteristically punctual, Hakim observed, struggling to remain calm.

His game was astir.

Yet somehow, it all seemed too easy.

Self-doubt, Hakim concluded. *It's only easy because of good planning plus being in the right place at the right time.*

By 8:40, fifteen limos had entered the garage and one thing was certain. This was no ordinary day for the New York Fed.

As had become his morning routine, Hakim picked up a few crackers and a pack of peanuts on his way out. After paying his bill, he walked across the street to the Louise Nevelson Plaza.

By the third day, the pigeons recognized him as a friend.

Escape from Manhattan
Thursday, Mar. 18, 9:03 A.M.
Liberty Tower

Hakim threaded the bomb onto the camera mounting plate, then locked the assembly on the head of his tripod. Once the softball-shaped bomb assembly was firmly secured to the tripod head, he ran the circuit board test one last time.

Perfect, Hakim thought. *Nothing has changed.* Instinctively, he raised the tripod legs and positioned it so that the bomb was situated inside the thin veil curtain in his picture window. So far, so good.

Then came the moment of truth. Shaking uncontrollably, Hakim couldn't steady his hands as he struggled to connect each detonator cable to the bomb. It could have been fear or adrenaline, but it really didn't matter. His hands shook like he was cold and wet, then, instinctively, his mind took charge. He'd use two hands to do the job of one. One hand held the connector, the other guided it into place. Once they were all locked into position, he took a moment to relax, then ran a low-current connectivity test, verifying that each cable was properly connected. This live-wire test left nothing to chance, testing all the components in the assembly. In less than thirty seconds, Hakim watched as a single green LED flashed sixteen times.

Perfect. Hakim smiled. Every detonator was reachable and operating within spec. Although he didn't fully understand everything he observed, he knew sixteen flashes was good. For practical purposes, this live-wire test reduced the probability of failure to zero. After he armed the bomb, it would detonate. That much was a certainty.

It was 9:16 when Hakim set the timer.

He didn't bother wiping down his apartment for prints, no need for that. Turning, he picked up his bag, switched off the lights, and walked out the door. His parting vision was of the bomb. It looked like the head of Medusa resting atop three long spindly legs.

Walking out the first floor of Liberty Tower, he wished the doorman a good day, then headed up Nassau Street at a typically hurried pace. His objective was to clear Manhattan with all possible speed.

Two blocks, Hakim thought as he checked his watch. Clipping along on Nassau Street, he passed Maiden Lane then soon disappeared underground into the Broadway/Nassau Street subway. His last mental image aboveground wasn't of the people—he'd learned to look right through them—it was of the Western Electric building across the street. Checking his watch again on his way down the subway stairs, the terrorist concluded the chances were good he'd just make it.

Six minutes later, he was riding the Eighth Avenue Express bound for Penn Station. In his pocket he held five Amtrak tickets to Boston and still, even with this five-ticket buffer, he had a problem. He'd missed his 9:30 departure and he couldn't wait to catch the 12:30 train. Feeling boxed in, he wanted desperately to get out of Manhattan. After arriving at Penn Station, Hakim went directly to the New York Metropolitan Commuter Rail ticket office and bought a pass on the next available outbound train. Though running the wrong way, he didn't care and took the coastline branch to Red Bank, New Jersey.

In Hakim's mind, only one thing mattered. The monitor read: NJ COASTLINE: NOW BOARDING.

CHAPTER TWELVE

A New York Minute
Thursday, Mar. 18, 9:46 A.M.
Liberty Tower

Three, two, one . . .

Sixteen precisely timed pulses raced toward the red mercury core, triggering a searing white-hot flash.

Everyone—thousands of people across the Financial District—exhaled as if they'd been hammered in the solar plexus.

A tremendous explosion rocked Liberty Tower, then entire city blocks fell deathly still.

CHAPTER THIRTEEN

Bird's-eye View
Thursday, Mar. 18, 9:46 A.M.
Manhattan

On the ground below, hundreds of people on the street dropped dead in their tracks, facedown, prostrate on the cold concrete. No one within five hundred yards and the direct line of sight of the flash lived to tell the tale, let alone see the fireball or small mushroom cloud rising above the city.

But fifteen airline passengers on the pilot's side of the twin-turboprop flight from Manchester to Newark had a bird's-eye view of the event. And it was their eyewitness account which would first be reported over CNN. At the time the telltale mushroom cloud formed over Manhattan, they were just west of the Financial District, flying over the Hudson on their approach to Newark International Airport.

"We didn't feel a blast or anything, just a bright flash followed by that cloud," one teenage witness reported.

But it was the eyewitness account from a Raytheon Missile Division employee which was most telling. "It was a nuclear explosion of some sort, of that much I'm sure. It had the classic mushroom shape of a low airburst, the toroidal circulation of hot gasses, the red-hot fireball and stem, it had it all. The fireball actually glowed and ascended skyward like a hot-air balloon; I never thought I'd live to see the day. I've seen a lot of film of this kind of thing, studied a good many pictures, but none of them were like this exactly. This cloud was pretty small compared to everything I'd seen. Its stem appeared anchored to the top of some building near the southern tip of Manhattan."

"The Financial District?"

"Yes, within sight of the Wall Street."

It was as if the top of the Liberty Tower suddenly disappeared into a boiling cloud. The building itself appeared to form the stem of the mushroom-shaped cloud; cool air, people, and debris were sucked up into the boiling frenzy like it was a giant vacuum cleaner, and then they were gone.

The speed at which the mushroom cloud cloud ascended into the sky would have shocked even the experts. From the Jersey side of the river, there was a brilliant, blinding flash, brighter than the sun, then the boiling fireball was seen rising into the heavens.

Hakim's ten-ton pure-fusion device had a blast radius of one hundred yards; however, more deadly than that, its lethal radiation radius swept a three-thousand-foot circle of death around Liberty Tower. Hakim's neutron bomb saturated this circle with nuclear radiation, which quickly incapacitated all those within range who were not adequately shielded. As expected, it didn't mangle anyone unless they were unfortunate enough to have been impacted by the direct effect of the blast. Like a conventional bomb, the blast wreaked havoc on those buildings immediately surrounding the Liberty Tower, and like a conventional explosive, the pure-fusion neutron bomb did not render the Financial District uninhabitable. Following the bomb's lethal release of neutron radiation, the people died, but unlike the Chernobyl nuclear power plant accident, there was no lingering radioactive contamination.

Over the next several weeks, doctors from New York, Washington, and around the world confirmed the Raytheon employee's claim. Time and observation revealed that New Yorkers suffered from three types of injuries: blast, heat, and radiation.

And by far, the greatest of these was radiation.

A fission bomb expends 85 percent of its energy in blast and heat, the remainder as radiation. On the other hand, a pure-fusion neutron bomb nearly reverses these percentages, releasing 80 percent of its total energy as radiation. The fusion reaction operates on the same principle as the sun and does not produce lingering radioactive contamination when triggered by a conventional explosive.

To trigger the fusion reaction, temperatures of several million degrees are fueled by a conventional explosion of red mercury. The fusion of hydrogen isotopes liberates a large amount of energy in a very short time and, because of their small mass, neutrons carry off most of the reaction energy. As a result, the red mercury is raised to temperatures comparable to the sun. The maximum temperature of conventional high-explosive is 9000°, while the red mercury explosion reaches temperatures of several million degrees.

Immediately afterward, the red mercury is converted into gas by heat, and since the gas is restricted at the instant of explosion, tremendous pressure is produced.

Less than a millionth of a second later, the sunlike mass radiates large amounts of energy, which forms the fireball—an extremely hot, incandescent spherical air mass. Since the temperature of the fireball does not vary significantly with yield, the brightness of Hakim's bomb was roughly the same as a 1-megaton nuclear warhead.

Immediately after its formation, the glowing fireball began to grow, engulfing the top stories of the Liberty Tower. As it grew, it rose above Manhattan like a fiery, ominous cloud. Less than seven-tenths of a second after its birth, the fireball from Hakim's grapefruit-sized neutron bomb had engulfed the top of the Gothic structure that had been Liberty Tower.

Down below, underneath the trees in the Louise Nevelson Plaza, Hakim's pigeons fell silently to earth, like soft loaves of bread dropping from the sky. Masked from the blast by the Federal Reserve Bank, Nevelson's sculpture remained intact, lifeless, but otherwise undamaged.

Inside Jon Bradley's, a barrage of neutrons came through the large plate glass windows, bounced about the interior, then lodged in the bone and soft, blood-forming tissues of its occupants. Mercifully, death was nearly instantaneous. The young waitress was carrying another gold brick breakfast from the kitchen when she saw the flash. Before the bright light fully registered in her brain, she dropped her food tray, fell to her knees, then rotated forward, facedown on the floor. Pancakes, syrup, milk, and sausage were strewn across the room. Unaware of the lady's distress, the guards and other regular customers keeled over and died as she dropped. Less than one second later, the blast shattered the picture windows, hurling glass shards and flying debris everywhere. There was no pain, only the darkness of death closing in around them, then they heard the explosion.

Before the flash, the cash drawer had been open. It would remain open for hours Thursday without threat of looting.

CHAPTER FOURTEEN

Get In and Get Out
Thursday, Mar. 18, 10:10 A.M.
CTC

"Listen up," Graham heard Commander Buck Harrison say. His deep baritone voice demanded the group's attention. "Right now, all we know is that twenty minutes ago, New York's Financial District was rocked by an explosion; it could have been nuclear and that's where we come in. By all accounts, lower Manhattan was the terrorist's primary target and Washington could have been a diversion. At this point, it's too soon to know. Telephone linemen working beneath the streets of New York called immediately after it happened, but we have only their initial assessment. They reported a blast and hundreds, maybe thousands of dead on the street, countless others wandering aimlessly around the Financial District in shock."

Buck clicked his handheld remote, and a large street map of the Financial District was projected on the wall. "There have been conflicting reports on ground zero, but from most accounts, the blast seems to have been centered in the vicinity of the Chase Manhattan Bank. We conclude this because eyewitnesses claim the Chase Manhattan building suffered the most structural damage from the blast."

Graham studied the map carefully, searching for hospitals

in the immediate area and not finding any. During his survey, he noticed the Chase Manhattan Bank stood across the street from the Federal Reserve Bank of New York and an alarm went off in his mind—Rosenberg, that article in yesterday's *Washington Post*.

"Since these early reports," Buck continued, "all two-way communication with New York City has been lost. Apparently, data and telephone circuits were overloaded and went belly up; all national television—ABC, CBS, and NBC— dropped off the air at 9:50 this morning due to technical difficulty, but within minutes, broadcasting resumed out of Los Angeles. What I'm saying is this: New York's been cut off. The power grid remains active, they've got that going for 'em, but their land and sat comm systems are off the air. As we understand it, direct trunks are being activated between Washington and New York as we speak, but for now, it's up to us to bridge the gap. We've got to break the logjam, set up mobile communications, and find out what happened so the president can know what to do."

An enormous, wall-sized satellite photo of the Financial District flashed on-screen.

"As you can see, lower Manhattan, everything below the Brooklyn Bridge, has been sealed off. No one's getting in or out of there unless they're on foot. And obviously, the rest of Manhattan's in gridlock. Bridge and tunnel traffic, all of it, has ground to a halt. There have been reports of people deserting their cars in the Lincoln Tunnel and walking out on foot. The panic started when the phones died. It's like a domino effect, the whole house of cards collapsed in on itself. Subways and trains are still moving, for a while at least, some of 'em anyway, packed to overflow capacity. Penn Station's a madhouse."

"Our job is to get in there with our gear, sweep the area, make our measurements, and get the hell out. Washington needs a radiological and biological assessment before committing additional government and military personnel to any major cleanup and rescue operation. Gentlemen, we have the dubious distinction of going in as the tip of the lance."

"We'll land here, on the *Stennis*," he said, pointing to an aircraft carrier anchored off the southern tip of Manhattan. "There's a no-fly zone being enforced over the area, so we're going in with an escort."

Buck noticed Graham looking puzzled and added, "We don't want to risk being shot down by friendly fire."

On hearing this, an icy knot formed in the pit of Graham's stomach. Over the course of the last few weeks, terrorists, grapefruit-sized nuclear bombs, and the prospect of friendly fire combined to make the world seem small and very, very treacherous.

"We'll take a chopper in and pull a sweep of the area," Buck continued. "For all we know, there could be more of these bombs waiting in ambush."

"If there's any more of these bastards buried in the city, we'll detonate 'em remotely before they kill anyone else," Russum said flatly. He didn't say they could get killed during the process. He didn't have to.

"Once we touch down," Buck instructed, "make your measurements, survey the damage, and determine if there's any biological or radioactive contamination in the area. We've gotta know before sending in our troops."

"Wyley, you're our man on camera and we'll need your eyes. Once we're on site, we'll need you to tell us if this is what you saw in Hama."

Wyley agreed, then asked, "What about motivation? Why would anyone do such a thing?"

"I have some idea," Graham offered, "but it's only a theory. We'll find out soon enough."

"So what's your idea?" Buck asked.

"I think the New York Fed was their target. Yesterday's *Washington Post* reported Jonathan Rosenberg would be in New York attending some international monetary conference. Today, he was supposed to meet with his board of governors in the New York Federal Reserve Bank. The president of the New York Fed made a statement to that effect in yesterday's paper. I'd be willing to bet they were in a board meeting at the time of the blast."

Buck reached for the phone to call one of his special forces buddies inside the FBI's counterterrorist organization. After a brief exchange, he hung up and looked Graham in the eyes.

"Your theory's gathering momentum like an avalanche, Doc. You were right. The board meeting was taking place on the top floor when the bomb went off."

Buck looked over at Russum and one horrific revelation jelled before their mind's eye.

Russum snapped into overdrive. "Show me the map again, and how 'bout roundin' up a set of architectural drawings of the bank."

Buck flashed the city map on-screen and sent his aide out of the room in search of the plans.

Russum checked the scale in the lower right corner, then drew a three-thousand-foot-diameter circle around the Federal Reserve Bank. "Assume that ten-ton-mini-nuke detonated here, somewhere inside this circle. It could have gone off in any one of these buildings. Chase Manhattan and Marine Midland are businesses—that'd be pretty tough; St. John's Methodist Church could be a possibility. Any burned-out or deserted buildings in the area?" He directed his question to Wyley.

Wyley queried Berndtson's New York database on his workstation. "Negative. Every square foot is either occupied, for sale, or under renovation."

"How about hotels or apartment buildings? Everybody's gotta have a place to live. I'm looking for a tall one, in sight of the Fed."

Wyley filled out the database query form then clicked.

A list came back, sorted by distance from the Fed. Fifty-five Liberty Street percolated to the top. "Liberty Tower's right across the street. Thirty-two floors."

"Can you bring up recent apartment sales on that thing?"

Wyley nodded, and clattered away.

"Liberty Tower; two apartment sales closed in the past three months, one in the past two weeks."

"Liberty Tower, that's how I'd do it. Tell me more."

"Twenty-eighth floor, four rooms. Looks like some kinda nice place. Corner apartment facing . . ." A pause as Wyley pulled up an apartment map showing the building's layout. This time, the map came off the internet, a URL to the real estate broker's leased website located somewhere in western New Jersey. Wyley blinked, as if he couldn't believe what he saw.

"Spit it out," Russum urged.

"It's a corner apartment facing the Federal Reserve and Chase Manhattan Banks."

"That bloody bastard . . ."

"Get in touch with that real estate agent," Graham suggested. "He should be able to describe the person who bought the apartment."

"Good idea," Wyley said, instinctively firing off some e-mail to the gentleman. Less than five seconds later, an error message appeared on his screen:

```
IP Host Unreachable
```

Looking across the room at Graham, Wyley reiterated what everyone already knew but hadn't fully appreciated. "His e-mail's out to lunch. The internet's down around the city so I guess his POP server must be in New York."

"You come to depend on it working without thinking about it," Graham acknowledged, then looked at Buck. "How about forwarding the real estate agent's name and number to the FBI?"

Buck was dialing before Graham finished the question. Moments later, he nodded satisfaction, hung up, then directed his next question to Russum. "They're on it, but we still need floor plans for the Federal Reserve Bank."

"We need more than that," Russum insisted. "We've got to have the architectural drawings for that building."

Buck and Wyley looked puzzled, so Graham jumped in to explain. "Shielding. He needs to know what materials the outside walls and roof are made of, and their thickness."

"And the windows," Russum added. "They're killers because they're like open doors to radiation entering the building. For practical purposes, windows pass neutrons like they pass light; they're transparent and can nullify the shielding effectiveness of even the thickest walls."

"I see where you're coming from," Buck said. "You're anticipating my next question."

"Yep. What are the chances some of the board members could make it out alive?"

Buck dialed his aide's cell phone number, apprised him of the situation, then addressed the group. "The Federal Reserve Bank of New York was built in 1924, but there's good news. We've got extensive documentation on-line for every nut, bolt, and stick of lumber in it. Wyley, check your e-mail. You should find two URLs, a log-in name, and a password; one URL links us to the bank's architectural drawings, the second points to an extensive set of floor plans; fourteen stories' worth, I'm told."

Moments later, Russum, Buck, and Graham were breathing down Wyley's neck, looking over his shoulder at the large-screen monitor. Wyley pulled up the architectural drawings first, consisting of hyperlinked pages. When you wanted to bore into a drawing for greater detail, you clicked on the object you were interested in, then additional pictures and tables appeared on-screen.

"Fourteen stories is correct," Wyley said, studying a series of outside views of the bank. "This place looks to me like an armed fortress surrounded by streets."

"That's right. She's boxed in all right." Russum pointed to an aerial picture of the building showing the wedge-shaped Federal Reserve bordered by Maiden Lane and Liberty, Nassau, and William Streets. "Click on the exterior masonry for me, will ya?"

A page describing the bank's immense stone blocks appeared.

"Built like the pyramids."

"What's that?" Buck asked.

"Massive sandstone and limestone blocks."

"Looks like a jail to me," Graham observed. "Iron bars cover the building's lower windows."

"Maybe so, but it's the fanciest jail I've ever seen." Buck grinned. "Those wrought-iron lanterns outside are gigantic."

"Take a look at this," Russum interrupted. "This is a killer. The entrance on Liberty Street is nearly thirty feet high. Those thick stone walls won't provide squat for shielding alongside a gaping hole like that. And look at all those bloody windows. Click here and look inside."

He pointed to the public entrance.

"Damn place looks like a cathedral inside," he continued. "Vaulted ceilings and look at the angles off those walls. I'll tell ya one thing: Those walls'll scatter neutrons all over creation. They'll bounce around in there like Ping-Pong balls until they find someplace to rest. And look at the size of those windows! Unbelievable, and so many of 'em. These people never had a chance. There's only one way anyone in there could survive if that mini-nuke went off nearby."

The group looked at him wide-eyed, as if to say, *Yeah, and?*

"If it were a dud. If the detonation was incomplete, someone on the main floor might survive the neutron radiation."

"I guess that makes sense," Buck reasoned. "It's an old building, built some eighty-five years ago, long before the days of fallout shelters."

A few more clicks around the building and Wyley spoke again. "Maiden Lane, this entrance over here, provides access to the building's garage and loading platform. This place even has its own post office."

"And zip code." Russum shook his head. "That's one hell of a lot of people trapped in there, something like twenty-four hundred of 'em."

"Look." Graham pointed. "Says here that closed-circuit television cameras continuously monitor the vault area and premises, inside the building and out. They have cameras monitoring the streets as well as the exteriors of surrounding buildings. That could prove useful."

"This must be guard headquarters," Wyley chimed in. "That room labeled 'Central Watch.' All the bank's security cameras must feed there."

"Yep, that'll be useful," Russum affirmed. "It's about three hundred feet from the garage entrance."

"Well," Wyley sneered sarcastically. "At least the gold is safe. The gold storage area's built on the bedrock of Manhattan Island, nearly eighty feet below Nassau Street. It's virtually impregnable."

"That's interesting." Russum squinted, cautiously studying the bank's cross-sectional view. "Below ground level? If they were sealed off from the surface, we could find some survivors down there."

"This changes things," Buck mumbled. He made one call, then another, and looked up. "Graham, this is where you come in. You'll enter the Fed through the roof with me. Get in, find the chairman and his board."

Graham nodded, then Buck spoke to Russum. "What chance have they got?"

"Top floor, right?"

"Right."

"None, they got no chance at all. They died instantly. Count the windows. The roof's not going to provide any substantial shielding at all."

"What about the possibility of a dud?"

"The probability of a dud is unknown. Insufficient data characterizing the detonation properties of the Russian mininuke." Techno-Russum sounded like a walking computer, but only for a moment. "Hell, at this stage, we're not even sure it was the pure-fusion device."

Buck thought for a few moments, then spoke again to Graham. "Do what you can to help 'em anyway, and get 'em out if they're still alive."

"What about the rest of the people? Those in the basement, the ones with a fighting chance below ground level."

Buck looked at all three men. "What state of mind do you think they'll be in? Would they be dangerous to us? Could they possibly hurt us or themselves?"

"Dead to delirious," Wyley quipped.

"I expect their feelings are scattered all over the map," Graham concluded. "Shocked, bewildered, disbelieving, desperate."

Russum agreed, adding, "Desperate's a little scary. There could be over a thousand survivors trapped inside that building, locked in tight."

"How so?" Buck asked the Texan.

"The building security system could've locked down on

'em, clamped shut when that bomb exploded. Wouldn't surprise me at all from the looks of their alarm system. If the security guards were dead, some of 'em might be locked in there with no way out."

Buck's forehead wrinkled up like a bulldog's. He called a friend in search and rescue, then reported his conclusions to the team. "We'll need to stay flexible. If there are a great many survivors in the building, we're gonna need some help. Trust me on this one. Our job is to assess the situation and get the hell out. If there are survivors inside the bank, and it's safe to do so, we'll call in the S&R teams immediately. They're one hell of a lot better at this than we are. They're trained and equipped for the job. In the final analysis, fifteen minutes one way or the other won't make any difference. We'll tell these people help's on the way and wait until the pros arrive. Unfortunately, I've got to eliminate the possibility of robbery before we leave."

"*Robbery?*" Graham, Wyley, and Russum reacted at once.

"Right. Like Russum said. We're only guessing, here. We could be wrong about this entire scenario. There could be a robbery in progress, we can't know for sure now, but we'll sure as hell find out. That much is certain."

"I think robbery's a long shot," Russum stated flatly. "Where're they gonna go with the gold? The area's sealed off tighter than a drum."

"I hope you're right," Buck responded. "If somebody's got balls enough to rob the Fed, who knows what we could be up against?"

"I think it'd be enough to kill the chairman and shut down Wall Street," Graham observed quietly. "In my opinion, this was a flagrant act of terrorism; robbery is out of the question."

"The Fed is dead," Wyley whispered, imagining the sensational headline. "Details at the top of the hour."

Wyley paused, then allowed a vengeful, acerbic tone to burn through his words. "Untold innocent dead and dying. All in all, not a bad day's work."

CHAPTER FIFTEEN

The Cloud Room
Thursday, Mar. 18, 12:46 P.M.
Helicopter approaching no-fly zone
New York's Financial District

Wearing his full-body radiation suit, Commander Buck Harrison looked like the Thing from Outer Space strapped in behind the controls of his Marine Corps Huey. Totally focused, Buck radiated pent-up energy, a kind of Jack Nicholson volatility—a relaxed, but-I-could-fly-off-the-handle-any-second persona.

Commander Harrison drew in a long, slow breath, then lifted the aircraft into a hover over the deck. Because he was isolated from the feel of the controls by the bulk of his radiation gloves, the helicopter felt stiff and clumsy. After making one final system check, he rotated the craft into the wind, dipped the nose, and increased the collective, heading the aircraft toward the city.

Above Buck's head, twin engines screamed at full rated power, delivering 2,800 shaft horsepower through the transmission to the rotors, transforming raw unadulterated energy into lurching, bone-shuddering speed.

Buck fat-fingered the radio, signaling the Navy's E-2 Hawkeye radar control aircraft circling high above lower Manhattan.

"Guardian, this is FedEvac 101. We are en route to station."

"Roger, 101, Guardian has you approaching pier fourteen."

Neither Buck's manner nor the bone-jarring ride helped relax his passengers. Russum rode up front alongside Buck in the copilot's seat, decked out in his radiation suit, carrying his black cowboy hat, an RF sweeper, and radio-controlled Geiger counter. The silver-suited pair of robots in the front seat would have made a frightening-looking twosome in any dark alley—a big-framed, bald fireplug of a cowboy paired with a fullback-sized burly nightmare from hell.

Russum claimed he could see better up front, but the truth was, he didn't trust Buck alone at the controls, not that he knew how to fly this thing. His job was to sweep the area for additional bombs and, hopefully, detonate them from a safe distance. If that went well, he was to enter the city, locate ground zero, and determine whether or not the damage had been caused by the Russian ten-ton pure-fusion device. The burden of identifying what type of device had exploded in lower Manhattan fell on Russum's back. It was the job he'd trained much of his adult life to do, and he was good at it.

Wyley and Graham sat ensconced in their radiation suits, strapped into the cargo section in the rear. If, in fact, they found the air contaminated, they had air enough in their tanks for a two-hour survey. Wyley's role, as it had been in Hama, was photojournalist for the U.S. government while Graham got stuck with the grisly work of coroner and video cameraman. Graham knew that, after a nuclear detonation, there would be little he could do as a doctor beyond documenting causes of death and easing people's pain. His primary job was to help the living, but he feared there'd be little he could do that would really make any difference.

Graham sensed the helicopter banking in an uneven lurch. It jolted him, bouncing him off his seat, and instinctively he tightened his seatbelt. Below them, he saw pier fourteen race past and heard Buck signal Guardian over the intercom, "Feet dry." About that time, he felt the helicopter suddenly slow, smoothly transitioning into a stable, even hover.

Except for a bank of smog lingering above the city, lower Manhattan appeared undamaged as far as the eye could see. From their inland position hovering near pier fourteen, Graham stared out the window, gazing at countless lights and neon signs still glowing. There seemed to be nothing wrong with the city—except there was no motion.

Moments later, Graham heard Buck tell Russum, "Go to it."

Billy Ray leaned forward, rotating a handle down and forward on the floor of the helicopter. Beneath the nose of the Huey, an array of different-sized antennas pivoted toward the city, pointing down Maiden Lane. Once the antenna array was locked in position, Russum threw the power switch on the wideband RF transmitter he'd jury-rigged to the floor.

Remarkably, the Huey began to lose altitude as the heavy electrical load caused the pitch of the engines to drop and the rotors to slow. Almost immediately, Buck pulled up on the collective, bringing the Huey back into stable hover.

A digital RF power meter told Russum he was on the air, radiating thousands of watts, but from the sound of the engines alone, he had a pretty good idea his transmitter was up and running. Next, he toggled the RF SWEEP switch on his equipment. Faster than you could blink an eye, the transmitter began sweeping its output power across a wide range of radio frequencies.

For practical purposes, the coded RF signal looked like the combined, serialized outputs of every garage door opener ever made. The idea behind this RF sweep was simple enough. If there were any bombs left behind in the city that could be detonated by remote control, this powerful signal should set them off. Twenty minutes later, after transmitting millions of coded RF signals at different frequencies in different directions, Russum declared his sweep complete. If there were any bombs remaining in lower Manhattan, he couldn't detonate them with his apparatus. That much he was sure of. After Russum killed the transmitter power and stowed the antenna array, Buck dipped the Huey's nose and accelerated toward the Federal Reserve Bank.

The five-block sprint down Maiden Lane clicked off quickly in the air, detached from events on the ground.

In the rear by the cargo door, air rushed past the open side windows. Wyley hung the long lens of his Nikon digital camera out the window while Graham sat, white-knuckled, without comment. The engine screamed so loudly there was no way to communicate without the use of a headset.

Still, they had good reason to feel hopeful regarding background radiation; so far no robotic drone aircraft had detected significant levels of radioactive contamination anywhere in the city. If their measurements turned up negative around the Federal Reserve Bank, they'd be out of their rad suits in a hurry.

Running this fast, skimming the building rooftops, everything looked normal enough on the ground through Wyley's digital camera lens. At first glance, countless yellow cabs and delivery trucks lined Maiden Lane as they would any business day. Graham watched Wyley's pictures flash on a TV screen near the rear of the Huey's cargo bay. Alongside the TV, another monitor displayed green infrared images of Wyley's shots in real time. These revealed that most of the engines below were warm and still running.

Forward, Buck eased the Huey into a lurching, jerky hover over the Federal Reserve Bank, next to Liberty Tower.

Once the aircraft slowed, Graham noticed a flickering video image of the street below on a third, smaller color TV screen. The TV and videocassette recorder were being fed by an external steady-cam pod and its camera controls were located alongside the screen. With the camera pointing down at the Nassau Street intersection with Maiden Lane, the pictures looked something like blurry gun-camera footage. Graham intervened, pulling the zoom lens into a tight closeup, adjusting its focus until an enlarged image of a traffic light showed clearly on-screen. Below them, one-way traffic was stacked up in both directions at the intersection, engines running. After forty-five seconds or so, the video revealed the traffic light changing, turning green.

But nothing moved.

"This is it," Russum spoke over the intercom. "Ground zero. No doubt about it."

Everyone's eyes were drawn toward the twenty-eighth floor of what had been Liberty Tower.

Smoldering before them, filling their field of view, were the charred, red-hot remains of Liberty Tower's upper stories. Hot air currents circulating near the top of the building made it nearly impossible to stabilize the helicopter. Heat quickly penetrated their radiation suits, causing the foursome to break out into a sweat. Four stories below the building's twisted Gothic roofline, a gaping wound lay open, blown outward, exposing its scalding interior.

"Wyley," Russum said through the intercom, "I'm ready up front. Would ya launch the probe?"

"Will do." Wyley laid down his camera and picked up a bazookalike device. After arming a high-pressure air firing mechanism, he positioned one end of the tube out the cargo window, pointing it toward the blown-out hole in Liberty Tower.

"Corner apartment, twenty-eighth floor," Wyley confirmed.

"How's this angle, Wyley? Can you shoot from here?" Buck wanted to know.

"The closer, the better."

"This is as close as we're gonna get. These hot air currents could slam us into the building if we move in any closer."

"Ready in the rear."

"Fire on my mark. Three, two, one, shoot."

THUMP-pssssssshure.

As the Geiger counter projectile rifled into the building, it transmitted a burst of data to the radio receiver plugged into Russum's laptop. In an instant, ground-zero radiation levels flashed on Russum's laptop display. "Radiation levels are acceptable, reading on the high side of the safe range. Judging from what we've seen so far, in all probability, this is the result of that Russian mini-nuke. I'd stake my reputation on it. At the very least, a pure-fusion neutron bomb was detonated here. Clearly, no conventional explosion would incapacitate so many people."

Buck nodded, then slowly circled Liberty Tower.

"Any reason to check for biological contamination?"

Russum shook his head side to side. "No, not here anyway. The air's safe to breathe."

Without prompting, all four men uncovered their heads so they could see without having to peer through the small transparent window on the face of their hoods. Then, as if running on automatic, the gloves came off. Even the hot air felt good

to Graham's skin. What really mattered was that the air was
moving.

After stowing his hood and gloves, Buck flew a survey pattern over ground zero, a top-to-bottom sweep of Liberty
Tower by columns. Up front, the pilot manned a bullhorn,
hailing the building for signs of life. From the copilot's seat,
Russum manipulated the Huey's large fuselage-mounted
searchlight, illuminating each apartment interior as Wyley directed. In the rear, Wyley held his camera out the open window in the Huey's cargo bay, working his low-light lens from
one apartment to the next; Graham shot backup video using
the steady-cam.

Liberty Tower residents, all of them including the doorman, died from the blast, heat, or radiation. Considering their
close proximity to the explosion, that came as no surprise.
Mentally, the team had hoped for the best, but prepared for the
worst.

Once their survey of ground zero had been completed,
Buck rotated the Huey toward the Chase Manhattan building,
facing the side that had absorbed the brunt of the blast.

Once again hovering over the Federal Reserve Bank, Buck
slowly changed altitude, lifting his craft to the top of the
building first, then descending slowly. The vertical winds running alongside the Chase Manhattan building were reasonably
calm, the air measuring a uniform temperature, so they risked
moving in close for better visibility.

"The glass was blown in," Russum observed.

From outside the building, emergency lights were visible
in the stairwells and over the exits. Bloodstains were evident,
spattered across many interior walls. Human limbs, clothes,
and occasionally a shoe rested atop the piles of office debris.
Bodies and office furniture were scattered willy-nilly, having
been slammed at incomprehensible speeds against the building's innermost walls.

"No sign of life," Graham said.

"These people were closer than fifteen hundred feet to
ground zero and had no effective shielding," Russum reminded Graham. "Considering all these windows, no one's

alive in there. Chances are, they never knew what hit 'em. If the blast didn't kill 'em, the radiation burst most certainly did."

"Well, keep your eyes open anyway."

"I'm with'ya, Doc." Buck pulled away to a distance of one hundred feet or so, took the PA microphone, and began hailing the shattered corpse of a building over the bullhorn. "We're here to help you. If anybody is listening, if anybody can hear me, please give us a sign."

Russum knew Buck was wasting his breath, but sat quietly, purposefully saying nothing more to discourage his team.

There was no motion, no human motion anyway, no sign of life whatsoever. The stillness screamed volumes through the shattered plate glass windows.

After methodically surveying the blast side of the building from top to bottom, Buck circled around to the back side of the Chase Manhattan Bank and began flying his search pattern again, a top-to-bottom sweep of the building by columns. Up front, the commander manned the bullhorn. From the copilot's seat, Russum manipulated the searchlight, while Graham and Wyley shot documentary footage.

The first thing Graham noticed as they circled around to the back side was that the building was leaning. The supporting building structure had suffered damage from the shock wave and seemed to be leaning away from both Liberty Tower and the Federal Reserve Bank. Furniture had been overthrown by the blast, much of it hurled out the windows, but none seemed to be damaged by heat. Again, they found many offices demolished by the blast and countless cold bodies. Signs that there had once been life—bodies, blood, shoes, and clothes—were strewn about the open office spaces, but they saw no evidence of survivors, even in those offices where the windows remained intact.

Eventually, they hovered outside a large, blown-out interior space which would later be called the cloud room. Bright, sky blue walls adorned with puffy white clouds drew Graham's attention like a magnet. Something was different here. Centrally located, this room had been the children's kindergarten and nursery school. Overturned children's furniture, sleeping pads, little easels, and toys were visible from the outside, but inside, nothing moved.

After a long protracted silence, Wyley asked Russum, "Would you hold your spotlight on the far inside wall?"

Billy Ray positioned his spotlight to illuminate much of the cloud room's interior, including a bulletin board attached to the far wall. Wyley zoomed in, filling his frame with the board, and drew a sharp focus. Pictures of those precious little ones lined the lower half of the board and remained intact. Recognizing this, Wyley tripped into autodrive. Their story, the story of these children, had to survive them all and must be told. Closing in at maximum zoom on their faces, his eyes flooded with tears. Not even the isolation behind his camera could protect Wyley from their haunting images.

The children were all there. Their happy, trusting faces clearly in focus now, their names written in colored crayon below their pictures. Their names and faces came crashing down on Wyley with such an emotional force that Graham saw him stagger, then collapse on his seat. After studying Wyley's anguished expression, he turned toward the TV screen to see the top half of the board featuring children's birthday's in March and April. Gazing at their faces, Graham felt weak kneed and knotted up inside. He read the bulletin board's theme printed in large letters across the top—March winds and April showers—and it catapulted him to thoughts of his youngest daughter.

This could have been her school. He imagined the cloud room as it must have been, once filled with singing and laughter, and refused to accept the world his eyes were seeing. He'd remember their faces as if they were alive.

And he'd do whatever it took to make sure nothing like this ever happened again; not on his watch, not in his lifetime. No matter what obstacles lay before him, he would not be distracted and would not lose his resolve. Few things in life are worthy of such limitless commitment, but insofar as this imperative was concerned, there would be no compromise, no reevaluation, and no looking back. Graham knew now why he'd been born. This was his destiny. From this point forward, he was in it for the long haul and, to this end, he'd either wipe this menace off the face of the earth or die trying.

Hama changed Wyley's life forever, but it was the cloud room that changed Graham. Although the foursome didn't recognize it at the time, it was the cloud room that bound Buck, Russum, Wyley, and Graham together as one; their experience outside the cloud room forged an inseparable team, filling each man with a selfless, unspoken resolve to make damn sure this would never happen again.

Once Wyley and Graham recovered their composure, they hovered outside the cloud room an extended period, taking additional photographs from the cargo bay, and surveying as much as possible. Over and over again, Buck's voice boomed over the bullhorn, but his best efforts revealed no visible signs of life. As the crew's spirits began to sink, the optimistic tone in the commander's voice faltered. Their Geiger counter indicated life was possible; from a distance, many offices looked normal in the spring sunlight. Instinctively, Graham felt sure there must be injured people in there, yet their infrared search revealed only the cold and dead.

Apart from the Chase Manhattan Bank, Liberty Tower, and literally thousands of shattered windows, the city looked undamaged for the most part. Through it all, however, one eerie, inescapable pattern emerged time and time again: The closer they looked, the worse, the more horrific the calamity became.

A morose sense of hopelessness engulfed the crew, sapping their energy, fatiguing them beyond anything they'd anticipated. The commander's voice sounded noticeably drained over the bullhorn, almost weary; Wyley struggled to lift his long camera lens and keep it in focus. Graham gazed at the infrared video on-screen, but felt numb. More than once, he found himself staring at the TV, but not seeing the images inside the Chase Manhattan offices. If there had been survivors, if there had been children alive in there, he could have easily missed them. Graham couldn't help being drawn into the disaster and the experience was debilitating; try as he might to stay detached, there was no escaping the enormity of this human tragedy.

Finally, once their building survey was complete, Graham decided to rotate his steady-cam downward, giving a bird's-eye view of the scene in the alley below.

To his horror, untold bodies, some of them small ones, lay crumpled like rag dolls on the asphalt. Broken bodies, shattered plate glass windows, and truckloads of office equipment had been blown out of the building, scattered like toppled doll house furniture. Graham zoomed in on an overturned child's stroller, and once again, his eyes clouded over. Thinking of his daughter and wife outside Washington, he turned off the TV monitor, his hands trembling, and looked away . . . .

Dear God in heaven, we've turned these monsters loose on our children. Over the intercom, the broken sound of a muffled cry.

Recognizing this, the commander spoke. "Listen up, gentlemen. Does anyone see any reason why we shouldn't bring in our mobile SATCOM unit and S&R teams?"

"The air's okay, but we haven't tested the water," Graham cautioned, after clearing his throat.

"I'll relay that concern. Anything else?" The silence told Buck all he needed to hear, then he radioed Guardian a qualified all clear for reinforcements.

"Let's wrap it up here." The commander pushed forward. "Remember, we've still got a job to do. Cut the cameras, we're touching down on the Fed."

"Did you see . . . below us?" Graham asked over the intercom.

"Yeah, and I don't want to talk about it."

Buck eased the Huey down on the roof of the Federal Reserve Bank and reduced power.

Wyley and Graham slid the cargo door aside—its gritty rollers grinding over a dirty metal track followed by a loud *bammm!*—and felt the smog-filtered sunlight on their faces.

Somehow, from somewhere deep inside, the foursome mustered an unrelenting resolve to forge ahead. After weeks of working together, Russum recognized that he finally had his dream team. Each moved with minimum words, renewed determination, and no nonsense. Instinctively, each sensed what the others were thinking. The whole now surpassed the sum of their parts and Russum knew they were ready.

Without an exchange of words, Graham slid a box filled with plastic explosive and primacord out the cargo door to Russum. Buck lined the heavily armored roof entrance with explosive as Russum crisscrossed the door and supporting metal structure with primacord. Judging from the architectural plans, this door was going to be a challenge, so they had come prepared. Their idea was that the heat from the fast-burning primacord would weaken, or possibly cut through, the door's vaultlike structure and surrounding frame, then the explosive would fracture the rooftop assembly into pieces. This method would bring down bridges, and Buck reasoned it would most certainly bring down a door.

Once the explosive was in place, Buck distributed several detonators around the rooftop assembly and buried them in the explosive. Finally, he wired all the detonators together, then attached them to a battery-powered radio receiver. Russum looked over his work, double-checking every connection, then signaled him an okay with his first finger and thumb.

"No one in special ops coulda done it any better," Russum would later comment. "SEALs love to blow things up, and Buck's as good as they get."

The foursome piled into the chopper, then Buck sounded a loud "stand clear" warning over the bullhorn. Satisfied they'd done all they could do, Buck increased power and lifted the Huey off the roof. After giving his instruments a final once-over, he flew them around to the back side of Liberty Tower, well out of harm's way.

Graham heard Buck speak to Russum in a short directive. "Go to it."

Russum lowered his antenna array, switched on the RF power, and . . .

BOOOM!

BOOM—Boom—*boom*—boom echoed off the skyscraper walls, sounding louder inside the cargo bay than even the Huey's screaming engines.

Within twenty seconds, they were circling a smoldering, rectangular-shaped, man-made crater on the rooftop.

"Well, that wasn't so tough," Buck admitted, a little embarrassed, "but you gotta understand one thing. Demolition, especially SEAL demolition, isn't an exact science." The door was demolished; so was the door frame, and the small room which supported the door frame. Where the room had been, there was now a smoking hole.

Minutes later, they entered the building without resistance.

Graham entered the bank president's top-floor office first and found himself drawn to the center of the large meeting room. Surrounding a sixteen-foot conference table, thirteen well-dressed senior gentlemen sat expressionless, open eyed, and frozen in time. The doctor stopped by the chairman's chair at the end of the table and felt for his pulse. "His skin's cold, about room temperature." Looking down, he noticed the man's bowels had let go.

Russum followed behind Graham and allowed his eyes to roam around the room. Above the oval table, two glass chandeliers remained intact and turned on, each set in what must have been a hand-forged wrought-iron frame. The room reminded Russum of many of Wyley's still shots, only the blast must have come in at a steep angle from overhead. The windows were shattered, but overall, damage due to the blast was minimal. Portraits of the bank's former presidents still lined the walls on three sides of the room. Only two paintings were slightly askew. The fourth wall showed no evidence of damage whatsoever; its carved oak paneling was in mint condition. Had it not been for the presence of death permeating the room, the fireplace near the door would have been most inviting.

Three large trays of uneaten breakfast food were situated on the table and near the fireplace. There was coffee, orange juice, pastries, doughnuts, muffins, and one or two open cans of Coke. On the floor, a tidy pile of *Wall Street Journals* lay undisturbed.

After surveying the scene, Russum pronounced his judgment with a confident tone that eliminated any question or doubt. "Death was instantaneous."

Less than two minutes later, Graham had confirmed Russum's knee-jerk. They were beyond his help. The Federal Reserve Board of Governors was dead and nothing was going to change it.

Graham sat down in the only available seat. He dreaded the thought of what they might find in the rest of the building; still, there could be survivors below street level.

Buck walked in a few minutes later with Wyley. Hurriedly, Wyley roamed around the president's office, camera and flash in hand, documenting the scene for the sake of the Washington authorities. As Wyley's flash went off, time and time again, Buck's expression turned grim as he spoke to Russum. "Look's like you were right."

"Yeah, I'm sorry to say."

"If the windows hadn't been blown out, the smell in here would kill you."

"You get used to it," Graham told him, sighing, "but it'll only get worse."

"I'd better warn the others. Search and Rescue will need to know." Buck paused, evaluating their next move.

Russum shoved the food aside, then laid the building's floor plans across the oval table. The trio looked over his shoulder, but Wyley and Graham appeared uneasy.

"I kinda wish you hadn't done that," Wyley said.

"Done what?" Puzzled, Russum wasn't sure what Wyley was getting at.

"In a strange way, it almost seems disrespectful," Graham added.

"Yeah, it's like we're violating the belongings of the dead or something."

"I don't think they'd mind," Buck said, "and besides, if anyone was left alive in the building, they'd sure as hell want us to help 'em,"

"Well, it does feel pretty damn eerie," Russum admitted. "Like working in the morgue, I guess."

"Standing here, studying the building's layout before the open eyes of thirteen dead men, would make anyone's skin crawl," Graham observed.

"Yeah." Wyley relaxed for the first time since he'd entered

the building. He felt a bit better having heard someone else say what he was thinking.

"You know, for some reason, the situation in here reminds me of the Last Supper. For the life of me, I can't imagine why." Graham laid out his impression before the group as a diversion, something to lighten their load, if only for a moment.

"What last supper?" Buck looked perplexed.

"You know, the one in the Bible. It reminded me of that story, but I can't imagine why."

"Maybe it's the table," Russum said. "Ya know, what with the food and all."

"It's the headcount, thirteen dead men," Wyley uttered quietly. "Once Judas left the table, there were twelve."

Graham concurred. "Yeah, that's it. Twelve disciples plus Jesus. I think you're probably right."

"Makes sense to me. Now if we're good and finished with our stories of biblical prophecy come true, can we get back on the horse here for a minute?" Once again, Russum turned to the floor plans, only this time he pointed to the room labeled CENTRAL WATCH.

"Go ahead," Buck urged.

After talking about their concerns and impressions out loud, for some incomprehensible reason everyone felt better. Nothing had changed, but the thirteen open-eyed dead men didn't seem nearly so unnerving.

"Central Watch is like the nerve center for all the sensors in the building. Hundreds of security cameras feed there. If anybody's alive in this place, chances are, we can see 'em from there."

The trio agreed.

"All right, gentlemen, our work's finished here, let's stick with the plan. We'll set up our operations inside Central Watch," Buck said, ready to roll.

"Elevators working?" Russum asked his SEAL commander.

"Yep, they're golden. Four doors down the hall and on the left." Buck pointed to the small, silver-haired man at the head of the table. "Rosenberg?"

Graham nodded. "The board is dead, every one of them."

"You ID'd 'em all?"

"Yeah, I checked their wallets. Nothing we can do will change it."

Silence fell as the commander pondered the ramifications of this situation. He wasn't sure how the death of these thirteen men would impact the stock market, but he had a hunch that things would get worse before they got better. Punching PUSH TO TALK, he concluded, "I'd better inform Washington."

"Doc, we found somebody alive down here!" Buck's voice boomed over Graham's walkie-talkie. "A lady, maybe thirty, thirty-five."

Russum's eyes met Graham's from across the Central Watch room. He'd heard it too. "A live one!" He grinned ear to ear.

"How is she? What's her condition?"

"We need you here PDQ, Doc. She's in a bad way, weak and disoriented, but she's breathing. We found her collapsed on the floor here at the loading dock. From the looks of it, she tried to . . . claw her way out through the steel garage doors."

"Anyone else?"

A pause. "No one else alive, Doc. The guards are dead, all of 'em."

"Yeah, we found that here, too. They died at their posts, and as best we can tell, if anyone else is alive in the building, they've been trapped inside like caged animals. We weren't able to bypass the security system at this end. Billy Ray said it'd take an encrypted key and password to unlock the bank doors and open the place back up."

"Figures, that sounds about par for the course." A pause. "I tell you one thing. Doc. If there's folks in here that need help, we can damn sure open this place up. I can take out the steel garage door, I guarantee it."

"Excellent, I'll be right there." Graham looked at the floor plan, then cut his eyes back over to Russum. "You going to finish up here?"

"Yeah, I'm going to gather up these videotapes and move 'em to the chopper. I'll join you in the garage in ten or fifteen."

Graham picked up his map of the building, hurried out of Central Watch, and headed to the garage.

Meanwhile, Russum continued working in the surveillance center, doing his dead level best to bring the building's computerized surveillance system back on-line. Overall, the room looked much like a TV recording studio with everything of interest visible from two control consoles. From a distance, the room reminded Russum of a miniature version of the Combat Information Center he'd seen on the *Stennis*. As he had expected, the room layout consisted of three walls filled with TV screens, computers, and monitors, plus racks of video recording and playback equipment. Finally, like many organizations eager to put forward a high-tech persona, the back wall was glass so tourists who visited the Fed could see themselves on TV.

Russum's problem, however, was that the screens—all of them—were black. Somehow, someway, the software that controlled the building's surveillance cameras had gone belly up sometime since the explosion. All Russum could do was restart the surveillance control system, then wait and see if that solved the problem.

After cycling power to the workstation, he didn't have to wait long before a UNIX system log-in window appeared on-screen. Fortunately, Russum had a keen eye for this type of situation and immediately recognized the significance of the tattered yellow Post-it Note stuck alongside the monitor. The security guards had taped, and retaped, a faded, handwritten note to the monitor listing the system password and login.

Once logged on, Russum soon understood the layout and organization of the TV screens before him. The forward wall of monitors showed activity inside the bank, another smaller array of screens was wired to display the buildings surrounding the bank, another showed sidewalk activity, and a fourth set was used for selective playback. The bank interior screens were organized by floor: the bottom row revealed both inside and outside the vault, and the top row showed the top floor, including three camera feeds from Rosenberg's meeting room. As it happened, the fourth and smallest group operated much like a programmable bank of VCRs, only their control screens were displayed on the monitors, and guards selected with a mouse what they wanted to play back.

Russum saw his job as one of selecting the right cameras and sorting through the right tapes. Not only could he see what happened before, during, and after the explosion, he could survey the entire building interior from this one central location.

Starting at the bottom, below ground level, first thing Billy Ray did was search inside the building for signs of life. His first look took no more than three seconds, then he punched his radio.

"Buck, you're going to need to blow that garage door sooner than we expected."

"Talk to me, Billy Ray."

"I got the surveillance system on-line back here and we hit the jackpot. There must be thirty to fifty people in the vicinity of the vault. From the looks of it, there was a bank tour under way when the vault slammed shut."

"Roger that, Russum. Garage door is history. Graham and Wyley have the lady; they're moving her back to Central Watch. They figured she'd be safe there, in case we had to blast."

"What's the latest from Search and Rescue?"

"Good news. Based on your recommendation, the Pure-Fusion contingency plan has been fully activated. Marines are moving in to guard the Fed. Hundreds of military and reserve rescue personnel are entering lower Manhattan as we speak. They'll be here any minute. I'll signal them to stand clear of the loading dock entrance."

"FYI: I can see outside the garage door from here, Buck. Radio me and I'll confirm an all clear before you blow the door."

"Will do."

"Once the smoke's cleared, rescue vehicles are going to need the loading dock."

"Yeah, so?"

"So don't destroy it."

"Give me a little credit, Cowboy. This job'll be done with all the finesse and style of a fine artist."

"Just go a little lighter on the plastic and take down the door."

"Will do, Billy Ray." A pause. "By the way, can you see me?"

"I'm watching over your shoulder like a hawk."

Buck exaggerated his reaction, rolling his eyes for the camera. "Believe me, that's a great comfort, Cowboy."

While Buck laced the garage door with primacord, Russum searched the building for signs of life. After studying the camera's control panel for a few moments, he noticed an intriguing radio button labeled MOTION DETECTOR. After reading about the button from the help menu, he decided the security guards must arm each camera for motion detection at night, once most of the occupants left the building.

Instinctively, he decided that was his key to an automated survey of the building's interior. In one fast sequence, he depressed the MOTION DETECTOR button in the control panel, then APPLY ALL.

As he'd expected, the rooms below ground level lit up first, confirming his radio button hunch as a good idea. Soon, one of the main lobby monitors began flashing, then several more flashed on the main floor. Billy Ray's heart began to race at the prospect of finding people aboveground. He looked around the lobby; nothing. Countless dead, but no one alive, no one moving. Swiveling the lobby camera about its base, he still found nothing.

Then suddenly, monitors started flashing on the fourteenth floor, then the twelfth, thirteenth, and tenth. There could be no life there, no way, not that close to ground zero. He scanned the fourteenth floor only to see Rosenberg and his board exactly as they'd left them. Then, after studying a few more screens, he found others, all dead. On the screen labeled BULLPEN, he counted over one hundred dead in a room that looked similar to the stock room trading floor. Still, the motion detectors went off relentlessly, demanding he look at each of them and determine the reasons why. Each time a detector triggered, an alarm bell rang near Russum's ear. Instinctively, he'd pound an Alarm Cut Off switch, only to hear it clanging again within seconds. This was all wrong; technology was supposed to help, not hinder his search for survivors; the bells were driving him crazy to an extent that he couldn't search a single room without being distracted by them.

This has gotta stop, Russum thought. He turned off motion

detection, then began a meticulous, well-ordered search. He looked again, back to the main floor lobby. Almost unbelievably, each camera revealed nothing whatsoever.

After a few moments of uncluttered thought, pieces of the puzzle fell into place: Nothing human was moving, but the windows had shattered and there was an abundance of airborne debris, blowing on the wind.

His motion detector idea would have worked had the windows not been blown into the building.

Setting this mystery behind him, he focused on a set of TV monitors labeled ROOFTOP CAMERAS. Next, he selected two of them, Liberty Tower and Chase Manhattan, entered today's date, and typed in 9:45 A.M. Less than two minutes into the playback, the screen labeled LIBERTY TOWER flashed bright white.

Not surprising, Russum thought, quickly recalling that video was captured at thirty frames per second. *The events I care about occurred in less than one-thirtieth of a second anyway so this probably won't be much help after all.*

Next, he began examining individual Chase Manhattan image frames, one at a time. To his dismay, every frame that might have revealed some reflection of the fireball had been washed out, saturated white. It was as if both cameras had been blinded by the surface of the sun.

"How's she doing, Doc?" Russum wanted to know. By now, the woman had drifted off and was unconscious.

Graham looked at Wyley. He nodded and, without an exchange of words, Wyley agreed to take over. Graham moved away and outlined her situation quietly to Billy Ray. "She's hurt really bad; I think she's dying."

"How long she got?"

"A few hours, maybe a few days at most. She suffered a head wound from the blast and cuts, most probably from flying glass and debris. No flash burn, but I suspect her radiation injury is fatal. I can't know for sure without bloodwork, but her legs and clothes show signs of extensive internal bleeding. More than once, she's coughed up blood. When you put it all together, it doesn't look good for her. The hemorrhage could be due to the blast or the radiation, but I expect it's a combination of the two."

"What happened to her hands?" They were coated in dried blood; the tips of her fingers were bleeding profusely even now.

"Her blood won't clot. I couldn't stop the bleeding even with a tourniquet. There was blood all over the garage door too. Buck was right, she nearly bled to death trying to claw her way out."

There was a long, protracted silence, broken only by the commander's voice booming over the walkie-talkie.

"I'm set in the garage. The door's ready to blow."

Relieved by the distraction, Russum replied, "Give me thirty seconds; I need to get back to the control room and check the street."

Wyley and Graham moved the woman to a sheltered place inside Central Watch as Russum scanned the sidewalk and immediate area outside Buck's garage. On-screen, he saw Jon Bradley's Restaurant across the street, its windows imploded, but no motion of any sort. Most important, no rescue workers had arrived in the area, not yet. No doubt, if any search and rescue teams were within a few blocks of the bank, Buck's fiery blast would draw a crowd like moths to a flame. From the looks of the surrounding sidewalks, there were a few people wandering the streets, near the bank's public entrance, but that was well away from the blast area.

Through the dispassionate eye of the security cameras, the stone-faced people in the street looked like the living dead, walking zombies, apparently seeing death in the streets, but not feeling.

"They're most likely in shock," Graham said, looking over Billy Ray's shoulder. Some left trails of bloody discharge, one collapsed in his tracks, convulsed, then lay completely still.

"There's nothing we could have done for him," Russum lamented, picking up his walkie-talkie. "Buck, now hear this. You're all clear to blow the door."

On-screen, Graham and Russum saw Buck shoot them a thumbs-up, then he took shelter in a small enclosed room, closing the door behind him.

They saw the flash on-screen before they heard the explosion.

Once the Marines occupied the bank, civilian and military rescue teams began the slow, arduous process of removing victims from the building. Predictably, the survivors emerged first—there were hundreds of them trapped below street level—followed by the injured and the dead. Judging from the monitors in Central Watch, most of the tourists and employees trapped below ground level looked to be in the best shape, so the first wave of rescue workers focused there.

Happily, the guards who worked the night shift came to the rescue in Central Watch. First thing, they placated the bank's security system and unlocked access to the vault room beneath the street. If there was a bright spot in this horrific affair, it came in the form of joy expressed on the survivors' faces as they were escorted out of the garage into the sunshine.

Working the basement rescue operation soon became a production line affair; other than the shock and stress that comes from being locked inside a building, most of those trapped below ground level didn't know what happened topside, but nevertheless, they emerged to tell their story. Many described their experience as being trapped like an animal in a hole, some described it as suffocating, like being buried alive, but most emerged unharmed, genuinely thankful to be alive.

Once Search and Rescue took over, the foursome decided to get a view of the city from the street. Long ago, Buck had stripped down to his fatigues. For their journey, he carried along a couple of friends for the team's protection—a Beretta 9mm pistol and the H&K MP-5N submachine gun. Wyley carried his camera, Graham took a small case filled with medical equipment—gadgets mostly—and medicine, and Russum brought along his Geiger counter, water sampling kit, and black cowboy hat.

Once they walked out of the bank's garage, Russum feigned admiration for Buck's handiwork. "Nice job with the door, SEALman."

"Ya see this, Cowboy?" Sporting his I-got-it-and-you-don't grin, Buck raised his machine pistol. "It's the world's greatest submachine gun and I'm your bodyguard for this trip. I don't think you wanna upset me at this juncture."

"The man makes sense," Wyley agreed, snapping a picture of the burly SEAL, machine gun in hand. His backdrop was the smoking garage entrance to the Federal Reserve Bank. In a way, the shot felt surreal; in another, it seemed perfect, like one of the best personality shots he'd ever taken. Suddenly, an idea crystallized in the camera viewfinder before his eyes. He visualized Buck in this smoking gun bank photo on the cover of his book. Recognizing this, he made Buck put on his toughest look and fired off several more location shots. One day, if he could muster the courage to face this horror again, their experience had best-seller written all over it. As for now, his emotional wounds were fresh and they cut deep; he couldn't imagine coming back here again, even in his imagination.

Graham led the team across the street to a group of buildings, stores of some kind. Moments later, they came upon a downed sign which read JON BRADLEY'S RESTAURANT.

"Every window in the place has been shattered," Russum observed, jotting down the tempered glass type, thickness, and building location. Where the plate glass windows had been, there were gaping holes. After turning on his Geiger counter, he checked for radioactive contamination. As he'd expected, there was little difference from the measurements he'd made at ground zero. The equipment remained silent, reading on the high side of the safe range.

Walking cautiously through the restaurant's main entrance, Graham noticed some of the inside lights were still on. His eyes roamed around Jon Bradley's, surveying every detail. A young lady's body, a waitress, lay facedown, crumpled on the cold tile. Syrup and milk covered the floor. It was what Graham had expected to see, but the sight was difficult to accept.

Russum filled two small, sterile sample containers with milk and water from the kitchen as Wyley snapped off flash pictures in autodrive.

"Take a look at this." Buck pointed to the coffee machine.

Coffee had evaporated from the glass Pyrex coffeepots, leaving cracked, dry glass and smoking plastic handles on the red-hot electric eyes. He unplugged the power and continued his sweep.

Graham saw that there had been a small party going on here and brought Wyley over to shoot it. Six security guards—four men and two women—sat around a table; judging from the birthday candles on her stack of hotcakes, it must have been the brown-eyed woman's birthday. In the cool springtime air, Graham could see her hair gently blowing in the breeze. In a convoluted sort of way, the tilt of the lady's head reminded him of one of those shampoo commercials. On the table, there were five candles, a card in a pink envelope, and—Graham looked closer. A small, blue velvet–covered box . . . a diamond ring carefully tucked away inside. For a moment, he was intrigued and drew closer still, then he removed the card. This wasn't a birthday party at all; it was the brown-eyed woman's anniversary. Two of the guards had been married. Turning, he broke away, for he'd seen all he could bear.

He came to the kitchen, paused, then looked in. Miraculously, there was a carton of eggs on the counter with only two removed. Somehow, these fragile things had managed to escape the carnage. Out of the corner of his eye, Wyley's bright flash caught his attention. Once he'd captured the last of his wide-angle shots, Graham noticed he picked up an unopened pack of Lucky Strikes from behind the check-out counter, slid a five-dollar bill into the open cash register drawer, then headed for the door.

A puzzled expression crossed Graham's face. *That's odd; Wyley doesn't smoke.* After standing silent for a moment, Graham switched off the griddle, closed the cash drawer, and turned out the light.

Together, they moved on, walking out the door and across the street to the Louise Nevelson Plaza.

The few trees looked well—as New York trees go in the early spring—and the sculpture was unharmed. Below it, a small bronze plaque read SHADOWS AND FLAGS. Looking down, Graham noticed a pile of feathers amassed on the ground. He gently turned it over with a stick to find a pigeon.

Without really looking, he counted six dead pigeons within ten feet of where he stood.

No birds, or cats, or anything alive. Apart from that, every-thing's . . . He couldn't bring himself to finish his thought and walked away.

From the Louise Nevelson Plaza, facing the narrow end of the wedge-shaped Federal Reserve, Graham looked down Liberty Street toward the bank's public entrance. A few automobile horns were wailing; the smell of vomit permeated the air and four-man Marine rescue teams were feverishly working the street, removing the dead from their vehicles.

"What do you make of it?" Graham asked Buck.

"The emergency vehicles need to get in, right?"

"Yeah, but the roads are blocked."

"Yep, that's the problem. Most of what's going on here is focused on clearing the streets, removing the dead, then driving the taxis, buses, and delivery trucks onto the sidewalks out of the way. They got no place else to put 'em."

"Yeah, that makes sense. Which way do you think we should go from here?"

Buck pointed to their Huey parked near the edge of the roof on the Federal Reserve Bank. It was very nearly teetering on a perilous perch atop the cylindrical turret which marked the bank's roofline. "I think we should get the hell out. Our job's finished here."

"Mine's not, not yet anyway."

Wyley agreed, adding, "I'd like to get some shots further away from ground zero."

"That's right. I need to make a few more measurements myself. I got to verify the kill radius, and that's gonna take some walkin'."

Buck slung his machine pistol to his side and held up both hands. "Ya can't fight city hall. So which way you wanna go, Cowboy?"

Russum adjusted his black hat and surveyed the skyline. After a few moments' squinting, he commented, "It ain't so tough deciding which way to go in the chopper, with a bird's-eye view and all, only standing here on the street, I can't see nothin'."

Puzzled, Wyley asked, "What're you looking for?"

"Short buildings. I'm looking for a beeline running from Liberty Tower out over the shortest buildings we got."

"So you want to eliminate the effect of shielding when you measure the bomb's kill radius," Graham said, catching on.

"Yeah, to the extent it's possible. With buildings outta the equation, that leaves only moisture in the air to absorb the neutrons and I measured the humidity first thing after we got here."

"We could get back on the roof and scout it out, or take the chopper," Buck offered.

"The roof of the bank ain't tall enough to see squat, and I don't intend to keep us here all week looking for some optimum path. There's a lot of round-off in my business so I suggest we wing it." He surveyed the skyline one last time, then continued, "Let's head back to ground zero, then walk northeast up Nassau. Most of the buildings I can see from here look pretty short, or at least short by comparison to every other direction."

"Hold it," Graham objected. Across the street, to their immediate left, towered the Chase Manhattan Bank. Looking up, seeing the building from the street, Graham had no less reaction now than when they were hovering outside its offices and cloud room. He'd been there and didn't want to go back, not under any circumstances.

Many of the buses, taxis, and delivery trucks lining Liberty Street were still running, filled with the dead. A few had been parked on the sidewalk, but not many.

The foursome didn't talk about it; they didn't need to. Wyley took one look at the Chase Manhattan building and said it all. "I don't want to go there again, ever."

Graham agreed and led the team back toward Jon Bradley's. From there, they walked down Maiden Lane by the smoking garage door and bank employee entrance. On the Maiden Lane side of the Fed, the buildings were shorter than the bank, which had the effect of opening up the sky and letting in more light. Nothing else was any different except civilian rescue teams were working the street.

From the looks of it, telephone workers had emerged from their underground cable vaults and were lending an enormous hand on the surface. Cars and trucks were being driven onto the sidewalks there too, and the dead were being bagged and carried to the bank's loading dock, but the combination of civilian volunteers and additional sunlight made the northeast side seem brighter.

Along their way, the foursome helped the civilians clear Maiden Lane. Graham examined the bodies for signs of life while Wyley photographed their faces and license plates. Exposed out in the open, less than one block from ground zero, there were no survivors. Once they'd done all they could do, Buck and Russum gently repositioned each dead driver away from their horn and cut off their engine. The net result was that the city seemed a little quieter, maybe a little more humane.

At least it did for a block or so. Once the four turned northeast on Nassau Street, they came up on a dazed, well-dressed man in a soiled white shirt, weaving in and out of the stalled traffic, wandering aimlessly down the middle of the street. His manner clearly indicated he was very ill.

Russum yelled to the man to draw his attention, but got no response.

Without discussion, the four men maneuvered around the survivor, surrounding him, closing off any possible escape route. He offered no resistance and made no threatening moves. He simply stopped where he stood, and staggered slightly.

Graham studied the man's face as they closed in. He was middle-aged, but his skin looked like it belonged to someone much older; purple bruises marked his face and hands; dark circles surrounded his eyes. From the looks of his dried skin, it appeared he was suffering from dehydration. Even upwind, from a distance of a full car length, the man stunk of vomit. What was most telling were his eyes; they showed no sign of life whatsoever—his pupils unresponsive to light, unfocused, fixed in a distant gaze.

"Can you hear me?" Graham passed his hand in front of the man's eyes. No blinking, no reaction at all.

"Like the lady in the bank," Buck observed.

"Yeah," Graham said softly. "Much the same. Radiation sickness and shock."

Buck checked his wallet. His identification showed he had been an independent broker on the floor of the New York Stock Exchange.

Buck radioed for a stretcher team and Graham gave him an injection to help him sleep. Wyley photographed the man's injuries while Russum studied his map of lower Manhattan. Less than five minutes later, after calculating a good estimate of the distance from ground zero to the New York Stock Exchange, Russum surmised the crux of the survivor's situation.

"Wall Street's well inside the dead zone. The radiation footprint covered roughly eighty city blocks."

Reluctantly, Graham agreed with his conclusion.

Within twenty-four hours, the tabloid press would designate this survivor, and thousands more like him, New York's "walking dead."

As Russum had determined, people immediately outside the bomb's drop-dead kill radius—including everyone on the floor of the New York Stock Exchange—received a lethal, though not immediately incapacitating, dose of radiation. Brokers suffered severe physical distress much like patients undergoing chemotherapy treatment for cancer; they felt miserable and over the next several days their endurance would be reduced to nil until their final decline. Although it wasn't widely discussed for some time, the vast majority of the walking wounded brokers were doomed to die.

In that fraction of a second, over ninety-eight thousand men and women, most of them thirty to forty years old, were thrust into the final winter of their life. Their days were numbered and many among them wouldn't live to see the stock market reopen several weeks later. Of those who did, precious few would see the new year.

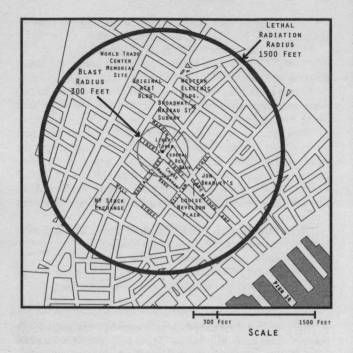

From day one, emergency medical personnel on the scene reported these people looked as though they had been subjected to megadoses of debilitating radiation and chemotherapy—potentially lethal poisons that destroy the body's immune system and the blood's ability to clot.

Resuming their walk up Nassau Street, the stench of bloody bowel movements and vomit suddenly reeked so strongly there was no escaping it. Graham felt dizzy, as if he were caught up in a cyclone, his head whirling around and around. A few moments later, all four men dropped to their knees and puked their guts out on the sidewalk. Oddly enough, when they were all done, they felt better and the smell didn't bother them as much. It was as if they'd paid their dues, and for the first time, they felt like they were part of it, at one with the city.

Once the four had regained their equilibrium, Graham's first reaction was to turn around and go back. After surveying the skyline, Russum suggested walking upwind, well clear of the stench.

"On the other hand," Graham reflected, "a stench like that could lead us to people in trouble, and after all, that's what I'm here for."

"Do what you have to do," Russum said quietly.

Buck and Wyley agreed, then, much to their chagrin, Graham tracked the stench straight to the entrance of the Broadway/Nassau Street subway.

From street level, looking down the stairwell into the bowels of the New York subway, Graham felt the full weight of the Financial District genocide crashing down on his shoulders. Tears welled up in his eyes; he couldn't breathe and felt a terrible emptiness such as he had never known, an ache in his soul he couldn't escape.

He looked back at Wyley, but he couldn't find the words. Below him, the subway was packed to overflow capacity with the dead and dying, stacked almost floor to ceiling, bodies heaped on top of bodies at the bottom of the stairwell. From what he could see, it looked as if people had crawled over each other in a futile, desperate attempt to reach the subway train.

Reaching deep within himself, somehow Graham found the courage and resolve to do what must be done. He tightly gripped the handrail, his knuckles white, his complexion ashen. As he descended the stairs, his head again felt light, spinning, overwhelmed by the abhorrent stink of involuntary bowel movements, urine, and vomit. In the dim light below, the stairwell looked like a clogged sewer pipe packed tight with bodies. This day had been the longest of his life and still he had to muster the strength to search for the living. In his heart, there was no alternative. He couldn't live with himself if he did otherwise.

Now near the bottom of the stairs, Graham paused, staring glassy-eyed and motionless, his senses overwhelmed by the vision stretching out before him. Transfixed by this endless, twisted logjam of corpses, pondering this calamity, he wondered how mankind had come to this.

And then he heard that sound: a faint, muffled cry.

"Mom-meeee."

It was more of a whimper really, distinctively female; then he heard it again.

"Mom-meeee."

It was that sound that flooded Graham's body with adrenaline and filled his heart with an unrelenting resolve. Those cries from the pit would not go unanswered.

Then there was a groan; female . . . older . . . "Katie," the voice said. "Katie, I'm here, baby."

The little girl's name is Katie and her mother, her mother must be alive! She's gotta be!

"Listen up!" Graham shouted. "A woman and her daughter are alive down here. They're trapped. We've got to help them!"

The trio came bounding down the steps and didn't ask questions. They arrived in time to hear the lady's tender cries, punctuated by the sound of a distinctly male, anguished groan.

"It sounds as if people below are suffocating," Graham said quietly. "They're retching on each other, running out of air."

"Mom-mee . . ." Katie's voice sounded weaker this time, as if she were fading away.

But every man heard it, and it was the sound of that faint little voice which drove the four men forward like a steamroller plowing downhill. There was no discussion, no distraction, and no alternative. Pairing off in twos, they wouldn't slow down from this point forward until they found that little girl and her mother.

With the first body lift, Graham felt he and Russum were working with the strength of forty men. He'd never experienced anything like it. Wyley put down his camera and joined Buck hauling bodies up the left-hand side of the steps. Graham and Russum moved full adult bodies, mostly male, up the subway stairs and out onto the street. If they'd taken the time to analyze their situation, they would have never started. An objective observer would have described their Herculean feat of strength as absolutely unbelievable, like Samson bringing down the temple.

Four adult men did the legwork of forty in half the time without a word.

Within fifteen minutes, bodies lined the street and subway stairwell. Then Buck and Russum heard Katie's cry again and, sensing she was growing weaker, they moved like men possessed.

Graham and Wyley joined forces hauling bodies up the steps, while Buck and Russum ran up and down the stairs as singles, corpses flung on their backs.

After twenty more minutes of sprinting the steps, the men were exhausted. Graham's arms shook and his legs trembled; still every man kept going, peeling the corpse wall back one body at a time. The subway was filled with hundreds, maybe thousands of dead. Graham couldn't know how many, and they couldn't save them all, but they could save that little girl and her mom.

And then it happened. Graham climbed to the top of the body heap and called, "Katie, Katie, can you hear me?" This time around, Wyley found the courage to join him.

Their eyes scanned the endless expanse of bodies stretched out before them under the overhead lights of the subway station. They looked and looked, carefully searching for some sign of motion, any sign of motion.

And then, "I want my mommy."

Graham's breathing quickened. Katie's voice was close. Tunnels could play havoc with sound, but he would have sworn she was close enough to reach out and touch.

"Katie, baby. Mommy's here."

That voice, it had to be close too. She sounded as if he were on top of her!

Alone, with a strength he had never known, Graham single-handedly slid a corpse from the top of the heap and placed it on the steps. Buck, Wyley, and Russum joined him in a huddle. "She's close, real close. We must be nearly on top of them."

The three men's eyes blazed with renewed vigor and hope. Buck shouldered a corpse up the stairs; Russum followed shouldering another; Wyley dragged his by the neck.

One more layer down and Graham called out, "Katie, Katie, can you hear me? Where are you?"

He saw something move toward the outside edge of the heap. Four little fingers wiggled only a few yards from Graham's outstretched arm. Then he saw Katie's hand; she was wedged between two dead adult men, but she was moving.

"Katie, your mommy. Where's your mommy?"

Katie's mother spoke for herself, her voice sounding stronger now. "You must be close; I feel as if you're right above me."

He was. Four layers of bodies down and four feet forward, Katie's mother lay facing sideways, her head up. Within two minutes, Mrs. Mary Marshall and her daughter, Katie, were gently lifted from their tomb. Tears filling their eyes, Katie clung to her mother as if she'd never let go.

Buck carried the pair up the stairs, gently placed them on the grass, then broke down on his knees and bawled like a baby. His breathing was staggered; he didn't know what had come over him, but he couldn't stop crying.

Russum helped his friend up, his own eyes tearing. Graham looked after the ladies as Wyley picked up his camera to document the occasion. Out of respect, he waited till Buck's tears had faded, for it goes without saying that SEALs, especially SEAL commanders, don't cry.

Later, back in Washington, Mary and her daughter would describe their four saviors as angels to the press. "They were our gifts from God," she would say tearfully. And she described her ascent with Commander Buck Harrison up the corpse-lined stairs like being raised from the dead. On this occasion, in light of her hopeless situation, even the most ardent skeptics kept their irreverent mouths shut. During their trip home, it was learned that Mary worked at the Chase Manhattan Bank. She'd been late to work that morning because of train delays and, as it happened, they'd gotten off the train only minutes after detonation; seconds after approaching the subway stairs, they were consumed by the rush of the crowd, swept up, then buried by a massive influx, a literal avalanche of flesh.

Once Graham had stabilized Mary and Katie, Buck signaled the Hawkeye for the last time. "We've got two live ones here and we're coming home."

CHAPTER SIXTEEN

The Aftermath
Thursday, Mar. 18, 8:55 P.M.
New York Federal Reserve Bank

Once Mary and Katie were safely strapped into the Huey's cargo bay, Buck spun up both turbine engines and engaged the rotor, stabilizing the craft. Meanwhile, down below in Central Watch, Russum and Wyley packed up videotape recordings of the bombing for further analysis back in D.C. After both men headed to the roof, Graham turned off the lights and they flew away, leaving behind a large contingent of Marines and telephone workers to finish the cleanup job.

From the air, things didn't look so bad as on the ground. You had to get down there and wallow in it, move among the dead to really experience how bad things were. For the foursome, one pattern repeated itself time and time again throughout the disaster. The closer they looked, the more vividly real and terrifying the New York bombing became.

This was not war. Nothing was glorified, no sacred cause was made holy; a lot of innocent people died—horribly. Some walked into the sea, some suffocated underground, others died in their tracks. Of those who remained alive, most wandered aimlessly about the surface, vomiting, looking for a place to die.

"Did you know much about New York before this?" Graham asked Wyley on their hop back to D.C.

"No, not really. I only knew New York from the movies, TV, and books. It seemed like everything you heard about New York was always big, overblown, or rude. I don't know, it's like they worship money and aren't happy unless they're pushing some moral limit."

"Yeah, I guess people are people everywhere, but New York seems to have more than its share of cold, greedy characters. Still, to be fair, they have to act that way to survive. It's like they trade away part of their humanity to live in the city. You know, before we came here, I had trouble visualizing it, all those buildings and nobody left alive. All those people. It's unthinkable even now, but I'll never forget it."

"That's the way it was in Hama, Graham. That's what I tried to tell you."

"Yeah, I know, I looked at your pictures and all, but somehow, they didn't connect. I didn't feel anything; it's nothing like being there. I don't know, maybe I had to learn it the hard way for myself. The whole thing's like my worst nightmare come true, it's unimaginable; it's unthinkable, so I chose not to think about it. Still, I'd rather remember the dead, especially the little children, like they were alive, the way they were, I mean."

"I remember my mother's face when she died," Wyley lamented. "Her eyes turned distant and I could almost sense her soul leaving her body."

"Yeah, but you don't want to remember her the way she looked when she died. You want to remember how she was when she was alive."

Wyley agreed, then shifted the topic to his favorite subject, photography. "You know, I've been giving a lot of thought to these still shots."

"What do you mean?"

"Stills don't convey the message; they don't telegraph the

horror because they look, well, like everything's too normal. I'll bet I've got a hundred shots of taxis lining the street, taken from every conceivable angle. None of 'em work, none of 'em convey the horror. It's like you said. They don't connect. You can't tell their engines are running and nothing's moving; you can't watch the traffic lights changing, you can't hear the horns, and really, you can't see that the people don't move. Still shots don't capture the experience; they document it, but they don't convey the feelings or touch your heart. Anyway, we're going to need your videotape more than ever. It captures the bizarre, something's-wrong-here feeling of the whole situation."

Graham nodded understanding, then Wyley stubbed out his cigarette. Judging from his squinting and red eyes, cigarette smoke did a number on his contacts.

"I didn't know you smoked."

"I don't; well, I haven't for years, but today provided some damn good motivation."

"The lights on Capitol Hill are burning late tonight." Russum spoke quietly to the airline stewardess.

Glancing out the window, she agreed then whispered, "The airphone's for you, sir. It's the New York chief of police."

Russum lifted the handset and, after a few seconds of conversation, the call had his undivided attention. "That sounds suspicious to me too, Chief. Give me a second. I gotta write this down. What's the name again? His alias, I mean."

"Trevor, Trevor Stevens."

"Yep, got it. Five one-way tickets to Boston, all departing today, each for a different time. I'd say Mr. Stevens wanted to get out of town today, no matter what."

"That's why we flagged him. We've distributed pictures of your suspect and have officers staked out all over the station. If he boards any train heading outta New York, we'll get him."

"He came in through Canada. My money says he's going out the same way."

"You're probably right."

"We'll alert the Canadian border patrol immediately. By the way, how'd your people pick up on this so fast?"

"Amtrak cooperated, computers did most of the work, and we just got lucky."

"Have they found anything else?"

"Not yet, but they will."

But Hakim had already left the city and was heading south, bound for New Orleans. Ultimately, with the help of bin Laden's al Qaeda network, he'd find his passport to freedom across the Mexican border, but his departure would not go without notice.

Encapsulating the structural damage, the blast from the ten-ton explosive force blew out every window on the twenty-eighth floor of the Liberty Tower and then some. Diagonally across the street, the blast wave focused on the Liberty and Nassau Street fronts of the Chase Manhattan Bank. Rocked by the shock wave, the structure reeled over like a green sapling, then sprung back, nearly righting itself. Stressed beyond its elastic limits, permanently deformed, its topmost story swayed a staggering arc from vertical, then returned to a slumped, windblown angle. Weeks later, architects would characterize the building as leaning like a great pine tree after being blown in a single direction by hurricane force winds. Looking up the corner bead of the building from the intersection of Nassau and Liberty Streets, the Chase Manhattan Bank building looked irreparably bent, bowed like a buckled I-beam.

Normally skyscrapers, like trees, depend on each other to break up the wind. Tragically on this occasion, the Chase Manhattan Bank absorbed the direct brunt of the ten-ton blast broadside, without advantage of a buffer.

Architects described the Chase Manhattan building as having taken the brunt of the blast on the chin. Glass on its two forward fronts caved in, glass on the backside walls blew out. Inside, people not killed immediately by radiation were, more often than not, decapitated by rocketlike shards of glass flying through the air at speeds of over two hundred miles an hour.

As the first tidal wave of neutrons smashed through the roof of the Federal Reserve Bank, unshielded organic life inside the building ceased to exist. Being closest to the radiation source, the people on the top floor—including Jonathan Rosenberg, the president of the New York Fed, and the Federal Reserve Board of Governors—were among the first to die. Mercifully, with little shielding from the roof and radiation doses in excess of five thousand rems, the group never heard the glass-shattering explosion which followed less than one second later.

But motion sensors feeding the bank's alarm system detected the shock wave before the earth tremors subsided. The security system tripped automatically, even as the security officers collapsed facedown at their stations. Metal doors clanged shut, steel garage doors slammed down hard, sealing off the auto entrance, exits locked all around the building, and the ninety-ton vault door closed.

Weeks later, when the New York mayor was struggling to cast a positive light on this tragic situation, he publicly stated that not an ounce of gold turned up missing during the unfortunate mishap. At the same time, he failed to mention that everyone with access to the gold—except those trapped below ground level—was either dead or incapacitated. Over twelve hundred people died that Thursday morning in the Fed alone; all totaled, nearly one hundred thousand individuals from the Financial District would die within a span of nine months.

Down the street at the stock exchange, the shock wave shattered the large glass windows alongside the public entrance on Broad Street. Neutrons bounced around inside of the building like billiard balls on a pool table, most coming to rest in the bone and soft tissues of the brokers, pages, and supervisors on the stock exchange floor. The electronics that supported the trading floor frenzy continued running, ready to trade, but the brokers fell silent at 9:46 that morning.

That day, the stock market closed early.

Two weeks later, government scientists and investigators would report that death varied as a function of two variables: distance from ground zero and shielding. Effectively, the more stone, earth, and water between the victim and ground zero, the better their chance for survival. It was an interesting analysis, but it really didn't get them anywhere. Who cared that death on such an enormous scale as this could be described mathematically?

Operating beneath the street, telephone and city sewer workers near the blast weren't harmed at all. Shielded by water-filled duct work, earth, and rock, workers in the city's cable vaults were among the first to witness the death and destruction overhead. As Wyley and Graham's documentary footage would later reveal, these telephone and sewer workers became the first in a long succession of unsung heroes digging out of the aftermath.

CHAPTER SEVENTEEN

Fear of Reprisal
Friday, Mar. 19, 11:10 A.M.
Onboard a civilian airline
En route to Syria

"Take a look at this." Graham showed Russum the *Washington Post* headline.

Manhattan's Nuclear Nightmare— Untold Thousands Dead and Dying

"Unbelievable how fast they pulled it all together."

"This story's plastered across every newsstand and tabloid from coast to coast. Even my internet search pulled up over ten thousand hits. The *National Enquirer*'s talking about New York's walking dead. The *Star*'s going on about mutants and zombies."

"It's like a flashback to those mutant movies made after World War Two," Buck said.

"Humanity's really come a long way," Wyley mumbled sarcastically.

"You've got to give 'em credit for one thing."

"What's that?" Wyley, Graham, and Buck raised a skeptical eye.

"The press correlated similarities between Hama and the New York bombing almost as quickly as we did."

"Yeah, well, the mass graves outside Hama don't seem so far away anymore, do they?" Wyley pinged his buddy.

"It's a small world," Graham agreed.

"Gettin' smaller every damn day," Buck added.

"I guess you heard that the evening news has expanded to an hour?" Graham asked Wyley.

"Yeah, I picked up on that in the morning paper."

"Then you've heard Hama's not a ten-second sound bite anymore." Graham directed his comment to Wyley, gracefully acknowledging he'd been right all along.

"It's a new ball game, gentlemen," Buck said. "The rules changed overnight."

"And the stakes shot through the roof," Russum agreed. "Everyone in the United States from the president on down has a stake in this now."

"It shocked everyone at first, but now that the shock's worn off, everyone I talked to is mad as hell," Buck continued. "From what I've seen in the old newsreels, it musta been something like this after the Japanese bombed Pearl Harbor."

"I don't know, Buck," Graham cautioned. "Pearl Harbor may have united us as a nation back then, but it sent us scrambling. We lost the Pacific Fleet and didn't have a leg left to stand on."

"We may be down, but we're not out." Buck was adamant on this point.

"Taking out the Fed was bad enough," Graham said quietly, "but nuclear terrorism in our own back yard makes it personal. It's one thing to bomb an American embassy in some place no one ever heard of, quite another to nuke the world's premier financial institution on American soil." The group unanimously agreed, then after a silent, protracted pause, the doctor concluded. "I don't know why this kind of thing hasn't happened before now."

"Fear of reprisal." Buck's tone was even, devoid of emotion and matter of fact. "You don't have to be a rocket scientist to figure that one out, Doc. Someone, or some renegade outfit, did this because they thought they could strike at the heart of our country and get away with it. They think we're weak; they think we'll sit back and take it, but mark my words, gentlemen. These people are wrong."

PART THREE

Urgent Fury

CHAPTER EIGHTEEN

Your Own Risk
Sunday, Mar. 21, 11:25 A.M.
Damascus

"We are eager to cooperate with our American friends," the ambassador opened. "Syria had nothing to do with the bombing and we are anxious to assist you in any way possible."

"So, let's cut to the crux, Mr. Ambassador." Buck looked like a new person, clean-cut and freshly shaven in his business suit and tie. "After the bomb went off in New York, the political roadblocks getting into Hama seem to have come down overnight."

"Yes, that is correct."

"Do you know anything else about it?"

"Come if you must, but enter at your own risk. As we've said from the start, your security on Syrian soil remains a very real concern to President Assad. We'll provide you protection as long as you choose to stay in Syria, but as I'm sure you know, our first-line troops are extended across the Turkish border. You may have heard, President Assad's personal secretary was kidnapped, tortured, and ultimately murdered by the Muslim Brotherhood only six weeks ago, within sight of our capital."

Buck considered the comment for a second, trying to read between the lines, then decided to just get to it. "Please be clear with your point, Mr. Ambassador. What's that got to do with us?"

"The twelve-man security unit protecting Assad's secretary was decimated during the attack. Four were killed during the kidnapping, their vehicle riddled with armor-piercing rounds and large-caliber machine-gun fire; three others were injured when their vehicle was hit by a shoulder-launched missile. The attack was timed like clockwork, more professional than anything we've seen in recent years. The rebels suddenly appeared out of nowhere, captured the secretary, then vanished into thin air before reinforcements could arrive. Our people were outgunned, outnumbered, and outsmarted."

Buck looked away; he'd heard similar stories from other countries in the Middle East. "What a terrible waste."

"That is so, my friend, but this is the truth of our situation. Ruthless brutality rules here and this is what we have tried to tell your government. Your lives will be in danger as long as you are on Syrian soil."

"So what arrangements have been made for our security?"

The corpulent ambassador rubbed his soft face thoughtfully, all the while measuring the man and his three colleagues. Against his better judgment, he decided to speak plainly. "The squad which once protected Assad's secretary has been restored to full strength and is now responsible for your security."

"The hell you say."

Ticket to Nowhere
Sunday, Mar. 21, 11:55 A.M.
Gas station near the Mexican border
Somewhere outside Del Rio, Texas

Hakim stepped off the bus onto the dusty asphalt, squinting in the bright Texas sun. Stretching out before him, an endless expanse of flatland conveyed the inescapable, desolate feeling of being stuck out in the middle of nowhere. High overhead, an infinite sky blanketed the featureless terrain like a canopy. To his right, the tallest thing on the horizon was a perfectly straight row of power poles that disappeared where the sky met the earth. To his left, the run of power poles continued, vanishing into the horizon, punctuated by a single rusting water tower far off in the distance. *This must be the place,* he thought, *power poles, water tower, and one lonely gas station.*

Scanning the landscape, Hakim took a moment to take in the fleeting lushness of a southern Texas spring. Green grasses and flowers adorned the flatland as far as his eyes could see.

After double-checking the sign, the gray-haired gentleman nodded to the driver, convinced this was it. With suitcase in hand, he entered the station and approached the wrinkled old man behind the counter.

"Howdy, stranger. Can I help you?" Hakim heard the station attendant ask. "You look a little outta place."

"That may be so, but I've traveled a great distance to get here."

"You gotta be kiddin'."

"No, I have family here."

"Really? Who?" The station attendant studied Hakim's gray hair and face carefully, then, in the filtered sunlight, he noticed the man's eyes looked younger than his skin. They shifted quickly, uneasily, constantly scanning the room. "You don't look like anyone I know, and I know most everyone."

"Jed Fassad."

"Come again?"

"Jed Fassad. I was told he is the manager here."

"No, I am the manager. I have always been the manager."

Almost instantly, the tension disappeared around Hakim's mouth. His appearance subtly transformed, his posture was now erect. "God is great."

"Yes. Yes he is. I have been expecting you. If you'd like to wash up, the rest room's out back."

After removing his makeup, Hakim cut a markedly striking figure when he again entered the front office. Sharp, angular features, dark eyes, black hair—handsome by no stretch of the imagination.

After downing a Texas-sized soft drink and sandwich, Hakim reviewed the station manager's plans for their border crossing. The manager was also a fishing guide in the area and explained that they would be less likely to arouse suspicion at the border if their purpose was obvious. Pleased with the fishing deception, Hakim went outside and looked over the old pickup truck that would carry them across the border. The truck wasn't much to look at, but the manager claimed it'd been well maintained and ran like a top.

But that wasn't enough for Hakim. He needed to see it for himself. Lifting the hood, he was pleased to see the engine appeared spotless, as if it had been recently steam-cleaned. After checking the oil, water, and the age of the battery, he cranked it and watched the temperature and oil pressure gauges rise to their normal operating range. Five minutes later, they leveled off and stayed there. Finally, he checked the air in the spare, then loaded the manager's fishing tackle, two life preservers, and a paddle into the truck. Satisfied, he had one thing left to do so he returned to the front office and asked one final question.

"Do you have internet access from here?"

"Our ole computer's out back," the manager said.

Moments later, both men entered a small windowless room which reeked of hydraulic fluid.

Hakim believed he knew the answer before he asked, but he asked anyway. "Do you have any picture software installed?"

"Naugh, none that I know of."

Hakim grimaced, recognizing the computer as old and already low on disk space. Carefully lifting his camera from the suitcase, he placed it gently on the table.

Surveying the back side of the computer, he quickly found the special camera port he'd been looking for. Without wasting motion, he ran a cable from his camera and plugged it into the computer. Less than two minutes later, Hakim had downloaded a dozen pictures into a folder named NEW YORK. As soon as his folder was uploaded to an internet mail server, Hakim disconnected this camera and began taking screen shots—pictures of windows on the screen. After each shot, he'd print it out then delete the file. Three pictures later, with the precision of a laser printer, the methodical man recorded a precise set of instructions which the station manager was to follow when conditions were right—once the stock exchange reopened in New Jersey. The pending move had been reported in the news and Hakim intended to take full advantage of it. Once satisfied, he removed his files, deleted the log and history files, then powered down the whole thing.

After meticulously reviewing every detail, the manager powered the computer back on and executed Hakim's instructions from start to finish on an empty dummy file. In effect, the manager played back his instructions line by line, convincing

Hakim that he fully understood. Without hesitation or praise, the terrorist nodded approval, then pulled his makeup kit out of his suitcase. Twenty minutes later, he added the crowning touch to his disguise with a can of costume paint for his hair. Once his now familiar drill was through, Hakim emerged into the bright Texas sun, a gray-haired man looking thirty years older.

When he entered the front office, the station manager commented, "I don't think your own mother would know you."

Hakim's expression remained unchanged. "You are correct. She would not. My mother was killed by American bombs during the Gulf War, along with my father. I have been told that I was found wandering in the debris."

"I'm very sorry, I didn't know." The manager looked down, wishing he had not said anything, but then something crossed his mind he felt he should say. "Their deaths have been avenged, my friend. You have seen to that, and they would be proud."

"Allah be praised."

Later that afternoon, after the manager had Hakim's visa in order, the manager's wife showed up to pull her shift at the station. Once the manager had arranged for their fishing licenses and motel, both men headed south, bass boat in tow, bound for the border.

Claiming Credit
Monday, Mar. 22, 2:35 P.M.
Washington, D.C.

"But no one has claimed responsibility, Mr. President."

The president of the United States gazed across the sea of reporters, seemingly stoic in his resolve to speak calmly. "Yes, to my knowledge, that is true, but this type of situation is not without precedence. As many of you know, bin Laden was linked to the World Trade Center bombing seventeen years ago, back in 1993. Then, five years later, his terrorist organization bombed two American embassies in Africa, killing nearly two hundred and fifty people. Finally, following 9/11, we went after them."

"Bin Laden is said to be ill, Mr. President; sources once

closest to him claim he's been dead for years, but his protégé and organization live on."

The president nodded to the reporter, clearly signaling that he was aware of bin Laden's alleged demise.

"Are you saying bin Laden's organization is behind the bombing?" the reporter continued.

"No, I'm not saying that at all, but even if we did believe it, I wouldn't state that publicly at this juncture. What I said was that this type of situation is not without precedence, and as a result, our law enforcement, special forces, and intelligence communities have learned a great deal from previous experience. Our response was formidable back in 2003, and we've had time to practice since then and get it right. Our Counterterrorist Center operates out of Langley and it's the best organization of its type in the world.

"Bin Laden has moved against New York's Financial District before; that much we know is true. He was indicted for masterminding the bombings of two U.S. embassies in Kenya and Tanzania, that, too, is a matter of public record, but the fact is, there are hundreds of terrorist organizations worldwide pitted against us today. There are a lot of people out there who don't like us, and they don't play by our rules. Our people in the Counterterrorist Center monitor these organizations around the clock, twenty-four hours a day. Every government agency that can bring something to the table is involved with this investigation. The FBI, CIA, local law enforcement, special forces, even the Treasury Department's involved. The outrage and upwelling of support across the globe has been almost unbelievable. Friendly governments around the world have offered their unequivocal support for tracking down these faceless cowards and bringing them to justice. There's even been some discussion among our allies about declaring a world war on terrorism. It'll take some time, but we may come to that."

"You believe, then, that there was more than one person behind the New York bombing?"

"I do. No one person operating alone could have done this." The president scanned the room. "Use your own judgment."

"So what do you intend to do?"

"I'm not at liberty to say what we'll do; we don't know who's behind this atrocity, but we'll find out, and once we do, we'll evaluate our options. Let me assure you, the fiends behind this outrage will be found. The free world will not rest until these vermin are brought to justice. Even now, our people are following up leads from all over the world. As president, it's my job to represent all the people of the United States, and the American people are outraged by this callous act of cowardice. As president of the United States, I vow that we will hunt these terrorists to the ends of the earth.

"It's a small world; there are only so many places to hide, and we'll be there, relentless, moving against our enemies with an urgent fury not seen since the Iraq war. I have instructed every branch of government to cooperate in this matter, the resources of the United States government are fully committed to this end, and privately, I've been informed that law enforcement organizations around the world have mounted a global campaign against every known terrorist leader on the face of the earth."

"What do they intend to do?"

"I can't speak for our allies."

"As I understand it, Mr. President, the British prime minister has been quoted as saying that they intend to wipe them off the face of the earth regardless of what we do."

The president smiled slightly. "No one wants something like this happening in their own back yard."

"How could something like this have ever happened in the first place?"

"When the time is right, we will tell you."

"With all due respect, Mr. President, what do you mean, 'when the time is right'?"

"Once we know how it happened and our people are out of danger, we will tell you." The president paused, then acknowledged a senior reporter near the front.

"Is it true that a Russian neutron bomb similar to the one detonated in New York was recently analyzed at Los Alamos?"

The president dropped his facade, looking a bit shocked by the question. Still, Los Alamos was a big place and leaks were inevitable in situations such as this.

"A Russian neutron bomb of extraordinary design was recently analyzed at Los Alamos, that much is true, but it has not been detonated. We're reverse-engineering the weapon now with the willing assistance of the Russians. We have not confirmed and frankly, at this early stage of our investigation, we don't know if this bomb was similar to the one detonated in New York. We're exploring this possibility and many others as well. More than this, no one can say."

"What about Wall Street? When will it open again?"

"That question is being evaluated as we speak. Repair of the New York Stock Exchange will get under way this week, but the exact date it will reopen is still in the planning stages. Fortunately for us all, New York's financial records remained intact after the blast, and in the interim, Wall Street operations have been moved to New Jersey. As most of you know, our Federal Reserve Board is already back in business, navigating these uncharted waters with acting chairman Epstein at the helm. Every banking region of the country is back in operation, including New York. They're not operating out of the Fed's main office, but at their secure East Rutherford facility, thirteen miles away in New Jersey."

The president cupped one hand over his ear, then raised the other as if to signal, *One moment, please.* After taking his cue through a small, nearly invisible earphone, the president announced, "Something unexpected's come up back at the White House and requires my immediate attention. There's time for one more question, then I must go." The president acknowledged the patient hand of a reporter near the back of the room.

"What role will the military play in our global pursuit of these terrorists?"

"That depends largely on the situations we encounter along the way. The details are still being worked out, but in principle, their role will be largely intelligence collection, covert surveillance, and execution. They'll help us find these fiends, and they could play a role in bringing them to justice. Following advice from the Joint Chiefs of Staff, I've escalated the defense readiness condition for all United States forces to

DEFCON Three. All leave has been cancelled, all forces have been recalled and they're on standby, awaiting further orders. Please, I ask that you make no mistake regarding our response to this unprovoked nuclear attack against the American mainland. We, the people of the United States and freedom-loving people around the world, consider the bombing of New York City a despicable, calculated act of war—and that's all I've got to say."

I Still Can't Believe It
Tuesday, Mar. 23, 12:14 P.M.
Lunch on the *Yorktown*

"Attention. This is the captain speaking." The intercom rang to life inside the *Yorktown*'s wardroom. "Effective immediately, all leave has been cancelled. Our orders are to resupply, take on additional provisions for an extended tour, and complete our sea trial posthaste. That is all."

"I can't believe it," Eion Macke exclaimed, his countdown to on-shore bliss put on indefinite hold.

"Don't take it too hard," Dr. Pappasongas said in a supportive tone. "In light of what's happened, we got off pretty easy. I don't know if you heard, but one of the junior officers had a father who worked in Manhattan. They don't know if he's alive or dead, but it doesn't look good so far."

"I hope he's all right." Eion sighed, reflecting on his own parents' situation. "Ya know, most of my family's in Texas, about a thousand miles away."

"Really? I've never lived in Texas. Tell me about it. What's it like?"

"It's so big, it's like its own country. Some parts of it are beautiful. I love the green, rolling hills around Austin in the spring, but in the panhandle, where I lived, springtime means dust season. My theory is that the whole world turns green in the spring except the panhandle of Texas. Springtime brings tornadoes and dust storms you wouldn't believe. Dust so fine you can't escape it. It comes through the windows, piles up on your windowsills, sandblasts your car, and gets into your sheets. At night, it gets in your mouth when you sleep. Take a shower and you still feel gritty. Nothing I can say really conveys the experience; you have to live through it to understand. God knows, I'm glad to be outta there, but maybe that's enough said. What about your family, Doc? They're not living in Alaska, are they?"

"No, my family lives on a farm in Virginia, southwest of Washington. Alaska's winters are too long for the kids and my wife needs the sunlight. She gets depressed without it."

"Yeah, I hear a lot of people are like that. I thought your office back in the States was somewhere around D.C. Where do you live?"

"I've got a small apartment in Washington, but I get home on the weekends, most weekends anyway. Washington's a terrible place to raise a family—too crowded and too mean. My wife and I don't like it much, the traffic, the crime, but for now, my job requires that I live close to D.C."

"I'll bet you miss your kids."

Andreas nodded. "Sometimes I wonder if I'm doing the right thing. They're growing up without me and I feel I'm missing the happiest years of my life just to fulfill a dream I've had since childhood. It's hard on my wife too, being a single parent. She's gotten used to making all the decisions without including me, but the kids seem fine with it."

"I've never had kids, Doctor, so I can't directly relate to what you're saying, but if you sense you're making a mistake living away from them like this, maybe it's time to call it a day. From everything I hear, HAARP's positioned to take off now. I think this long-wave imaging technology will really make a difference to all of us, and in our lifetime. It's a fantastic achievement. You've actually made the world a better place and you didn't have to die in the process. Gary Ellie believes that good ideas like this one have a way of bubbling to the surface and creating momentum on their own. Maybe it's time to let go of your baby and reclaim your family."

"I've been thinking the same thing myself, but it's reassuring to hear you say so. What happened in New York really hit me like a wake-up call. When I was your age, I never thought about dying because I believed I'd live forever. I don't think about it much now, but what happened in New York really drove it home to me. We need to make the best of the time we have and focus on the people that matter most. It's the relationships that matter when it's all said and done. I suppose people learn these lessons at different times in their lives, but it seems to me I should have picked up on this years ago. My father often said that no one ever wished they'd spent more time at work, when they were on their deathbed, but somehow, his message didn't sink in."

"Well, as the saying goes, your work won't keep you warm at night."

"No, quite the contrary; it keeps me awake." Andreas grinned. "It gives me a place to sleep with a roof over my head, and some satisfaction, but even that is fleeting. Truth is, our funding could dry up overnight for any number of reasons."

"All things considered, I don't think that's very likely."

"I hope not, but you never know. How about you, Eion? How're you holding up? You haven't touched your lunch and you seemed pretty upset a few minutes ago. What's on your mind?"

"We were so close."

"Close? Close to what?"

"Shore leave and women."

"Ah, yes. What cruel fate is this? Your countdown to all that is London put on hold and even we civilians roped into temporary active duty." Andreas nodded understanding. "You may find it hard to believe, but twenty years ago, I was a great deal like you."

"You're kidding, right?"

"No, not at all. I'm perfectly serious. I remember feeling many of the same frustrations you feel today. From the outside looking in, I'd call it female-centric."

"Yeah, I guess that's a pretty good one-liner, Doc. You got any advice you think would do me any good?"

Andreas thought for a moment, then looked at Eion through

compassionate eyes. "No, I don't have any advice that would make any difference, but I will tell you one thing. My hope is that you survive it all and come out the other side with a woman who loves you."

CHAPTER NINETEEN

House of Cards
Tuesday, Mar. 23, 9:40 P.M.
Hama, Syria

"Yeah, I hear you, Chief, but if I were you, I'd keep a low profile," Russum said quietly into his satellite phone. "You don't stick your head up when somebody yells incoming." Moments later, he ended the call, then looked at Graham across the hotel room.

"I hope you don't have your retirement money hard-wired into the stock market."

"About two-thirds of it's in stock. Why?" Graham looked apprehensive, not fully understanding where Russum was headed.

"The stock market's like a house of cards."

"I don't follow you."

"It reopened today under a cloud of uncertainty."

Looking up from his laptop, Buck's eyes narrowed. "Yeah, but everyone expected a shaky start the first day. Spit it out, Billy boy, what's the problem?"

"Pressure inside the CTC is exceeding crush depth and Washington's demanding results."

"Yeah, so what else is new?"

"Somehow the press got wind that there may have been more than one bomb and it caught everyone off guard. They even got pictures of 'em on the news; two identical briefcase bombs squirrelled away in some apartment. It hasn't been confirmed, but the CTC believes they were taken at ground zero."

"You've gotta be kidding me. Inside Liberty Tower?"

"Yeah, I wish it was a joke, but the CTC and FBI admitted the pictures looked viable."

"Viable? Whaddaya mean?"

"Well, I guess we'll just have to see for ourselves. Did you ever get your e-mail connection working?"

"It works, but it's slow as an old dog."

"How about logging on and checking your mail. The photos're in a file attached to some e-mail from CTC."

Buck lifted his hands from the keyboard and signaled Wyley. "You're our picture and computer expert. Have at it."

Once Wyley started the picture file download, Russum continued.

"It was described to me like a photo album of the crime scene. There's supposed to be a half dozen shots of the city taken out the apartment window and six more of the device itself. From what I was told, they were taken from different angles and, by all accounts, they could be legitimate. It's as if these photos were designed to convince us—people on the inside, I mean—that they were authentic. They even included the detonator electronics."

"Close-ups?"

"Sounds like it."

"What about the detonator cables? Did they count 'em?"

Russum grimaced. "Yeah, they did. One shot even showed 'em sequentially tagged and numbered. It's like they knew we'd be counting cables and they wanted to make sure we got it right."

"So they made it easy for us."

"Download's complete," Wyley announced.

Click; click, click . . .

"Dear God in heaven; they're right." Graham sighed, looking over Wyley's shoulder. "It's a photo album of ground zero. I'd recognize it anywhere; the Chase Manhattan Bank, the roof of the Fed. This is as real as it gets. These photos are legit all right, they've gotta be."

"They've even got a date and time stamp on 'em," Wyley added.

"Those bastards hung a ruler in the picture for scale," Buck seethed, "like it was some kinda scientific study or something."

"Let me guess," Wyley pitched in. "The bomb's diameter is the same as the Russian mini-nuke."

Russum nodded. "And these pictures were made public only an hour after the New Jersey stock market opened."

"Classic," Wyley vented.

"Well, I'm sure the timing was no accident," Russum agreed.

"What a piece o' work." Buck sounded bitter. "Seems like premeditated market sabotage to me."

"They're saying they did it before and they'll do it again," Graham whispered.

"Good God."

"Once is not enough."

"They're not finished with us yet, and they want us to know it." Buck's face was beet red now. "It's like they're toying with us; they've got us where they want us and we're dangling by a string."

"Anyway," Russum continued, "Washington's going ballistic."

"Now that's a surprise," Wyley quipped.

"No, you don't understand. It's worse than that. Apparently, the head of the FBI spoke off the record about the pictures and made matters worse, much worse. The chief's never seen anything like it."

"Why? What's the problem?"

"Most of our agents are straight shooters, not politicians or stock analysts. Their director acknowledged it could happen again, and understandably so; America's a free country, not a gestapo state, and our borders are wide open. There are no guarantees in this life."

"Sounds like the former head of the FBI to me."

"The man's got integrity," Russum insisted. "He spoke the truth, but his timing was unfortunate."

"I still don't follow you. So the head of the FBI spoke out of turn. What of it?"

"Let me spell it out for you, SEALman. Today, the New Jersey Stock Exchange opened under a cloud of uncertainty. Early on, the market appeared to rally, but it stalled mid-afternoon, floundering as foreign investors pulled out to cut their losses. The slide began slowly at first, then rumors spread that OPEC may announce an increase in the price of crude. American confidence was shaken, and all this happened with the head of the FBI outta the loop. Then, outta the blue, these pictures showed up on TV and the director confirmed a reporter's concern that this could happen again. Word spread like wildfire, panic hit, and the bottom fell out."

"Sounds like a pretty volatile situation."

"It was that, but from what I heard, the frenzy has subsided a bit."

"Why's that? What changed?"

"The president got involved once he understood the reasons behind the panic. His reasoning was pretty simple, really. He said if his administration could help start a panic, they could help end it. They're taking steps to ease people's concerns in the interim, until the market reopens."

"What's next?"

"Damage control—divide and conquer. The president convened the energy commission to formulate an emergency response to OPEC's threats. They're considering making America's strategic oil reserves available if they'll help stabilize the situation. And this time it looks like our terrorists screwed up. Those bomb photos were an intelligence gold mine and they're crawling all over 'em back home. They could have been easily doctored to the point they revealed very little detail at all, but they weren't. God only knows why not, but those photos were either scanned in at some kind of high resolution or taken with a digital camera. They weren't compressed or run through any kind of lossy filter. Our lab thinks somebody either got in a hurry or wasn't properly trained."

"That makes sense," Wyley confirmed from firsthand experience. "Taking pictures on a digital camera is pretty much a point-and-shoot affair. That's the easy part, but editing the pictures requires learning the tools and knowing a lot about picture formats. That takes time, patience, special picture software, and a fast computer, one fast enough to process images anyway."

"All that really matters is that we've got the goods. They've already identified the electronics manufacturer who made the detonator from the logo on the circuit board. It's some quick turnaround outfit in New England."

"It's about time we got a break," Buck concluded. "Any chance they'll be able to trace the source of those pictures? Who developed them or where they came in over the internet?"

"I asked the same question. They feel it's possible, but not likely, not anytime soon anyway. The pictures came into ABC News indirectly over e-mail, by way of some proxy server at the edge of the internet. It's as if they'd worked out a way to hide the source of the e-mail, but they hadn't thought through how to filter the pictures."

"Thank God. That worked out good for us anyway."

"Ya know, I can't seem to shake that little kid." Buck eyed his laptop display intently.

"I've been thinking about her too," Graham said. "I'm afraid it's going to be difficult for them to put New York behind them and move on."

"Yeah, but somehow they've got to get on with their lives."

"What about Mary's husband? Do you know anything about him?"

"Yeah. She said she's made some bad calls in her life. He was one of them."

"Really? I'm sorry to hear that."

"The way she explained it, her dad never liked this guy, but she wouldn't listen. Her dad said he was no good, that this boy didn't really care for her and never showed any sense of commitment. The guy was selfish and self-centered, but he had a charm that was disarming. It made up for everything until the chips were down. She can see it clearly now, but she wishes she'd listened then."

"Live and learn. That's the way life is sometimes. We all make mistakes," Graham said, suddenly feeling a knot in the pit of his stomach. "Man, I'm not looking forward to the time when my daughters start dating."

"Me neither," Wyley added. "Some things I'd simply rather not think about."

"There're so many fine young men out there," Buck sighed. "I don't understand why the prettiest girls inevitably end up with the biggest jerks on the face of the earth."

"Maybe the jerks have something the nice guys don't," Graham reasoned.

"And what's that?"

"Courage."

"Courage, yeah right; like Mary's husband who left when he found out she was pregnant."

"No, that's not it. Courage isn't the right word, maybe it's confidence. I think these guys have the confidence to approach the prettiest girls when they're young because they've already learned to deal with rejection from their parents and teachers. Most thrive in situations of rejection and conflict. They don't have as much to lose and they're willing to risk it all. It's that rebel without a cause image, stand alone, stand apart, reject the establishment. You know what I mean."

"Faint heart never won fair lady. I guess that makes sense."

"The sad part is, the girls buy into it. I know a hand surgeon back home who told me his daughter enjoys rubbing his face in it. It's like she goes out with losers to spite him."

"So you're telling me that some teenage girls limit their own future to spite their parents? That doesn't make any sense at all."

"Not to an adult, it doesn't. Maybe the nice guys finish last because they're too damn nice and they're inexperienced. It never occurred to me before now, but it's really an issue of maturity. That's it; that's the problem. In one respect, the jerks are more mature than the young men you could feel good about."

"That makes sense, I guess. It's like the nice guys are just finding their way in the world."

"That's right. The good guys are too damn nice and the girls don't have the experience to understand their hearts or see the truth. They see the good guys as immature, and I guess they're right. Somehow, the girls need the ability to read a fella's thoughts and know his heart. I don't know, I think God could have done a better job with this girl-boy relationship thing."

"Yeah, I gotta give God low marks on that score. I don't think there's any good reason why growing up has to be so painful."

A long pause, then Graham summarized the crux of the matter. "Hormones rule."

"No doubt about it."

"How'd you find out so much about Mary's husband any-way?"

"E-mail."

"E-mail?" Graham cocked his eyebrow.

"We've been sending each other e-mail; what of it?"

"Oh, nothing." Graham craned his neck around Buck's shoulder, staring at his laptop display. Focusing on his e-mail inbox, one pattern was obvious at a glance—Mary Marshall had sent "SEALMAN" a long list of messages and, from the looks of it, he'd answered every one. *Now that's an interesting development,* Graham thought. "You heard any-thing recently?"

"Yeah. Mary's decided to move back in with her parents for a while, far away from New York and the big city. She thinks the change of scenery will do them good and I think she's probably right."

"How's Katie doing?"

"Not so great actually, but I'm hoping she'll be okay. She drew me a picture of their new house and family. Take a look." Buck pointed to her hand-drawn, colored picture on-screen. "That's her grandfather there in the middle. See his wrinkled skin; she says his face is crushed. It cracks me up. That little girl has a way of getting under my skin."

"Yeah, I know what you mean."

"Katie's not really aware of what happened in New York. Mary kept her away from the TV. Her goal was to move to an environment where Katie could experience all the love and at-tention she could stand."

"Grandparents are good at that." Wyley smiled.

"Mary said her parents had been asking her to move in with them since her husband left. I told you that jerk pulled out on her when he found out she was pregnant, didn't I?"

"Yeah, you mentioned that. Seems like they're on your mind."

"There's a real man for you."

"I'd say his behavior vouched for his character."

"I tell you what. I'd like to cut that bastard's balls off, maybe change his outlook on life a little."

"Were there any extraordinary circumstances?"

"Not from what I heard. I guess he didn't wanna be a father."

"I'd be willing to bet it's been tougher on Mary than her daughter. Small children are resilient. I'd like to think Katie could bounce back from anything."

"Well, maybe. Kids, even little kids, can be pretty mean. Katie's already had one setback in her new school."

"Setback? Nothing too serious, I hope."

"Well, I don't know. It sounded pretty serious to me. Seems that even in kindergarten little kids set you up. You know Katie loves to color, just loves it, and some of the kids in her class told her it was okay to color in their big picture storybooks. They told Katie they did it all the time. Anyway, Katie was sitting at the table, all by herself, coloring in her storybook like she thought she was supposed to when her teacher walks up and screams at her because she was coloring in her *schoolbook*. Katie was devastated because she thought she was doing such a good job, you know, staying in the lines and stuff. Mary said she was even coloring in red, her favorite color. All the kids laughed at her for getting in trouble, and I don't know if she's ever going back to that school again."

"She needs to get back on the horse."

"Mary asked me what she should do and that's what I told her too. You can't run from your problems, even if you're a little kid. And I told her something else, too. I said if I was there I'd dress down that teacher for hurting my little girl's feelings like that."

"You said 'my little girl,'" Graham observed.

"Yeah, well, she's really gotten under my skin and that made me mad as hell. No teacher, especially a kindergarten teacher, has any business stomping on the feelings of a little girl who thinks she's doing the right thing, especially on her first day. Hell, I'd buy the school a truckload of new story-books before I'd let that happen again to Katie, or anyone else's kid, for that matter."

"Maybe the teacher was having a bad day," Wyley countered. "You don't know, her husband might be dying of cancer or something."

Buck remembered the loss of his own wife, and knotted up inside. "Yeah, you're right. I shouldn't come down so hard, I guess. It just made me mad, the way those little kids set Katie up like that. They knew she wasn't supposed to write in the book, but they told her to just to get her in trouble her first day."

"You seem pretty wrapped up in all this," Graham said. "I'll bet Katie'll get over the shock of her first day and she'll be fine."

"Yeah, maybe she'll get over it, and maybe she'll make some friends there, but I'll bet she'll remember that day, and those kids, and that teacher for the rest of her life."

Graham thought back over his own childhood experiences and said, "She may remember the event, she may still feel the hurt, but she probably won't remember their faces."

"I hope you're right. You hear about things like this sometimes scarring a kid for life. After what happened in New York, that little girl needs a break; hell, we all need one."

"I expect she'll be fine. I only hope Mary can put New York behind her and get on with her life. At least she's got Katie to worry over and it sounds as if you're doing enough worrying for both of 'em."

"I don't know. I'm having trouble shaking New York. I'm flying off the handle at anything that moves. How 'bout you, Doc? How're you holding up?"

"I haven't recovered from New York, if that's what you're asking. I don't think I ever will."

CHAPTER TWENTY

First Sighting
Monday, Apr. 5, 1:08 P.M.
Somewhere on the Persian Gulf

"What do you make of it?" Russum wanted to know.

"Something's under there all right," Buck replied, looking across the light table at Andreas, "but I'm not sure what."

"Judging from the thickness of the reinforced-concrete walls, I think we're onto something. It's an underground installation housing some kind of manufacturing facility."

"Is that some kind of big pipe?" Buck pointed to an annex attached on the side of the building with two dark lines emanating from it. One line ran upstream, another down.

"Yeah, probably metal pipe surrounded by reinforced concrete. Looks like a pair of aqueducts to me. Something for channeling cooling water through the building. They're using the river as a big heat sink."

"Really. That sounds like a factory, doesn't it. What's that big rectangle inside there?"

"Since it runs the length of the building, I'd guess it's some sort of mezzanine."

"A what?"

"A partial story between floors inside the building."

"Really?" Buck sounded concerned. "Does it have open walls?"

"I don't follow you." Now Andreas looked puzzled.

"You know, half walls, like could someone stand up there and look down over the production floor?"

Andreas nodded. "You're asking for more detail than I can see here, but probably. I can't tell from these pictures, but it's

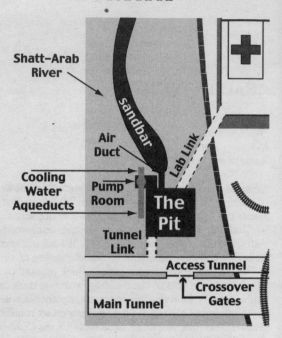

not unusual for a factory mezzanine to be built with open out-side walls. The ones I've seen were always built with an open walkway and handrail running around the outside periphery. I think they're called catwalks. Why do you ask?"

"Just trying to get the lay of the land, Doc. From what you've said, that mezzanine sounds like high ground."

Andreas's expression turned blank, so Buck spelled out his concern.

"Anyone who holds it could either pin us down or pick us off one at a time."

"Oh, I see. I didn't think of that."

After a long pause, Russum circled the area of the picture he was most interested in. "Look at the layout of this large equipment."

"It just looks like a lot of squares laid out in a grid to me," Buck stated flatly.

"Judging from the clarity of the image, I'd wager that manufacturing equipment is built out of a good conductor, maybe steel or some other metal, and it's well grounded to the earth."

"Considering their size, they must be massive pieces of equipment," Russum speculated.

"I'd agree with that."

"Any possibility that some of that heavy machinery could be industrial-grade milling equipment?"

"It certainly could be, but we can't know for sure without someone going in."

"Why else would they go to the trouble and expense of hiding this facility underground?" Graham asked what everyone was thinking. "And look at the thickness of those walls."

"That structure's built more like a bunker," Andreas observed quietly. "It's built to withstand far more than outside water pressure."

"You know, you're right. Look at this." Graham pointed to the middle of the river. "The tunnel's buried much deeper than the bunker, but still, the bunker's walls are at least three times thicker. What do you make of that?"

"They're up to something and they're going to a great deal of trouble to keep it a secret," Andreas summarized.

"Why would they tunnel it to the basement of the hospital?" Eion queried his mentor.

"If nothing else, it's misleading, like camouflaging a military facility alongside a school. Once you identify the school, you tend to stop searching there and move on."

"And that tunnel construction project, that'd provide a perfect cover for the dig." Graham's mind was running ahead of the pack now. "The tunnel's being worked anyway, there's no way we could keep track of the amount of dirt they take outta there."

"True enough."

"What else can you tell us from those pictures?"

"We can give you better size and number estimates of the larger equipment. Beyond looking inside, we can analyze what type warhead's best suited for taking out this bunker with minimum damage to surrounding structures."

"Like that hospital?"

"That's right. And once the strike's complete, we can fly by and assess the damage minutes following the attack."

"What if this were our neutron bombmanufacturing facility; could you count the number of bombs inside?" Russum wanted to know.

Andreas raised his eyebrows and decided to probe. "Let me verify my assumptions first. These bombs are made of metal, correct?"

Russum nodded.

"And their size? They're physically large, yes?"

"No, I'm sorry to say, that's not the case."

Andreas furrowed his brow. "All nuclear bombs require an inordinate amount of shielding. They must be large."

"That's the rub, Doc. These devices aren't shielded."

"Then they're lethal poison to everyone in their vicinity."

"No, and that's part of the problem. They don't require shielding and they're extraordinarily small, smaller than a basketball, not much larger than a grapefruit really."

Andreas narrowed his eyes to a skeptical squint. "Then these nuclear devices are unlike any I know."

"They are. I only became aware of them within the last two months, and nuclear devices are my business. When it comes to dealing with this problem, we don't have many options, really. Your long-wave imaging technology wasn't available twenty years ago, but it's the best tool I've seen for detecting these underground weapons facilities. Somehow, someway, we've gotta continually inspect these clandestine facilities for red mercury or else."

"You're saying either we destroy these bombs at their point of manufacture or risk being held hostage by terrorists?"

"Yep, that's the way I see it because it's impossible to detect 'em once they're in circulation."

"Didn't the U.N. have weapons inspection teams inside Iraq following the Gulf War?"

"Yeah, and in my opinion, that was one of the best things the United Nations ever did. Judging from what I could find out, the U.N. inspection teams were always hunting for red mercury, but back then, they kept it under wraps. I read a lot about it, and you never saw anything about red mercury in the news. If it was ever mentioned in print, it was always as a footnote, like it was some sort of insignificant detail. Anyway, to make a long story short, we had U.N. inspection teams in Iraq back then, and one day, they just packed up and pulled out."

"What happened?"

"I'll be damned if it makes any sense to me, but I think Saddam simply wore down the resolve of the free world. The inspection teams would try to do their jobs, Saddam would protest, create an international crisis, and as a result, he'd strain the resolve of the political coalition inside the U.N. It's the damnedest thing in retrospect, but it looks like the U.N. just got fed up with Saddam and quit."

"You're telling me the threats of one single tyrant wore down the resolve of the United Nations?"

"That's the way I read it. They got fed up and left."

"You'd think Saddam's protest would've strengthened their resolve."

"Wrong, Doctor. You may be the world's expert on long-wave imaging, but you're politically naive. And to make matters worse, the U.N. found tons—we're talking about thousands of pounds—of red mercury in Iraq that had come down from Russia. Russia needed money, Iraq needed red mercury, and the U.N. inspectors went ballistic when they were recalled."

"I would've gone ballistic too. What happened when they returned?"

"Their protest fell on deaf ears. The world had grown tired of Saddam and simply lost interest."

"Unbelievable that one tenacious dictator could outlast the world's attention span."

"Well, anyway, twenty years ago, no one had ever seen a pure-fusion bomb, so everyone wanted to believe it was some kind of crackpot theory."

"I guess I'm guilty too. If I hear something really frightening, something I don't want to believe, I look for ways to discredit it. It makes everyone feel better, especially if you can write off a menacing threat as technical nonsense. Tell me more."

Russum went on to summarize for Andreas the Russian neutron bomb plus their New York and Hama observations. When Russum believed that Dr. Pappasongas had absorbed the enormity of his story, he asked again, "Can you count the number of bombs inside that bunker?"

"We can't resolve anything that small. I wish we could."

"So someone's gonna have to go in there and take a look."

"Oh yeah. That'll be easy," Buck quipped from across the room.

"Buck, what can you do for us? Can we use the river?"

"Are you serious?"

Russum nodded.

"How deep is it?"

"Twenty to thirty feet."

"Get me some optical surveillance in there and we'll sure as hell find out."

"Something else unexpected fell outta those bunker pictures."

Buck looked up at Russum. "What do you mean?"

"You have mail." Russum pointed to Buck's laptop. "Turns out, the CTC's been monitoring that tunnel dig for several weeks, but they couldn't figure out what was going on from satellite surveillance alone. As soon as they saw the bunker, they forwarded us several surveillance clips."

After waiting for the computer to boot up, Buck displayed his e-mail.

```
To: SEALMAN
Subject: The number of vehicles entering the
access tunnel does not equal the number of
vehicles leaving.
```

"What's that got to do with the price of tea in China?" Graham asked, looking over Buck's shoulder.

Buck double-clicked one attachment, and played back a time-compressed movie on-screen. Everyone crowded around the big man's shoulders, hunching forward, struggling to see the screen. What appeared was a small, two-by-three-inch moving picture.

"Judging from the timestamp in the opening credits, it covers a one-week period," Graham observed.

"The size and picture quality are disappointing," Andreas added. "Wyley, is there anything you can do to make it bigger?"

Buck looked at Wyley with a smile. "Have at it."

Wyley took Buck's seat and winged through a few mouse maneuvers. After a couple of clicks, the picture expanded to fill the full display.

"Hell, that looks a hundred times worse." Buck squinted, talking to the screen. "It's jerky and blocky as all get-out."

"It looks like a tiled, claymation movie." Andreas smiled.

The group fell silent as the movie jittered and jerked forward. After watching access tunnel traffic come and go for a few minutes, everyone was quickly running out of patience. Listening to the team sigh and groan, Buck could stand it no longer. "It's worse than that; it's boring as hell, like watching grass grow."

"Even popcorn couldn't save this one-star loser," Wyley joked. "It's the worst." Instinctively, he clicked the file attachment named BOTTOMLINE, and the meaning of CTC's cryptic one-liner became clear in a text message on-screen.

```
Reports from CIA satellite surveillance
group confirm suspicious traffic pattern near
bunker access tunnel. Most vehicles dwell
in the tunnel a few minutes at most then
exit, but there are outliers who violate
this short-time-in-tunnel rule on a sched-
uled basis. In summary, the number of cars
entering the access tunnel never seems to
equal the number leaving. At times, cars en-
ter the tunnel, then come out days later. A
few vans stream in and out on a daily basis
in what could be a staggered twelve-hour
shift.
```

"It's not conclusive proof of anything, but it does support our suspicion that something's going on in there twenty-four hours a day."

"And it gives us a pretty good idea how many people are involved," Russum observed.

"Don't forget about the tunnel link back to the hospital," Graham cautioned. "If the hospital were being used as office space for manufacturing, those vans might represent only the tip of the iceberg."

"What do you think, Buck? Can you get in there to take a look?"

"Where are the entrances?" he asked, looking over Wyley's shoulder.

Click, click . . .

Buck frowned as he studied several black-and-white snapshots of the access tunnel entrance. "I'll give it a good, hard look, Billy Ray, but I can tell you up front, it won't be easy. Judging from what we've seen so far, we don't have many options. We either get in through the access tunnel, the main tunnel, or the hospital. Either way, they'll know we're in there, and unless we overwhelm them, we'll have hell to pay on the way out. What's our objective?"

"Survey the site. We gotta know if red mercury's involved and if they're manufacturing neutron bombs in there."

"You're saying we've got to secure the site and bring in a noncombatant, some kinda bomb expert."

"Yeah, that's what I'm saying and my guess is that you're looking at him. And if they're producing these bombs, we need to know how many they've made, how many remain on-site, and how many are in circulation. If they've got computer records, we need 'em."

"A computer expert too?"

Russum made eye contact with Wyley, then nodded. Anyone could see Wyley didn't look happy, but he wasn't surprised.

"Is that it? Are you expecting us to move any other non-quals in there?" Buck was referring to noncombatants.

"We're going to need a corpsman."

"Yeah, I figured as much." Buck glanced at Graham, rubbed his face in his hands, then pressed on. "I understand what you need, but SEALs don't operate that way. We need to get in there, set our charges, and get the hell out before they're on to us. SEALs don't analyze industry, we blow it up."

"We won't do anything you don't support, Buck," Russum said quietly. "I'm asking that you study our situation, understand what we need to bring back from there, then give us a plan. Tell us what we need to pull this off and the best way to go about it."

"All right. Give me some time on this and I'll get back to you."

"Do you need anything from us? Is there anything we can do to help?"

Holding his hand up, Buck feigned a gesture of caution. "No, no. You've done quite enough already."

CHAPTER TWENTY-ONE

Angel of Mercy
Monday, Apr. 5, 5:50 P.M.
Basra, Iraq

The first thing Hakim noticed was the bullet holes. From where he stood outside the Huey's cockpit, casual inspection revealed al-Mashhadi's medevac chopper had taken small arms fire—probably from Kurdish rebels—and recently. Older hits had been patched with duct tape and circled with black permanent marker, but the shiniest new holes—and the terrorist counted at least ten on the copilot's side alone—had not.

The next thing he noticed was his bulky Kevlar flight suit and body armor resting on the copilot's seat. After crawling inside the helicopter's titanium cargo bay, the terrorist first strapped down his suitcase. Next, he moved forward, picked up his flight suit, and carried it back to the cargo bay. After climbing into the ill-fitting garment, he continued his inspection, studying the chopper's maintenance log. To his surprise and relief, it was current and as complete as any he'd seen in his limited experience with the Iraqi army. Even the most recent bullet holes had been noted in a diagram and earmarked for repair.

Painted white with a big red cross across its side, this armor-plated Huey wasn't pretty. Thick flat angular plates formed its body, there wasn't a smooth aerodynamic line to be found along the exterior, but regardless of how his boxy bird looked, Iraq's minister of information insisted it would fly and his pilot was the best in the Iraqi army.

Still, it seemed to Hakim that this helo was a sitting duck. Largely armed with hope, the only visible weapons it carried for defense were a forward-facing Gatling gun and twin 50mm machine guns in its tail.

Moments later, the terrorist heard a truck approaching and checked his watch. They were late, but as far as he was concerned, the later, the better. The extra time had given him the breathing room he'd needed for a thorough once-over, and further, their tardiness randomized their departure time, making their flight less predictable.

Climbing down onto the concrete runway, Hakim watched as al-Mashhadi and his khaki-clad pilot approached the chopper. Already sweating inside his Kevlar suit, the pilot ran his hand through his hair, then used two fingers to squeegee the perspiration from his eyebrows. *Hot, but undaunted,* Hakim thought.

Ten minutes later, with the pilot's preflight complete, all three men climbed aboard. Hakim had been impressed with the pilot's uncompromising thoroughness; apparently there was nothing he hadn't checked. Although he remained a little apprehensive, Hakim strapped himself snugly into the copi-

lot's seat on the right-hand side of the cockpit and tried to relax. Once the pilot released the rotor brakes, the blades began
spinning, slowly at first, but soon, they'd come up to speed.
After scanning his instrument panel and watching his rotor
tips for a bit, the pilot checked off the last two items on his
list. Finally, he announced over the intercom that they were
ready, then placed his right hand up on the throttles.

Hakim drew in a deep breath as the pilot pulled up on the
collective, increasing the pitch of his rotor blades. Smoothly,
evenly, with all the finesse of a fine artist, the Iraqi pilot lifted
the craft off the ground into a hover, making one last check to
see that there were no red lights staring him in the face. The
Huey vibrated and shuddered during takeoff, but the pilot
sensed nothing out of the ordinary.

In one smooth motion, Hakim felt the nose dip as the pilot
increased power, transitioning the Huey into forward flight.
Accelerating into a climbing turn, they banked right, then
continued their climb to one thousand feet. Below them,
greenish streetlights marking the road to Basra clipped by at
breakneck speed. Ahead, on the horizon, a yellow glow
marked the outskirts of the city.

Ten minutes later, Hakim could see a dark, shimmering,
winding ribbon on the ground, its banks lined with streetlights; it had to be the river. Moments later, Hakim flinched as
the pilot suddenly banked the Huey and plummeted to an altitude of fifty feet. They hovered so low, Hakim could see chop
on the water created by their rotor downwash.

Then, for the first time, Hakim sensed the pilot had tensed
up. There was something different in his tone when he
spoke.

"Watch the rooftops for sniper fire," was all he'd said, but
that was enough.

This evening, he'd chosen the river run from the north for
their approach to the Basra teaching hospital and Hakim was
riding shotgun.

It was dusk. The pilot drew in a deep breath, increasing
both throttles to full-rated military power. Forcing the aircraft
into forward flight, he dipped the nose, then ran wide open,

hugging the deck in an all-out, bone-jarring sprint down along the Shatt-al-Arab River.

Twilight
Monday, Apr. 5, 6:05 P.M.
Rooftop
East Bank, Shatt-al-Arab River

"We're ready," the youngest rebel said, ending his cell phone call, then signaled his squad, relaying the alert message by flashlight to the surrounding rooftops.

Whop, whop, whop, whop, whop.

As had so often happened in the past, the rebels heard the chopper long before they saw it. The riverbanks had been leveed through the city, creating a sort of sound duct which channeled the chopper's distinctive rotor beat and alerted the troops long before the Huey became visible.

Then, only a few breaths later, there it was on the horizon, backlit against the twilight sky, a low-flying faint white dot, racing toward them downriver.

Ambush
Monday, Apr. 5, 6:07 P.M.
Basra, Iraq

"Hold on," the pilot said, but Hakim and al-Mashhadi read it as an order.

As they approached a bend in the river, a white flash erupted from a flat rooftop.

"Small arms fire." Hakim pointed to the west bank.

Instinctively, the pilot stomped the pedals and pitched nose over, yawing the craft into a steep dive to the east. Hakim's helmet slammed into the door, and the terrorist felt his brain flattening to one side, then rattling around inside his skull.

Suddenly, a shuttering burst of muzzle flashes erupted from a row of rooftops lining the east bank and Hakim saw three separate tracer streams reaching skyward like fiery fingers to strangle them.

"Ambush!"

Hakim's pulse pounded hard as the pilot yanked the collective, hurling the helicopter skyward, hoping to climb above the incoming rain of death.

Before Hakim recovered his stomach, he felt the helicopter lurch laterally as the massive wavefront of lead slammed into the titanium plate bolted to his door. A loud metallic screech signaled the door's sheet metal was failing, then, in the blink of an eye, a gaping hole ripped open as the armor plate tore off and fell into the river.

Hakim swallowed hard and forced his gaze down. He could see the river through a hole opened up near his right foot. For practical purposes, his door had been reduced to a mass of cracked Plexiglas and sheet metal flapping in the wind.

No Rush
Monday, Apr. 5, 6:08 P.M.
East bank, Shatt-al-Arab River

Steady on, the missileman thought, purposefully releasing a slow breath.

Within seconds, his buddy patted him on his back, signaling his shoulder tube was loaded, armed, and ready to fire.

Low on the horizon, the seasoned veteran saw the chopper's heat signature on-screen now, approaching in the distance.

"Steady, there's no rush, let them come to you." The veteran spoke to himself out loud, quietly, in a calm voice.

Burr-rump-pomp-pomp-pomp-pomp-pomp-pomp-pomp . . .

"What's that?" The missileman looked up, pulling his aim off target. *Tracer streams. All right, focus, crosshairs on the mark . . . release the safety and target lock—five, four, three . . .*

Suddenly the chopper changed course, swinging about and turning head-long, streaking directly toward him.

Light of God
Monday, Apr. 5, 6:09 P.M.
Basra, Iraq

Plink, plink, plink, pazinnnggg!!!

One round ricocheted off the instrument panel; metal fragments splintered, slicing through the pilot's left cheek like butter.

Undaunted, the pilot lowered his helmet-mounted sight in front of his right eye, activating his Gatling gun. "Hold on," was all he said.

Rotating his head slightly, he aligned his crosshairs on the rooftop muzzle fire. Beneath the cockpit, the Gatling gun tracked his head motion, and in an instant, fiery hot lead rained down from the sky.

Burrrrruppp, burrrrruppp, burrrrrrruppppp.

As the pilot opened fire, Hakim was thrown forward against his shoulder harness as if he were in a car slamming to a screeching halt. The gun recoil had the effect of an air break, hurling them skyward at the cost of forward air speed.

Moments later, the pilot spoke again. "Hosing the rooftops should keep their heads down."

On the ground, the white flashes seemed to disappear, but then another round clipped the cockpit. Hakim felt super-heated air near his face as a bullet shrieked by, nicking his forehead just above his right eyebrow. Blood ran down his face, blinding him. Lifting his right arm, he put pressure on the wound, then . . .

Thud, thud, thud, thump!

Hakim keeled over, feeling a sharp pain in his chest, as if he'd been bashed in the ribs with a sledgehammer. He tried to catch his breath, but breathing deep caused him to cough, and to cough hurt with such stabbing pain he couldn't believe it.

Suddenly, a red MISSILE light flashed on the instrument panel as an insane warble racked their ears.

"Find it!"

Hakim searched the rooftops below, but couldn't see any bright light streaking toward them.

Tripping into overdrive, the pilot's response was automatic. Toggling a row of overhead switches, he ham-fisted a big red button marked COUNTERMEASURES. Smoke canisters, chaff, parachute flairs, and an array of arc lights erupted from pressurized launch tubes in an instant. Stomping the pedals with a jerk, the pilot pulled a snap-rotate maneuver, turning the nose 180 degrees. Now with their back to the countermeasures, the pilot slammed the collective to the stops, hurling the craft skyward, climbing like a bat out of hell.

Then, before Hakim could speak, the outside air seemed to ignite with a brilliant radiant light.

From the ground below, the light in the northern sky was blindingly spectacular, as if the air itself had caught fire. As a result, all rebel sensors in the area—infrared, laser, radar, and optical—were useless, jammed by full-spectrum noise to the point that they were totally blind.

Less than a second later, following an augering corkscrew dive into the river, the shoulder-launched rebel missile detonated harmlessly, exploding below and behind the Huey.

In the blink of an eye, the chopper had disappeared, as if it had ascended into heaven, consumed by a light so bright as to defy description.

Moments following the flash, once the fireball had faded, the only visible evidence that remained of the event was a shimmering cloud of tin foil strips backlit by the glare from a half dozen parachute flairs.

As for the unfortunate rebels on the east bank, their lives were changed forever. Predictably, the pupils in their eyes had been heavily dilated by the dim twilight and those closest to the brilliant white flash were blinded, the fireball forever burned into their retinas. Even rebels on the far side of the river were temporarily blinded by the light, but their sight would return several days later, inside an Iraqi prison.

Pride Won
Monday, Apr. 5, 6:16 P.M.
Roof of the Basra teaching hospital

After slamming down hard on the hospital's heli pad, al-Mashhadi collected his composure and carried Hakim's suitcase inside the hospital, protected by four armed guards. Meanwhile, Hakim and the pilot circled the aircraft, inspecting it for damage. Though Hakim still had trouble breathing, he felt the pain was manageable, and besides, the wound above his eye had already stopped bleeding. As it turned out, the pilot's flight suit was saturated with blood and sweat, but the first thing Hakim noticed when they stepped out of the chopper was that the pilot reeked of hydraulic fluid.

"It was worse than I thought," the pilot concluded quietly, but his tone conveyed relief. After running his hand through that gaping hole, he continued, "Some of the hydraulics were shot out, but that door of yours is useless. You're going to need a new one."

Hakim remained silent for an extended period, struggling for the right thing to say. "Next time, I think I'll take a cab."

The pilot smiled lamely, then moments later, Hakim followed him through the rooftop entrance into the hospital. Hakim was interested to observe that the Iraqi pilot knew his way around, like he'd been there before and often. Further, he was treated like some sort of visiting celebrity; he seemed to know most of the doctors and nurses by face recognition, some by name.

As a result, they both received immediate medical attention. Hospital X-rays revealed Hakim had suffered a deep penetrating bruise from a sniper round in the lower side quadrant of his rib cage, beneath his right arm. Not surprisingly, the bullet was found buried in the body armor of his flight suit. Iraqi doctors stitched up Hakim and the pilot a few minutes later, then sent them on their way under armed escort, bound for the bunker.

When Hakim entered the connecting link, the stench made him think of a head-on collision. The smells of antifreeze, gasoline, burned rubber, brakes, and hydraulic fluid all melded together to form a vile, concentrated stench he'd never experienced in one place. Although it was stating the obvious, he felt he wanted to say something to the pilot. "Smells like your shot-up chopper in here."

The pilot inhaled, then scowled. He could have lived his whole life and not experienced this again.

Rushing quickly through the connecting link, Hakim and the pilot soon entered the bunker. Although well lit, there was clearly some problem with the air handling system. The air appeared hazy and felt oppressively humid, forming halos around the overhead lights, limiting visibility so that it was difficult to see more than eight or ten feet forward.

Nevertheless, Hakim saw al-Mashhadi and Kajaz waiting for them inside the bunker. Kajaz had already opened Hakim's suitcase and was studying its contents with an enthusiastic and curious eye. It contained detonation electronics for ten grapefruit-sized neutron bombs plus one live one.

Kajaz examined the live device carefully. Clearly, he was pleased and was not afraid to show it. "With the addition of your proven detonation electronics and the latest modification to our pit fabrication process, I'm confident we can demonstrate our first working prototype in a week, possibly less."

"It sounds as if you've made significant headway since I left," Hakim said.

"We have, but our progress has not come without setbacks. Our early device runs proved disappointing from a neutron yield perspective, but fortunately they were useful nevertheless."

"Are you saying your early devices didn't work?"

"As neutron bombs, they were failures, but as it happened, they were useful countermeasures."

"Countermeasures? How do you mean?"

"You saw it tonight," the pilot injected.

Hakim looked puzzled for a moment, then his expression revealed understanding. "That bright light?"

"That's right." Kajaz nodded. "We have corrected our materials problem now, but for reasons we don't fully understand, our earliest devices produced a blindingly bright light, but little else. The neutron radiation and explosive yields were negligible with over ninety-five percent of the weapon's energy converted to light."

"Ineffective tank killers, but useful nevertheless," al-Mashhadi agreed.

"You understand then what needs to be changed?" Hakim asked Kajaz.

Standing in al-Mashhadi's shadow, Kajaz was clearly uncomfortable with the direct question. A combination of fear, pride, and sadness played tug-of-war inside him, but in the end, pride won. "We will demonstrate our first detonation in less than one week. I am sure of it."

CHAPTER TWENTY-TWO

Turning Point
Monday, Apr. 12, 6:25 P.M.
USS *Yorktown*
Persian Gulf

Graham gazed intently at the laptop display. On-screen, he studied an infrared picture of the sandbar located alongside the bunker near the edge of the Shatt-al-Arab River. After a few minutes' thought, he printed it out, then circled a dark spot on the bunker side of the sandbar.

"What about air shafts?" he asked Buck. "They need fresh breathing air from somewhere."

"I suppose that hot spot could be an air duct, but it doesn't seem likely. No connecting ductwork shows up in any of our HAARP pictures."

"Maybe so, but they've still got to get air from somewhere. What do you think, Andreas?"

"I can't be absolutely certain, but we usually see metal ducts with HAARP, especially ductwork this close to the surface. Did you check with the recon group back at Langley?" he asked Russum.

"All they reported was dredging equipment in the area. From what they've seen, the Iraqis keep dredging equipment in operation continually just to keep the waterway open to the gulf."

"Well, I feel like we're missing something," Graham continued. "They have to move air, water, power, sewage, and trash in and out of that bunker. They gotta get life support from somewhere. And if they're manufacturing bombs, where's the loading dock? They've got to get them out of there too."

"They could siphon air, water, and power from the hospital," Buck offered.

"Sewage and trash removal too," Andreas added.

After a few moments' thought, Buck pointed to the rear of the hospital. "I think I'd use the hospital loading dock to move those bombs outta there. They're small enough, so why not? Don't get me wrong, Graham. I'm with you in spirit on this, but what I wouldn't give for one set of construction plans of that bunker."

"It's gotta go in and come out somewhere."

Buck agreed, but seemed lost in his thoughts, distracted by the HAARP images.

"What are you thinking about so hard?" Graham wanted to know.

"This bunker access problem is a bitch," he answered with a sigh, picking up a pencil. "There's three ways in and outta that hole: the hospital tunnel, the access tunnel, and the main tunnel. The main tunnel has a crossover section which ties into the access tunnel, and the access tunnel links directly into the bunker. I don't like the looks of it because it's more of an indirect access route, but the main tunnel is heavily involved in construction. From what I can see, it would offer us the best cover under fire."

"Cover? Fire?"

"Yeah, Doc. They're digging 'round the clock. We may get in and get out without calling in the calvary to save us, but don't count on it. I don't believe in fairy tales, and we'd need a miracle to get in and out without them cutting us off."

"So what's your plan?"

"They're still in flux, but one thing's clear. We're going to have to seal off access to those tunnels or reinforcements are going to swarm all over us. SEALs can blow that bridge across the river and cut off highway access to the hospital. That should buy us some time. I hope it's enough."

"What about air superiority?" Russum probed.

"No way, not if we're going to surprise 'em."

"Where does that leave us?" Russum fired off another question.

"Close-quarter small arms combat and, to make matters worse, Andreas thinks that bunker may contain a second floor, some sort of mezzanine. We've got to take it or they'll pick us off like rats. This setup has all the makings of an in-your-face shoot-out at the OK Corral."

"What's in our favor?"

"Surprise, stealth, and speed. Both SEAL and Delta Force operators have a talent for popping up where they're least expected, so we'll hold the advantage of surprise. We're better trained and we travel light. Chances are, we'll be in and out of there before they know what hit them."

"You don't sound convinced," Graham observed.

"I don't believe it for a minute. Complicated ops like this one look good on paper, but they have a way of going sour on you, know what I mean?"

"Yeah."

"Let me tell you what I think about this assault."

"Shoot."

"Counterterrorist ops are really Delta's stock-in-trade. Their men and women are going to get the call for this op. They'll assault the bunker. The SEALs have a few long-hairs left for a covert op like this, but it's not our strong suit. We'll provide a deception, throw 'em off the scent, then take out the bridge and cut off access roads to the hospital and both tunnels."

"Makes sense," Russum agreed. "Sounds like we need to confirm that there are no tanks in the area."

"That's right. No tanks or armored vehicles." Buck looked at Graham, then continued. "Russum's CIA buddies have already set up a special reception committee for us in Basra. Five days ago, this advance party infiltrated the city with a small contingent of foreign nationals and Kurdish rebels. They're setting up safe houses, local truck transportation, and they've already provided us photo recon from the main tunnel entrance."

"Can they get a close-up of that sandbar?" Graham asked, again studying the printout of his satellite picture.

"It'll take some time to get your request through to them, but we can check if you feel strongly about it."

"I think it'd be a good idea. They've got to get air in there from somewhere."

"Then I'll talk to them about it."

"Once we get their feedback, we could have a much better idea of what to do," Graham said. "I've been thinking about those bunker plans you wanted."

"Yeah, me too," Buck responded. "What about 'em?"

"Billy Ray said Kurdish prisoners are being used as slave labor to keep that tunnel dig moving twenty-four hours a day."

Russum confirmed he'd said that, then qualified his remark with some "based on the best intelligence we have" weasel words.

"The Kurds who work in the hole could be a big help to us," Graham observed.

"Yeah, that's true enough," Buck agreed. "What of it?"

"Any chance some of those prisoners might escape?"

Buck looked across the room at Russum for confirmation. His expression telegraphed Buck's knee-jerk. "No, not a snowball's chance in hell."

"If we help them, maybe they'd help us."

"You talking about a jail break or some sort of rescue operation?"

"That's right. Could you plan this bunker assault to look like some sort of hostage rescue operation to free the Kurds?"

"All of 'em?" Buck furrowed his brow.

"No, not at first. Only one or two initially, maybe some sort of covert swap where we plant our people with the promise of freeing more to come—and soon."

Buck nodded.

"What if this bunker assault started as a rebel prisoner revolt?" Russum probed, taking up Graham's pitch.

"What if it looked like it started on the inside, you mean? We stage a small jail break or prisoner exchange, maybe swap one rebel for another, then in the end, our bunker assault frees the rebels like some sort of rescue operation."

"That's right. Two birds with one stone." Graham's thinking became clear to the group now.

Buck looked at Russum, implicitly asking his opinion. "It's complicated, but I like it and it's worth considering. Recruit the locals for help and pull off an inside job. It sounds like something we'd do because it puts fewer of our own at risk," Russum said.

"Those Kurdish prisoners may already know what we need to know about that dig," Buck reasoned out loud. "Some of 'em might even know what's in the pit. Hell, they'd be a lotta help planning this operation. What I would give for a few rebels and a translator on my staff right now."

"Do you really think they'll help us?" Graham queried Wyley for his opinion. Wyley had remained silent until now, but he knew more about the people of the region than anyone in the room.

"If they're convinced we're helping them, they will." He sounded confident. "They could be our best hope for pulling this off and I like the idea. These rebel prisoners have a vested interest in this operation, and imagine the diversion they'd create."

Buck concentrated for a moment then asked Wyley, "Can you speak their language?"

"A little. The Kurdish language is similar to Persian. I can communicate with them, if that's what you're asking."

"Aside from backing off and blowing that bunker to hell, they're the best chance we've got," Buck concluded. His mind was racing ahead. "It's complicated, but you could be right about this one. We could send you in with an advance party of special forces to infiltrate the rebel prisoners. How'd you feel about that? You could be waiting for us as sort of a welcome committee and the diversion would keep our losses to a minimum."

What about the rebel losses? Wyley thought, stunned, slack-jawed, completely silent. Maybe he should have seen this coming, but he felt like he'd been blind-sided by a Mack truck.

"That's right. This idea has possibilities if you're willing," Russum affirmed. "It's requires timing and coordination, but you'd sure as hell goose up our chances."

"Hell, if we keep this up," Buck quipped, "this operation'll include every trick in the book. How 'bout it, Wyley? What's your gut tell ya?"

"I, I don't know what to say." There was silence for what seemed like an eternity. "I guess it's simple really."

"Simple?"

"I'm scared to death. My gut's tied up in a freaking knot, like I'm gonna puke."

"You've been trained for this kinda work, right?"

Wyley nodded, never looking up. "Yeah, about a hundred years ago."

"We could make you look like one of 'em."

"Yeah, I know, but I've been a photographer so long, I'm not sure I'm cut out for this anymore." Wyley made eye contact with Graham. "I've never been the warrior type, you know what I mean?"

"Me either." Graham sighed, feeling heartsick that he'd brought up the rebel prisoner exchange idea at all. *Why didn't I keep my mouth shut?* Initially, he'd considered his idea as fuel for an exploratory conversation, nothing more, but now suddenly, Wyley was faced with one of the most difficult decisions a man ever has to make.

"Well, Wyley, think about it anyway, will ya?" Russum asked quietly.

"Yeah, I'll think about it all right. I won't like it, not for a minute, but I'll think about it."

Wyley gazed into space. Memories of the little faces pictured on that bulletin board haunted him, flooding his soul, washing over him like an inescapable torrent that grabbed his heart with a meat hook and wouldn't let go. The next time he looked up, he spoke with a tone of sadness in his voice. "Well, I guess we've got a score to settle."

"I'll let 'em all know what you found out." Russum hung up the phone, turned off his encryption device, then spoke to the group. "Langley detected a flash, some form of nuclear detonation, only a few miles north of the bunker."

"A flash? So what does that mean?" Graham asked quietly.

"Any way you cut it, it's not good. One of our drones flew

through the area less than twenty-four hours later and measured normal levels of radiation."

"Normal levels sounds hard to believe," Buck observed.

"Yeah, Langley thought so too, so three days later they sent in two men from our welcome committee."

"And?"

"They reported the same thing. Our advance team measured no lingering radiation and no new deaths due to the flash. Apparently, the Iraqis rounded up a few blind rebels following the blast and that's about the extent of it."

"No deaths? Maybe that's a good thing," Graham said, searching for the sunny side.

"To our knowledge, no one else in the world has such a weapon as this and it can only mean trouble. It's clean, it's nuclear, and Iraq's got it. We gotta assume they developed it and its trigger's built outta red mercury."

"I see where you're headed and I'm afraid." Graham's voice was somber.

"If they can build this device, in all probability, they have the means to manufacture pure-fusion neutron bombs. I'd bet a month's salary that they're building 'em as we speak."

Silence; the group was stunned. Reality was closing in around them and there was no place to hide.

Following an extended discussion of their options, Buck concluded, "Then that's it. Time is of the essence. We go in PDQ and there's no alternative."

"Yep," Russum agreed. "They're building 'em somewhere. If not in this bunker, then somewhere else."

"You think they're already in mass production?" Graham asked, not really wanting to hear the answer.

"It's our job to find out."

"Dammit to hell," Buck snapped, looking at Wyley. "The devil's in the details, but for the life of me, I thought it was a good idea at the time. Truth is, it's too damn risky. I can't convince myself we can make it work."

"You're talking about that prisoner swap."

"Yeah. If we could plant you on the inside, you'd be worth your weight in gold, but I'll be damned if I can see how to pull it off on a short fuse."

"I knew it'd be tough, but I trust your judgment."

"There's no way we can do it. End of story. Even if we only snatched a couple of prisoners to help us plan, the guards would get suspicious. Chances are, they'd change their routine and that'd do a lot more harm than good. Our plans depend on their routine, and if they go to changing it, it could set us back for weeks."

"Yeah, I know."

"We've worked through decoy and diversion scenarios, even considered running an extra van into that tunnel to set you up on a late-night shift, but when push comes to shove, they're all too risky. If they get suspicious, we're sunk."

"Well, I'm relieved anyway. I haven't had a good night's sleep since you hatched up that half-baked idea."

"It seemed like a good idea at the time," Russum added in Buck's defense.

"As it stands, we'll go in behind Delta Force as a specialty team. Once they secure the bunker, we cover it with a fine-tooth comb."

"Kind of a rear-guard action," Wyley affirmed, playing back what he thought he understood.

"Yep. They'll bear the brunt of the battle and hold us in reserve."

"Mary is one of those women who don't need a man in order to feel good about herself," Buck said, clearly pleased with his conclusion.

In the middle of yet another no-place-like-home conversation, Graham and Wyley were nodding agreement when Russum entered the room.

"I hope I'm not interrupting anything important."

"Nothing that won't wait, Billy-boy. What's your story?" Buck grinned.

"The advance team took a look at your sandbar," Russum said, speaking to Graham. "They found pay dirt."

"Really," Graham responded, pleased to have surfaced on their radar screen.

"So spit it out," Buck pressed. "What'd they find?"

"Inconclusive result, but you could be right. It might be a ventilator shaft. They couldn't rule it out. And one of those units looked like a condenser; you know, the refrigeration part of an air-conditioning system."

"All that sounds pretty suspicious to me," Graham said.

"Me too," Buck agreed. "Good enough for a fallback plan anyway. Why couldn't they nail that sucker down?"

"Short of beaching on the sandbar and risking discovery, that's the best they could do from across the river."

"Yeah, that makes sense. Find out anything else?"

"Yep. They brought along some gadget that works like a supersensitive ear. Turns out, one of those big boxes sounds like a huge blower assembly. They couldn't see it because it was camouflaged by some fishnet, but the giveaway was that power substation and cellular antenna tower."

"The what?"

"You gotta be kidding."

"No, I'm completely serious. There in open view, out on the middle of that sandbar, the power company poured a concrete pad and built a substation on it. From the way they described it, that sandbar was fed some serious power, great big transformers and glass insulators stacked high, and all of 'em standing in the shadow of a huge cellular tower."

"Funny they didn't try to hide it." Buck smelled deception.

"Yeah, our guys thought the same thing at first, then they figured it looked commercial. In fact, they said near the hospital, it didn't look out of place at all. They've got high-voltage lines strung across the river as plain as the nose on your face and they all run to this substation that feeds the hospital and cell tower. Funny thing, though, that substation sounds big enough to feed a small city."

"Any other antennas on that tower?"

"What do you mean?"

"You know. Radio antennas, UHF, satellite dishes, that kind of thing."

"Yeah, that tower's stacked top to bottom with 'em."

"So if nothing else, we know their comm site and where they get their power," Graham observed. "And we might know where they get their breathing air."

Buck smiled. "They probably use a combination of gear, including landline for their comm backup, but that tower will be the first to fall. We'll have to be careful, though; we don't want to knock out their power."

"Their computers?" Wyley asked.

"That's what I was thinking anyway."

"When your SEALs take out that tower," Graham asked, "can't they check out the air conditioner? If it feeds the bunker, tear gas might save a lot of lives."

"My thinking exactly." Buck grinned. "I thought you'd be pleased."

"We're not there yet," Russum concluded, "but our prospects're looking a lot better."

"It's not perfect," Buck agreed, "but no plan ever is. Fact is, we're out of time. Either we go with what we've got or Washington will plan it for us."

CHAPTER TWENTY-THREE

Motion
Saturday, Apr. 17, 9:03 P.M.
Onboard a Sea Stallion
Flying low over the Persian Gulf

So far this evening, everything had gone pretty much as they'd practiced. With the exception of crosswinds and chop near the surface, even the weather was cooperating, thank God.

Outside, the moonless night was black as pitch; below them, the filthy gulf glistened from thick black crude, and overhead, an infinite black sky was filled with clouds they couldn't see.

Ultimately, they found themselves held aloft—suspended between heaven and hell—by wind, power, and noise.

But mainly noise.

Seven whirling forty-foot-long rotor blades provided the wind while three screaming engines provided power plus noise enough to airlift the crew, one armored vehicle, plus four fully equipped special operations troops to target.

Flying nine abreast in a tight wedge formation, they were cruising in lockstep at 150 knots, only two hundred feet above the Persian Gulf. This type of low-level formation flying reminded the Sikorsky pilot of his high school football days, but little beyond the wedge shape of the formation felt familiar. Their night penetration mission profile was schedule driven, timed down to the minute, and as a result, it left them no margin for error. Their mission was to penetrate Iraqi airspace undetected, ferry special ops forces to their drop zones, unload them near the entrance to the tunnels, then bring them back once the bunker had been breached.

The big Sikorsky Sea Stallion carrying them into harm's way, the MH-53J Pave Low heavy-lift helicopter, was one of the largest, most advanced helicopters in the world. Its terrain-following radar, infrared sensors, and map display allowed the pilot to follow terrain contours, making their low-level penetration possible. Easily recognized by its boxlike fuselage and large horizontal stabilizer, the Super Stallion boasted three redundant turbo-shaft engines. Armor plated and bristling with .50-caliber machine guns, in many ways it resembled a helicopter version of World War II's Flying Fortress.

Inside its cargo bay, a nuclear weapons officer tried to set aside his fear and imagine capturing the first pure-fusion weapon he'd ever seen. Beside him, a computer expert sat strapped to his seat, head rocking back and forth, sound asleep. Closest to the door, white-knuckled and looking pretty nervous, a doctor gazed outside into the darkness. As it happened, the officer in charge of the team didn't look much better, a captain best described as unblooded. He'd never experienced live combat, but on the other hand, everyone on this mission was in the same boat.

Their mission was clear: Get inside the bunker, find out what was going on, and get out.

Plug-and-Play
Saturday, Apr. 17, 9:05 P.M.
The Bunker
Basra, Iraq

Kajaz Hamandhani handed dark goggles to al-Mashhadi's advisors, confident that no one would be disappointed. After studying all the faces present, the weapons director was satisfied that everyone who mattered was there.

He looked up at al-Mashhadi on video link, made eye contact through the big man's dark black slits, then began his demonstration by first introducing Hakim Moussavi, the terrorist and most wanted man on the face of the earth, to the Iraqi dignitaries.

Cabinet members, old and young alike, nodded in homage to the young terrorist. His achievement in New York's Financial District was widely known, but his face was not.

While this conclave was smaller than the first such gathering, most believed it to be the weapons director's last chance. This wasn't the first such demonstration al-Mashhadi had assembled in the bunker, but this time, Kajaz was confident they were ready, and he was out to sway the Iraqi cabinet.

"Follow me, please," Kajaz said, addressing the group.

The weapons director led the group onto the factory floor. It was organized in a way that telegraphed industrial organization and simplicity. The factory mezzanine—a partial second story surrounded by a catwalk—provided storage cages plus conference rooms, computers, and office space for his engineers. By contrast, the factory floor housed the milling, test, and assembly equipment necessary to mass-produce, package, and ship pure-fusion neutron bombs to anyplace on earth. Not surprisingly, it was organized such that raw material came in the access tunnel entrance side of the bunker with finished product carried out the other to the hospital loading dock.

Kajaz led the group out onto the factory floor, close to the corner nearest the hospital. Stopping in the packing area, the weapons director drew Hakim's attention to a factory worker packaging a large tray of softball-sized bombs in cube-shaped boxes.

"As you suggested," Kajaz said to Hakim. As it happened, the worker was standing by a slowly moving conveyor belt, spraying an expanding viscous liquid in each box, encapsulating every bomb in a bed of foam before shipping. The young terrorist recognized his suggestion had been taken seriously and acknowledged satisfaction.

Kajaz knew this wouldn't be their first successful detonation, nor would it be their second, third, or fourth. As he'd planned, detonating neutron bombs was part of his factory's production process now and was strictly a matter of routine. Bombs were pulled off the production line on a daily basis, analyzed, and detonated to verify quality.

For the weapons director, this demonstration was like any other day at the office.

From the beginning, the weapons director had been obsessed with quality control, and to this end, he knew that when a bomb shipped from his facility, there was a 99.9 percent chance it would detonate on command. He proudly boasted his bombs were produced with three-nines reliability and described them as plug-and-play chaos you could count on.

Kajaz walked over to a pallet stacked waist high with white, cube-shaped boxes, then spoke again to Hakim. "Would you select a device for our demonstration tonight?"

Hakim looked at the weapons director, a bit puzzled. "Any device?"

Kajaz nodded.

Hakim walked back over to the factory worker's desk and picked out a fresh pit, one which had only recently been packed in foam. The worker handed the white box to Hakim and he returned it to the group.

Kajaz then led them to a pallet stacked head high with boxes containing detonation electronics. "Pick one," he said with his thin smile.

Hakim did so without comment. "What about batteries?" he asked as an afterthought.

"Batteries are included."

"Good."

Finally, the director escorted the cabinet members to his test facility alongside the pump room, against the bunker wall nearest the sandbar. It was a small room centered around a thick viewing glass portal overlooking the blast chamber. Culling Hakim from the group, he escorted him through a massive, submarine-grade hatch, into a thick-walled metal test chamber. Inside, Kajaz pointed to a heavy, slate-top table occupying most of the room. "Please assemble the bomb for us, here, in view of the group."

Hakim could see the cabinet members through the thick glass and again looked puzzled.

"It's exactly like the one you assembled in New York," the director assured him.

Hakim nodded understanding, then laid both boxes on the table and went to work. First thing he did was remove the battery from his remote control, and then he assembled the bomb. Once the detonator cables were attached, he placed the Medusa head assembly on a heavy pedestal, picked up the remote control, then joined the others.

Once the terrorist cleared the chamber, the director checked the hatch's watertight seal. Overall, the blast chamber was constructed like the breech of a water-cooled rifle barrel. Water surrounded the explosion while the blast force escaped upward to the surface, following the path of least resistance. Satisfied with the hatch, the director opened the vents, flooding river water into the tanks surrounding the chamber.

After joining the others, he reinstalled the battery in Hakim's remote control, then explained his actions. "The water jacket will shield us, absorbing the neutron radiation and heat. Force from the blast will be vented away from us, toward the surface."

Al-Mashhadi narrowed his squint and spoke for the first time over video link. "You've tested this before, correct?"

"Yes, many times," Kajaz responded. "Put on your goggles and stand clear of the portal. As you know, our manufacturing facility is mechanically isolated on springs. You will feel a slight tremor and hear a muffled explosion, that is all. Our detonation is successful as long as we achieve an eighty percent conversion to neutron radiation or better. We measure conversion efficiency several ways and it's displayed here, on this screen." He pointed to a TV monitor, mounted on the wall, showing three numbers.

Looking through the portal, Kajaz could barely discern the distorted outline of the Medusa's head. Turning away, he preferred to watch his TV monitor. Scanning his instruments for green lights, the director made sure his measurement equipment was operational, then set a timer.

"We are ready," he announced. "Ten seconds to detonation and counting. Five, four, three, two, one."

Kajaz depressed the remote.

A fantastic bright light flooded through the portal as a ball of superheated steam streaked toward the surface. Less than five seconds later, the event was over and their American-made measurement equipment flashed a message on-screen in English:

```
Data Acquisition Complete
```

There were only three indicators the weapons director took seriously. They read simply:

```
85% 86% 85%
```

The weapons director looked his boss in the eye, feeling vindicated by the numbers. "Our manufacturing process is well in hand, our testing is complete, and we're ready to ship."

Al-Mashhadi's eyes widened on video. "How long have you been in production?"

"We've been in limited production for two weeks and have produced nearly four hundred pure-fusion pits. We're fully trained and ready to shift into full mass-production now. My organization has its arms around this problem and we have the quality controls we need to produce these bombs by the thousands. Considering the stockpiles of red mercury available, there's no limit to the number of bombs we could produce over the next few months. Even with production running around the clock, my Basra facility could manufacture ten pits per hour, maybe more."

"And the detonation electronics?" the big man asked, thinking ahead to his next problem.

"Detonator electronics can be manufactured anywhere in the industrialized world."

"How many bombs are here, in your facility, now?"

Kajaz clattered several keys on his computer keyboard, then responded, "Ninety-six. The rest have been shipped, dispersed to weapons warehouses across Iraq."

"Excellent, my friend. That is excellent." Al-Mashhadi's eyes narrowed, then he seemed to relax for a moment. "You know, I look at you and think of your dear father. What a man he was. He would be proud of you were he alive today. God is great."

The group agreed, acknowledging the director's astute judgment regarding this matter. Though they'd bullied him for immediate results from the very beginning, they admired his toughness. He'd stood by his principles, prevailing with an achievement comparable to the development of the first atomic bomb.

After their approval had been expressed, the Iraqis grew silent and, once again, al-Mashhadi addressed the group by video link. "Is there any problem supporting our weapons director during his transition to full mass production?"

The minister of defense, a broad-shouldered, leathery-looking man, thought for a moment, then added one suggestion. "We should duplicate this facility now that we know how to make the bomb."

The lab director agreed, but deferred his comments to al-Mashhadi. "We intend to do exactly that. New plant construction is already under way."

The group's reaction could best be described as one of unanimous, overwhelming support.

They'd wanted this for years . . .

Changes
Saturday, Apr. 17, 9:17 P.M.
Onboard a Sea Stallion
Flying low over the Persian Gulf

They had been airborne only twenty minutes. Back in the cargo bay, it seemed more like twenty hours. As they flew closer to land, the adrenaline began pumping, and time seemed to stand still.

Forward in the cockpit, the pilot looked at the clock on the instrument panel, then back at his gauges. Seemed like that damn clock was stuck, but everything else looked normal.

Suddenly, a siren howled as a yellow indicator began blinking a warning message that the main rotor could fail.

In one smooth motion, the pilot squelched the siren and cleared the alarm. Before he could speak, it went off again, and this time, it turned red and wouldn't be quieted.

```
Main Rotor: Failure Imminent
```

One minute, the Sea Stallion appeared on tracking radar as a blip. On-screen, air traffic controllers watched nine dots closing on the coast.

And then there were eight.

Night Eyes Rule
Saturday, Apr. 17, 9:34 P.M.
Outside the access tunnel entrance
Basra, Iraq

It was dark inside the tin maintenance building and the place smelled like dirty engine oil.

Unseen by anyone outside, a SEAL cameraman removed a night-eye reconnaissance device from his equipment case. Its critics back in Washington called it cute. In the field, reconnaissance practitioners called it a technological miracle. It was show time, and he had to make sure their flying eye was operational after their wet ingress to target.

First thing, the cameraman connected a battery to the small ball and signaled the pilot sitting on the dirt floor.

He sat and watched his flat panel display, one hand on the rotor collective control, the other on a joystick. Studying the screen, the young man felt satisfied that the night eye's data link and autopilot were working. "Ready to rock." He grinned.

Holding the ball-shaped body of the miniature helicopter in one hand, the cameraman slid the shaft from his handheld starter over the main rotor of his tiny chopper. Squeezing the starter switch, he spun its two-inch rotor up to speed in the blink of an eye. Its micromotor caught on the fourth revolution, but unlike a model airplane engine, it made almost no audible noise. About the size of a human eye, the gyroscopically stabilized flying machine looked like a miniature version of the McDonnell Douglas Little Bird helicopter—an eyeball suspended beneath a two-inch main rotor, stabilized by its tail boom and tiny tail rotor assembly.

Once he sensed it was ready, the cameraman felt the gyroscopically stabilized camera pivoting inside the ball as he lifted the lilliputian helicopter over his head for launch.

As the pilot increased the pitch of the blades, the cameraman felt the rotor downwash blowing the hair on the back of his hand.

Once the chopper's twisting motion faded, he released the night eye with all the care of a fragile hummingbird. Through his night-vision goggles, he made sure it hovered where he released it, six feet off the dirt floor.

As its automatic pilot trained, it bobbed a bit, dipping slightly, overshooting its original altitude, then settled back to its original release point.

"Stability looks good," the cameraman confirmed. Once he'd gotten comfortable behind his own control console alongside the pilot, he took off his goggles. From that point forward, neither he nor the pilot could see their micromachine, and that took some getting used to. He punched a VCR function key and started the videotape recorder running. Adjusting the camera's focus, he backed off the zoom, yielding a wide-angle view of the building's interior. The infrared image revealed vivid detail through the darkness, and soon the cameraman nodded to the pilot. "Let's rock."

The pilot headed his tiny chopper toward a broken window, tilted his joystick slightly forward, and flew out of the building.

A quick survey of the urban landscape rendered the main and access tunnels as two black, circular-shaped holes set in a cold, concrete wall. Without hesitation, the pilot dipped the nose and streaked toward the access tunnel. As he neared its entrance, he climbed near the top of the curved wall and darted forward with a series of quick abrupt motions, similar to that of a hummingbird flitting from flower to flower—a sort of sprint, dwell, sprint pattern.

Near the entrance, everything looked normal enough, much like any civilian tunnel construction project back in the States. The tunnel walls appeared like most under construction, some sections dry, others dripping water between the seams, but overall, the scene could best be described as a flight down the inside of a leaky pipe whose walls were lined with tile. The pilot and cameraman recorded no hidden gun emplacements, booby traps, mines, or gas vents, nothing out of the ordinary except for the fierce headwind.

And when you're smaller than a hummingbird, a killer headwind is significant.

The pilot adjusted the autopilot to compensate for the headwind, and it took everything the control system could deliver to hover the little bird in the midst of the gale.

Ahead, in the distance, the cameraman could make out people: guards and rebel prisoners from the looks of them. Guards had guns; prisoners, most of them anyway, had shovels. They could play back the videotape and count heads later; what was important now was that they run their sweep through the bunker.

As the night eye darted over the guards below, the picture suddenly froze, breaking up into tiles. As fast as humanly possible, the pilot pulled back on his control stick, commanding his lilliputian chopper to halt.

Flying blind, with his visual frozen, the pilot's control link remained operational, he hoped. His heads-up display showed him hovering near the top of the tunnel, slowly drifting backward, twenty feet above the floor. He couldn't analyze the picture problem now, he had to get out and get out now, undetected by the guards below.

Twisting the control handle through a series of short, tail thruster bursts, the little bird's pilot rotated his chopper around toward the tunnel entrance.

Although the pilot felt none of these twists and turns firsthand, he felt good about his prospects for getting out undetected. The readouts on his display weren't like being there, but they were the next best thing. In a sense, flying on instruments was like flying blind through a storm cloud without the bumps.

His readouts showed him drifting toward the entrance.

Still, no picture.

Next he punched a navigation function key, pinging the floor and tunnel walls with ultrahigh frequency sound to verify his position. After centering the tiny craft near the top of the tunnel arch, he switched the positioning system to continuous ping, constantly updating his position. It wasn't stealthy, it could be detected by intrusion equipment, but he'd seen no evidence of extraordinary security measures here. Humans couldn't hear the batlike sonar signal and he had to hope the tunnel security·systems hadn't been equipped to hear it either.

He dipped the nose slightly, edging forward toward the entrance, all the while maintaining constant distance from the tunnel wall and floor. Constantly fighting a stiff tailwind, it felt like a losing game of three-dimensional chess.

He inched the craft forward, pushing the stick slightly, then easing it back.

Nothing.

Forward again.

Nothing, the picture was wasted.

Again.

Nothing.

He'd retreated almost twenty feet now; he had to be getting close.

Checking the videotape, the cameraman confirmed his intuition. He was within three feet of the spot where they'd first lost picture.

Push, pull.

Nothing.

Push, push, pull.

The video appeared looking out toward the tunnel entrance, and almost as quickly, the cameraman noticed something telling about the picture. Once the video signal was reacquired, only a trace—the thinnest sliver—of the tunnel entrance showed on-screen.

"The tunnel's interfering with our signal," the cameraman concluded. "When we lose sight of the entrance, we lose picture."

"High tech," the pilot grimaced. "Ya gotta love it."

"Technology's a blessing and a curse."

It was eerie. No sooner had the cameraman stated his observation than he felt the satellite phone in his pants pocket vibrating. Pulling it from its holster, the young SEAL rolled his eyes. The caller ID said it all—Washington area code.

He answered to find some admiral's aid at the other end dead set on telling him how to do things.

"Your signal's garbled, sir, breaking up." The young SEAL sounded convincing. "Some kind of interference. I only got two bars at my end. Must be the building."

Click!

"Oh, too bad, man. I lost signal." The cameraman snatched the battery from his phone and shoved it in his pocket. "I feel a lot better knowing they're back there running my business."

CHAPTER TWENTY-FOUR

Something's Wrong Here
Saturday, Apr. 17, 10:05 P.M.
Approaching Nightstop station
South of Basra, Iraq

Whop whop whop whop whop.

By now, the sound and shake of their Huey felt familiar to Graham, much like that of an old friend, but unfortunately that's where the familiarity ended. Flying treetop level somewhere over the grasslands of southern Iraq, shrouded by the pitch black of night, everything else about their situation felt outside the box—*way outside.*

Scariest of all—the thing that really caused Graham's pulse to ratchet up a notch—was flying in this low, this fast, for this long in absolute darkness. He still couldn't believe it. Fact was, they were hauling butt, screaming in wide open, throttles to the firewall, flying so low they kicked up a wake of dust and flying debris behind them.

Forward in the cockpit, Buck scanned his instruments with clockwork precision, but didn't look worried. He shifted a little on his rock-hard seat then headed the helo down the final leg of their journey to Nightstop station. The way he figured it, considering everything they were facing tonight and all the things that could go wrong, flying was the easy part. All he had to do was hug the nap of the earth and stay beneath Iraqi radar coverage. Besides, at low altitudes, Iraqi radar coverage had as many holes in it as a piece of Swiss cheese.

While Buck manned the flight controls, Russum sat to his right in the copilot's seat, riding shotgun, continuously scanning the horizon for hills. Not that he needed to; Buck and his terrain-avoidance radar had the situation well in hand, but it made him feel better to see a clear horizon ahead and also kept him out of trouble. Buck noticed when Russum was really nervous he unconsciously scanned the horizon and kept his hands off the instruments. *One less thing to worry about,* Buck mused.

Watching Buck's relaxed, professional manner helped Russum keep his fear in check. He considered Buck a natural inside the cockpit, a flesh-and-blood extension of the Huey's control system. A man of minimum words and motion, there was nothing that happened inside the cockpit or out that he didn't notice.

To the rear, from inside the cargo bay, Wyley and Graham scanned the Iraqi grasslands for signs of life and an occasional tree. Outside, the blackness extended horizon to horizon as each man surveyed the endless terrain below through night-vision goggles.

Over the intercom, Graham heard Buck key his radio and worried that they could be detected. What he didn't know was that radio silence was a thing of the past because their transmission looked like noise and only friendly forces could detect, let alone reconstruct, their signal. "Nightstop, this is Nightrider 101. We're feet dry, approaching from the southwest, bearing two one four. Request IR beacon and permission to land."

"Roger, 101. Set down on your mark and stand by. Our situation has changed."

Ahead, Graham saw a bright greenish light suddenly appear, penetrating the inky black gloom like a torch. Streaking toward the infrared beacon like a hurling rock, Buck banked in at fifty feet then leveled out. Beneath them, Graham watched the greenish light draw closer. In a matter of seconds, Buck slowed to a hover directly over the beacon and Graham could see the light illuminating a circular section of flat grassy field.

Nightstop station was a hastily assembled staging area, refueling and supply depot for their raid and rescue operation. It was set up after dark earlier that evening, and it would be taken down once their operations concluded before dawn. Nightspot consisted of a makeshift hospital, a drop site for supplies, and a grass landing strip for tanker aircraft, troops, and helicopters. But most telling was that there were no visible lights, none whatsoever. Without night-vision goggles, Graham couldn't make out anything with any degree of certainty, yet to his surprise, he could make out the hot, greenish hulks of their attack force—at rest—neatly organized in rows on the ground below.

Something's wrong here, he thought. All the rotary and fixed-wing aircraft were parked as if they were sleeping, yet they should have lifted off over half an hour ago and already be deployed around the tunnel. Positioned around the outside of the staging area's perimeter, he counted seven big Sikorsky Sea Stallions and six Hercules HC-130 tanker aircraft.

Graham knew they'd started with nine Sikorskys and two were missing. Besides that, having the tanker and supply aircraft on the ground was a dead giveaway that something had already gone seriously wrong. Originally, the tanker crews planned to remain airborne, circling well outside Iraqi airspace, on call for refueling the choppers during their return run over the gulf.

Once on the grass, ground crews came rushing toward them ferrying fuel and three palettes stacked high with supplies.

"We've had a change in plan," Graham heard a young officer tell Buck.

"I gathered as much," Buck replied, stepping down out of the cockpit.

The young officer handed him a supply list and he scanned it, looking for the load's total weight. "You're loading us to the max, Lieutenant. What the hell happened?"

"I've got some bad news, Commander."

"The night's young." Buck tried to smile. "Can't be as bad as all that."

"There's been an accident and we've lost three outta nine choppers. One's missing and two are down for maintenance."

"How 'bout the crew?"

"Don't know yet. They were flying low and dropped off-screen. Seven men all told: three crew, four mission specialists. They're still searching for survivors."

"What happened? Did anyone see anything?"

"They saw her go in. Not much margin for error at that altitude."

"Tell me about it. We'd expected to lose one Stallion to maintenance, two at most; I mean, we know the ole horse has got some problems, but we never planned for thirty-three percent attrition en route to target."

"We're critically short of transports, Commander, no doubt about it, and they need you in medical."

Buck checked through their supplies—there was enough gas here to put New York to sleep—then the foursome set off for the medical tent.

As expected, the six fixed-wing aircraft on the ground were configured as tankers or troop transports, for hauling in the fuel, assault teams, and ground support. Curiously, Graham sensed a considerable amount of movement surrounding each aircraft, and intuitively, he surmised the assault may be late, but hadn't been aborted.

Entering medical, the foursome weaved their way through a whirlwind of soldiers coming and going, then headed to the center of the storm. Recognizing the sweaty officer in charge, Buck interrupted his discussion and cut to the crux. "What's the situation here, gentlemen?"

The ops officer went silent and studied Buck from top to bottom. Decked out in desert camouflage and face paint, the officer didn't recognize Commander Buck Harrison at first, not without his long hair and beard. Still, one aspect about the big man stood apart immediately. He had presence; you knew when he walked in because he commanded attention. And the guy had to be a SEAL because nothing about his uniform struck the operations officer as standard issue. From his hood to his Israeli combat vest and boots, this big SEAL struck the ops officer as a custom piece of work. Once he drew closer, Buck's eyes revealed his identity and the officer's expression revealed both relief and recognition. "Am I ever glad to see you, sir. This mission may have cost us seven lives already—one helicopter crew plus our nuclear weapons specialty team. On top of that, we've lost one Super Stallion plus two are down for maintenance. Our primary strike forces are on hold and we're an hour behind schedule already."

"What's the situation forward?"

"On schedule. The trucks and supplies are across the bridge, positioned near the hospital. Bridge and tower have been wired; they're ready to blow."

"Good. Any problem placing the charges?"

"No; so far, they're undetected."

"How about tunnel recon? We got our night eyes in there?" Commander Harrison wanted to know if his SEAL recon team had flown their miniature Unmanned Aerial Vehicles into the tunnel for a look-see.

"Yes, the insertion team's operating out of an equipment shed near the tunnel, but they've got problems. The tunnel clobbers their signal."

"You seen any video?"

"Enough to know we can't count on it. Bottom line is those little UAVs don't work very well in the tunnel. Not enough range."

"Hmph. So let me play it back the way I see it," Buck said. "We're below minimum transport strength outta the chute and our tunnel recon's been ineffective."

"I've got to push back on your assessment, Commander," Ops countered. "We're down, but we're not out. It's more like we've straddled the fence; we could go either way. We've got a work-around, but if we delay any longer, we'll miss our strike window." The officer went silent for a moment and Buck grew impatient.

"Spit it out. We can't abort this mission if we've got any chance at all. The stakes here are staggering." Buck recalled the gas being loaded on their chopper, then continued, "You're using the Huey, right?"

"Yeah."

"And? Give it to me straight."

"Bottom line is this, Commander. We need you and your Huey, but we can't order these civilians to the front line." The officer pointed to Graham, Wyley, and Russum.

Next, Ops looked at Russum, singled him out, then asked, "You're that guy from the CIA, right? That nuclear weapons expert?"

"My name's Russum, Billy Ray Russum. I work for the

government and nuclear devices are my specialty." After making eye contact with Graham and Wyley, he continued, "We'd planned on moving into the bunker as a team, once it'd been secured."

"Yeah, I know, but we're fresh outta transports, Mr. Russum. Would you fly in with the main force and help off-load the Huey?"

Russum looked at Wyley's face, but his typically animated expression now telegraphed nothing. Next, he looked at Graham and noticed how fear had a way of showing through his eyes. "Is this the only alternative we got?" he asked Buck. "Can't you pick us up once the dust settles?"

"No time to off-load and run a round-trip."

"If you're in, we go," Ops said to Russum. "If not, we'll need to rethink our situation. Chances are we'll have to abort the mission."

"Count me in, Buck. I brought you this far, and I'll be damned if I'm gonna turn back now." Looking at Graham and Wyley, he continued, "You two need to speak for yourselves."

"I remember the dead." Wyley sighed. "I'm not cut out for this, but I've been in it since Hama."

"I can't forget the children," Graham whispered. "I'm not cut out for this either, but just promise me one thing."

"What's that?"

"If I get hurt, don't leave me there. Don't leave me there alone, to die with them."

Buck put his large hand on Graham's shoulder. "We don't desert our own."

A long silent pause followed, then Graham released a sigh. "Well anyway, if I get killed, at least I know what I'm dying for."

"Don't talk like that, Graham. It won't come to that. I won't let it come to that."

"Nightstop, this is Nightrider 101," Buck said into his throat mike. "We're airborne."

"Roger, 101, Nightstop has you loud and clear. You're good to target. Godspeed."

Click, click.

Buck shifted a little in his seat, then sighed resignedly. Another change in plan after the show started.

Packed in the rear cargo bay like sardines, Wyley and Graham studied their monitor as if their lives depended on it. Watching the early action over video link, Wyley and Graham could see how the strike was going and, so far tonight, it looked bad. Even before the strike force touched down, the night sky over Basra lit up like a fireworks display. Once chopper pilots started calling out Triple-A warnings, there was no doubt about it. It was really dangerous in there.

Forward in the cockpit, Buck and Russum could only hear audio of the action—they had no video screen—and imagined the worst.

"What the hell's going on?" Buck demanded, still focused on his instruments. "Where'd that Triple-A come from?"

Russum looked forward, clearly concerned. Well ahead, on the distant edge of their horizon, the sky suddenly lit up like a beacon, easily visible to the naked eye. "We have no information about antiaircraft guns in the area."

"I can't see what's happening on the ground," Graham said, struggling to stay calm, "but no one's been hit in the air. Stick to the original plan; come in low over the river and we should be okay."

"I agree," Wyley added.

"The original plan, you say," Buck said. "Now that's a switch." After listening to Triple-A chatter until he could stand it no longer, he spoke again to Graham. "What do you see? What's it like over target?"

"It reminds me of those night videos taken over Baghdad during the Gulf War."

"Yeah, I know what you mean. I see a red glare in the distance, like the sky's on fire."

"Tracers are lighting up the night, but our boys are flying in low. Flak's exploding high over their heads."

"Uncoordinated?"

"Yeah, I think so. It's like an all-out effort to fill the sky with shrapnel."

"They're fighting the Gulf War again," Buck said softly. "That'll be useful."

"You're right," Russum acknowledged. "Same tactics."

"They're geared up to take out stealth fighters, but no one's gunning for choppers, not yet anyway."

"That makes sense," Graham agreed. "I never thought about it, but that's the way I'd read it too."

"Well, that's one thing we got going for us anyway," Buck mused.

"What do you mean?"

"If they continue to do what they've always done, we're golden. They're cooperating so far, and fact is, we're depending on it. They're not expecting us to come in quick and low, and their defense forces aren't equipped to counter it."

"These people aren't like us, but they're not stupid," Wyley cautioned. "They learned from both wars and they've been watching us ever since. Believe me, I know these people. They won't make the same mistakes twice."

CHAPTER TWENTY-FIVE

Bridge and Tower Down
Saturday, Apr. 17, 11:46 P.M.
Basra, Iraq

They were entering the last leg of their river approach; bright flashing lights on the antenna tower marked the target vicinity. Buck had just increased the Huey's throttle to full military power when suddenly a red light started blinking and a loud high-pitched warble echoed about the cockpit.

"Launch detection," Russum snapped. Looking out behind him, down over his shoulder, his blood ran cold. A jerky pinpoint of light streaked toward them across the darkness. He felt absolutely helpless. "Missile coming in at five o'clock."

Instinctively, Buck heaved the chopper's collective and stomped the pedals hard, spinning them through a high-torque, one-eighty turn and hurling them skyward. They were sitting ducks for any kind of missile strike and he knew it; too close to the river to maneuver and too heavily loaded to respond with any agility. Simultaneously, the Huey's defense computer tripped into overdrive, dumping a rapid-fire sequence of flares and chaff in their wake. As Buck and Russum rotated through their one-eighty, an array of heat flares ignited the night like pyrotechnic projectiles, saturating their night-vision goggles, masking the riverbank below them, rendering both men temporarily blind. For a few seconds which seemed like an eternity, Buck flew by feel and feel alone.

Meanwhile, back in the cargo bay, Graham and Wyley were both stunned after being thrown against a wall of metal gas cylinders. Neither had been trained for this and it would take a few moments before either regained his wits. Temporarily blind in front and dazed in the rear, the foursome hung suspended over the river, floundering lethargically at the mercy of the Iraqi missile launch operator on the ground below.

Unseen in the darkness, rising below them from onshore, a shoulder-launched missile had the coordinates of their engine exhaust locked in its memory. Spooling out behind the guided missile like a tether, a thin strand of glass fiber linked the missile's control surfaces to an Iraqi soldier's thumb-controlled joystick on the ground.

He'd been patient, biding his time, waiting till the chopper passed him by before letting loose his weapon. Looking up the Huey's skirt, he held his crosshairs on the chopper's engine exhaust, set his mark, then squeezed the trigger.

Beads of sweat appeared on his brow as he held his breath, struggling to steady his aim. For better or worse, his shoulder-launched missile was not a fire-and-forget weapon and it wasn't foolproof; it required a cool head, intense concentration, and all the nerve one man could muster to hold it on target. While the missile remained in flight, he knew it was imperative that he track the chopper's position with his crosshairs. He was, in effect, driving a large, screaming bullet to target . . . but his trouble was obvious. Driving a bullet requires a steady, practiced hand and, above all else, clear vision.

But all he could see were flares.

Given no alternative, he guided his missile to the vicinity where he judged the chopper should be and . . .

BAROOOM!!!

A blazing fireball ignited to one side and below the cockpit, the shock wave slamming the Huey laterally to one side with a lurch.

Buck's heart was thumping now, his chest about to explode, and he smelled hydraulic fluid. Moments later, once his night vision partially returned, he scanned his instruments. A maze of red lights summarized their plight. Their hydraulics had taken a hit, and they were flying in on backup. If nothing else went wrong, they'd make it in, but flying out of there . . . well, he couldn't think about that now. His rotor control was fading fast, already feeling spongy, but the target was in sight. He felt like he was riding in on a wounded bronco, heading for the last roundup.

Buck could see their landing zone rushing up at them, a flat parking lot behind the equipment shed, bordered by bright klieg lights, just outside the entrance to the main tunnel. Pulling his control stick back into his lap, Buck tried to level the chopper. The main rotor's tilt responded sluggishly, slowing their forward progress. Their descent was level now, but they were plummeting from the sky like a rock.

"Hold on," he yelled, wrestling the rotor collective to its stops to slow their descent.

The crooked stripes on the parking lot were clearly visible when the rotor finally yielded to Buck's will. Refusing to give up, he demanded maximum pitch from his lethargic rotors, and finally got it. He didn't have time to think about it but he knew a miracle when he saw one.

In his windshield, towers of bright klieg lights rushed up to meet them, and in an instant, their overloaded Huey slammed down on the asphalt with a resounding *clang*. The metal gas cylinders in their cargo bay didn't take impact without complaint.

Still, they hit the pavement hard but didn't roll over.

No fire, the landing skids remained intact . . . but what about Graham and Wyley? They carried enough gas to put New York City out of commission. Buck punched his throat mike. "You okay back there?"

"Yeah, I think so."

"Damage?"

"Nothing obvious, not yet anyway."

Buck and Russum looked at one another, then exhaled in relief. They would walk away from this landing shaken, but not broken.

No sooner had they climbed out of the chopper than the night sky seemed to ignite overhead.

A staccato of explosions reverberated across the parking lot, shaking the ground. With each explosion, another red-orange fireball lit up a smoke-filled sky.

What followed next was the explosive, gut-wrenching sound of twisted steel buckling under stress. After a few moments' pause, Graham felt the earth tremble beneath his feet—something enormous was falling into the river. It was the bridge, collapsing into a twisted, crumpled mass.

Boom! Boom!

Suddenly, the blinking lights on the antenna tower went dark over the river, consumed by two fireballs. Backlit by a red-orange glow, Graham watched the tower listing badly, tilting precariously toward them onshore, and he was concerned. As it happened, they had landed much closer to the antenna than the bridge, too close by Graham's way of thinking; no more than one hundred yards to its base. It held fast for a moment, then, like a gigantic California redwood, it yielded gracefully, almost majestically, under the strain. In one protracted, slow-motion descent, the five-hundred-foot tower lay over, creating a bridge of twisted steel between the shore wall and sandbar. The enormous tower missed them coming down, but fell closer than anyone ever expected.

Before the dust settled, Graham and Wyley began off-loading weapons and gas cylinders from inside the cargo bay, carefully, without wasting time. The payload had shifted, but for the most part, it had been well secured before liftoff and their work proceeded without incident.

Forward in the cockpit, Buck and Russum surveyed the situation unfolding before them like generals overlooking a field of battle. Upriver, less than fifty yards away, they could see a Super Stallion lowering a Marine light armored vehicle (LAV) near the access tunnel entrance. In addition, they saw two boxy heavy-lift helicopter transports unloading Delta special forces out the rear down a fast-rope. Both aircraft converged on the access tunnel entrance ramp simultaneously, from different directions, and began hovering overhead. Then, as if operating in locked mechanical step, each chopper began off-loading thirty armed, fully equipped troops. Almost unbelievably, less than three minutes later, all sixty Delta Force troops had disappeared into the darkness of the access tunnel and both helicopters were gone.

Another hundred yards farther north, hovering just above the roof of the Basra teaching hospital, Buck and Russum saw this off-load scenario play out again with a slight variation. Airspace over the rooftop helipad was limited, so the first chopper flew in and off-loaded ahead of the second. Nevertheless, in less than six minutes, 180 men and women from Delta Force began converging on the bunker through every known entrance.

Though they couldn't see it from their vantage point, they knew this same scenario should be playing out in synchronized lockstep across the river, at the west bank entrance to the access tunnel.

Buck confirmed this over the radio and learned their troops were closing in at breakneck speed. In less than ten minutes, they had secured the west bank perimeter to the access tunnel, confiscated an electric locomotive, and driven the LAV thirty meters into the tunnel. To everyone's relief, their surprise had been complete, and as a result, initial resistance had been unorganized, off balance, and largely ineffective.

Timing, speed, mobility, and overwhelming force were the

linchpins behind this strike and its orchestration left as little as humanly possible to chance.

Although the size of the strike force alone wasn't necessarily overwhelming, the element of surprise combined with Delta's counterterrorist training should paralyze much of the resistance on the ground—at least that was Buck's thinking. In theory, cutting Iraqi communications, combined with the element of surprise, should create chaos, chaos should beget panic, and panic is the father of paralysis.

Buck picked up his two-way radio and spoke to his Delta and SEAL commanders on the scene for another assessment of the situation. After several short conversations, Buck confirmed that the construction railway leading into the east entrance to the access tunnel had been secured, Iraqi radio and satellite links were jammed, all communication links had been cut, the Basra telephone office had been destroyed, and American special forces were on the move, advancing in the tunnels. With their perimeter secured around the hospital and tunnel entrances, American troops were storming toward the bunker.

Their surprise had been complete; the general tone of his commanders was confident, optimistic, and invincible, but Buck was concerned.

Though extensively trained, none of his commanders had ever operated with real bullets flying by, not one had firsthand combat experience. More to the point, none had seen their friends die, not yet anyway, and none felt vulnerable.

Still, there was good news. Early advances to target met with little resistance, but they weren't there yet. In spite of their initial losses and setback earlier that evening, their mission was picking up momentum now and running under a full head of steam. Buck knew the importance of time and judged it most important his team move, and keep moving, toward the bunker.

Meanwhile, across the parking lot, Wyley hot-wired a pickup truck, then drove it back to their Huey, traversing the concrete access ramp that marked the entrance to the main tunnel. On first inspection, the scene looked like any other tunnel construction project after dark. Klieg lights threw a harsh glare across an otherwise urban landscape. Minutes later, with the truck loaded, they were ready to clear the area.

Without skipping a beat, the four men pulled Nomex ski masks over their heads, fastened their Kevlar body armor, and headed toward the equipment shed.

By the time the foursome approached the main tunnel, all digging had stopped—the bad news was that the guards and rebel conscripts had been alerted by the explosions overhead.

As they drew nearer, the entrance to the tunnel loomed over them like an all-consuming black hole. Even in daylight, Graham felt the cavernous black mouth would look forboding. Buck had said he expected the bunker to be defended with suicidal frenzy, and for the first time, Graham reluctantly agreed. There was something about this place, something menacing; experiencing it firsthand was markedly different than analyzing the pictures.

Still, one thing was consistent with their aerial photos. The main tunnel entrance was wide enough to allow two lanes of traffic while the access tunnel was smaller, one lane of traffic occupied by railroad tracks.

Cluttered with heavy earth-moving equipment, a line of dump trucks sat parked near the main tunnel's entrance, waiting their turn beneath the conveyor belt. Studying the trucks' engine compartments through his night-vision gear, Graham concluded that the digging had stopped, but only recently. Every engine stood out on his thermal screen as hot.

Buck entered the main tunnel cautiously, several feet ahead of the group. Angling downward beneath the river, the predominate characteristics of the concrete tunnel were its glaring construction lights, wind, and noise.

Wind howled out of the tunnel as if a Canadian cold front were roaring through, stirring up an endless dust cloud of small debris along its way. Russum said something about springtime dust storms on the Texas panhandle, but the others couldn't make it out over the machinery noise. Squinting, Graham and the others moved forward, pelted squarely in the face by the dust. Harsh carbon lights hurt their eyes, nasty-tasting dust coated their teeth, and flying debris only made it worse.

Graham reasoned that air handlers were blowing fresh air into the tunnels from somewhere and venting out each entrance. More than the wind, he noticed the boring machine was still running and so was the long earth-moving conveyor belt. He could hear it. Still, as best he could determine, the forward progress of the boring machine had stopped.

Like a curious child, Graham climbed the single flight of metal stairs leading to the maintenance catwalk overhead. It ran alongside the conveyor, and Graham confirmed that the belt continued to run, but carried no dirt to the trucks waiting outside.

Graham recognized the view from the catwalk offered their team an eyeball advantage, so he proceeded cautiously as Buck, Russum, and Wyley moved along the road below. A few minutes later, Graham saw one armed man walking toward them, then counted seven more guards moving their way slowly, with deliberate purpose. As smoothly as possible, he dropped to his knees, signaled Buck by radio, then slipped off his backpack.

Buck felt his radio vibrating in his pocket and pressed the transmit key twice.

He'd seen them too.

Without words, Buck dispersed Wyley and Russum to cover. Moments later, they were concealed in the darkness behind the framework of steel girders supporting the conveyor. Overhead, Graham lay still, frozen in place, thirty-five to forty feet forward of their position.

Once hidden, Buck crawled out of the steel maze, scanned the slow traffic lane again, then pulled himself back into the darkness. "They've seen us," he radioed Graham, then signaled Russum and Wyley, holding up three fingers.

Wyley followed Buck's lead, moving low and to his left, scanning the fast lane from behind a concrete barrier. Twenty yards ahead, three men moved slowly toward them, one at a time, continually maintaining their cover behind a maze of construction material and steel girders. This wasn't going to be easy. Wyley pulled his head back in and nodded tightly, holding up three fingers.

Unfortunately, what they couldn't hear was more important than who they could see.

Graham felt them approaching first through his fingertips, footsteps . . . one pair of boots, then two, stomping up metal stairs leading to the catwalk.

"I've got company up here," he said into his radio.

Still kneeling on the catwalk, he could feel each step through his legs now; they were getting closer—and fast. His heart pounded so hard it felt as if it would erupt from his chest.

"I was afraid of that," Buck answered. "How many? I got two missing down here."

"I think I found 'em both. I can't see them, but they're coming, fast."

"Listen up and stay low. You got my forty-five with ya, right?"

"Yeah, but—"

"No buts. If the time comes, don't forget to release the safety; you may have to use it. How 'bout tear gas?"

"Good idea," Graham said, feeling better now about his prospects. *I can't shoot but I can throw.* "What do you see on your side?"

"Tight group, three men at twenty yards."

"Left?"

"Three men, widely dispersed behind better cover. Closest man's forty feet away. Deep man's out sixty feet, tops."

"Should I center one in the lane?"

"Roll 'em as close to the conveyor belt as you can. They're hugging the center line directly below you."

"Tell the others, Buck. I'm on it."

In one smooth motion, he edged over the side of the catwalk, scanning the road below him with one eye. He saw them, not clearly, but three men were making their way up the right-hand side of the road, beneath the catwalk.

Pulling his gas mask from its pouch, he slipped it over his face, secured the straps, then removed three baseball-sized metal spheres from his pack. He felt better with something to do, and besides, he was good at this. Years ago, he'd been a

Little League pitcher. Rising to his knees, he pulled the pin, lifted the gas grenade above his shoulder, and hurled it into the midst of the three guards.

Seeing, but not understanding, Graham watched the gray gas cloud come rushing back toward him.

Suddenly, a deafening barrage of bullets erupted toward the catwalk from the road below—six in rapid succession, the seventh a split second later. The last round clipped the handrail above Graham's goggles, ricocheting off the galvanized pipe, streaking past his gas mask.

Pinned down by a wall of sparks and splintering metal fragments, Graham watched the gas cloud engulf him, dissipate, then blow past.

The wind, it was the wind; shielded by the mask, I forgot about the wind!

"Again," Graham heard Buck say. "Watch for the guys on the catwalk and keep your head down!"

Burrddddddddddruppt . . . Burrddddddddddruppt . . . Burrddddddddddruppt . . . Burrddddddddddruppt . . .

Heaving his heavy M60 machine gun to his shoulder, Buck laid down a blanket of lead to pin the guards on the ground and draw their fire.

Moving fast while he had a second chance, Graham pulled another pin and threw the grenade deep against the outside wall. He wouldn't miss twice.

The tunnel was shaped like the curved, inside wall of a giant pipe. Once the baseball-sized gas grenade came into contact with the wall, it clung to it, rolling down toward the center of the tunnel beneath the catwalk.

Forty feet forward, two gunmen caught a glimpse of Graham and froze on the catwalk, dead in their tracks. The younger guard with oily black hair lay on the metal grate, steadying his pistol from a prone position. Behind him, the larger man braced against the inside handrail in a kneeling position and held his sights on Graham. Smiling, the big guard's shot was clear now.

Graham could see the tear gas cloud closing behind them, but he couldn't wait for that. Instinctively, he pulled another pin, lifted himself off the grate, and chucked the grenade toward them. It rolled down the catwalk like a candlepin bowling ball rolling down the alley.

BAM!!! BAM!!!

Graham saw the muzzle flashes before he felt the fire—searing hot lead hammered him in the ribs. Winded, reeling in pain, he felt as if he'd been punched in the solar plexus. Knocked back, then recoiling forward, he fell facedown on the catwalk behind his pack, unconscious.

Even as Graham fell, a hail of bullets and orange tracers pounded the catwalk from the road below, ripping it open, laying large sections to waste. Two rounds caught the smaller guard in his chest, severing his spinal column and boring a one-inch hole through his back. A third round took down the larger guard, catching him under his jaw, blasting off the top of his head. Having been totally focused on Graham's chest, he never knew what hit him.

Buck stood poised below them long enough to make sure both men were dead. His gas mask had fogged up so he waited till the gas dissipated, then pulled it off to examine the scene. He turned away quickly when he found their blood dripping from the catwalk onto the concrete road below. Nobody moved up there except Graham, and he was moving pretty damn slow.

Two guards were dead—the remaining six, debilitated by the gas, their hands strapped to steel girders with nylon cable ties.

Before Wyley could reach Graham, he was moving again, coughing, spitting up blood. Taking account of himself, Graham knew his ribs were bruised, he was bleeding internally, but thanks to the Kevlar, he was alive. After recovering his wind, he dropped a rope over the rail, rappelled down, and joined the others. It hurt like hell, but for now, Graham elected to grin and bear it.

"We'd better keep moving," Buck said, once they'd reloaded. "I wish I could understand what these guards said. One of them had a radio and I got a real bad feeling that there's more where these came from."

"Shouldn't we interrogate the prisoners first?" Wyley

pressed. "I speak their language well enough and I can tell you one thing already. These men are scared, really scared."

"I'd be scared, too, if I'as in their shoes," Russum observed dryly.

"I'm not sure what they're scared of, but I don't think it's us."

"What then?" Buck wanted to know.

"Could be the Kurdish prisoners," Graham surmised. "I expect the rebels feel they've got a score to settle."

"That'd make sense," Wyley agreed. "Shouldn't we interrogate them before we move on?"

"Well, no one's learned anything from any guard so far and we need to know what we're up against. We need numbers: how many guards? how many troops? how many rebel prisoners? And we need a map. They could have something set up for us in there that we're not counting on." Buck then looked at Graham. "Got your stuff?"

Graham nodded, then asked, "What about their uniforms? Things might go easier for us if we disguise ourselves to look like them."

"Yeah, it's possible, but I doubt it. If Delta doesn't kill you, the rebels would. Remember, we got one hundred eighty special forces operating around us and we gotta consider friendly fire. They're discriminate shooters, but this is their first live combat and I wouldn't want our lives depending on their discretion. Besides that, you and Wyley could probably pull it off if you kept your mouths shut, but Billy Ray and I would stand out like the front line of the Chicago Bears."

Graham thought for a moment, then admitted to Wyley, "He's right, but I still think we could use their clothes, maybe not for long, but we should carry them with us."

"Be prepared," Wyley agreed, then stood for a moment, studying the build of each guard. He and Graham picked out two guards about their size, then he asked again, "So, should I interrogate the prisoners?"

The commander stood in silence considering his request, then replied, "Have at it, but we've got to move quickly."

Buck cut loose the Iraqi who looked most likely to cooperate—a wide-eyed kid who reeked of cigarettes and couldn't have been over twenty. He culled him from the group at gunpoint, led him beneath the conveyor belt, then tied him once again to a steel I-beam with another nylon cable tie. Once the tie was secure, Buck nodded to Wyley.

Wyley spoke to the young man in his own language. "What are you afraid of?"

Silence. The young guard mustered his toughest look of defiance.

Wyley didn't have time for this so he unbuttoned the guard's pants, slid them down around his ankles, then held the warm barrel of his gun against the boy's groin. He didn't look so tough anymore.

His eyes widened to the size of quarters.

"What are you afraid of now?"

The guard eyed the end of the rifle barrel, and Wyley pulled it away.

"What is it? What are you afraid of?"

"We failed to stop you and we're going to die; we're all going to die."

"We're not going to kill you. You'll be safe with us."

"There's nothing you can do to stop it. We're all going to die."

Pressured by the ticking mission clock, Buck and Graham discounted the young guard's concern, then Wyley shifted his questioning, focused on the numbers.

"How many guards in this complex?"

"I don't know." The young man shrugged.

Wyley nudged him again with his rifle barrel. The guard's eyes were open wide, his most cherished possession in peril, but he didn't speak.

"Give it a rest," Graham whispered. "He doesn't know anything."

After a couple more minutes, Wyley agreed, then the doctor injected the young man with enough sedative to knock him out between twelve and twenty-four hours. Its effect was immediate. Once he was asleep, Graham and Wyley removed the remainder of his uniform, then tucked it away for safe keeping. The kid's clothes smelled like a burning cigarette factory.

Buck chambered a single round in his forty-five caliber automatic Colt pistol, fired it into the sand, then went to fetch another prisoner with his handgun still smoking. The blast echoed through the tunnel. He returned a few minutes later with the lead guard, one of the older men in the bunch. His hair was thinning, his skin tough as leather, and if any one of them knew anything, he should be the one.

Wyley repeated his numbers question.

Ten feet away, the young sedated guard sat straddling a steel girder in his underwear, slumped forward on the ground, hands tied around the column, not moving. Through the dim light, dust, and smoke, he didn't appear to move at all.

It was no accident that the guard could smell burned powder from Buck's forty-five.

The guard sat quietly considering his situation with his head tilted to one side. A few moments later, he decided to buy himself some time. He'd been told that time was on their side, and he believed it. He'd recognized this from the beginning.

"I can tell you very little, but I will tell you what I know," he said to Wyley.

"How many guards?"

"Fifty, maybe fifty-five."

"Military? How many soldiers and civilians are in the bunker below the river?"

"You mean the Pit?"

"Yes, the Pit. How many in the Pit?"

"I don't know; never been there. I work in the tunnel behind the boring machine; oversee a wall construction crew."

"How many Kurdish rebels are on your crew?"

"Six, only six. Most rebels dig and haul dirt. My prisoners have the best job, building tunnel walls."

"How many rebels are here in the tunnel tonight?"

"One hundred, no more."

The guard revealed no more, and Buck pointed to his watch. They were out of time so Graham put the older man and remaining guards to sleep.

"We'd better get moving," Buck said. "I got a bad feeling about this."

CHAPTER TWENTY-SIX

This Can't Be Happening
Sunday, Apr. 18, 1:14 A.M.
Inside the main tunnel
Basra, Iraq

"Take cover." Buck's direction was explicit. He signaled Russum and Wyley with his fingers, and they brought their silenced MP4 submachine guns to firing position. Graham followed them into the darkness beneath the conveyor belt, tear gas in hand.

"What's that noise?" Graham heard voices, Iraqi or Kurdish voices, he didn't know which. And footsteps, many footsteps, stomping, sometimes sloshing through the tunnel muck, moving closer.

"Sounds like a herd of elephants," Buck muttered. "I think they're rebels."

Graham squinted, trying to make out their numbers. "They're carrying white flags."

The rebel leader, a bearded, rough-looking sort, directed one group of men to the right of the conveyor belt; another group dressed in prison garb continued with him up the left lane. Although Graham couldn't understand what they were saying, their appearance and behavior were revealing.

First, the men looked emaciated, exhausted, and filthy, as if they'd been underfed and overworked for a long time. Unlike the guards, they weren't stalking anything. More important than this, they carried no visible weapons. In fact, judging from their informal demeanor and constant chatter, they weren't really concerned about anything except waving their dirty white rags and drawing the attention of the Americans.

About the time they moved close enough for Graham to

make out their numbers, yellow-white flashes of muzzle fire backlit the rebels. Suddenly thunder, lightning, fire, and smoke saturated the tunnel. Men's screams filled the air, and for a few moments, Graham stared with eyes wide open, but couldn't comprehend what he saw.

Faceless silhouettes dropped to their knees toward the rear of the pack; blown over like rows of wheat, trampled, broken, they staggered, then fell. Shot from the back, mowed down with callous precision, row after row of rebels lay dying, but still, the machine-gun fire wouldn't stop.

Hakim didn't stop until the last man fell. There was no chaos, no panic, no time to react. A few rebels tried to run, but to no avail. It happened too quickly.

It was like watching some horrific scene from *The Deer Hunter* playing out in slow motion on-screen; there was nothing Graham could do but close his eyes and wish it was over.

Moments after the guns went silent, Graham and Wyley emerged from beneath the conveyor belt to aid the wounded. Buck radioed for backup, then he and Russum moved forward in the shadows, never showing themselves, hoping to wipe out the cowards behind this carnage.

Ahead in the darkness, Hakim set a timer and disappeared behind an eight-inch-thick wall of steel.

Almost immediately, Graham heard the gritty sound of dirty gears turning and squeaky, steel wheels rolling over iron rails. Above the noise of the conveyor belt, he heard electric motors stalling, straining under the load, moving something massive. Then there was a final metallic clang, like large aircraft hangar doors slamming shut, and the wind died.

Ahead, to their right, two enormous eight-inch-thick steel fire-wall doors pulled together, then locked tight.

"They're closing the gates, making a run for it," Graham said softly.

"They've got no placc to go." Wyley sighed. "I expected a last stand, but nothing like this."

"It's not over yet," Graham cautioned, his voice still shaky. Using a small, concealed penlight, he and Wyley carefully examined an exit wound on a rebel boy's inner thigh. The bullet had caught him just below his groin, penetrating the fleshy part of his leg. The boy was in shock, suffering from loss of blood, but with proper attention, his wound shouldn't be life threatening. The exit wound was a clean, small red circle which looked like it'd been created by the skilled, precise hand of a surgeon.

Graham instructed Wyley to put pressure on the wound then moved on to the next victim. Almost immediately, the doctor noticed the exit wound looked much the same. Another clean leg wound. Without slowing down, he checked the next rebel, a harsh-looking, weather-beaten man. He hadn't been so lucky. The bullet had shattered his thigh bone, severing an artery. Something had to be done to stop the bleeding so Graham wrapped a blood-soaked rag around the man's leg, tied it in a knot, and created a tourniquet using a piece of steel rebar. Graham believed the man might make it, but he'd need a transfusion and fast.

Moving quickly, he surveyed the rest of the rebels. In total, twenty-six men were down, moaning in agony, but all were alive, suffering from leg and hip wounds.

"What do you make of this?" he asked Wyley.

"Steel-jacket bullets and leg wounds. I don't know; they got something up their sleeve."

"What do you mean?"

"They're delaying us here for some reason. They know we'll take care of the rebels."

Graham surveyed the scene for some clue, some hint as to what was going on. The wounded men reminded him of New York, then suddenly, a cold chill ran down his back. He knew what was happening here, what was coming. "They're setting us up."

"I dunno, they're buying time for something," Wyley said, lost in his own thoughts. Once Graham's words registered, the reporter seemed to collapse in on himself. "This can't be happening."

"See that intersecting tunnel section ahead?—by the fire doors," Buck prompted Russum. The crossover gates loomed in front of them to their right. "Watch for an ambush. They could be trying to draw us in."

Russum nodded from behind his infrared binoculars, searching the fire-wall doors for anything suspicious. From his vantage point, he could see both enormous plate steel doors and the control panel used to operate them. "I don't see any people, but . . ."

"Whatdaya see?"

Suddenly, Russum's pupils expanded and he turned to Buck, ashen white. "Holy shit!"

"Russum? What is it?"

"Medusa!"

"Hot?"

"Yes! yes! Hot as hell!"

Buck's heart was pounding, his stomach stuck in his throat. "Cover me!"

"No time, damnit, get down!" Russum's blood was pumping now, his instincts kicked into override. Lifting his submachine gun, he launched a barrage of 9mm bullets streaming across the tunnel. Orange tracer rounds guided him, fiery sparks flew off the plate steel doors as the big Texan converged on target. A single bullet shattered the detonation electronics, then another demolished its battery, rendering the bomb harmless. Once Billy Ray had his mark, he held it fast, emptying the clip. Once the circuit board shattered and separated from the bomb, the ball rolled along the floor, but Russum didn't stop. He kept firing, blasting it across the gateway, severing its cables, trapping it in a corner between the concrete wall and massive plate steel door.

Click, click, click . . .

Russum reached for another magazine and slapped it in place.

"Ease off, Billy Ray. It's over." Buck grasped Russum's hands. They felt like hot steel, holding his gun in an iron grip. Watching Russum's face, Buck could tell his adrenaline was beginning to ebb. Slowly, his hands relaxed, then began to shake. "The doc's got something for that, if you need it."

"I'll be all right." Russum held up his hand and watched in disbelief as it shook. Try as he might, he could not stop it from acting like it had a mind of its own.

About that time, Buck's radio vibrated. It was Graham calling to relay what they'd learned.

"We figured that much out," Buck confirmed the doctor's fear. "Billy Ray disarmed it."

"There's one more thing, Buck. I need to speak plainly about it; I couldn't live with myself if I didn't."

"Sure, spit it out. What's on your mind?"

"I wish you'd pull your people out, Buck. Get them out of the tunnels now, before another one of those things goes off."

Buck's guts wrenched inside. "The stakes are too high, Graham. We gotta keep the pressure on."

"These people are desperate. They'll do anything."

"Yeah, we knew this could happen, but we can't give 'em the chance to regroup. We've gotta keep 'em running, scrambling for cover, or we'll lose everything. I hear what you're saying, though. I'll get the word out and reduce the size of my forward teams—but we can't stop. We gotta break through and we gotta expect they're gonna defend that bunker like fuckin' fanatics."

"Yeah, I think you're right. It's going to get worse before it gets better."

"Anything else?"

"No. That's all I wanted to say."

"I heard you, Graham, and I'm telling you, people with nothing to live for scare the hell out of me."

"Yeah, me too."

"Cut it, cut the lock." Commander Buck Harrison guided a Delta technician to the hangar doors.

The soldier eyed the quarter-inch plate briefly, lowered his eyeshield, then struck a spark to his cutting torch. "Piece of cake."

A blinding light reflected off the doors, and soon, the metal latch glowed a dull red-orange. Seconds later, a wall of sparks waterfalled down the steel doors and the latch melted under the heat.

Standing by the control panel, Russum held the switch down, hoping to roll open the doors.

Nothing. The electric motors remained silent. The door controls had been shot up by the guards during their escape.

Dangling from a long length of flexible conduit, a switch box hung suspended near the doors. Russum tried it, but it was dead too. Running out of options, he tried turning a hand-wheel and felt the worm gear engage. Slowly, the doors began to part and fresh air rushed in, blowing against the flexible conduit, sending the switch box swinging back and forth like a pendulum, banging against the door.

Several hundred feet away, closer to the main tunnel entrance, Graham, Wyley, and a few Delta medics tended the wounded, but they felt the wind rushing through the vertical opening once the doors parted.

As Russum spun open the doors, Buck slid up close to the opening, staying low. To his surprise, he saw rebel prisoners streaming toward the access tunnel entrance. Like the others, they looked gaunt, but were walking of their own accord. Still, something was missing. There were no guards in sight.

As the hangar doors parted, dim, hazy light from the access tunnel filtered in through the tall, narrow slit. Buck could see American special forces approaching in the distance, trailing behind their LAV. While smaller than a tank, the light armored vehicle provided them a mobile shield, a bullet-proof wall on wheels, rolling down the tunnel straddling the railroad tracks.

Yet, even though the LAV was a sitting duck for a shoulder missile, Buck noticed Iraqi resistance had vanished. It didn't make any sense. Where were the fanatics?

Buck radioed the LAV, told his position, and arranged a rendezvous by the fire doors. He knew they'd be expecting an ambush by the doors and he didn't want to get shot.

Once the rebels passed, the LAV rolled to a stop alongside the fire-wall doors.

"Hold your fire," Buck yelled. "We're Americans." The commander moved cautiously through the slit to meet Bob Townsend, the Delta team leader.

Buck had chosen Townsend for the job and knew him as a tough, no-nonsense warrior who would waste zero time trying to impress him. He didn't. The soldier went straight into their situation, rapping on the LAV personnel hatch to get the attention of the night-eye recon team working inside.

In response, the cameraman raised his hatch and handed Buck a flat panel display, tethered to the VCR inside.

"I heard the night eye didn't work in the tunnel," Buck commented.

"We found it works as long as the bird and control station are both in the tunnel. The tunnel behaves like a wave guide or something like that."

Buck watched the tunnel video as Townsend gave him the summary. "We're good to the connecting link that runs to the bunker. So far, all we've found is tunnel sprinklers for fire control, and video cameras. We've flamed 'em all to this point, but we gotta assume they feed some central security complex somewhere, probably in the bunker."

"Yeah, that makes sense. Let's keep moving."

Inside the bunker connecting link, it looked abandoned. The overhead lights were off, and except for occasional emergency lighting, it was black as pitch.

Buck sent the night eye ahead of them, surveying the link, making its way to the bunker. The first thing the pilot noticed was the increased headwind. It was stronger in the link than anywhere else, twice as strong, making it impossible to hover with any stability whatsoever. As a result, the video quality suffered because of the short dwell time on areas of interest, plus the video was jerky. Even the gyros and autopilot couldn't compensate for the headwind. There was markedly more turbulence near the walls, so the pilot flew down the center of the tunnel. Both operators were concerned they would miss something, but there was little they could do but tuck the nose of the little bird, and plow forward against the wind.

The LAV rolled to a stop as the night-eye team maneuvered the little bird nearer the bunker.

Ahead, Buck could see a single emergency light, and expected where there was light, there could be real danger. Unlike the civilian access tunnel, the bunker link felt dangerous. Maybe it was the darkness, maybe it was the proximity to evil, but there was something here that made Buck's hair stand on end.

Buck, Russum, and Bob Townsend watched the flat panel display as the little bird probed ahead. As it approached the emergency light, Buck saw a blue glint. "Hold it."

The image jerked up and down, then the little bird attempted another pass at the dark rectangular opening recessed in the wall. Townsend froze the shot on-screen and zoomed into the dark recessed area.

Buck sensed no life there, only death. He couldn't see it, but there was something there, maybe the blue glint off a barrel. Regardless, it was something hot.

Examining the video screen, Russum pointed out what could be twin cameras mounted either side of the tunnel. Buck and Townsend agreed.

"Zoom in there," Russum instructed the cameraman. The hot spot grew larger.

After a few moments, Russum stated his opinion. "Judging from what we can reconstruct, it's not a gun barrel at all. Far from it. It's the pilot light on a flamethrower—you can see it flicker—probably remote-controlled, two of them mounted across from each other so they'll engulf the tunnel in cross fire."

Over his headset Buck heard the pilot's voice. "Not a problem, gentlemen. We have the technology."

Back inside the LAV, a second drone pilot sat ready behind his flight control station. The cameraman removed another micromachine from his bag, then stood up so his torso extended through the open personnel hatch.

The little bird looked like a night-eye recon device, but it wasn't.

Although shaped like the night eye and carrying a camera, it didn't have its range; its fuel was replaced by plastic explosive and hollow steel pellets filled with ricin.

The cameraman started its micromotor. Once the pilot signaled all was well, the cameraman told everyone near the

LAV to stand clear. No one hesitated to give the flying bomb a wide berth and the cameraman let loose his miniature killing machine.

Like the night eye, the bird bomb transmitted a picture back to a flat screen on the pilot's remote. Up the tunnel, about five feet from the rightmost flame thrower, the cameraman zoomed in to target. The picture was jerky, the hover unstable due to the wind. Thankfully, they didn't need to take out the concrete pillbox, it was only necessary to destroy the weapon's control system.

"We're good to go," the second pilot said, a bit unsure of his own words. This stiff headwind was a killer.

He positioned the bird bomb alongside the pillbox and crabbed laterally toward the dark opening. After three passes, the pilot was frustrated and running out of patience. Every time he'd crab right, he'd drift back, ultimately missing the hole in the wall. Low on fuel, the pilot knew he was running out of time and that didn't help either. So far, it seemed like it'd taken an awfully long time and he wasn't there yet.

It was the first pilot who suggested that he fly the bird bomb into the wind, beyond the pillbox opening. When sliding sideways, the micromachine would drift back no matter what they did, so they'd compensate for it by flying forward of the hole. The tough part was getting inside the pillbox without smashing into the wall. Once in the box, the air would be calm so hitting the target should be easy.

The pilot tried again, hovering about three feet upwind of the opening and two feet out. Once the cameraman centered the pillbox on-screen, the pilot jinked his control stick quickly. In the blink of an eye, the concrete wall filled the screen and he jerked away only inches from impact. The playback tape showed he'd almost made it, so he fine-tuned his initial position before starting his next pass. Once set, he jinked his control and broke through the turbulent boundary layer into the hole. For a moment, the calm air surrounding the weapon felt like a safe haven, but that didn't last.

Maneuvering the bird bomb toward the rear of the weapon,

the pilot could see control valves and circuit boards mounted in a shelf on the floor toward the rear of the pillbox.

With his confidence renewed by the calm air, the pilot reduced his altitude, aligned his camera alongside the control shelf, and squeezed the red detonator button on his control stick. At that moment, the bird bomb spent its energy with a sudden flash of light and explosive force.

A reddish-yellow fireball erupted from the hole, flooding the area with flames; but in a moment, it was gone, the flames contained, retreating back to the pillbox.

Outside the LAV, Buck and Russum watched the tunnel light up.

"Bull's-eye!" Buck said, anxious to move on. "One down, one to go."

Once the pilot learned to compensate for the turbulence, flying into the box became easier. Less than three minutes later, the left-hand torch was extinguished and Delta Force rolled forward another forty feet toward the bunker.

The night-eye pilot continued to operate the little bird well ahead of the pack, probing, all the while battling the wind. Six more pillboxes were disabled without incident, but the recon pilot sensed they were moving too fast. He couldn't help but feel rushed. At best, their video was blurred and jerky and his concern was that they would get in a hurry and miss something, something dangerous. As his team's recon scout, he felt responsible for their safety and didn't want to get anybody killed.

On the other hand, Buck's concern was the Iraqi army. The United States had its satellite eyes watching their every move, and so far, well, so far, they'd been lucky.

It was only a matter of time. They would come, he didn't know when, but he knew they would come and he didn't want to be there when they did.

It was this concern that drove Buck to take risks that he might otherwise have considered uncalled-for.

Buck took the point now, leading his special forces down the link, nearing the bowels of the bunker. Russum urged caution, but Buck sensed they were running out of time.

As it happened, both men were right.

CHAPTER TWENTY-SEVEN

Katie Needs a Daddy
Sunday, Apr. 18, 2:37 A.M.
Inside the link connecting the access tunnel to the bunker

"We're in, Commander. We've breached the bunker!" the cameraman yelled.

Finally, at long last, the night eye had flown into the bunker, with special forces no more than fifty yards behind.

Inside the LAV, the cameraman saw a bird's-eye view of chaos and mayhem sweeping across the factory floor. Guards running between large manufacturing tables, heading for the hospital, factory workers bolting out the door like it was the end of their shift. If any single emotion shone through, it was panic.

Panic unlike anything Russum had ever seen.

He worried that these people would do something desperate—they'd done it before—and it was this concern that drove him to ask Buck to stop his advance and take a look.

The commander didn't argue, returning to the LAV to get a glimpse inside the bunker.

"Looks like what we expected, but worse. They're already in full production." He pointed to an area near the hospital connecting link. "Check out those pallets, all those boxes. That's gotta be shipping."

Moments later, the camera eye shifted from the factory floor to the mezzanine. The pilot maneuvered into the second-story office space with amazing speed and agility. He was into it, flying his recon probe as if it were an extension of his own reach; every motion fluid, every turn, seamless. Flying through the windy link had been difficult, but once he'd broken into the bunker, running the night eye down office hallways felt like a cakewalk.

Traveling down the corridor, he saw a glass-walled office that immediately caught his eye. Instinctively, he flew in and began looking around. It had to be their nerve center, their security complex, because he saw eight armed men sitting behind monitors, studying the events unfolding below. First thing, he videoed their faces, weapons, and body armor, then studied their monitor screens.

It was weird.

He froze for a moment, not knowing exactly what to think. Before him on-screen, he saw a picture of them looking at Commander Buck Harrison standing by the LAV.

He told his cameraman to stand up, stick his hand through the hatch, and wave. He did, and the pilot saw him on the Iraqi screen. This was too weird. It's one thing to look over someone's shoulder. It's another to look over their shoulder to find them looking over yours.

Outside the LAV, Buck recognized himself on-screen, and at that point he decided he'd seen enough.

Heading for the point, he spoke to Townsend. "Let's move."

"We need to neutralize that security complex."

"Go ahead, throw everything you got at it, but don't let those bird bombs slow us down."

Moving forward toward the bunker, Buck signaled the LAV driver to follow him. The final assault was on and nothing could stop them now.

Pumped with adrenaline, Buck could see the factory floor before him and it was exhilarating. It was well lit, most of the factory workers had cleared out, and it looked like a fruit ripe for picking.

In one smooth, continuous motion, he glided toward the bunker entrance; he looked up and eyed the catwalk, expecting to see snipers at the ready on the handrail, but there were none.

He checked the ceiling and overhead cranes.

Deserted.

Excellent! The time to strike is now!

Waving the others forward, he felt a low-frequency vibration shake the building and knew he'd missed something.

Behind him, a massive twelve-inch steel door plummeted to the floor, sealing off the link.

Russum rushed the door, thrusting his weapon in its track, but the tremendous force flattened his submachine gun like a hydraulic press.

Buck was cut off, isolated from the others.

Instinctively, he looked for a way out, first eyeing the hospital link across the way. It was dark now, sealed like the door behind him.

It was lockdown time and there was no escape. *I'd better find a place to hide, get the lay of the land, and wait for the others.*

Suddenly, he sensed movement and looked up toward the mezzanine catwalk and overhead cranes.

Snipers.

They were all over him.

Two LAVs rolled out of the main tunnel, laden with wounded rebels, bound for their makeshift hospital in the equipment shed.

"I still can't believe it," Graham said, walking out through the tunnel. "What are we going to do? We can't leave him in there."

He could be dead, Wyley thought, but held his tongue. There was no good to come from stating the obvious.

After a pause, Russum summarized Townsend's plan as brute force with no nonsense. "They're plastering C4 explosive around the door now, lacing it together with primacord. I don't know, though, that door's gotta be at least a foot thick. One of the guys said it looked like the blast door in Cheyenne Mountain. They're trying to blow it down, but I think they're going to have to blast through the wall and dig around it."

"That could take hours," Wyley reacted.

"No," Russum corrected. "It'd take days."

"What about big guns?" Wyley asked.

"We don't have any big guns. The LAV's 25mm cannon is the biggest we got."

"And?"

"The LAV's gun didn't scratch it."

"I still can't believe it." Wyley grimaced. "What are we gonna do?"

"I dunno, if the C4 fails, we're stuck."

"What? What are we wasting our time here for?" Graham shook his head emphatically. "There's gotta be another way. I don't know how but we've got to think of something. What would Buck do?" Graham racked his brain, trying to put himself in Buck's shoes and think out of the box.

"He'd blast the door down," Russum answered, sighing.

"No, no, he wouldn't. You know him better than that. He'd exhaust every alternative, and wouldn't stop until he found something he believed in." Graham closed his eyes, trying to imagine Buck's reaction if they had been the ones trapped inside the bunker. Frustrated, the doctor got mad at himself for not having any imagination. "I don't know how he'd do it, but he'd save us or die trying; he wouldn't leave us in there with them."

A few moments later, Graham, Wyley, and Russum emerged from the tunnel on foot and spoke to Townsend outside in the shadows. "That's the last of them. Everybody's out. The main tunnel's clear."

Bob Townsend nodded, then yelled into his radio, "Clear the tunnel!"

"Clear on the west bank, sir."

"East bank is clear."

"Fire in the hole!"

Townsend knelt down on one knee, rotated a T-handle, and the earth shook.

Once the smoke cleared, Townsend sent his explosive specialist inside to examine the door.

A few minutes later, Townsend's radio crackled. "I can't believe this shit, sir. I've never seen anything like it. What the hell are we gonna do now?"

Townsend knew he was in over his head and called Washington. He'd learned a long time ago that you could be successful as a lone ranger, but if you fail, you'd better go down as a group.

* * *

"So what are we going to do?" Graham struggled to think, but found himself haunted by thoughts of Manhattan, Mary Marshall, and her little girl, Katie.

Concentrating hard, Russum stroked his mustache. "We've got to get him out of there. The question is how."

"You know he's nuts about Mary and her little girl," Graham lamented. "She's invited him up to stay the weekend when we get back to the States. She wants him to meet her father."

"That sounds very promising," Russum said. "I wouldn't want to disappoint her after what they've been through."

"I had a feeling something was going on with them," Wyley observed. "What with the phone calls and e-mail and all."

"They write each other every day," Graham confirmed, thinking of his own family.

"Seems like this happened pretty fast," Wyley said.

"I'll say," Russum agreed. "It'd be nice if something good could come out of that New York bombing."

"Buck told me that people like Mary are the reason he wanted to be a warrior."

"Warrior? What are you talking about?" Wyley asked.

"You want to know what I thought about Buck when I first met him?" Graham asked Wyley.

"Yeah, I'd like to hear it."

"I'm ashamed to admit it, but when I first met him I thought he was the kind of person that I'd never invite to my home. He looked like a terrorist from hell, more bear than man. On the other hand, if my daughter were ever kidnapped, I'd feel good that the United States chose him to rescue her. I mean, I'm glad he's on our side."

"I know what you mean." Wyley nodded. "At first, I thought Buck enjoyed this macho military crap because it was some kind of power trip for him."

"I guess we were both wrong. You know, I once asked Buck why he stayed in the military. It doesn't pay much, he's a natural leader, and I'm convinced he'd do well in the civilian sector. Know what he said?"

Russum and Wyley shrugged.

"It wasn't the money that attracted him to the job; he wanted to protect people, the weak ones who couldn't protect themselves."

"That's really admirable, but I'm convinced he's not so tough as he seems."

"He's a big teddy bear in Mary's hands and he's crazy about her little girl."

A long silent pause followed.

"Failure is not an option."

"Hell no," Russum agreed. "Katie needs a daddy."

Russum entered the equipment shed to find Graham and Wyley deep in conversation with a wounded rebel prisoner. From the looks of it, Graham was asking the questions, with Wyley doing the translating. Another thing Russum noticed was that both men were surrounded by moaning, bandaged rebels. It was depressing, the place oozing an aura of bloody defeat. Russum signaled them from across the room and they joined him alongside a greasy workbench.

"Looks like we've ground to a screeching halt," Russum reported.

"So I've heard." Graham seemed lost in his thoughts. "I think we may be on to something with these rebels."

"What do you mean?"

Graham showed Russum a rough, hand-drawn blueprint of the bunker. Nearest the sandbar side of the structure, an X was scratched over something the doctor had labeled COOLING TOWER. It connected to a pump room, an escape trunk, and an underground test facility.

"What's all this mean?"

"We're not positive, but I think it means we found a back door into the bunker."

"Through the river?"

Graham nodded. "We were running this map by the rebels when you got here. This X marks a maintenance hatch on the cooling tower. If we can get in the cooling tower, we can get in the bunker."

Russum eyed the drawing suspiciously. "Where'd you get this?"

"The rebels. They said we were breaking in the wrong way."

"That's all very interesting, Graham, but Townsend got orders to pull out. The Iraqi army's on the move three to four hours from here."

Graham responded as if he hadn't heard Russum. "I still need to see that night-eye video."

Russum plugged in the tape and laid the flat display on the bench. Impatient, he pressed FAST-FORWARD. "You guys need to get moving, choppers're already inbound. We're pulling out."

A few seconds later, Graham punched PLAY and looked puzzled once the picture came into frame on-screen.

Again, Russum punched FAST-FORWARD, Graham punched PLAY and frowned. "What's wrong with this picture? Why's it so jerky and blurred?"

"Wind. Once we entered the connecting link, the night-eye pilot said it was blowing twice as fast. He couldn't hold his little bird stable, had a hell of a time with it."

Graham thought back. When the fire doors closed, the wind died in the main tunnel. When the blast door had slammed shut at the entrance to the bunker, the wind died again. "What's the story on the wind now?"

"Dead still, why? What are you thinking?"

"So why'd the wind die?"

"The door shut, Sherlock. It don't take a rocket scientist to figure that one out."

Graham made eye contact with Wyley.

"Yes, it follows," was all he said.

And then the revelation occurred to Russum. "So where's the air coming from?"

"It could be the sandbar. We never got confirmation about that blower one way or the other."

"Yes, it's possible," Russum acknowledged, thinking ahead to their next step. "We could check it out. That downed antenna tower is made to order, gives us a bridge."

"Won't even get our feet wet." Wyley grinned.

Graham knew the people in that bunker had to get their breathing air from somewhere and felt this could help them gain entry. He punched PLAY again and watched the tape. When the night eye flew into the light of the bunker, he backed it up, studying the last few feet of the tunnel walls.

He didn't have to look long or hard. There were two vertical seams of tile encased by a metal frame. They didn't look any different from any other tile seams except they were continuous, floor to ceiling, and it broke up the tile's checkerboard pattern. Graham backed up the tape and played it again as the camera swept by the two seams. Finally, he looked at Russum and said, "Steel doorjamb."

"We could see the lights from the bunker. What can I say? We got in a hurry and missed it."

Graham nodded, and punched PLAY.

This time, Russum left his VCR controls alone.

Graham and Wyley watched in amazement as the night eye entered the security complex undetected, like a fly on the wall. Even with a wide-angle shot of the glass-walled room, one young man in civilian clothes stood out among the guards.

Immediately, the camera eye zoomed in on his face and the doctor punched PAUSE.

Graham sensed something frighteningly familiar. "That's him."

Wyley nodded, typing a name into their video player's tiny keyboard. In less than a second, their computer relayed his request over satellite link to a CIA file server in Virginia, then a picture of Hakim crossing the Canadian border appeared onscreen. "There's something about his eyes."

Graham studied it carefully, positioning both pictures alongside each other on-screen. Hakim's mouth was obscured behind the driver's side window, but his eyes were vividly clear.

Graham nodded, then looked to Russum.

"Same eyes," Russum agreed.

"It's the same man." Wyley was sure of it.

"Let's pick up with Ali where we left off," Graham said softly, referring to one of the more knowledgeable rebels. "Maybe he can help us or knows someone who can."

CHAPTER TWENTY-EIGHT

No Turning Back Now
Sunday, Apr. 18, 4:02 A.M.
Basra, Iraq

Graham swallowed hard and started maneuvering toward the downed antenna tower. His eyes were in constant motion, darting from shadow to shadow, searching out. "The evac choppers will be here in half an hour. Let's move like we have a purpose."

Smiling, Billy Ray looked at Wyley. "I'm supposed to say that."

All three men moved slowly toward the river, each straining under a ponderous load of weapons, tools, batteries, and scuba gear. Surveying the tunnel entrance, Graham knew the whole area would soon be swarming with Iraqi troops. Behind them, a flurry of activity was under way.

Bob Townsend had his troops organizing the wounded, rounding up their vehicles and weapons, making ready to pull out. Near-panicked retreat was never pretty.

What would they do with the wounded? What about the guards? And they needed to get their equipment out. No need to leave it for the six o'clock news.

Graham was glad that wasn't his problem. He had enough to think about and understood why he couldn't plan on support from Bob Townsend. He had his hands full just evacuating his troops before the Iraqis came.

Besides, our plan's a long shot, Graham thought, his wife's remarks haunting him. *A one-in-one-hundred chance and it won't make any difference.*

Keeping their backs to the river, the doctor led the trio the long way around to the downed antenna tower on the shore wall.

Winded, they moved alongside the metal structure and Russum examined it in darkness. After a quick once-over, he climbed on the tower and walked out over the river about fifty feet from shore. There was a long drop to the river below, but he felt confident enough to use his jump-on-it-and-see-if-it-breaks method of structure evaluation.

Walking the length of the downed tower might have been drier than swimming, it may have been faster, but Graham was convinced it wasn't any easier and it scared him to death. Each crab step sideways, each bounce, twist, dip, and sway of the tower caused his heart to pound like there was no tomorrow. His backpack and equipment were constantly shifting. At times, he held them so tightly his knuckles turned white. It reminded him of crabbing down the long sides of an enormous ladder turned up on its edge, and each step between the rungs stuck a hard steel edge in his shins. Off balance and dizzy, Graham found the tower bobbed and swayed in the middle more like a rope bridge than a steel trestle.

But it could have been worse. No one was shooting at them.

Hearing the roar of blowers, his pace quickened. Looking ahead toward the sandbar, he could see the bunker's air-handling system. Set alongside a concrete slab and power substation, the blowers were surrounded by a camouflaged chain-link fence.

Graham broke out his torch, clicked it alight, and began cutting through the wire fence. Red-hot molten metal dripped to the sand as the flame melted the wire like butter.

In the background, Graham heard the roar of American Super Stallions closing from the south. Only minutes away, Graham knew their journey to the sandbar had taken much longer than they'd anticipated and he had no idea how they could make up the lost time.

Graham had the top and side of the entrance cut when Russum said, "Step aside, Doc. We gotta move."

Russum kicked hard and a jagged door-shaped section of chain-link fence bent open.

Without hesitation, Graham grabbed his flashlight and tools, then plowed through the opening to a narrow walkway encircling an enormous metal box riveted with pipes and conduits. Climbing a ladder to the top of the blower assembly, Russum and Wyley followed Graham to the access walkway overhead.

On top of the assembly, Graham saw two metal stacks, cylindrical ductwork funneling air to and from the blowers. The roar alongside the stacks was deafening.

Standing on the service walkway above the blower's twin thirteen-foot fans, it became obvious where the wind in the tunnels came from. This had to be the place. It felt like a wind tunnel.

"I don't understand why we didn't see air ducts running to the bunker," Russum wondered out loud. "Andreas said they could see 'em beneath the surface."

"I don't know, but we can't worry about that now," Graham said, collecting some colored smoke grenades and tear gas.

Wyley agreed, pointing to a Super Stallion hovering near the main tunnel entrance. "We've got to move, or we're going to miss our ride."

We're going to miss our ride no matter what we do, Graham thought, but saying it would do no good.

Russum wrapped primacord around the blower power cables while Graham and Wyley returned to the access walkway above the intake blower.

Pulling the pin from a tear gas grenade, Graham tossed one over the side onto the fan intake grill. It slammed down hard but they couldn't hear its impact over the blower noise.

Wyley aimed his flashlight down the enormous cylindrical duct and found the gas bomb impaled on the grate. Drawn down hard, it had smashed into the grate and never bounced; every cubic inch of gas sucked into the blower was sent racing toward the bunker. They didn't know exactly how many they'd need to saturate the bunker and didn't care. They tossed in more than enough, then waited for a trace of the gas to show in the air return.

After nearly emptying their backpack of tear gas, they grabbed a sulfur smoke bomb and rolled it over the side. Graham watched orange smoke stream downward from the device for a few seconds, then waited for a trace to emerge from the exhaust stack.

Meanwhile, Wyley climbed down the ladder to help Russum finish setting their explosives.

After a time, it seemed the orange smoke would never show in his flashlight beam, so Graham pulled the mask to one side of his face and, almost instantly, his eyes flooded with tears.

He joined the others below, saying, "We may have overdone it with the gas."

Russum look puzzled.

"The gas out the exhaust is really concentrated," he went on to explain. "The bunker's saturated. Let's do it."

The threesome knelt down outside the camouflage fence and Wyley twisted the detonator handle. There was a flash, but no explosion. In the blink of an eye, the fast-burning primacord cut through the power lines running to the blower assembly. The roar of the fans was hushed, replaced with the hum of the nearby power substation.

Russum led the trio back to the blower. One side of the metal box was smoking, and the scorched outline of a door was apparent where there had been none before. The big Texan braced himself against a chain-link fence post and kicked.

The metal yielded and a door-sized hole opened up into the side of the blower assembly beneath the intake fan. Inside the box, Russum saw something that looked like the primary air duct running vertically, connected to the intake fan at the top and disappearing into the ground. Unlike the other ductwork he'd seen, this was made of some form of plastic. He scraped it with a sharp piece of metal and a curled shaving peeled off. "It's not metal."

"I think you've found the answer to your question," Graham affirmed. "That's the reason Dr. Pappasongas couldn't see it."

"Stand back. We'll open another hole."

Minutes later, Russum and Wyley had outlined a door shape with duct tape and primacord. Once they were ready, Wyley twisted the detonator handle, then Russum kicked the smoldering panel in while the material was still molten. Almost immediately, the trio recognized the distinctive odor as fiberglass, no doubt about it.

Before descending the dark passageway, the trio put on their climbing gear, a combination of black Nomex coveralls, Kevlar vest, rappelling harness, and leather gloves. Dressed in respirator and hood, each man looked like a black rat.

Approaching the smoky passageway, Graham slowed to a halt and tested the air in the shaft for gas. Near the intake blower, tear gas fumes weren't detectable so he removed his mask and examined the shaft with his flashlight. "It's a steep descent, and a long one," he told Russum. "About thirty feet down, the corridor angles toward the bunker, but the sides are smooth and slippery. We're going to need the rope."

Russum nodded. "No surprise." The big Texan tied one end of their rope to the fence post nearest the hole, then tossed the other down the chute.

Entering legs first, Graham braced himself against the treacherously slick surface of the shaft. It was coated with a thin film of something slippery, probably fine dust, and there was no way to get his footing. "Going down's the easy part," he said, nodding to Russum.

Billy Ray released Graham's arm and he rappelled down the chute, passing the rope under one thigh and over his shoulder. Paying it out gradually at first, once he got the feel of it, he pushed away from the wall and dropped quickly to the bottom.

In the main duct below, Graham saw only darkness, an endless black abyss. He could see Russum at the top, but down the main duct, his flashlight provided only a column of light which tapered off to nothing.

Instinctively, he lowered his night-vision goggles, peering into the darkness. They made it feel more like daylight, but no matter what technology he put between himself and the night, darkness took some adjustment.

The size of the primary duct was easily as large as the vertical chute, at least fourteen feet on a side, with pipes and sump pumps installed to keep the duct dry. *At least we won't have to crawl or wade,* he thought.

Overhead, he heard Russum yell down the shaft. "Heads up. Scuba coming down."

After lowering their equipment and weapons, Wyley followed.

Satisfied they were ready, Billy Ray met the trio at the bottom, guarding their rear.

Fifty yards or so down the primary duct, the tunnel split into smaller ducts and narrowed. They didn't know how far they had to go or how small the ducts would become, but they weren't worried. Earlier that evening, they'd experienced gale force winds through the connecting link so they felt confident the ducts didn't reduce down too fast.

It was pitch black inside the duct. Night-vision gear helped, but there was no hint of visible light anywhere. Moving through the fiberglass duct, Graham noticed the well-grounded sound of his footsteps was changing to a hollow, almost cavernous noise.

The doctor reasoned they could be suspended above the factory floor, but from the sound alone, he couldn't know for sure. Should they stop to cut a hole, and risk giving their position away? He hoped every one in the factory was incapacitated, but again, he couldn't know that for sure. After a few moments' thought, he decided to keep moving and probe later.

Once the tone of their footsteps changed, Graham noticed the number of small connecting tubes began increasing quickly. As a result, Graham found their main duct stepping down in size again and again. Finally, he came to a juncture where he could see light near the end of one of the smaller tubes.

Graham crawled in to find that he had second thoughts once he got inside. Very soon he learned he could crawl toward the light, but would have to back out. There was no room for a man, even a small man, to turn around. He distracted himself by focusing on the dim light at the end of the tube, imagining what it could be coming from. Surely they must be over the factory floor by now.

Fumbling to unlatch the vent, he swung it open, then his eyes began tearing. Scrambling, he placed his gas mask over his face, then picked up where he'd left off.

Moving slowly, he stuck his head out of the vent and found himself suspended fifty feet above the factory floor. Across the ceiling, he could see the main feeder duct running toward the mezzanine, and there he determined they should cut their way out. It was closer to the floor and well concealed behind the office walls.

After planning their escape route, he counted the number of smaller ducts between their position and the mezzanine, then made a mental note of it. Next, he scanned the factory floor for movement or any signs of life. There were none, the floor appeared deserted, but from here, he couldn't see what was taking place inside the security complex. The catwalk surrounding the mezzanine was deserted, he could see that clearly enough; the overhead lifting cranes were deserted too, but he could only see the open manufacturing spaces. He couldn't see more, not from this vantage point anyway.

Slowly, painfully, Graham Higgins backed out of the tube on his knees. All in all, it felt like it took an awfully long time. Coughing, he tasted blood again and knew the gunshot had caused either his lungs or stomach to hemorrhage, maybe both. He kept spitting up blood, and when he'd burp, the distinctive taste of blood haunted him with a vengeance.

Once out of the tube, he stood upright and found himself feeling light-headed. Regaining his balance after a moment, he gathered Russum and Wyley for a review of what he'd learned.

Encouraged, they started walking down the main duct heading for the mezzanine. Before long, the trio had checked off the last of six ventilator tubes Graham had expected to pass along the way.

"Stand clear," Graham said, pulling his miniature cutting torch from his backpack. Striking a spark, his torch blazed to life, and the doctor burned a small hole through the duct. Once it was melted, Graham slid a circular pipe into the smoldering hole and looked outside. They were standing over a supply stockroom with just enough light coming in. He could see several large boxes below them containing computer monitors and fans. This was perfect.

Graham moved quickly now, melting the fiberglass duct walls with his torch with machinelike speed and accuracy. One side, two, three, four sides later and he was done.

Putting his finger in the hole, he pulled up on the smolder-

ing panel and set it to one side. Before the molten fiberglass
cooled, he put his foot on the large box below, climbed down,
and Wyley followed. Russum passed him their gear, then
climbed down as well.

Closer to the floor, tear gas was present. It wasn't overpowering, but their eyes began tearing once they began moving
about the room. No one talked about it, but all three put on
their respirators, trading the nuisance of their gas masks for
visibility through the goggles. Even through his respirator,
Graham smelled the stench of molten fiberglass and hoped no
one else in the bunker would notice.

Covered in black Nomex from head to toe, the trio moved
forward, searching for Buck and physical evidence to reveal
just how far along the Iraqis were with their nuclear weapons
manufacturing process.

Graham reasoned that the bunker's eyes, ears, and nerve
center must be its security complex; its heart, the manufacturing floor; and its brain, the computer center. They'd seen the
security complex, but knew if anyone was moving in the
bunker, chances were good that they could be seen on closed
circuit TV. Here, the possibility of finding Buck was greatest,
and here, the trio decided to make their mark.

Russum took a deep breath and let it out slowly, steadying
his hands for their upcoming ordeal. Almost immediately, his
respirator goggles fogged over and he found himself waiting
for them to clear. Moments later, he glanced toward Graham
and Wyley, conveying that he would lead them now.

In one fluid motion, he pulled open the door, leaned forward scanning the hallway, then pulled his head back inside.
"It's clear. Follow me."

Wyley nodded. His gaze darted left, then right, his silenced
submachine gun at the ready.

The doctor's load was largest of the three. A bandoleer of
grenades and night eyes fit neatly across the front of his harness, but the little bird's controls were bulky. On top of that,
he couldn't shoot straight, so, on Russum's suggestion he carried a flamethrower as a get-it-in-the-ballpark alternative.
Graham primed it and made sure it was full, just in case.

Billy Ray moved out into the hallway, keeping low, his eyes constantly moving from side to side, checking every shadow. The hall light was on, illuminating offices on both sides of the corridor. Around the first corner, Russum found a map of the mezzanine posted on the wall. He couldn't read the words, but recognized security by its glass walls and monitor screens. He reasoned that the red X on the map meant *You are here,* then charted their shortest path to security.

Looking to his right, Russum visualized the glass-walled complex down the hallway, around the corner, toward the end of the corridor. Looking behind them and overhead, he saw a small fixed video camera covering the catwalk. Up ahead, the halls were clear of cameras as far as he could see. *Halls clear, perimeter covered,* he thought. *Makes sense.*

Silently, Russum glided down the hallway. Keeping low, he peered around the first corner, looking for a glimpse of the glass walls surrounding security. He could see it. The lights were on. He wasn't sure, but thought he saw a shadow move inside the room.

Signaling the others forward, he held up one finger as a warning.

Suddenly, feet stomped on the catwalk surrounding the mezzanine. A man's gas mask and shoulders appeared down the corridor heading for security. Without seeing his face, Russum recognized him at once by his build and civilian clothes. Those were the same clothes the terrorist was wearing in the video.

Russum's heart was racing now—this was big.

Drawing the others near, Russum relayed the danger. "They're moving, I can't see how many's in security, but our terrorist is in there. He's one of 'em, and he's still here."

"Your worst-case scenario." Graham sighed, looking at Russum. "State-sponsored nuclear terrorism."

"Everything we feared and more," Wyley added quietly.

"Looks like it." Russum's voice was muffled behind his mask.

Thinking ahead, Graham pulled a flat video screen and joystick from his backpack then signaled Russum. The big man saw it and immediately took to the idea.

It was like flying a remote-controlled model helicopter, only smaller, the little bird pilot had explained. *Well, we'll see about that,* Graham thought as he took the controls.

Wyley started the little bird's motor as Graham got comfortable behind the controls. First thing he noticed was that they felt awkward and twitchy—nothing like driving a car at all, where you could feel the road. Other than the camera's video, there was no tactile feedback beyond the instruments shown on the flat screen. The doctor thought those instruments didn't reveal any feeling at all; numbers on a screen meant nothing to him.

Untrained and unknowing, Wyley released the little bird too early, before Graham had countered the main rotor's twisting torque. As a result, the night eye started spinning uncontrollably beneath its main rotor once it was released.

Wyley and Russum took cover in the supply room, but Graham stayed put, riding the night eye down. The minichopper spun countless three-sixties at breakneck speed, with no hope of recovery. Graham twisted the joystick, jinking it, then jinking it again, trying to regain control. The spinning slowed, but the little bird never achieved stable hover. Seconds after its launch, the night eye spiraled down, bouncing hard off the wall and smashing into the mezzanine's tile floor.

Once the rotor hit, forces inside its tiny transmission and micromotor sheered the rotor drive apart, scattering tiny pieces of rotor, engine, and transmission across the corridor. Fortunately, only a few of its internal parts erupted from its shattered carcass and they rolled harmlessly away, along the floor.

Graham examined the crushed corpse of the little bird carefully. Next time, they'd launch it after he'd gotten a better feel for the controls.

Without delay, Wyley spun up another night eye and handed it to Graham. He could feel it twisting round, and countered by jinking the control stick through a series of short twists. The effect was cumulative, and soon, the torque was countered by the tail rotor. Next, the doctor adjusted the collective to achieve stable hover. After adjusting the trim thumb-wheel on the collective, the little bird felt weightless, suspended in air. Handing the little bird back to Wyley, Graham felt ready for his second solo flight.

This time, when Wyley released the little bird, it lifted only slightly then transitioned into stable hover immediately. Watching the screen, Graham moved his stick back and forth, getting the feel for the little bird, then he sent it down the hall and around the corner.

His flight to security wasn't graceful, he didn't bank the little chopper around the corner, but he did execute his turn as a series of stop, rotate, and go maneuvers.

His flight to the security complex took no more than thirty seconds, then the doctor eased the little bird into a stable hover outside the complex. Twisting his controls, he panned the camera across the room, but through the glass walls, he couldn't get a good look at anyone's face.

But it didn't matter, really. All nine men were wearing gas masks anyway, but only one was American-made.

Mainly, he saw the backs of their heads, shoulders, and waistlines, but that was telling enough. The thinner man in civilian clothes was their terrorist all right, and the linebacker of the bunch dressed in black had to be Buck. Commander Harrison stood out as a giant, broad-shouldered hunk of a man among the portly security guards.

Unsure of his piloting skills, Graham attempted to fly into the room and found the door shut. His little bird rapped into the window glass, pecked at it a couple of times, then the doctor sensed the little craft becoming unstable. Shaking violently, it was dropping like a rock.

Looking over Graham's shoulder, Russum and Wyley had seen enough. They knew what to do and urged the doctor to recall the little bird.

Graham lifted his collective, kicked its tail around, then headed down the corridor.

Shaking, the little bird barreled down the hall at breakneck speed and failed to negotiate its final turn, clipping the outside wall. Much like his first flight, Graham sheared off the nighteye's rotor, then smashed into the floor.

"That could've gone better." Graham sighed.

"Not to worry. You found out what we needed to know. The way I see it's like this. There's eight of 'em and they got Buck."

"I count six guards," Wyley added, "and I don't think they're professional shooters. Judging from their bearing and the way they move, my bet is they watch security cameras all day."

"What about the other two?"

"One's our terrorist. The gas mask obscures his face, but he's wearing the same clothes."

"Yeah, and the other?"

"Unknown. He's a wildcard."

Graham played back the videotape and zeroed in on their wildcard. "He's not carrying a gun, not that I can see anyway."

"Excellent." Wyley examined the man's clothes on the small screen. "He's a manager. Looks like he dressed to impress somebody."

"So we've got one shooter out of the eight."

"Yeah, but I could be wrong. It sounds too good to be true."

"I hope not."

"I think you're right," Russum supported Wyley's conclusion.

"What about Buck? How are we going to get him out of there without getting him killed? It looked like he was handcuffed to his chair."

Graham paused the videotape to reveal a large, broad-shouldered man seated in the back corner of the glass-walled room, his hands bound behind his back. Something white and shiny, like thick plastic straps, was wrapped around each wrist.

"So what are we going to do?" Wyley pushed.

"We've got to think of something. I don't know how, but there's got to be a way." Graham forced a determined smile, but his voice sounded as if he had a frog stuck in his throat.

"Don't forget, there's only three of us," Russum cautioned. "And we don't know anything about the factory area. They could have an army down there."

"I checked out the factory floor from the air duct, and didn't see anyone. I couldn't see everything, though."

"We don't know if anyone's on the factory floor, so assume the worst." Russum's point was conservative.

The doctor thought for a moment. "I guess that means whatever we do, we should confine it to the mezzanine."

"That'd make sense."

"So let's draw 'em out of there, pick 'em off one by one," Russum said. "Surprise is on our side. We should take advantage of it to divide and conquer."

"We've got two things going for us," Graham said. "Surprise and disguise. They don't know we're here and we've got their clothes."

"We could walk in masquerading as guards, take out the terrorist, and . . ." Wyley went silent, reading Graham's expression.

"That sounds pretty risky to me. I'm not trained for this and chances are high that some of us would get killed in the cross fire."

"That kinda defeats the purpose, don't it?" Russum quipped. "We could rush 'em . . . I dunno, though. That takes practice and teamwork. I'm afraid we'd end up shooting each other."

"Yeah," Wyley affirmed, "and there's eight of 'em. We can't use the flamethrower with Buck in there."

"So what can we do to improve our chances?" Russum wanted to know.

Graham felt the warmth from the pilot light in his flamethrower, and an idea began to coalesce. Looking overhead, he saw the ceiling was laced with an array of smoke detectors, temperature sensors, sprinkler heads, and water pipes. *Perfect,* he thought. Next, he double-checked the lumps in his bandolier—it was filled with smoke bombs. Finally, he was almost positive that he remembered seeing cooling fans in the supply room, so he checked again to be sure.

They were there as he'd remembered, several room fans for cooling people and equipment. Visualizing his plan from start to finish, he concluded they had everything they needed. Graham returned to the others and explained his idea.

CHAPTER TWENTY-NINE

Lock 'Em Out
Sunday, Apr. 18, 5:28 A.M.
The Bunker

Wyley and Graham took off their black coveralls and hoods, exposing their guard uniforms. After changing into black shoes, they could have easily been mistaken as Iraqi guards behind their goggle-eyed masks.

Once Wyley was ready, he and Russum kept low, slipping outside the supply room, down the corridor to the wall-mounted map of the mezzanine. Wyley studied it carefully. Knowing the language, he quickly found what he was looking for. Translated, it read simply: ELECTRICAL UTILITY.

He studied the path to the room, then pointed toward a junction down the corridor. A second hallway crossed theirs; the mezzanine electrical utility room was around the corner.

Russum nodded and ran his eye back across the map. "Where's the brains of this operation?"

"Their comp center's here, on the far back corner, diagonally opposite the security complex."

They turned the corner, bound for the electrical room. It wasn't locked. Their first impressions: harsh glary lighting, and conduits running in and out a central breaker panel on the back wall. Wyley studied the electrical circuit markings on the door of the breaker box, a bit unsure what to make of it. "This one should kill the hall lights," he said, pointing to the top breaker in the rightmost column. He marked it with a grease pencil. "This'll kill the lights in security and the one below it'll take out their wall power."

"I want to black out that quadrant."

"This breaker should do it."

"That's it then. That's what we need." For the second time, Russum tried to rub his mustache in vain. "I'll kill power when the smoke gets thick."

"They've got emergency lights covering the exits, but the combination of smoke and darkness should create the confusion we need. We'll get in and out before they know what hit them."

"I hope so." Russum couldn't decide what was missing, but felt they'd overlooked something. "What about batteries? They okay?"

Without discussion, Wyley changed batteries, then checked his ammunition clips for the third time. "Got bullets and batteries. Radio and night-vision goggles are good to go."

"Don't leave home without them."

Wyley keyed the throat mike in his gas mask three times to get Graham's attention. "Billy Ray's set at this end."

Click click, Graham acknowledged.

Wyley headed back to supply, leaving Russum standing by in electrical.

Inside the supply room, Graham hoisted two room fans through the hole he'd cut in the feeder duct, positioning them where they sucked air from supply and blew it down the vent toward security. Turning both fans on high, the motor noise was noticeable, but not obnoxious. Next, he covered the supply room smoke detector with a plastic bag he'd found inside one of the computer monitor boxes. Once he'd secured it with a rubber band, Graham climbed up on a chair, lit his torch, and scored the outline of a hatch on the return air duct running parallel to the main feeder. Within seconds, the smell of molten fiberglass and smoke permeated the room.

Pushing the side of the air return with his gloved hand, Graham felt the fiberglass yield with a *crraaackkkk*. He pushed harder, putting his shoulder behind it, and the hatch collapsed inward to form a two-foot-square hole. Satisfied, the doctor watched smoke boiling from the smoldering opening, streaming toward the fans in the primary feeder. The smoldering fiberglass made a kind of snap, crackle, and pop noise as the fiberglass strands glowed, smoldered, then eventually gave way.

Knowing a stench this strong couldn't be ignored, Graham's plan was to plant the suspicion of fire in the minds of the security guards, then give them cause to panic.

Wyley appeared at Graham's side and both men began rolling smoke grenades into the overhead air duct. A wall of thick black smoke funneled its way down the duct toward security. From the factory floor below, the mezzanine looked on fire, black smoke boiling from the overhead vents.

Minutes later, Graham heard three clicks over his headset and knew that Russum had seen the smoke in electrical.

In security, thick black smoke boiled through their overhead vents and Hakim was concerned. Within seconds, halos formed around the lights, and visibility dropped inside the room like flying into a cloud.

Wyley continued rolling smoke grenades into the feeder as Graham strapped on his flamethrower and headed for the catwalk. Overhead cameras maintained watch over the stairway approaches to the mezzanine, and Graham was careful to move slow, low, and quiet, outside of their view.

Suspended in plain view of one camera, Graham found what he'd been looking for, a chrome sprinkler head and temperature sensor. From an intersecting corridor near the catwalk, he squeezed the trigger, slowly at first, but once the flame erupted, there was no stopping it. Yellow-orange flames streamed from his weapon, dancing across the camera's field of view, laying a billowing layer of smoke and blazing napalm on the metal catwalk.

Klaxons sounded as a bright red light began spinning above the smoldering sensor. In the blink of an eye, a single sprinkler drenched the flames; seconds later, the steady rain became a torrential downpour, as four, sixteen, then thirty-two sprinklers opened to extinguish any blaze in the area.

Once Russum heard the Klaxon, he knew what to do.

Inside security, Hakim jumped at the sound of the alarm. His gaze darted to a computer screen showing the mezzanine floor plan flashing brightly, lit up like a Christmas tree. The smoke was thick, and before the guards could sort through the situation, their overhead lights went out. Pitch black darkness engulfed them, then emergency lights kicked in, dimly illuminating the way to the exits. Hakim grabbed Kajaz by the arm and bolted for the door, shouting into his headset as he ran.

"Meet me at the catwalk!"

Carrying fire extinguishers, the plant manager and the terrorist felt their way down the hallway with single-minded purpose.

Outside security, masked by the howling siren, smoke, and darkness, Graham and Wyley watched the men working their way toward the catwalk through night-vision goggles.

Graham pressed his throat mike, signaling Russum. "Two coming to you, the terrorist and manager."

Click click.

The situation on the catwalk was mayhem. The Klaxon continued howling, smoke boiled from the overhead vents, molten plastic fixtures smoldered about their feet, and water soaked both men through and through, shorting out their radios, making it impossible to communicate. Hakim's clothes clung to him like a second skin as sprinklers drenched the catwalk and everything on it.

Concealed behind a wall of boxes, Russum knelt on the factory floor below, aiming up toward the catwalk. Through the downpour, he could see the manager approaching, but where was the terrorist?

Suddenly, a hot vapor trail whipped past the big Texan's face as a bullet screamed by.

Shit. He yanked his head back, dropping behind the boxes.

The terrorist was out there, but where? Scanning shadows beneath the mezzanine, he caught a glimpse of motion and snapped off a shot. Sparks flew as the bullet ricocheted off a metal column, but Russum couldn't find any trace of the gunman.

Something scraped against the metal above his head.

He whirled, expecting to see the terrorist. Nothing. Were there two gunmen?

A metal crash followed one second later, then a clatter.

Glancing up, he saw the manager hosing down the catwalk with his fire extinguisher. Every instinct told him to grab the man, but Russum knew this was no time for heroics. He swallowed hard, forcing his breathing back to normal, then scanned the area.

Alert to danger, he rushed up the stairs toward the man, with his weapon drawn.

Dropping everything, the manager's hands shot over his head.

Deafened by the sirens, Russum's eyes darted from shadow to shadow. Where was the terrorist?

Shoving the manager away from the catwalk into the hallway, he cuffed him with cable ties and, from there, began searching the factory floor below.

Instinctively, Wyley took the lead now outside security, pulling Graham into a telephone wiring closet.

Once inside, Wyley told the doctor what he needed to do, and climbed an access ladder into the ceiling. Concealed by conduits, cable racks, water pipes, and smoke, he positioned himself over the corridor outside security.

Below him, Wyley saw the complex in chaos. Only minutes after Hakim and Kajaz had bolted, two more guards scrambled for the exit.

Wyley took a deep breath, releasing the safety on his silenced submachine gun.

The first man's head appeared in the open door.

Gazing through the smoke with his night-vision goggles, Wyley braced himself on a steel cable tray, finger on the trigger. The first guard carried a holstered pistol on his right hip.

Below him and to one side, Graham played out his role as the distractor. His heart pounded so hard he felt it would explode. He stood paralyzed, his senses overloaded by the chaotic extremes of his situation. Instinctively, Graham wanted to run as the dark, shaggy-haired guard charged toward him, but his feet felt frozen to the floor.

The large man almost ran over him, but stopped short, yelling out something in Arabic.

Wyley understood the language and knew the guard's question demanded a response, but he remained silent, hidden overhead in the black, smoke-filled shadows. Bringing his weapon to his shoulder, he hesitated, centering the crosshairs on the first guard's neck and shoulder.

Standing squarely in Graham's face, the guard got a better look behind his goggles. He froze for an instant, then drew his gun.

Unfortunate, Wyley thought. Both Iraqis were only yards away with the closest fixed in his front sight.

Pop pop.

The first guard fell to the floor in a heap like a fifty-pound bag of potatoes.

The second guard panicked.

THOOM!!! THOOM!! THOOM!

The short fat gunman with skinny legs and an enormous gut turned and fired blind into the darkness, pounding Graham once in his chestplate from close range.

Distracted, Wyley saw the muzzle flashes and wavered off target, brushing the sights of his own gun across Graham's back. Startled by almost shooting his friend, he froze long enough to see his friend stagger backward and fall to the floor.

"NO! NO!! NO!!!" Wyley screamed at the top of his lungs.

Below him, the round man raised his pistol and shot toward the shout. The bullet ricocheted off a water pipe, then slammed into the concrete ceiling.

Moving quickly, Wyley swung his submachine gun toward the round man and squeezed.

Grabbing his gut, the man staggered momentarily, then his toothpick legs collapsed like a house of cards. Once down, he didn't move.

Fearing the worst, Wyley radioed his friend. "Graham, Graham. Can you hear me? Pull back, man. There's more coming."

Unconscious, Graham lay perfectly still below him. Wyley thought he heard breathing over his headset, but with all the noise, he couldn't be sure.

From that point forward, the Iraqis came quickly. Emerging in pairs with weapons at the ready, they were disorganized, ill-equipped for night fighting, and half-cocked.

Wyley, knowing the guards couldn't hit what they couldn't see, climbed back into the jungle of overhead pipe, conduit, cables, and ductwork.

Having heard the gunshots, the next few guards emerged cautiously into the corridor crouching slightly. Judging from their independent styles, Wyley concluded they weren't trained as a team. Still, they wouldn't be taken by surprise as easily as the first two.

Checking only what they could see at eye level and around their feet, both guards were distracted by the obvious smoke, noise, and bodies. As Wyley had expected, neither one of them searched overhead for danger, but even if they had, it wouldn't have made any difference.

Wyley could see two gunmen making their way down the dark, smoky corridor through his night-vision goggles, yet even if they'd been looking overhead, they couldn't have seen him.

Technology was both a blessing and a curse, but Wyley knew as long as his batteries held out, he owned the darkness.

Studying the carnage strewn across the floor, Wyley concluded the first to examine the dead would be the next to die.

Gazing down at his friend, Wyley wanted to see motion, some sign of life. Graham's arm twitched first; then he heard a gasp over his headset, and a wonderful, God-sent wheezing sound. *If anyone so much as touches him, they'll die in their tracks.*

A pressing sense of urgency gnawed at him; he knew there were at least two more guards where these came from—and Russum had missed the terrorist. What were they doing while he hid here, suspended overhead, beneath the ceiling?

Whatever I do, it'd better be fast, Wyley thought.

Below and forward, the point man knelt between two fallen guards, checking their condition. He checked the round man's pulse first, then his buddy's.

Wyley exhaled slowly, holding his aim steady on the target, then noticed someone moving to the right of his front sight.

The rear guard's the immediate threat here, Wyley thought, suddenly shifting targets.

Turning toward Graham, the man was only yards away from his friend and closing fast.

Wyley swung his gun toward the top of the guard's head

and shoulders, but the man was moving quickly and a sprinkler blocked his shot.

By the time he lifted his gun barrel up and over the water pipe, the guard was kneeling alongside Graham, examining his respirator and night-vision gear.

Wyley tripped into automatic, fixing his thermal sights on the guard's rib cage, just below the fleshy part of his arm. Try as he might, he couldn't steady his aim, his sight drifting high and perilously close to Graham's head. He exhaled slowly, commanding his hands to relax and his heartbeat to slow. Moments later, both hands flushed with warmth as his front sight stabilized on target. *Now!*

A subtle pop followed, inaudible above the screaming sirens.

The rear guard slumped forward and to one side, lying over Graham's stomach in a heap.

Moving quickly, Wyley swung his MP4 submachine gun back toward the point guard, working his eight-inch silencer between the clutter of cable and pipes. With the remaining gunman surrounded by corpses, Wyley felt no need for pinpoint accuracy, a focused sweep would do, and besides, there was no time; his target was climbing to his feet, about to move.

Wyley squeezed the trigger and held it firmly, saturating his field of fire with an extended burst of 9mm rounds. Five seconds later, once the target dropped, Wyley slapped in a fresh clip.

Coughing echoed in Wyley's headset.

"Graham, can you hear me?"

Click click.

"What's your condition?"

"I think one of my ribs is cracked. I don't know for sure, but it hurts to breathe deep."

"If all you've got's a cracked rib, then we've been mighty lucky so far."

"How long was I out? What's our situation?"

"Four of the eight guards are down. I think they're dead, none of 'em are moving anyway. Russum's captured one, but the terrorist got away. He's armed and could show up anytime."

"How about Buck?"

"He's okay. He's still in security with two guards, but from what I can see, they're not paying much attention to him. They've got problems of their own."

"Anyone else in the bunker?"

"We don't know yet. We'll find out once we're in security. Can you move? Can you get to the wiring closet?"

"Yeah, I was thinking the same thing."

"How about your flamethrower? Think you can carry it?"

"Yeah, I believe so. How about you? Are you injured?"

"I'm okay, but my contacts are killing me, Doc." Wyley squinted inside his gas mask, his vision blurring a few seconds. *The last time my eyes felt this scratchy was in New York,* he thought. *Cigarette smoke did a number on 'em. Cigarettes—that's an idea. This uniform reeks of cigarette smoke. Maybe . . .*

Rubbing both hands outside his pants pocket, he felt a hard lump. Pulling it out, he gave it a flick and a steady yellow flame blazed from the plastic butane cylinder.

Wyley looked down the maze of water pipes and found a temperature sensor located above a conference room down the hall from security.

"I'm ready," Graham reported from inside the wiring closet.

Wyley summarized his intent, then began crawling down the cable tray toward the conference room. Unfortunately, the cable tray wasn't a tray at all, it was more like a long steel ladder laid horizontally, suspended from the ceiling by half-inch threaded rod. To Wyley's dismay, every ladder rung notched into his shins like a knife. He'd never known such pain. *I'm getting too old for this shit,* he thought, but no good would come from complaining. Finally, after what seemed like an eternity, he inched forward to within reach of the sensor.

Seconds later, sprinklers drenched the room and adjoining hallway. Once the smoke cleared, glary red rotating lights revealed the gruesome spectacle in the hallway below.

Meanwhile, inside security, a flashing alarm warned the two remaining guards of a fire much too close to ignore. In response, the lead gunman crawled out of his smoke-filled sanctuary with pistol in hand; the second dragged an extinguisher. Further down the corridor, drenching rain cleared the smoke around four bloodstained corpses.

One look at the four dead men and the hostage rescue operation was over. Both guards recognized the bodies, then reversed direction, bolting for the catwalk.

Casting caution to the wind, Graham hurried into security as fast as his sore ribs would allow. In the far back corner, through the smoke and darkness, the doctor saw Buck struggling to escape. Tied to the chair with four of his own nylon cable ties, he hadn't given up, but felt little hope for freedom.

With Graham still wearing his Iraqi uniform, Buck didn't recognize the doctor through the smoke, but noticed the guard's movements were a little wooden, as if it hurt him to bend or turn quickly.

Closer inspection convinced the commander that the guard's respirator and night-vision goggles were not only familiar, but Delta Force standard issue. Studying the eyes behind the mask, Buck finally recognized his friend.

Without further delay, the doctor severed the nylon cable ties binding the big man to his chair.

Buck's hands were purple, but within seconds, they flushed beet red. Feeling better about his prospects, he pointed to the deep gouges on his wrists and joked behind his gas mask. "That's going to leave a mark."

Graham saw the commander's jaw move, but couldn't hear him speak.

Standing, the big lineman squeezed Graham in a bear hug and continued talking. Graham's ribs were bruised near the sternum, so the embrace caused him to cry out.

Signaling time-out, Graham opened the battery compartment of the commander's battlepack and slid in a new set.

Before he could complete his first sentence, Buck interrupted over his headset. "I guessed you were behind the tear gas."

Graham nodded.

"What about Wyley and Russum? They okay?"

"They're fine. Be here any minute. Russum's got a prisoner."

"Prisoner?"

"An Iraqi civilian."

"The one who took off outta security with the terrorist?"

"Yeah, he's the one."

"That civilian, my good doctor, happens to be the weapons director. He knows more about what goes on in this bunker than anyone."

"It's about time we got a break."

"What about that terrorist? What happened to him?"

"He got away clean."

Buck grimaced. "Armed?"

"Yeah, he's still inside the bunker somewhere."

"Man, with that murderer on the loose, we'd better watch our backs. I've worked with a lotta young people over the years, and I tell you, this kid is frightening. He's carries himself like a seasoned soldier though he's not a day over twenty-five. I couldn't believe it at first, but I've watched him. Somehow, he's got the judgment of a mature adult in the head of a young body. If I hadn't seen it with my own eyes, I would never have believed it."

Buck paused, then changed the subject. "Take this seat here. There's something I've gotta show you."

Graham sat down in front of a poster-board-sized, flat-screen computer monitor showing a floor plan of the factory.

Next, Buck went on to explain what he'd learned about the bunker. Walking from one surveillance screen to another, the commander related different video camera shots to positions on the factory floor plan. Very quickly, Graham got a good sense of the layout.

"Drill down here." Buck pointed to a small, brightly flashing section of the factory floor plan.

Graham double-clicked, opening a new window containing a video camera shot of the area. "Jackpot."

Buck pulled a double-take. To his surprise, the video surveillance camera showed a wide-angle shot of the terrorist and four guards moving an overhead hoist toward the mezzanine.

"What the hell're they doing with that dumpster?"

Both men leaned forward, scrutinizing the video. Attached to the crane's lifting hook, the commander saw a large steel dumpster.

"Motion detectors picked up their movement. That much is clear."

"Yeah, but it doesn't get us anywhere. We can detect their motion and see 'em coming. Hell, the factory's covered with cameras and motion detectors. Looks to me like they're regrouping," Buck observed. "If that terrorist is half as smart as I think he is, they'll either try an ambush or pin us down."

"That makes sense. I'd guess they're going to pin us down and wait for help. They don't have any information to help them set up an ambush. I mean, they don't know how many of us are here, how we got in, or where we're going."

Buck agreed and continued to study the terrorist moving across the screen. He was working a control box dangling by a long flexible conduit from an overhead crane, walking it across the floor as the hoist traversed an I-beam suspended from the ceiling.

Positioning the dumpster over an open space, he released the chain brake, allowing it to slam down hard on the concrete.

Once the empty container settled, four guards converged on it with cutting torches blazing. Waterfalls of sparks streamed down the dumpster's exterior, dancing across the hardened floor. Within minutes, narrow slits on all four sides telegraphed their intent.

Buck read their purpose like a book. "It's a gun platform. They're planning to hole up in there and pin us down."

As Buck reached this conclusion, Wyley and Russum appeared in the doorway, completing their reunion. Wyley entered security first, limping on both legs; Russum followed, leading the weapons director on a makeshift leash. The civilian prisoner—named Kajaz according to his picture ID—was shackled with three cable ties where he could walk, but couldn't run.

Increasingly alarmed by their situation, Buck pressed his concern. "Kajaz speaks English. Tie him to my chair back in the corner, then we need to talk."

Wyley complied immediately, fearing the Iraqi army

would arrive any minute. Not knowing their exact whereabouts created an almost crippling anxiety. Each second that
ticked off felt like another spin of the chamber and squeeze of
the trigger in a losing game of Russian roulette.

Graham handed Buck a backpack containing his weapons
and scuba gear. The commander pulled his Colt .45 pistol
and ammo clips out first. Holstering his Colt, he slipped a
few full clips into his vest. Next, he scrutinized the MP4 submachine gun. "It's no M60," he quipped, "but it'll do in a
pinch."

"That's big of you," Graham said. "Your machine gun and
ammo would have broken my back. I don't know how you
carry that thing."

"What can I say? It lays down a suppressing fire second to
none, but it don't come for free. What's with the scuba
gear?"

"There's a maintenance hatch below that leads to the
river." Graham sighed, imagining how the water pressure
would hurt. "We're planning to use it."

"Good. Can you take it? You're moving pretty stiff."

"I think so, if I take it slow. At least it's not too deep,
twenty feet or so. Besides, it's not like I've got much choice."

"So what's the plan?"

"We get in the comp center, gather evidence, and get out."

"What about the Iraqi army?"

"They're breathing down our neck." Graham pressed his
sense of urgency.

"How long we got?" Buck asked.

"They'll be here any minute."

"I expected their recon scouts would be here before now,"
Russum added.

Graham grimaced; he hadn't thought about that possibility.

"I was afraid of that." Buck checked the motion detectors
covering both tunnel links into the bunker. "No sign of 'em
yet, but if we don't act now, we'll have hell to pay once the
smoke clears. Billy Ray, did you bring my boom bag with
you?"

"Yeah, a stripped-down version, det cord, blasting caps,
and a little C4. I had a feeling you'd need it."

"Enough C4 to disable the motor drives on those two steel blast doors?"

"The big doors blocking each entrance?"

"Yeah. Can we disable 'em? I want 'em locked shut."

"I think so, but go easy on the C4."

Buck looked puzzled.

"We're inside a sealed bunker here—the shock wave's got no place to go."

"Good point," Buck agreed. "Can we lock 'em shut?"

"If we can get to the gearboxes, we can disable the doors. You buying time? Locking us in and them out?"

"Locking them out's the idea, but unless I missed something, we're not locked in. We've got two ways out, right? The air duct or the river."

"Our chances are better if we can find that maintenance hatch and run wet. We left an obvious trail topside. A blind man could follow the path we cut."

"So we run wet. Everybody good with that?"

"That's been our working assumption from the start," Russum agreed.

"Good." Buck pointed to two small toggle switches on the control console near Graham. "These open and close the blast doors, and you gotta believe when the Iraqi army gets here, they're gonna want in."

"Are these the only switches controlling the doors?"

"I don't know. I thought about it and I honestly don't know."

"Well, I can tell you one thing," Russum observed. "Those little switches control those big doors indirectly. They're too small to switch power directly to the electric motors so they probably drive some large relay or control logic which powers the doors."

"I don't follow you."

"Well, the way I read our situation is like this. When the Iraqi army arrives, our terrorist will be under pressure to get those doors open. He may or may not rush security to gain access to the door control switches."

"No, I think we know more than that," Graham insisted.

"He's a survivor, calculating and deliberate. Tell me, how would you handle this situation were you in his shoes?" Graham asked Buck directly.

"I'd ask the guards. If another switch existed, I'd use it. If not, I'd hot-wire the door."

"I think that's your answer, Buck. They're going to pin us down, run a bypass, and throw open the gates."

"I see what you mean. If they're using their heads, that's what they'll do."

The foursome agreed, then Wyley asked the obvious question. "What if they panic?"

"That's no good. Their response becomes more difficult to predict."

"Then we need to control their panic button," Graham concluded.

"That's right. Based on your scenario, Doc, you'll probably be safe alone here as long as they feel they have the upper hand. You sit tight in security and cover our floor surveillance. You know the drill. Keep us posted. If anything changes, let us know."

Click click. Graham toggled his transmitter.

"I know the way to the comp center and both blast doors," Buck said, taking the lead. "We need a tail gunner, someone to cover our backs. Wyley, you up for it?"

Wyley nodded, making eye contact with Russum and Graham. His expression telegraphed his feeling that it was good to have Buck back in the driver's seat again.

"Good, now we've got another problem to sort through. We need to stay together, but our situation demands we split up. We need Graham in security as our eyes and navigator; he'll be safe here, he knows the ropes, and he's got his flamethrower, just in case we're wrong. Agreed?"

Three nods.

"Good, then as I see it, disabling those blast doors is our top priority. We've got to lock those doors no matter what."

"Most blast doors are finely balanced so they can be operated by hand," Russum said. "There's usually a manual and automatic method for controlling them."

"I hear you, Billy Ray," Buck said quietly. "Let me play back where I think you're going. Unless I'm missing something, this operation is a job for a few ribbons of C4. It should boil down to cutting the power conduit to each motor and severing the manual controls."

"That's the idea."

"Excellent. Sounds fast and straightforward."

"Keep it simple, stupid, but the devil's in the details," Russum cautioned. "We need to take a close look at those doors."

"Can do." Graham drilled into the factory floor plans by double-clicking the tunnel link leading to the hospital. A grainy video picture of the blast door appeared. Using his mouse to navigate around the plans, he double-clicked on the video image and opened a detailed blueprint of the door and surrounding area. The mechanical assembly drawing showed a large flywheel mounted on the wall near the door for manual operation and another switch mounted nearby for motor control.

"I've seen what I need," Buck said. "How 'bout you, Billy Ray?"

"Yep."

"Good. Next, we've got to get what we came for. Collect whatever evidence and records we can find, then get the hell out."

Buck had the uneasy feeling that he was missing something important. "Tell me one thing. Where's that maintenance hatch? I gotta know my way out before I got my bases covered."

"Somewhere in the pump room."

"Let's pull it up. I need to see it. It's gonna be a hell of a dark swim outta here and I got a feeling we're gonna need to leave in a hurry."

Without wasting time, Graham drilled into the pump room, revealing the escape trunk and maintenance hatch. After plotting their escape route, the team was primed to go.

"Let's get it done. Check your ammo and batteries. Wyley, grab the boom bag. Billy Ray, leave your prisoner with Graham and follow me. I'll grab the grenades and take point."

CHAPTER THIRTY

Mass Production
Sunday, Apr. 18, 6:40 A.M.
The Bunker

Buck's instincts told him to move to the service elevator and move quickly, but an inner voice insisted he heed Russum's warning regarding the shock wave from exploding C4. As a result, all three men deliberately detoured by the comp center and propped open every door entering the complex. Inside the room, they ran through a duct and cover drill, lowering workstations to the floor, positioning them under heavy desks. Satisfied, they hurried down the hallway and around a corner to the elevator. Tucked away against an outside wall, its retracting doors were well concealed from both the mezzanine and the factory floor.

Fortunately, the elevator was already on the second floor, well lit and empty. *A good sign,* Buck thought. *One less thing to worry about.*

The trio entered, placing their backs against both side walls of the enclosure. Buck punched the bottom button and set the safety on his MP4. As the cage closed, he thrust the butt of his submachine gun up into the electric light. Following a shower of fiery sparks, the elevator fell dark and began its descent. It was slow going and the single-story drop seemed to take forever. The sluggish pace allowed the trio time to engage their night-vision goggles and Buck to make one final check with Graham in security.

"Any motion toward the elevator?"

"Negative, they haven't seen you, but their shooting house is nearly ready. Once they hoist that thing into position, they can cover most of the factory floor, both blast doors, plus the catwalk."

"They want the high ground, but they can't hit what they can't see."

"You're thinking about the lights?"

"Yeah. Can you search the plans for the bunker's main electrical panel? I saw it on the north side of the bunker in the pump room."

"Right. I saw it too." Graham double-clicked a small section of the floor plan and a blueprint of the pump room appeared on-screen. "It's between the maintenance hatch and primary cooling pump. I'll bet you can control power to the crane and overhead lights from there, but I can't read the labels."

"Not to worry," Wyley broke in over the intercom channel. "I'll translate when the time comes."

Buck sensed the hydraulic freight elevator whining to a stop, his heart pounding in his chest. Sirens still howled throughout the bunker, red lights rotated overhead, sprinklers rained down, smoke and tear gas lingered in the stagnant air, emergency lights illuminated the blocked bunker exits; yet from the relative calm of the factory floor, the chaos appeared largely confined to the second-floor mezzanine.

The elevator hit the metal stops with a thunk. Buck raised the muzzle of his submachine gun as the safety doors clanked open. Russum and Wyley followed Buck without a word.

A dark, empty vestibule lay before them. Adjoining the freight chamber, crossing to the right, a dimly lit passageway turned the corner and emerged from the shadow of the mezzanine into the factory lights. It was here they were vulnerable; here in the light, Buck sensed danger.

"It's clear." Graham's words played out like music over the trio's headsets. All three men rotated their night-vision goggles away from their line of sight.

Clothed in black from head to toe, the trio moved with stalking, almost animal precision across the floor into the light. Buck stayed low, turning left, then right against the bunker's south perimeter wall. The south wall linked up with the access tunnel, and it was here Buck expected the Iraqi army would gain entry. This was the shortest, most direct, and best developed route, so it stood to reason they'd come there first.

Looking behind them and overhead, the mezzanine catwalk surrounded an intricate maze of dimly lit, smoky hallways and office space. Although no fires were visible from the floor, sprinkler water spray interacted with the overhead lighting to form haloes and rainbows near the ceiling. Even in the midst of chaos, in a cold, mechanical way, there was beauty in this godforsaken place.

Staying low and out of sight, the commander stuck his head around the corner leading to the blast door which had first imprisoned him here. Thinking ahead, he visualized the doors locking shut, entombing his captors. He wasn't sure of the best word to describe their little four-man operation, but something about it felt like justice.

"They're staying together," Graham reported, "still clustered around the dumpster. Keep moving while the going's good."

Click click.

Eclipsed by the massive blast door, Buck and Russum went to work with Wyley covering the rear.

Wyley's gaze darted high, low, left, then right. He was struck by the hard shapes and harsh shadows. The factory floor was a maze of electronic manufacturing machines, boxes, packing material, milling machinery, and test equipment— much of it made in Japan and the United States.

Two aisles away, his eye was drawn to a massive assembly table. Suspended vertically on its edge, a familiar doughnut-shaped silhouette caught his attention.

Further down the line, each ring had detonator cables attached. From a distance, they reminded him of snakes.

At the end of the production line, inside a clear plastic chamber, red, green, and yellow lights flashed across countless detonators under test.

Realizing this, memories of Manhattan came flooding back. Wyley's knees felt like jelly.

Closer inspection revealed that this factory wasn't geared for producing a few of anything; this was a mass-production facility geared for creating thousands of production-quality, pure-fusion neutron bombs.

Wyley felt crushed by the inescapable reality of this revelation. It was one thing to speculate it could happen, but quite another to experience it happening before your own eyes.

Overwhelmed by the vast scale of it all, the *Times* correspondent dropped his guard and followed his instincts. "Pictures."

"No flash," Graham responded tightly. "You're clear down the line, but keep your eye on the shoot house. Go!"

Back by the blast door, Buck pinched off a piece of plastic explosive, flattened it into a ribbon, then wrapped it around the power conduit running to the door's motor drive. Next, he wrapped another ribbon of C4 around the shaft attaching the manual door wheel to the drive shaft in the wall.

Russum electrically primed two ten-foot lengths of det cord and handed them to Buck. Without words, he buried them in each ribbon, attached both wires to a small, wallet-sized box, then ran through the math. Checking the time, it had taken nearly three minutes to move from the mezzanine to the access tunnel link, and five minutes to rig the door with explosive. *Six minutes to the hospital link from here, five minutes to rig the second door—eleven minutes to boom time.*

Besides, if the Iraqi army arrived earlier, he could remotely detonate the door using his handheld control. Rubbing his remote control across the top of the detonator, it trained up, flashed green, and they were ready to roll.

"Graham, hospital link. Gotta move. How's it look?"

"Not good. They're cutting off their torches, hosing it down. Steam's boiling off the shoot house. They finished it; four guards climbing in."

A pause.

"Buck, hold everything. I got motion!"

"Say again."

"Motion in the tunnel. Something's happening in access."

"Drill down. What do you see?"

"Nothing. Black screens. Cameras are wasted, but I've got motion down the tunnel, multiple signals. They're close, it's gotta be them."

"What do we do?"

"Mezzanine. Head under the mezzanine. Pump room, breakers . . . Stay low. Go! Go! Go! Go!"

A rifle shot cracked from the shoot house above Buck's head. The bullet ricocheted off a massive metal table by his right arm, severing a high-pressure air line. The hose undulated over the trio, broadcasting their position for all to see.

In sight of the mezzanine's shadow, the three men kept moving.

Inside the dumpster, one gunman drew his best bead and fired again, this time off to the left. Squeezing the trigger, he emptied the clip of his automatic, unloading it wildly off the mark.

Under cover of darkness, Buck went down on one knee, sighting on the gun port. His aim was true, but his laser pointer kept drifting off the mark.

He saw a barrage of muzzle flashes blazing from two sides of the shoot house. The dumpster gave the appearance of a metal pillbox, with one subtle difference.

It was moving, dangling by four chains from a single hook, swinging slowly back and forth, twisting side to side. Tracking the gun port's motion with his laser pointer, Buck could see the shoot house was unstable. As the gunmen moved about, the dumpster swung. As they fired, the dumpster rotated back and forth like a carnival ride set in slow motion.

Bullets plinked haphazardly around the trio on the floor below, but none came threateningly close.

Suddenly, the shoot house began gliding horizontally, accelerating toward the mezzanine. Below and behind the dumpster, Hakim worked the crane controls, driving the hoist laterally along its overhead support beam.

"They're trying to stabilize it, pinning it to the catwalk," Graham reported. "Move, move now while they're off balance."

Buck didn't need to hear it twice. All three men sprinted down the aisle underneath the mezzanine. Without stopping for breath, they rounded the corner, broke out into the light near the north wall, then headed for the pump room. Hobbling on both legs, Wyley brought up the rear, and managed to finish a distant third.

Inside the dangling container, the gunmen braced for impact, but it didn't do any good. Their guns fell silent as the dumpster smashed into the catwalk.

On the floor below, Hakim's handheld squad radio began vibrating. Pulling it from his pants pocket, a short message flashed on display: RAISE THE GATES.

In the pump room, Wyley slammed open the master panel. Breakers were marked, but poorly and in pencil. Flipping four that looked suspicious, he was rewarded when the bulk of the overhead lighting went out.

Seconds later, sixty feet from the blast door, Hakim was running toward the tunnel, darting through the shadows, guided by whatever emergency illumination remained.

"Heads up, Buck. He's bolting for the door. Blow it now!"

"Wait till he gets there."

"No! No! No! Now! Blow it now!" Graham screamed, diving under the desk. Instinctively, he covered his ears and opened his mouth wide.

Grabbing Wyley by the shoulder, Buck's speech was clipped. "Get in the trunk." Russum was already inside the chamber. The commander followed, pressing his remote as he stepped into the hatch.

The resulting shock wave slammed the escape trunk hatch closed with a resounding clang, barely missing Buck's foot. Less than a second later, the vacuum created by the expanding air blast sucked the hatch back open, evacuating the chamber, then in an instant, whammed it closed again with the force of spring steel. Inside the trunk, the three men were stunned by the rapid changes in pressure, their ears ringing, but otherwise unharmed.

Not everyone had been so lucky.

Hakim saw the flash, felt the blast and searing heat, then experienced the expanding fireball pass over his body, scorching his hair. The subsequent concussion shattered his radio, knocked him off his feet, and hurled him like a rag doll into a stash of cardboard boxes across the aisle. The hearing in his right ear was destroyed.

Inside security, much further from the explosion, the shock wave compressed everything for an instant, initially scattering debris away from the blast. Office glass shattered across the mezzanine, TV monitors crashed to the floor, but inside both the comp center and security, the doors had been propped open. With the pressure equalized, most of the glass walls remained intact and the impact of the explosion had been minimal.

Hakim and the guards had absorbed the brunt of the concussion. They emerged shaken, but still armed and dangerous.

"Graham? Can you hear me?"

A pause.

"Graham?"

"Stand by, Buck. I hear you. My ears're ringing, but I'm okay."

"What about the access tunnel?"

Graham crawled out from under the desk. "We got movement, tunnel's crawling with soldiers, motion detectors're going off all over. That's gotta be the main force."

"Good. Let's keep 'em there."

Stepping out from the escape trunk, Buck spoke to Wyley. "Turn off the factory lights."

"They're off. I'm ahead of you this time."

"Right." All three men lowered their night-vision gear into position. Beyond the pump room door lay dimly lit silhouettes defining the factory floor, mezzanine, and shoot house. "Let's hang our gunmen out to dry."

Under cover of darkness, Buck took control of the crane and manipulated the dumpster away from the catwalk to the center of the factory floor. After hoisting it up near the ceiling, he shot its dangling control umbilical, severing power to the crane, trapping the guards like rats.

Straightaway, Buck and Russum began wrapping ribbons of C4 around cut points on the remaining blast door.

As they rigged the door, Wyley's worst nightmare was confirmed. The packaging facility was located near the hospital link and there, in the dim light, he counted ninety-three neutron bombs, each individually serialized, packaged as Edam cheese balls.

Instinctively, the *Times* correspondent photographed the packaging area, then collected several bombs and detonators as evidence.

Before they left, Russum assembled one bomb and placed it out of sight in the pump room. "That should cover our butts."

"It's the only way to be sure," Buck agreed.

Five minutes later, the second blast door was blown and the trio reunited with Graham in security.

Once Hakim saw the three men climbing the stairs to the mezzanine, he moved with calm presence and precision to take them down. In the back of his mind, he had hoped he'd be joined by Iraqi forces, but with both doors out of commission, even they couldn't help him now. He had to lower the dumpster and release the guards, but failing this, he was on his own.

Meanwhile, on the sandbar above, a young Iraqi patrol leader radioed his commander concerning the man-sized openings his platoon discovered cut through the security fence and blower. Once he described the baseball-shaped gas grenades they'd found, his commanding officer recognized them as American, radioed Baghdad immediately, and took action. Ropes, tear gas masks, and troops were rushed by barge to the sandbar. Less than forty minutes later, the air ducts were swarming with Iraqi troops.

Inside the comp center, a yell rang out above the roar of a hundred equipment fans. "Russum! Come here! I need you."

Billy Ray grabbed his headset with both ears ringing. "Damnit, Wyley. I hear you. Whaddaya got?"

"Good news. If we can't find what we're looking for, we can take it with us."

Gazing over Wyley's shoulder, the big Texan squinted behind his goggles, struggling to read the small print on-screen. "You talking 'bout the database?"

"Yeah. I copied it on this." Wyley held up something that looked like a credit card, then tucked it away in his shirt pocket.

"Hell, it's about time we got a break."

"We're running on borrowed time as it is." Wyley sighed, his fingers flying across the keyboard.

From experience, he expected the database contained the information he needed. In addition, he understood better than most, the trick was finding it, wading through the irrelevant muck and culling useful data from the abyss.

While beginning his information hunt, he heard Graham on his headset, calling Buck with a heads-up from security. "The terrorist is moving, he's on the factory floor now, by the catwalk stairs."

"More distractions." Wyley grimaced, his concentration derailed again. "Man, I can't focus, working like this."

"Listen. Do the best you can and don't worry. I'll cover it." Buck said. "Graham. Talk to me. Where is he, exactly? Which staircase?"

"Near the south wall."

"I'm on it." Buck grabbed his gear and headed out the door. "What's he doing?"

"He's armed, carrying something with him, some kind of box."

The headset went silent for a moment.

"He's seen the surveillance camera, taking it out. Picture's gone."

Wyley looked at Russum as Buck left the room. His expression conveyed an urgent sense of "let's get on with it." Without an exchange of words, Russum cut his prisoner loose and brought him forward.

"Sit down." Wyley instructed the Iraqi weapons director to log in to the manufacturing database.

Kajaz had experienced both explosions and reasoned the Iraqi army must be outside the gates. Rescue was only a matter of time and all he needed to do was stall.

He sat down, giving an impression of cooperation. Without prompting, he entered his log-in name and typed a series of letters and numbers for his password. Satisfied, he clicked SUBMIT.

PASSWORD REJECTED flashed in a gray box.

Acting flustered, he tried again and failed, but Wyley didn't buy it. "We need your bomb inventory, manufacturing, and shipping records. We can get this information with or without your help. You have five seconds to decide."

"Bombs? You're mistaken. We have no bombs here." The weapons director responded in English, most insistently.

"We're attached to a teaching hospital. We manufacture radiation equipment for the treatment of cancer."

Russum shook his head. "We don't have time for this. Give him one more chance, but let's show him we're sincere." In plain view, he removed a donut-shaped circuit board and metal ball from Wyley's backpack and was gratified to see Kajaz freeze—a look of disbelief on his face.

While the nuclear weapons expert assembled the bomb, Graham spoke to Buck again over his headset. "Hold it. I see him. He's moving again, got both hands full, running to the center steps now."

"What's he doing?"

"Lost him. He took out the camera."

The commander examined the metal steps through his thermal binoculars, hoping to see some fleeting ghost of a trail showing where he'd been. "Hmmmm. No trace of him at the south wall."

Moments later, careful scrutiny revealed a group of hot spots across the bottom steps. They could be footprints, or indicate something worse. "Negate that. I think I got something."

Zooming in, he noticed duct tape wrapped around the third step. It looked too new, and he needed to see it up close. Slowly, carefully, Buck began his descent down the stairs.

"He's moving again."

"Shit, Graham. Where is he? I'm halfway down the stairs."

"He's under the mezzanine, by the elevator, against the side wall."

"Good," Buck said, gingerly kneeling short of the tape. Closer inspection showed a thin metal trip wire, about midcalf high, tightly strung between the handrails. As Buck had guessed, the wire ran to a grenade taped beneath the third step. "He's wiring our exits. What about the camera?"

"It's history. I can't see anything around the elevator."

"There's only one more stairway to the mezzanine, right?"

"Right. He knows we're up here."

"Three down, one to go. He's blinding us, then setting trip wires across every path to the mezzanine."

Back in the comp center, Russum struggled to steady his hands, wedging another detonator connector into place.

Kajaz looked on in stark terror, gripping his chair so tightly his knuckles turned white. He had to say something. "Remove the battery."

Hearing this, Russum knew he'd won. Removing the dead battery from the detonator ring, he slid it into his right pocket.

Gently, firmly, the weapons expert pushed the final connector into place. It locked with a reassuring click. Pulling a good battery from his other pocket, the big Texan looked to Kajaz for approval.

The Iraqi shook his head from side to side.

Billy Ray was not convinced, but he was careful. He understood that this was an unquestionably dangerous step, for once a live battery was inserted, the bomb was armed. He snapped it in place with a frightening sense of confidence and detachment, but internally, the big man was a nervous wreck. Still, he was determined the Iraqi wouldn't see him sweat.

Finally, he started the timer and announced, "Thirty minutes."

Kajaz could see the timer flashing away the seconds, but with the Iraqi army at the gates, it was only a matter of time until they blasted through.

Will they break through before thirty minutes is up? Kajaz wondered. *Clearly not. Will the Americans disable the bomb if I help them? No, but if I drag this out, they'll have to.* Logging in, he asked, "What do you want to know?"

"How many bombs have been produced? How many shipped? And where'd they go?"

Kajaz displayed one report after another, but none answered his questions. Staring over his shoulder, Wyley began to see a pattern. The weapons director was going around in circles, deliberately skipping reports he felt could be important.

Seconds protracted into minutes, and finally, they'd seen enough.

Kajaz felt Russum's gun barrel on his temple.

Moments later, he produced a report summarizing their bomb production. "Ninety-three devices remain here. Twenty-four were exploded for testing purposes. All total, we produced approximately four hundred pits and six hundred detonators."

"Jesus Christ."

Shaken, Wyley froze, contemplating the consequences. Like an overwhelming torrent, memories of the Manhattan subway came flooding back. *The corpses stacked like cordwood; Dear God in heaven, what has man wrought? Three hundred bombs shipped, how many more Manhattans?* Wyley felt a cold chill that cut him to the bone, then he remembered Hama: *the little boy's shoe buried beneath the rubble, the dogs, and the mass grave. How many more would die?*

A kaleidoscope of emotion overpowered him, and suddenly, he didn't feel dread or sadness anymore. He felt raw, uncontrollable rage—an anger welling up inside him unlike anything he'd ever experienced. Making eye contact with Russum, Wyley sensed that he felt it too.

Grabbing Kajaz by the scruff of his neck, he yanked him out of his chair with the strength of ten men. "Shipping records! Show me your goddamn shipping records and show me now!"

Stunned, Kajaz fell limp. Slowly, he turned his head and looked at Russum. Behind the gas mask and black Nomex, the huge man telegraphed menace, filling him with fear. Looking down the wrong end of his gun, the weapons director felt death looming one breath away.

Crushed by the anger, crippled by fear, he collapsed on his chair. "This is what you're looking for."

"Copy it on this." Wyley shoved the storage card in the weapons director's face as Buck entered.

Squinting to read the small print, the *Times* correspondent leaned forward behind Kajaz. "Most remain in Iraq, thank God," he said finally.

"Whereabouts?"

"Not far from here, in a Basra warehouse near the river."

"What about the rest of 'em?"

"Four are on a tanker bound for Mexico, four already made it to Canada." Wyley paused for a second, then directed his next question to Kajaz. "Are there more factories like this one?"

"No. This is the first."

"I've been through your files and they're extensive. I've seen your manufacturing documentation and factory blueprints. Your people wrote this down for a reason."

"Our facility is well documented. I don't deny it. We've had many discussions about duplicating this facility, but we're only in the planning stages."

Wyley looked at Buck with his assessment. "There's nothing in this factory that doesn't show up in these files."

"Spit it out. What are you telling me?"

"He's lying. This place is documented to this extent for one reason. Using this information, we could duplicate this factory from the ground up. Either they've already done it or they're well on their way."

Wyley looked at Russum for consensus. "I can't read these files unless they're translated, but from what you're telling me, I think we've got all we're gonna get."

"Good, then strap that sonofabitch to a chair and lock him in the storage room, outta sight," Buck pushed. "Let's copy their files, grab a few bombs, and get the hell outta here."

"What about the bomb?" Russum asked, pointing to the blinking timer atop Medusa's head.

Buck eyed the device warily. "Reset it to three, no, make it three and a half hours, and hide it, get it outta sight. That'll give us time to swim clear."

CHAPTER THIRTY-ONE

They're Here!
Sunday, Apr. 18, 7:47 A.M.
The Bunker

The three men grabbed their weapons, heading for supply.

Across the mezzanine, inside security, Graham turned to the guard's armory and began loading his backpack and pockets with anything that'd smoke, make noise, or blow up. Grenades, smoke bombs, tear gas, mines, and more . . . anything that might goose up their chances of getting to the maintenance hatch.

Following their rendezvous inside supply, all four men shouldered their scuba gear. Gazing at the hole he'd cut in the air duct overhead, Graham muttered his thoughts out loud. "If we got in, they could too."

"Right now, their commander's doing exactly what I'd do," Buck surmised. "He's looking for another way in, and he won't stop until he finds it."

"A blind man could follow the trail we left topside," Russum said with a sigh.

Wyley shook his head from side to side. "I gotta believe that they have access to the bunker blueprints."

"No doubt about it," Buck agreed. "So what's stopping 'em? Where are they?"

Graham climbed up a stack of boxes to the air duct and stuck his head inside. Stunned, he questioned his own hearing. Placing his hand on the tube, he couldn't feel any vibration, but felt sure he heard a noise. "I hear something."

"Quiet," Buck said, climbing alongside Graham.

"Do you hear it?"

Buck stuck his head inside the duct, then pulled it back. "Hell, yeah. Sounds like a herd of elephants." Instinctively, he thought of his boom bag, then spoke to Russum. "You string the trip wire, I'll set the charges."

From the floor below, Billy Ray could see bolts mounted to the right and left of the man-made opening, perfect points for fastening a trip wire. "Can do. There's not many problems that can't be solved with a good high explosive."

Buck flattened his remaining C4 into a ribbon and wrapped it around the duct. Once secure, he laid det cord over it, encircling the tube. "We coulda used some more C4."

"I brought this from security," Graham offered. "It looks like a mine."

Smiling, Buck examined the contents of his backpack. "Good man. It looks a lot like a claymore." Satisfied, he added Graham's coup de grâce to the mix, a mine rigged to explode when anyone approached the supply door. When detonated, it sprayed steel pellets that'd kill anyone within 150 feet.

"That's the best we can do," Buck concluded, grabbing his rope and leather gloves. "I'll divert him to the south wall while you three rappel down over the handrail on the north."

In front of them, with the catwalk lit up by emergency lights, Graham, Wyley, and Russum knelt near the north wall, waiting for Buck's signal.

Graham primed his flamethrower, checking its fuel level for about the fiftieth time. Nearly four-fifths full, he hadn't had to use it much, and hoped he wouldn't have to use it again. Moments later, he noticed he could still hear the Klaxons howling. Already breathing heavily, his legs trembled under the weight of his scuba gear and flamethrower.

"Heads up." Buck's voice echoed through their headsets as he tossed an office chair down the stairs. The shock wave from the explosion was powerful enough to shake the mezzanine floor.

Graham tried to move quickly, but his ribs screamed in protest with every step. The doctor took point, covering the factory floor with his flamethrower; Russum filled in as waist gunner, staying low, protecting against an attack from either flank.

Overlooking the bunker, a dimly lit, cluttered factory lay stretched out before Graham, offering a thousand places to hide. In addition to emergency lighting, reddish glows emanated from behind dark metal silhouettes. Air hissed from ruptured hoses, sparks flew from damaged circuits, but nothing moved.

Hanging his head over the handrail, the doctor checked again. He saw nothing moving through the shadows, nothing at all. There was a steep vertical drop over the handrail to the floor, but not a terribly long one. Dim light marked the end of their descent, the tiled floor leading to the pump room and maintenance hatch.

"It's clear, Wyley. Hurry."

Wyley hitched his rope on the handrail and swung his foot across. First thing he noticed was the slippery metal surface, still wet from the overhead sprinklers. Pushing away from the mezzanine, the *Times* reporter felt the rope tighten beneath his leg. Releasing it little by little, he began his descent to the floor below.

Still, the doctor could see nothing moving, but it felt as if the entire floor were alive, like there was life in every shadow. Staring into the distance, he saw the reason why. The dumpster was down.

Suddenly, without warning, he saw the flash of muzzle fire and felt a rush of hot air streaking by his ear. *That was close, too close.* Backing away and behind the handrail, he knelt, focusing on the darkness below.

Below and forward, he caught a glimpse of a guard through his night-vision gear, looking down his rifle barrel at Wyley. He knew he had to do something.

Against every instinct and everything he'd ever been taught, he moved forward to the handrail and squeezed the flamethrower's trigger, laying down a blanket of suppressing fire whose tentacles reached out more than fifty feet. The dimly lit factory glowed brightly, their position illuminated by a napalm beacon. There could be no doubt about their location now.

"Graham, Graham! He's behind me," Wyley screamed. "Behind the boxes."

There he was, a second guard, below and behind the reporter. Russum fired and missed. The man ducked out of sight.

It was up to Graham. Once the first fuel flowed, it came easier for the doctor. On spotting the second guard, he pointed his weapon in the general direction, then squeezed the trigger.

Yellow-orange fire rained down from overhead as a two-legged torch was set ablaze on the floor below. Almost as quickly, the factory sprinkler system kicked in, drenching the area with a soaking downpour.

But it came too late for the guard.

From the catwalk overhead, Graham sanitized their pathway to the pump room. Fiery napalm tentacles rained down, engulfing the area. The torrent of rainfall which followed cooled the flames, but if anything had been alive near the pump room, it was dead now, charred and blackened.

"Graham, hold your fire," Buck ordered, joining Wyley on the fuel- and water-soaked floor below. "Billy Ray, you next."

Russum looped the rope through his descending link, bolted over the handrail, and dropped like a rock.

Surrounded by smoldering debris, fuel, fire, and rain, Wyley moved slowly down the aisle, submachine gun at his shoulder. Before him, three twisted, blackened corpses lay prostrate, facedown in a flaming pool of napalm. Surrounding them, smoldering silhouettes outlined an almost biblical vision of hell. Beyond the smoke and smoldering bodies, he could see the pump room entrance.

Sensing he wasn't alone, he remembered Buck's law. *You can't hit what you can't see.*

Suddenly, a shot rang out from nowhere, glancing off a metal conduit near his face. Sparks flew and the reporter ducked out of sight. Looking to his right, the shot could have come from a hundred places. Evaluating his options, he signaled his intent. "I'm smoking the north wall."

Reaching into a bag strapped to his leg, he removed three smoke grenades. Holding a baseball-shaped grenade in his right hand, he pulled the pin, let its safety lever fall away, and he was ready to roll.

With the pump room hatch in sight, he rolled the first one beyond the entrance. Thick dark smoke surged outward, churning, boiling in every direction. He rolled the second midway down the aisle, and the last only a few feet from the mezzanine.

On cue, Hakim and two guards moved through the shadows, toward the smoke, and into position, waiting in ambush.

Buck saw movement and followed Wyley's lead, releasing a smoke grenade immediately beneath Billy Ray. "Graham. Somebody's moving by the north wall and it ain't Wyley."

Graham thought he saw movement too, but couldn't make out anything definite. The only thing he could see clearly was the well-defined trail of smoke and fire leading to the pump room. From his vantage point on the catwalk, the smoke wall telegraphed both their whereabouts and their intentions.

Checking his fuel level didn't make him feel any better—down to a quarter tank. "Pull back to the catwalk, Wyley. I'm hosing the north wall again."

Suddenly, shots rang out behind Graham, deep inside the mezzanine.

"They're here!" Whirling about, Graham raised his flamethrower and opened fire, torching the corridor to supply.

"Graham! Get down!"

The doctor heard Buck's warning, but ignored it, blasting the corridor with his flamethrower, saturating it with napalm. After hosing down the hallway, he took cover behind an outside office wall and began scanning the large air duct overhead for signs of life.

Then it happened.

The explosion rocked the mezzanine as an enormous fireball erupted from the hallway, thrusting a blistering tongue of flame out above the factory floor.

Most of the explosive force escaped through the path of least resistance—the air duct—flattening those soldiers nearest the supply room, impaling others with flying shards of debris. The remaining energy blasted office windows from the inside out.

In the blink of an eye, the mezzanine transformed into one horrendous vision from Dante's inferno.

"Graham! Graham!"

Hollow, piercing, human screams filled the air, emanating from the air duct overhead, rising above the wail of the emergency sirens and hissing air lines. One inescapable fact became clear immediately. The main feeder was crawling with Iraqi soldiers.

Unseen by the Americans, power saws began frantically ripping through the fiberglass duct. Klaxons blared wide open as ropes appeared hanging down from the dark, man-made openings overhead.

"Graham! Graham!" Where was Graham?

Inside supply, as dazed Iraqi survivors stumbled through the smoky darkness, a larger, more powerful blast shook the mezzanine, crippling or killing everyone in the room. Once again, with the steel door locked shut, the lion's share of the shock wave surged out the air duct, mowing over the soldiers trapped inside.

In the blink of an eye, Iraqi soldiers burst through the man-sized holes they'd cut in the duct like they'd been blasted out of a cannon. Riddled with holes, the long fiberglass duct served as a human scattergun, hurling bodies in a parabolic arc, sending them plummeting down to the floor below.

Exactly what had happened wasn't clear to the Americans and most Iraqi soldiers never knew what hit them. Still, the feeder had been packed with people, and, though stunned, most over the factory floor survived.

"Graham! Can you hear me?" There was a desperate tone in Buck's voice, now. He began pulling himself up the rope using only the strength in his arms.

Rocked by both blasts and off balance, Graham had been thrown against the handrail. Dazed, the doctor felt lost in a fog. Squeezing his trigger, flames erupted from the weapon, coating the ceiling overhead with fiery rain.

Heaving himself up the rope to the catwalk, Buck saw the doctor sitting with his back against the handrail. Bolting over the rail in a single leap, he sprinted to his side.

Kneeling, Buck could see him breathing, but he seemed disoriented, like he'd taken a blow on the head. Examining him, he found only one bump on the back of his head, and at first glance, it didn't look too bad.

Water. Instinctively Buck knew Graham needed some water.

Sprinklers rained down all over the factory, so he didn't need to go far to find a downpour. Grabbing Graham by his flamethrower, Buck dragged the doctor beneath a sprinkler head. As the water poured down, he removed Graham's mask long enough to saturate his hair and face with cool spray. The effect wasn't instantaneous, but within a few moments, the doctor was gagging with both eyes wide open.

Graham would never know it, but the man who saved his life was damn glad to do it.

After strapping his gas mask back on, Buck saw Graham's eyes flash recognition.

"Graham."

A cough echoed over the commander's headset, a wheeze really, then he heard the words he wanted to hear.

"What happened?"

"Later. How you feel?"

"Aside from one helluva headache, I think I'm okay. Nothing's broken, anyway."

"Can you walk?"

Graham stood with Buck's help. He was a little shaky, teetering backward with the weight of the flamethrower, but after a few steps, he got his balance again. "I'm okay."

"Stand back!" Russum's voice echoed over their headsets. "Clear the north steps. They're gonna blow."

Another smaller explosion followed, then moments later, Wyley and Russum sprinted to the top of the steps.

With Wyley taking point, Graham put his arms over Buck's and Russum's shoulders, and together, they began their descent down the twisted metal staircase.

One shot cracked past the foursome, lodging in the wall behind them. Then another.

Without pausing, Wyley scanned the floor below for muzzle flashes, but saw only thick smoke, fire, and darkness. The factory was a continuous maze of smoldering silhouettes he couldn't identify. Someone was out there somewhere, but there were a thousand places to hide.

Looking up, he saw movement, an endless row of ropes dangling from the ductwork, seemingly alive, crawling with dark, antlike silhouettes descending against the backdrop of a smoky, white ceiling. "They're here!"

Recognizing this, the four men ran like hell down the stairs, taking cover behind the screen of smoke below.

Never slowing to catch their breath, sprinting around the bend on the north wall, their smokescreen remained thick and intact. Instinct told them to keep running or be overrun.

Behind them and to one side, voices yelled out something in Arabic.

Wyley took the point, Buck and Russum pushed him hard, but Graham remembered something the others forgot. "Hold it! Someone's by the pump house."

Down the corridor, one of the guards caught a glimpse of movement through a swirl of smoke. A barrage of bullets streaked past them, pulverizing everything in their path. Like a wave of hot lead, a wall of gunfire washed back and forth across the smoke-filled passageway.

Grabbing Wyley by his backpack, Graham shoved all three men facedown into the watery muck, out of harm's way behind a large metal lathe. Winded, Buck skidded in first, then Russum went down, a slug lodged in his Kevlar armor. In less time than it took to breathe, all four slid to safety and stayed down, bullets screaming overhead.

"We gotta move," Buck pressed.

Without pausing, Graham slid out into the corridor, belly down, through the watery muck. Scanning for any signs of movement, the doctor noticed he couldn't see.

Wyley followed close behind, his submachine gun held tight in his hand, dripping wet. "Graham, you got any fuel left in that thing?"

"A little."

"Burn those bastards."

Sliding behind a large milling machine, Graham felt the nozzle of his flamethrower. *Cold and wet.* "Nothing's working. My night vision's shot and my pilot's out."

"I can't see either," Wyley said. "Damn water."

"Grenades?"

"No, nothing."

"Got a light?" Graham primed his weapon and held the business end within Wyley's reach.

Pulling the Bic from his pocket, he gave it a flick. Touching the lifeless pilot to the warm, yellow flame breathed new life into the weapon. "How much fuel you got?"

"Not much. I hope to God it's enough."

Down the corridor toward the pump room, the smoke was so thick, neither man could see more than ten feet.

Gunfire erupted down the hall; bullets glanced off the milling machine, fiery sparks raining down.

Panic pushed Graham to take chances; his heart was beating so hard his ears were pounding. Peering around the corner, he could see muzzle flashes diffused by the smoke.

Twisting his weapon's fuel nozzle, he adjusted its beam to form a wide, horizontal spray. Pointing his wand toward the muzzle flashes, Graham extended his arm, holding it out around the corner, his body shielded behind the milling machine.

Wyley was watching him now, waiting for his signal.

"Punch it." Graham's voice echoed over everyone's headsets as he squeezed the trigger.

A blanket of flaming fuel surged forward, igniting everything in the corridor to the pump room and beyond.

Gunfire was replaced by the bloodcurdling sound of human cries as two living torches ran screaming toward the sprinklers.

Behind the wall of fire, Buck and Russum sprinted to the entrance and spun open the hatch.

As the heavy metal door swung back away from the wall, a clear view of Buck's broad chest appeared over Hakim's front sight. As the big man stepped through the hatch, the terrorist pulled the trigger. His target fell to the floor, writing in pain.

Russum saw the flash, then whipped his weapon to his shoulder. Stepping in front of the door, he blasted the vicinity with a hail of bullets. Sparks flew in every direction, but through the chaos, Billy Ray recognized something familiar about his target's civilian clothes.

Hakim pulled his head back behind the maintenance trunk, waiting for the bald gunman to either rush or reload.

Once Russum's submachine gun fell silent, the terrorist fired back. His bullet clipped the metal bulkhead near the Texan's head, spraying hot sparks across his gas mask and goggles.

Jerking his head away from the hatch, Russum slapped a full clip home, then signaled Graham, holding up one finger. "It's him. He'll stick his head up when I reload. Get him."

Behind them, Iraqi gunshots exploded above the wailing sirens. Two twisted bodies lay smoldering on the floor, their cries now silent.

More yelling; the voices were close.

And gunfire. Bullets streaked down the corridor, ricocheting off the hatch.

"Shit!" Russum rushed in first, his submachine gun blazing, hammering Hakim high and low.

Graham followed close on his heels and Wyley pulled up the rear, spinning the hatch shut behind them. Picking up a piece of metal pipe, he shoved it through the flywheel, locking the hatch shut tight.

Russum emptied his clip, then whirled away behind a large electric motor to reload.

Seeing shadows move behind the cylindrical trunk, Graham squeezed his trigger. A small, low-pressure ball of black smoke puffed forward, igniting nothing. Frantic, he pumped his tanks and squeezed again. A flickering blue flame spewed and sputtered, with all the menace of a flaming jet of hairspray.

Graham saw Hakim's head and shoulders appear from behind the large metal cylinder for the first time. It was him, no doubt about it.

Focused only on his defenseless target, Hakim was confident, smiling behind his gas mask, extending himself beyond the cylinder to get a better shot.

How fortunate, Buck thought. Below and behind Graham, the commander lay poised on the floor, the sight of his Colt .45 fixed squarely beneath the man's chin.

To Graham's left, Russum steadied his aim on the terrorist's rib cage, just below his shooting arm.

And to his right, kneeling behind a large pump, Wyley positioned a red dot on the side of the man's neck.

Hakim never knew what hit him.

Buck's round struck first, taking off the top of his head, blowing out his brains, spattering them across the pump room wall.

Wyley squeezed his trigger and held it down. Countless 9mm rounds ripped through the mass-murderer's neck, severing his head near the base of the skull.

And Russum bored a hole through his heart.

Graham felt stunned, disbelieving. He couldn't speak, but Buck didn't give him time to think. "The maintenance trunk. Move. Move."

In an exhausted, no-nonsense fashion, the four men made ready their escape. Graham felt fatigue in every bone, but knew in the next few minutes, they would rid the world of this godforsaken man-made hell. As Graham, Wyley, and Buck crawled through the hatch into the maintenance trunk, Russum carefully placed a fresh battery into another Medusa head, setting its timer for three hours. Once the timer began flashing, the Texan concealed the bomb and joined the others.

"A little extra insurance?" Buck asked.

"It's the only way to be sure," Russum said, then, for the first time in what seem like an eternity, the four men removed their gas masks.

Peering through the hatch, they surveyed the pump room one last time. Within arm's reach, the terrorist's bloody body lay spattered across the wall. Across the room, hidden behind a pump access panel, the neutron bomb flashed, counting down the seconds.

"Complacency is the enemy here," Graham said quietly. "We shoulda never let these people get away with this. How many more will die?"

"How many have died already? And for what?" Wyley snapped. "There's more factories like this out there, and if we sit back on our butts and do nothing, mark my words, it'll happen again."

Russum felt the need to remind Graham of his own words, then smiled, like a father would smile at his son. "It's halfway around the world. If these people want to blow themselves up, I can't stop 'em. What's that got to do with me?"

"You're preaching to the choir." Graham nodded, recognizing he had changed. Russum had been right all along, but some things you have to learn for yourself. "We've got to keep on top of this one. The stakes are too high and we can't let it happen again."

Russum nodded. "Let's get the hell outta here."

Buck slammed the hatch behind them for the last time. There was no sense of exhilaration, only survival to fight another day.

Once the hatch sealed shut, the four men stood beneath the donut-shaped air pocket lining the top of the cylinder. Fluorescent lights surrounded the four men, breaking up the darkness.

Buck looped his rubber air hose and rebreather around his neck, then put on his mask. Next, he checked his flashlight, snapped the tow rope in place around his waist, and that was it. Without conversation, his beleaguered team repeated his every move in a monkey-see-monkey-do fashion. Unfortunately, no one brought swim fins—no one had space for them. Buck, Russum, and Wyley carried MP4s slung at their sides, and Graham carried their factory plunder in a backpack.

Once everyone was ready, Buck opened the flood valve, filling the cylinder with river water. The water felt cool at first, but not terribly so. As it flooded, the men kept their heads inside the air pocket near the ceiling. Once the chamber filled, Buck opened the upper hatch with the spin of a wheel. Now completely underwater, the three men lined up behind him. Leading the way and joined together at the hip, the commander tethered his men with a rope.

Once the pressure inside the trunk equalized with the river overhead, Graham adjusted quickly and felt relieved to find he could breathe without the distress he'd first imagined. Maybe the pain from his ribs was masked by everything else that hurt, but he was glad he could breathe underwater.

Buck signaled the others with his flashlight, then ducked under the metal flange centered on top of the chamber. Once inside the lip, he swam slowly toward the surface, waiting for the others. As he'd expected, before him lay an enormous water outlet, an exhaust pipe extending vertically for a short distance, then horizontal, running downstream with the current.

Though the current wasn't strong here, every man knew that following it would take them home.

Slowly, sometimes painfully, Commander Buck Harrison and his team swam their way downstream, unnoticed in the midst of the chaos on the surface. With lights from the Basra oil refineries still visible in the distance, the four men surfaced and radioed for rescue.

Still, in reality, nothing's ever as easy as it looks on paper. Iraqi tankers maneuvering the shallow waterway to the Persian Gulf presented helicopter rescue crews with the very real problem of visual detection in broad daylight.

Seeking solitude and isolation, the exhausted group was

ordered southwest, away from the river into an enormous flooded marsh. Several hours later, they came upon a seemingly endless expanse of grassy flatland, surrounded by nothingness for as far as they could see, and it was here they rested and waited extraction.

The Delta Force rescue crew flew their Super Stallion in fast and low, parallel to the river, hugging the deck. Buck radioed their final coordinates and, once spotted, they were hauled aboard without further incident.

Following a short rest and debriefing, Harrison, Russum, Ramsi, and Higgins returned home to CTC headquarters with their stolen pillage of bombs, information, and photographs.

PART FOUR

The Junk Room

Two Weeks Later

CHAPTER THIRTY-TWO

The Marshall Farm
Saturday, May 1, 10:38 A.M.
New England seacoast
Near Plum Island, Massachusetts

"We'll be landing in Boston shortly. Please make sure your seat backs and tray tables are in their locked and fully upright position," the flight attendant recited over the P.A.

Buck couldn't wait to see them. Outside his window, a solid overcast sky telegraphed a dreary, gray day on the ground below, but it didn't matter. For weeks, he'd dreamed of this reunion and had played it over and over in his head. Mary and little Katie had kept him going—they were his reasons for living and now he wanted them to know it.

Across his lap lay pictures and paper, recent photographs of the girls, copies of Mary's e-mails, and printouts of Katie's artwork. Staring at a picture of the young artist, he wondered if she would recognize him without his long hair and beard. After all, she'd never seen him when he didn't look like a terrorist and little ones could be so shy. He'd e-mailed Mary several pictures of himself and his buddies, but wondered if Katie'd been able to make the connection. On the one hand, he looked ten years younger and Mary liked that, but on the other, meeting her little girl again dressed as a spit-and-polished naval officer might not be the best plan. He had a hunch he might scare her away in this getup, but the gold braid on the sleeves and hat really sparkled. Who could say? She just might go for it.

Since he'd gotten back to the States, he'd talked to them on the phone at least once a day. Maybe that'd help too. She might recognize his voice even if she didn't know his face. Only time would tell.

And what about Mary? It wasn't complicated, really.

She's my gift from God, Buck thought, believing this with all his heart. Something good, something magic, and something wonderful had come out of Manhattan, and her name was Mary. She came into his life that day and he hadn't been the same since. He remembered breaking down, sobbing on the grass alongside her, like it happened yesterday. He hurt inside just thinking about that subway.

God, I don't know what came over me then, but it changed me. Life's so short, so fragile. I can't seem to shake it. I think about her every day and she's gotta know I miss her.

Buck heard the wheels set down on the tarmac. Thinking back, he remembered that she'd liked the pictures of him in uniform, at least she'd said she did, and besides, her dad was an old Navy man.

Now that's gotta count for something.

It was a soaking wet morning in May, and the wind whistled around their New England farmhouse. Mary had gotten up early to go to the airport in case there was any traffic. She hadn't slept all night, but it didn't matter. She wasn't tired.

She couldn't put her finger on it exactly, but she felt nervous, excited, and a little apprehensive, all at the same time. More telling than this, her heart was beating so hard she heard it pounding while she sat stuck in traffic, stalled north of Logan.

As happens almost every day, there'd been an accident somewhere in Boston. One accident led to another, and as a result, traffic was stacked up north, west, and south of the greater metro area. She heard about it on the radio, then turned off the distraction so she could think without interruption.

There's so many things to talk about: Katie, his medal, his promotion, Iraq, C-SPAN, Manhattan.

And him.

Finally, after all this time, she'd get to know him face-to-face and could decide for herself if he was the man he seemed to be.

She couldn't help thinking of him as her guardian angel, and she recalled being carried up the subway stairs, in his arms, in textured detail. Every sense was heightened then, as it was now, and she remembered feeling as if she'd been raised from the dead.

Would he be easy to talk to face-to-face? Probably, why not? He'd been wonderful over the phone.

Would he think she was as pretty today as he did then, on that horrible day in Manhattan? Mary's eyes clouded over reliving her experience of being buried alive, smothering, not knowing if she would live or die.

And panic.

Oh, God! I lost my baby, she'd whispered in a muffled cry for no one to hear. That moving, faceless wall of flesh descending on them, tearing them apart, and burying them alive. Replaying the experience over in her mind's eye, she felt the sudden, overpowering terror she knew then. She'd never forget that feeling for as long as she lived and deliberately chose to set it aside and think about the positive.

She'd made it, Katie'd made it, and Buck had survived.

Startling her, a car horn brought her back to reality and the traffic started to move, slowly at first, but moving.

Soon, she'd be there, and could see his face, feel his warmth, touch his hands.

She had missed him and wanted him to know that something wonderful had come out of the carnage. Mary hadn't been the same since that day, but she'd blocked out the horror and was looking forward to the rest of her life, hoping it'd be with him.

Bolting out of the jetway, Buck gazed at row after row of nameless faces seated outside the gate and his pace began to slow. Where was she? She said she'd be here.

After studying the traffic pattern of passengers leaving his flight, he noticed that no one met anyone at the gate, then remembered that things were different since Manhattan. Down the corridor, past an endless succession of passenger gates, a black sea of security guards stood out from everyone else and their message was clear.

Grapefruit-sized neutron bombs wouldn't be flown into the United States, or across it.

Logan International Airport reminded Buck of a police precinct under siege and for deliberately obvious reasons. Security guards were visible everywhere, screening passengers, pets, carry-on luggage, airline employees, and anyone else who looked suspicious. These days, Buck knew that airport security had been tightened far beyond the point of inconvenience. It was stifling. Anytime you flew, your privacy was violated and there were no exceptions.

Ahead, Buck saw a line of passengers from his flight awaiting exit screening, so he dutifully took his place behind them. And it was there, waiting in line, that he saw her face on the far side of the turnstile.

He bolted through the turnstile like he had a plane to catch, ran to her side, then stood there, towering over her, speechless. He'd thought about what he'd say for hours, replayed it a hundred times, but it didn't matter. He drew a complete blank; his carefully crafted words were gone.

Nervously, Mary leaned forward and touched his hand.

Being so near this beautiful creature, seeing her face again, the smell of her hair, Buck's knees felt like jelly. With his head out of the picture, his heart took over.

Reaching out, he held both her hands and smiled, gently.

Looking up, she faced him, unsteady on her feet.

Buck noticed the tiniest twitch on her cheek and knew he must do something to put her at ease.

Tongue-tied, he couldn't speak, so he did what he wanted most to do. Hugging her tightly, drawing her close to him, he held her as if he'd never let go.

Mary gasped, then seemed to melt. Her relief was so intense that for a moment, she felt faint. "You're finally here," she whispered.

"I've been living for this moment," Buck said softly, savoring the scent of Mary's hair. Unknowingly, he'd lifted her off the ground, but it didn't matter. She wasn't going anywhere without him.

And it was then and there something wondrous happened, the kind of thing that transpires when two people fall in love. Even airport passersby took notice.

As their hearts touched, the throngs of people surrounding the couple seemed to fade away, if only for a few moments. They were two together, only seeing each other, and no one else existed.

"I hear that I should congratulate you," Mary said finally.

"Where'd you hear that?"

"Daddy. We heard about it last night on CNN. They said you'd been promoted to some think-tank job in the Pentagon."

"It's nice of you to congratulate me and all, but I'd just as soon skip it," the commander said with a ring of sadness in his voice.

"All right, but I wish you'd explain why."

"I'm afraid it's not going to work out so well for me there."

"What do you mean? It sounded impressive on the news."

"I can't see being chained to some Navy desk in Washington. I'm just not cut out for it."

Mary nodded understanding. "How are you doing otherwise?"

Buck gazed into Mary's eyes for a moment, then hugged her again. "I'm doing a lot better now," he said, smiling. "How 'bout you and Katie?"

"We're both doing much better now that Katie's made a few good friends at school."

"Friends make all the difference," Buck acknowledged. "Did she recover from her picture book fiasco?"

Mary thought for a moment. "I think so. She looks forward to school every day now and that's probably the most important thing."

Buck agreed. "Does she still remember it?"

"Yes, but I don't think she dwells on it like she did at first."

"Good. What about Manhattan? Does she remember much about the subway?"

"No, she doesn't, but I think about it. I think about it a lot, especially at night. I can't help it. I lost friends there. Sometimes, early in the morning when dreams seem so real, I go back there and wake up in a cold sweat. I want to scream, but I can't breathe; I can't catch my breath. It's like I'm smothering. Then I wake up and think about you, about how you saved us, and I feel better. But I'll never forget it. I'll go to my grave with that."

"You might feel better if you saw it again now."

Mary frowned. "I'll never go back there."

"Sometimes closure on an experience like that is the best way to put it to rest. It's like with Katie and her picture book. Getting back on the horse made all the difference. I went back there one day last week and it made me feel better about the whole thing."

She paused. "You didn't tell me about that."

"No. I was afraid it might upset you, but the truth is, I did it for me. I wanted to see what happened to New York. It's like the rest of the story. How are the survivors coping? How are they getting along? I wanted to see for myself."

"Oh . . ." The young woman went silent. "Well then, tell me about it. You said you felt better. What'd you find?"

Buck smiled, and a gentle twinkle shone in his eyes. "Jon Bradley's is back in business."

"Really? I know that restaurant. It's by the Fed."

"That's right. I ate there and got a gold brick breakfast too. It was good. And those New Yorkers are unbelievable. I'm serious. I never thought I'd hear myself say that, but from the looks of it today, you'd never know they took a hit."

"Unbelievable," Mary interjected.

"It is. They told me that everybody's been pulling together and you simply could not imagine what they've accomplished in forty-four days. It's incredible. They said Wall Street would be back on-line by June and I was stunned. I've got to hand it to these people. I don't live there and I was proud of 'em. Talk about triumph of the human spirit, I was almost giddy; felt like wrapping myself in the American flag and walking down Wall Street."

Mary stood quietly for a few moments, absorbing his words. After a long pause, she concluded, "I think you're right. I would like to see that. I'd like it a lot."

They arrived at her parents' farm three hours later. Katie was waiting to welcome her mother and the big stranger with a bright fire in the den.

Hearing her mother's voice, Katie ran to her.

Mary knelt down on both knees and hugged her daughter tight. Standing, she introduced the tall stranger in the dark suit with sparkly stripes. "Katie, I'd like for you to meet a very dear friend of mine. You saw him once when we lived in the city, but he looked different then. This is the man I talked to you about yesterday. He's the one that saved us."

Timidly, the little girl took shelter behind her mother's legs, looking up at the stranger from behind her dress.

Buck sat down near the fireplace on their wide pine floor, meeting Katie eye to eye. Opening his briefcase, he laid everything out on her little child-sized table. Its contents didn't look like any Mary had ever seen in a briefcase before, but it caught her daughter's attention immediately.

Emerging from behind her mother's legs, Katie stood beside him, studying the objects with genuine interest. On the table, she saw her favorite cookies, drawings, crayons, and coloring books.

The first thing Katie zeroed in on were the little boxes of Nabisco animal crackers. Buck handed one to her and asked that she deliver it to her mother.

Katie looked the box over carefully, then complied with the big man's request. She didn't recognize his face, but his voice she knew.

With animal crackers in hand, Mary joined Buck on the floor, sitting down alongside him by the fire.

Buck gave Katie her animal crackers and they were set. She pulled her chair to the table and began asking questions. "Are these for me?" She was referring to the crayons and coloring books.

"Yes, I brought them especially for you. I know you like red. There's lotsa red." As the commander reached across the table, the gold braid on his sleeve glistened in the firelight. The sparkle caught Katie's eye and she rubbed his jacket to see if the sparkle would come off on her hand.

Buck held his arm still while she rubbed it. Her hands were so tiny. He didn't think his hands had ever been that small.

While he had Katie's attention, he showed her one of her

drawings Mary had sent him. It was a red Christmas tree with a small photograph of Katie's face on top. "Have you seen this picture before?" he asked.

Katie recognized her face and smiled.

"Your mother sent this to me. I showed it to everybody and they loved it. They said you were a beautiful little girl and they all wanted a Christmas tree just like this one."

Katie understood that she could be a helper trees and went straight to work drawing more red trees for the nice man's friends.

While Katie labored, Mary listened and gradually the Iraqi story came out. Buck thought it was pleasant to be fussed over, and found it increasingly easy to relax.

At first, Mary could not believe the words she heard, but later, as incredible as it sounded, she knew he was telling the truth.

Later that evening, after Katie was put to bed, they talked before the blazing log fire, grateful to be alive, listening to the patter of the rain outside.

What followed was a very revealing week for Buck Harrison. He wasn't the same man he had been, and after his experience in Basra, the change did him good.

On the second morning of his visit, Mary found him standing at the doorway of a space she affectionately called her junk room. It wasn't an attic really; it was a large, second-story back room which had evolved into a storeroom for old trunks, children's furniture, and toys of every description—a storeroom for junk that was too valuable to throw away.

Buck was standing at the door, looking with genuine interest at the assortment of treasures inside. Thinking back on his own childhood, he recalled his aunt had just such a room as this on the third floor of a dear old southern home, one with a tin roof and front porch swings. He hadn't thought of those days for a long time, but the smell and character of this room brought his memories flooding back.

Mary spoke to him, bringing him back from his reverie.

"This is where we put all the things we can't bear to part with. We always say we'll put them in a yard sale, but when the time comes, we never do."

Buck smiled. "My aunt had a room like this. It was my favorite place when I was growing up. I'd visit her for a week and wind up staying all summer."

You could do that here too, she thought, taking his hand.

About that time, Katie came bounding up the stairs and met them outside the room. She seemed to know her way around splendidly, and skipped in ahead of them with a hint of excitement in her step.

Buck entered the room reverently, as if it were a church sanctuary or some magic land filled with wonder and mystery.

Inside the room to his right, Buck noticed an old, hand-cranked wooden telephone mounted low on the wall. It must have been at least a hundred years old and he judged it was mounted low on the wall for a reason—Katie. Kneeling down on one knee, he lifted the receiver off the hook, placed it to his ear, and turned the crank.

Ring . . . ring . . . ring . . .

After all these years, the bells of the old Western Electric phone still rang clear.

Katie's ears perked up and she joined him right away. The telephone mouthpiece just fit her height and he handed her the handset.

Ring . . . ring. . . . ring . . .

Smiling sheepishly, he looked up at Mary. "This place is wonderful."

Even the smell in this room was distinctive, not stale or moldy, almost inviting, like leather and cedar with only a hint of mothballs.

Beyond the telephone, Buck saw several trunks, just waiting for someone to explore. He guessed they must be lined with cedar. After examining the latches on one of the larger trunks, he found it unlocked and opened it carefully. Impatiently, Katie urged him on, knowing in advance it was unlocked. As he'd hoped, Buck found it filled with childhood treasures, piled high to overflowing with small dolls and stuffed animals. "Whose dolls are these?" He looked to Mary.

"They were mine when I was little. Mother and I saved them for Katie."

Katie riffled through the top shelf of the trunk, finally finding whom she was looking for. "This is Rainbow Bright," she declared proudly, showing him her little orange-haired ragamuffin.

"It's very nice to meet you," Buck said, studying the little doll's face and well-worn clothes. After a few moments' thought, he asked, "Do they all have names?"

"Yes!" Katie beamed, then introduced them, each and every one.

In Buck's heart, this child was what his passion was all about. He'd trained all his adult life to protect those who couldn't protect themselves, and this little girl personified the best reasons on the face of the earth to be a warrior.

Several minutes later, once all their introductions were exchanged, Buck stood again and spoke to Mary, his eyes smiling as he pointed across the room. "How about that little red wagon? Whose Radio Flyer was that anyway?"

"It was mine first, then my little sister's."

"How old were you then?"

"We've got videos of my father pulling me to the beach when I was only two or three years old. He said he turned a corner too tight one time and accidentally dumped me out on my face. It made me cry, but I don't remember it, really."

"I'll bet he does."

"He says he remembers it like it happened yesterday."

"I'm not surprised. How about all those toy horses? They look so real."

"When I was little, I loved horseback riding and dreamed of owning a horse. I still love horses. I loved them then and I miss them now. There's something about the feel of a horse that causes my spirit to soar. I don't know why exactly, I just feel better being around them, that's all."

"Does Katie like horses, too?"

"She loves to draw them, but she's too small for a horse. She loves ponies, though; they're more compact, more her size."

"Shetlands?"

"Yes, I wish she had one now, especially after what happened. It would give her a friend to take care of and think about."

"A distraction?"

"No, a responsibility, a pet to take care of, love, and look after."

Buck continued his exploration around the junk room, then together, they walked outside and surveyed the barn and pasture. "So what's stopping you?"

"From getting a horse?" she asked, as if she could read his mind.

Buck nodded. In front of him, a wide expanse of marshy pasture opened up to meet the sea.

"Money and maintenance. Daddy can't keep our fences mended as it is, let alone raise hay to feed a pony through New England winters."

Later that day, following a conversation with Mary's father, Buck began mending fences. As it happened, both men spent the next three days mending fences—with Katie's help.

Each night, Buck went to bed early, slept hard, and woke up refreshed the next day. The company was good, no one shot at him, and he slept better than he had for as long as he could remember. There was something satisfying about being plain old physically tired. He could get used to this.

On the fourth day, Mary found hay stacked in the barn, hauled in with a new horse trailer.

And on the fifth day, she discovered a horse in the barn. Katie found a pony.

Finally, on the last day, Mary asked her father, "Do you like him, Dad?"

"I do, I like him quite a lot. He treats you nice and he's nuts about Katie. He's interested in your hopes and dreams, what you care about, what you stand for, and where you came from. Yeah, I think he's a keeper."

PART FIVE

Epilogue: The Journey Home

CHAPTER THIRTY-THREE

Surveillance satellites first detected the fireball. The brilliant light persisted beneath the river surface for a few thousandths of a second, then disappeared as the bubble of superheated, high-pressure steam breached the surface.

Predictably, the explosive force tried escaping through the path of least resistance.

On the sandbar overhead, the shock wave blasted the blower assembly skyward with the force of a battleship's sixteen-inch gun. As with any detonation, the bulk of the energy had to escape quickly, but the fireball found itself restricted, throttled back by the limited size of the duct.

Erupting upward, the fireball incinerated its own path to the surface, rupturing an outlet through the bunker's steel-reinforced ceiling.

Back at Langley, Virginia, analysts studied super-slow-motion playbacks of the event with a detached, clinical sense of wonder. Watching the fireball reduce the bunker to chalky ash, one CTC analyst remarked offhandedly that, by contrast, Dante's inferno didn't seem so bad.

As the fireball expanded underwater, the bubble of superheated steam launched a visible shock wave recorded by satellites overhead. It showed itself as a rapidly expanding ring of black water, resembling an oil slick, racing out across the surface. More noticeable than this, trailing the black ring, white water filled in, taking its place.

Unbelievably, only four-hundredths of a second following the explosion, two hundred thousand tons of water heaved skyward in a column the width of a football field.

Looming over the bunker like the giant Tower of Babel, the colossal water column collapsed on itself once it reached its frenzied peak. Tumbling back into the river, it formed a gigantic wave of mist much like the spray at the base of Niagara Falls. Inside the mist, the cauliflower-shaped cloud contained water and chalky white aftermath from the factory.

The collapsing water column created a series of enormous waves streaking outward from the explosion. Ten seconds after detonation, the first fifty-foot wave slammed over the river wall, smashing through the bottom three stories of the hospital, flooding its lower floors and every tunnel link leading to where the bunker had been.

As Russum had expected, the unprecedented flooding which followed played havoc with warehouses along the river. Once the waves settled back down, CIA analysts noticed that the sandbar slightly north of the bunker was gone.

Less than an hour after detonation, the Kwajalein and Gakona HAARP sites ramped up to full power and, working together, they steered their combined radio beam toward Basra, halfway around the world.

South of Basra, somewhere on the Persian Gulf, computer screens came alive inside CIC, dancing with data. Across four adjacent screens, HAARP's chief scientist and his team saw a panoramic view of the Basra teaching hospital transmitted from their RPV's cockpit. Images of flooding and devastation were sobering. Submerged flatland dominated the area where Basra's great river levy once stood; every tunnel entrance now lay below water from the great waves.

Dr. Andreas Pappasongas, Eion Macke, and Gary Ellie went to work analyzing the data, and in less time than it took to place a phone call, both Washington and the CIA at Langley were viewing a three-dimensional cross section of the river bottom revealing a craterlike depression where the bunker had been. After four low-altitude passes, their flyby damage assessment revealed that no follow-up strike on the bunker was necessary.

There was no bunker left to target.

Not surprisingly, things changed for Andreas and his team following HAARP's high-profile technology debut. By all accounts, HAARP's flyby underground imaging and damage assessment capability was considered an unprecedented breakthrough by everyone in government from the president on down.

From that day forward, with the Pentagon, CTC, FBI, and Washington watching, HAARP became the premier technology of choice for combating terrorism around the world. Having achieved this de facto standard status overnight, HAARP's future and the integrity of Dr. Pappasongas's dream were assured for years to come.

Before the chief scientist and his team could return to the American mainland, HAARP received its next round of funding and Andreas received a long overdue sabbatical with his family. Hearing this, he sold his apartment in D.C. and returned home to his wife and family in Virginia.

The time had come to let the next generation take the reins. His dream was airborne now, sailing the political winds on an unprecedented wave of technical success. It was time to let go and allow someone else to steer the ship.

In a military ceremony in Arlington, Virginia, Dr. Andreas Pappasongas was awarded the Department of Defense's highest civilian award. Complete with a cannon salute and military band, the chief scientist was presented the Department of Defense Distinguished Public Service Award for his enormous contribution to America's future and security.

Air Force First Lieutenant Gary Ellie, handed responsibility for more computer technology than he'd ever dreamed possible, was promoted to captain, transferred to a warmer climate at Kwajalein, and placed on the fast track inside the Air Force's Electronics System Division.

Naval Lieutenant Junior Grade Eion Macke was promoted and received his long-awaited shore leave in London. Predictably, he enjoyed coming to know the British better and found their hospitality unforgettable. Soon after returning, he transferred with his friend to Kwajalein.

Without fanfare, the United States military assimilated the Iraqi manufacturing database into its industrial bloodstream, and less than eighteen months later, the next generation of enhanced radiation devices began entering the American arsenal.

Remarkably, one of these was a small black ball, nearly

identical in size and appearance to the night eye. By all accounts, it flew like the little bird, but was a miniaturized pure-fusion neutron bomb. Political planners and military strategists alike considered it the next generation smart bomb and a sniper's dream come true. Arguably, the most effective assassination weapon the world had ever known, the black ball gave new and personal meaning to the concept of selective targeting, meaning, you wouldn't want one to find you with your name on it.

As the *Times* correspondent had expected, Wyley's pictures from the factory floor moved more people and politicians to action than everything else combined. Although pictures moved the masses, it was hard physical data that swayed the scientific and engineering communities.

Later that month, the four gave sworn testimony before a joint congressional committee which aired on C-SPAN. Once word got out, it filled the United States and all the free world with an insatiable resolve to carry on the hunt for red mercury.

Commander Buck Harrison was promoted to a SEAL think-tank command inside the Pentagon after receiving the Congressional Medal of Honor, the highest military award bestowed by the United States. Mary, Katie, and both her parents traveled to Washington to witness the presentation.

Buck didn't look forward to the prospect of being chained to any desk, even a Navy desk in Washington. As a result, he retire from active duty and began spending more time in New England on the Marshalls' farm.

Wyley and his family returned to Beirut, where he resumed his work as bureau chief. Eventually, he had laser surgery on his eyes, got rid of his contacts, and quit smoking altogether—again. The following year, once the emotional pain began to numb, he wrote that book about the Manhattan bombing and put Buck's picture on the cover.

There was no one better qualified to write it. He had the photographs and he could write, and later that year, his book won the Pulitzer Prize. Understandably, regrettably, inescapably, the spirit of the book was dark, and Wyley knew it wouldn't sell very well. Hoping to capture the public's attention, in spite of the morbid topic, he entitled it *The Hunt for Red Mercury*, in honor of his favorite author's fantastic submarine thriller.

It was a cute gimmick, but gimmicks don't sell books. Neither do Pulitzers. Word of mouth sells books, and the word on this street was "a well-written story, but depressing as hell!"

Not many want to read a book that makes them feel bad.

Once the dust settled in Washington, Billy Ray Russum was promoted to CTC director, and took over another floor of the CIA building. To no one's surprise, Russum spearheaded America's relentless hunt for red mercury. Inside CTC, and around the globe, he filled people with a ceaseless determination to carry on the hunt for terrorists and their weapons factories.

Graham returned home to his medical practice and family a changed man, and never looked at the evening news the same way again. In a manner of speaking, he'd been right all along too. Somebody's gotta do it.

Along with Dr. Pappasongas, Dr. Graham Higgins was awarded the Department of Defense Distinguished Public Service Award for his enormous contribution to the nation's future and security. In the end, his wife had underestimated her man. According to the president of the United States, Congress, and a grateful nation, Graham was the hero type, only he didn't know it. Whatever it took was inside him, lying dormant, all along.

Overseas, no mention of any nuclear explosion ever appeared in the Iraqi press. Rapidly melting snows in the northern mountains were cited as the explanation behind the sudden disaster in Basra. The flooding was considered unfortunate, but it happens.

Although the United States captured all the bombs shipped to Mexico and Canada, the whereabouts of the remainder were never accurately determined. Much like terrorists who planted them, they kept showing up in the worst possible places, unexpected and uninvited. America was a free country, but the ominous menace posed by terrorists and these grapefruit sized neutron bombs threatened to change all that.

Al-Mashhadi and Kajaz both knew that most of the bombs had been delivered to warehouses scattered all across Iraq, not the single warehouse chronicled in the factory database. Kajaz took this information to his grave, but al-Mashhadi prospered from it.

After revealing this to the Iraqi president and his cabinet, al-Mashhadi began construction on two new factories, identical to the bunker in every way. Perceived as a man who produced results, he was considered one of the few surviving heroes of the catastrophe at Basra and leapfrogged quickly up the ranks. In addition to nuclear terrorism, he was awarded responsibility for a new high-tech program which targeted computer controlled weapons fielded by the United States military.

Al-Mashhadi was placed in charge of Iraq's viral R&D program. Their mission: create a new strain of battlefield-grade computer virus which incapacitated, but could not be detected or cured. Under his leadership, the Iraqis soon became the preeminent authority on computer virus infections. Although originally developed by organizations inside the United States government, the mutated Iraqi strain held the very real promise of unprecedented worldwide calamity in three to five years' time.

This was important, for the U.S. government had come to rely on "High Ground," its space-based missile defense system. Built on the Star Wars technology first envisioned by former President Ronald Reagan, High Ground was an orbiting satellite armada—that depended completely on computers.

ACKNOWLEDGMENTS

Pure Fusion portrays the next generation of terrorists, a new generation more frightening than any we have known. Under contract in August 1999 and completed in January 2001, it was written to sound an alarm against complacency, a reminder that we must be vigilant for state-sponsored terrorism will not go away.

It took a great deal of help from some very gifted individuals to bring this story to you and I would like to thank them.

My heartfelt appreciation to Dr. Dennis Papadopoulos, chair of the committee on HAARP research and applications and professor of physics at the University of Maryland, College Park, for reviewing the manuscript and offering his vision of where HAARP will be in ten years' time. His technical leadership, attitude, and ability to articulate complex problems in plainspoken English are both exhilarating and inspirational.

And to Olga Wieser, Tom Colgan, and Leslie Gelbman. Olga, for her insightful comments which always touch my heartstrings; Tom, for his editorial feedback; and my publisher, Leslie Gelbman, for her belief in the story.

Special thanks to Bing Bridges, retired FBI agent extraordinaire, for offering the benefit of his guidance and years of experience in law enforcement. Suzie Buchanan, for sharing her reactions to the story. Kenneth Brock, for conversations about oilfield technology, acoustical surveys, seismic acquisition, and image processing.

I would like to express my appreciation to friends who reviewed and helped improve the manuscript: Harry Mildonian, for providing comments regarding the thematic importance of red mercury; Pete Massey, for summarizing his impressions;

and Tommy Gambill, for conveying his reactions, suggestions concerning character behavior, and enthusiastic support of the story.

Most of all, I would like to thank my family—Janet, Amy, and Laura—for their ideas, support, and editorial assistance. Your input and experiences helped breathe life and heart into *Pure Fusion*.

Books like this are written in the hope they will make a difference. I pray this one does.

ABOUT THE AUTHOR

Other novels by Bill Buchanan include *Virus* and *ClearWater*.
He lives with his family in Mississippi where he's writing his
next novel.

"Fasten your seat belt! *Carrier* is a stimulating, fast-paced novel brimming with action and high drama." —Joe Weber

CARRIER

Keith Douglass

U.S. MARINES. PILOTS. NAVY SEALS.
THE ULTIMATE MILITARY POWER PLAY.

The Carrier Battle Group Fourteen—a force including a super-carrier, amphibious unit, guided missile cruiser, and destroyer—is brought to life with stunning authenticity and action in high-tech thrillers as explosive as today's headlines.

**AVAILABLE WHEREVER BOOKS ARE SOLD OR AT
WWW.PENGUIN.COM**

B384

DAVID E. MEADOWS

JOINT TASK FORCE: AMERICA

Terrorist Abu Alhaul is bringing mass
destruction to America's east coast.
Alhaul says he is retaliating for the death of
his family, which he blames on one man:
U.S. Navy SEAL Commander Tucker Raleigh.

0-425-19482-5

"David Meadows is the real thing."
—Stephen Coonts